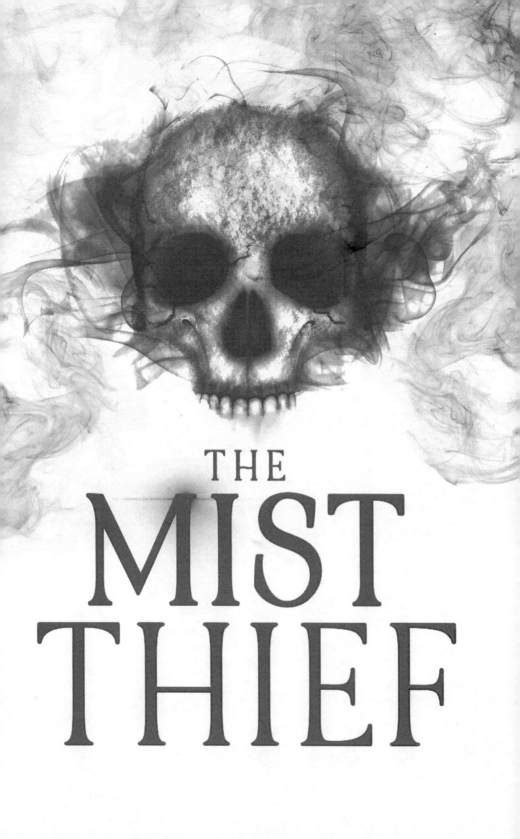

THE
MIST
THIEF

For rights inquiries email Katie Shea Boutillier ksboutillier@maassagency.com

Cover design by MerryBookRound design

Edited by:

Sara Sorensen

Megan Mitchell

Jasmine Mckie @faye_reads

Interior Art:

Samaiya Beaumont @samaiya.art

Kate @lepra.art

Chapter Headers/Maps:

Eric Bunnell

*To the sweet cinnamon rolls who
have burnt edges.
Be monstrous, my darling.*

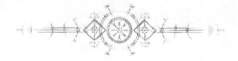

Content Warnings

This book contains content that some
readers might find triggering such as:

descriptive scenes of torture

talk of past manipulation

emotional/mental abuse

threats of harm

past dubious consent

self harm

thoughts of self-harm

explicit sexual content

gore

violence

dark themes

murder

forced marriage

past loss of loved ones

misogynistic behavior

Forest of Limericks

Felstad Ruins

Jagged Grove

Sk

Black Palace

Alver Lands

The Falkyn Nest

Hunt Arena

Furen

lockglas

Natthaven

Natthaven

Watch Point

Night Market

Alver Mesmer

HYPNOTIK KIND

Masters of Illusion, power found in conscious thought.

MEDISKI KIND

Masters of healing, power found in natural healing

PROFETIK KIND

Masters of senses, power found in sight, taste, and sound

ELIXIST KIND

Masters of alchemy, power found in blood and herbs

RIFTER KIND

Masters of breaking bone, power found in pain

ANOMALI KIND

Masters of unknowns,
power found in emotion & combinations of Kinds

Elven Clans

LJOSALFAR CLAN

Light Elven.
Summon light through sunlight, moonlight, or fire.
Some generations in the royal bloodline have the
ability travel short distances through light or fire.

DOKKALFAR CLAN

Shadow Elven
Summon medicinal properties in herbs
and plants. Craft talismans and charms
to ward off illnesses.

*Rare affinities summon a void where matter can
be taken and faded into nothing.

*The affinity of taking instead of summoning is
considered dark and dangerous.

AUTHOR NOTE

Welcome back to the dark world of the Ever Seas. I hope you enjoy this book and the unexpected, passionate romance between Jonas and Skadi. The elven lore in this book uses the names of Norse Mythology, but liberties have been taken with the appearance, culture, and magic system that might not align with the myths.

Now, while books 1 & 2 spent a great deal of time in the land of the sea fae, this story takes us to several lands, including some realms that were built in the first generation series, *The Broken Kingdoms.*

The Broken Kingdoms follows the tales of the earth fae kings and queens, the stories that built the Ever and this expanding world.

It isn't necessary to read that series first, and the Ever Seas is designed to stand alone from it, but several characters from The Broken Kingdoms will be prevalent in The Mist Thief.

For readers who have gone on both journeys in both series please keep in mind, to avoid Broken Kingdoms spoilers, certain beloved faces who didn't make it out alive are not mentioned in The Mist Thief. Just know they are looking over us from the great hall of the gods. Don't blame me for their absence, blame the tricky Norns.

No matter if you're new to this world or not, I hope you enjoy falling into tricks and schemes with some royal thieves all the same.

Without further ado, welcome to our prince of nightmares and a thief in the mists.

THE EVER SEAS RECAP

The Mist Thief brings a new couple, and while this book is arranged to stand as a new story, their tale does have connections to events in The Ever King and Ever Queen, books 1 & 2.

For those beginning here, or who want a refresher, here are a few events (mild spoilers) that took place in the battles of the Ever Queen.

Fae lands consist of four kingdoms in the earth fae realms, then the Ever Kingdom of the sea fae. Earth and sea fae were once enemies.

Livia Ferus, daughter of one of the earth fae kings, was taken by and fell in love with Erik Bloodsinger, the king of sea fae. But traitors in the Ever Kingdom stole Livia away to a fading isle called Natthaven. The isle belongs to a clan of elven people, the Dokkalfar, or shadow elven.

While imprisoned, Livia meets the Dokkalfar princess, Skadinia, who has the power to steal away anything—life, magic, matter, even entire lands—with dark mists.

Skadinia is trying to protect her people from Arion, prince of the Ljosalfar, the light elven, along with Ever Kingdom traitors who stand with him.

Her mists leave her heart cold if used for vicious reasons, and as she tries to help Livia, she is forced to use her magic for cruelty. When Livia finds her way back to the Ever King, the sea fae unite for the first time with the earth fae realms which include a magical clan called alver folk.

The alvers and fae attack Natthaven to defeat traitors and Arion before the elven clans can rise against them.

During the battle, it is discovered the king of the Dokkalfar is bespelled in a sleep, and his granddaughter, Skadinia, is trying to protect him.

Sander, one of the alver princes, is nearly killed by her blade, and his twin brother, Jonas, uses his ability to force nightmares into the mind to overpower the elven princess.

Traitors are defeated, and Arion flees back to the light elven territories, leaving Skadinia and her grandfather to face the fae. Livia insists the elven princess tried to help her before her mists made her cold, and she only battled to protect the elven king.

The Dokkalfar king confesses that Skadinia's dark magic cannot be used against any person bonded to her through kinship lest she suffer corruption to her soul. Since the fae realms share many bonds and familial connections, Prince Jonas of the alver clans petitions her grandfather to take her as his wife.

The prince swore a magical oath to protect every kingdom in the earth and sea fae realms, and from the compulsion of that bond, he believes that to marry the elven princess will keep her dark power from harming his people should Arion ever return to use her again.

In the end, the king of shadow elven, heartily agrees.

PROLOGUE
BATTLE COSTS

HER GRANDFATHER MADE THE ANNOUNCEMENT WITH A TOUCH OF GLEE: by week's end, the princess would have a husband.

Her vows would be given to a prince from realms of curious magics who stood on opposite sides of a battle between fae and elven.

An advantageous match was always meant to be her fate. Still, the elven princess did not anticipate her future husband to be a man she faced on a battlefield. He was a man whose family was nearly destroyed by her magical affinity.

In truth, the princess knew this was no match of convenience—this was done for revenge.

For the damage caused by her people, the princess would serve as the sacrifice for all the transgressions of elven folk.

Her husband, his people, and those he loved, would all be protected from the wicked magic she kept inside once he claimed her as his wife. She would never be permitted to harm them. No laws of this alliance demanded her future husband do the same.

Cruelty, hatred, and anger were all she expected from her new household.

But what the princess never expected was the touch of an enemy thawing the ice in her heart, a kingdom of cutthroats becoming home, and a prince of nightmares loving the monster in the mists.

CHAPTER 1

THE MIST THIEF

BEING ON THE LOSING SIDE OF A BATTLE WAS SHIT.

Victors always chose the reparation prizes, and they were wretched, in my limited experience. Prizes like unwitting brides to vicious princes with a score to settle.

I blew out a long breath. Some of the elven plum wine I kept tipping over my lips churned in my belly. One palm braced against a stone wall, I waited for it to settle before continuing down the dark, cobbled path. With the moon half-hidden by soupy clouds, now was my only chance at freedom.

When fae armies attacked the isle of the shadow elven—my folk—there'd been no choice but to raise a blade. Now, my life had been purchased for glory and a bit of petty revenge.

By tomorrow's sunset, I would have a husband.

I was already drunk enough that the thought now brought out despondent chuckles more than hidden tears in the night.

What a tale I would recite to the littles someday—for there was no doubt heirs would be part of this damning alliance—bright-eyed young ones looking up at me as I told them the romantic tale of the day their father came for me.

Maj, tell me your love story.

3

Ah, little one, let me tell you how your father whisked me away into the sunset, complete with shackles and promises of blissful hate for the rest of our days.

I snorted and took another foolish sip of wine before tossing the small vial into the dark leaves of a briar shrub, then pulled the woolen hood over the starlight silver of my braids.

My future husband was taking me as a wife for no reason save my former betrothed was the prince of the Ljosalfar, the light elven clan. Prince Arion was the one who raised battle against the sea fae—allies to my future husband.

All I could puzzle through was since Arion fled after the battles, it meant I became the next best target for enemies to exact revenge.

Heated frustration boiled in my veins. I nearly stumbled when I tried to kick at a pebble in the soil, wine still heady in my skull.

My crimes in all this were being wholly naive and not seeing Arion's moves before he made them. But I was dangerous in my own right.

Arion desired me as his wife for the same reasons as the fae—to use the darkness in my blood as his blade. Doubtless, my future husband would claim my affinity for himself after he'd broken me.

My affinity—the magic the gods saw fit to curse me with—was too unstable, too treacherous, to be left untethered. But to bind me through vows would create an unbreakable bond with my new kin.

There was a long-standing belief in our lore that elven could not bring harm to their kin without marking their souls in darkness.

I wasn't certain I believed it anymore. Seemed like there was plenty of kin-harming going around as of late.

My fists clenched until my fingernails ached across my palms.

Fae and other curious clans of magics were tangles of familial connections throughout their kingdoms. To make me their kin, in theory, would keep the whole of their realms protected from any threat of my dark affinity.

I ducked into the hedge, careful to avoid any main roads; I cursed Arion with every prick of a thorn, every snag of a branch in my silver braids.

This was his bleeding fault. Perhaps the cowardly prince should be the one being sold off as the pawn in a vow alliance. But Arion was tucked away in his glittering palace in Grynstad, the isle of the light elves, probably still sulking he didn't get his way while leaving me to shoulder his stupidity.

Tomorrow fate would deliver her sharp knife, but tonight was mine to live as I desired.

I emerged from the thorny hedgerow on the backside of a longhouse made of pale stones. Perhaps, if I were to get caught, my new clan would see me as too disorderly and rescind their offer of vows.

I snickered with bitterness.

No mistake, should I be caught by my future husband or his people, they would simply tighten the tethers.

Outside the back door, I removed the hood and secured a linen scarf over my head, the way most of the sea fae kept their hair free of their eyes. I plucked out the silver rings lining the whole edge of each of my sharply pointed ears.

With the tip of my thumb, I ran inky kohl under my eyes—a style of most sweaty sailors on the ships of the Ever Kingdom.

The land of sea fae was playing host for the alliance signing in a show of good faith, so it was the sea folk I would pretend to be tonight.

My borrowed boots were too large and heavy buckles clinked on every step. With a silk scarf, I fashioned a patch over one eye.

When a twig snapped in the hedgerow behind me, I spun around. The night was empty. There was nothing but the vibrant stars, the glitter of the tiered golden palace of the sea fae on the hill, and a few splashes from playful merfolk in the surf near the docks.

Inside the tavern, boisterous sea fae sang cheery shanties of sirens and spirits of the far seas. Privateers, merchants, off-duty guards, dock men, and a few unashamed pirates filled the tables. Some tossed wooden dice, others clanked polished drinking horns against the other. There were women who sat on the laps of lovers, while others looked as brutish with their blades and trousers as any man.

Since the Ever Queen stole the heart of the wicked king and was crowned, the women of the Ever Kingdom were bolder.

Or so I heard.

I took a bit of strength from them tonight.

The docile, obedient elven princess could crawl into the shadows for now and make way for a bold sea fae woman fresh off the tides who was looking for a bit of debauchery and diversion.

When no one glanced my way, when no palace guards rushed from the alcoves to drag me back to my chambers, I accepted my disguise as adequate and approached the long counter, sticky with spilled ale and what smelled like old bile.

Tables were filled, but most seats at the counter were empty. Only the aleman stood behind the edge, scrubbing drinking horns. On the last seat, leaning one shoulder against the wall, was a hunched man in a thick canvas cloak with a straw hat tipped low on his brow.

I aimed for the far end away from the drunkard.

A man with a floppy brim hat grunted a rough, "Pardon," when we collided.

I skirted around him, on the path nearer to the center seats. Fine enough. All I needed was a bit of bold sea fae rum and a few game pieces to join in at one of the tables.

The moment I carved between two game tables was the moment the players decided to verbally attack each other.

"You be damn cheats!" A man with a matted beard and two heavy rings pierced in his tapered ears shot to his feet.

He blocked my path, so I skirted around him.

"Calling me a cheat?" The second voice was younger, smoother. He stood at the opposing table, forcing me to side step.

In another breath, the two opposing players lunged at each other. Chairs skidded over wooden floors, tables rocked as men raced for the tussle. With a shriek, I spun away from the chaotic tables to avoid being yanked to the floor in a rowdy battle.

"Move," a disapproving voice said. Strong hands took hold of my arms, shoving me aside so another fae could slip around me. He wore a black scarf over his head, a gold ring in an ear, and a vicious gleam in his gaze.

This might've been too reckless.

Back home on the isle of Natthaven, I was not allowed a great deal of independence to wander. In the palace of sea fae—former enemies who trusted few things about elven folk—I certainly was not left alone without a watchful eye.

I blew out a long breath. No mistake, I was merely overthinking, unsettled by the noise and being alone for the first time in turns.

With all the shuffling, I was now three seats away from the drunkard at the counter.

He likely wouldn't even know I was there. Still, I shouldered him out and took my place on a crooked stool.

"What'll it be, lady?" asked the aleman, scrubbing the same horn when he approached.

I cleared my throat, lowering my voice to sound like a smoke-soaked rasp to match many of the sailors. "Brown rum. And a few pieces." I tossed over the only coin I had—juvel—elven currency.

If the aleman cared, he made no note of it. Then again, with the approaching alliance, more and more Dokkalfar elven had stepped foot on fae lands whenever the king came to visit me, his somber grand-daughter.

I was the caged creature when all I had done was try to keep my folk safe. I should've known, if I fought and revealed how my mists could swallow entire lands, the fae folk would see me as the fearsome princess the same as many elven.

What was I to do? My grandfather had been bespelled by one of Arion's minions into a sleep during the battle. He was defenseless, vulnerable. I had to stand between the fae warriors and the king.

"What's a wee lady doin' out here in a place like this?"

It took me a moment to realize the drunkard hunched three seats down had spoken.

I frowned, scanning my disguise. "Do I not look like I fit? Just got off the sea."

"Did you now?" He chortled, thick and rough. "Most folk come here when there're troubles on the heart. What's troublin' you?"

"There is nothing troubling. Merely want a drink, if you please."

The drunkard slapped the table. "Drink for milady, Tonguetaker!"

Tonguetaker. The aleman perked at the name. Sea fae had the strangest surnames. Each one different and named for the magic they kept in their song or their prowess with a blade.

Tonguetaker could be skilled at anything, but none sounded entirely pleasant.

"I was getting to it." The aleman clapped a horn in front of me in the same moment the drunkard scooted down a seat.

I swallowed, embarrassed how the hair lifted on the back of my neck, and raised the drinking horn to my lips. Gods, it burned. I winced against the satin fire, feeling it drop down my throat to my belly.

"You runnin' from something, lady?" asked the drunk. "Looks like you might be."

I forced down a second sip. "There is nowhere I can run. I came to enjoy my last moments of independence. Not that I had much of that before."

"Always the good girl then?"

"Always." Another drink. It was getting simpler to stomach.

"What be so horrid that you chose to spend your last bit of independence, as you say, in a piss-hole as this?" The man waved his hand at the aleman. "No offense meant, Tonguetaker."

I clapped the drinking horn over the tavern counter, gasping through a swallow. "I'm to be sold off in vows."

"Hmm." The man paused. "Thought most of the lady folk liked the notion of a mate."

"Ha." The laugh broke from my chest like a kind of warbling sea bird. "A mate? More like a jailer."

"Now that's taking it too far."

Was it the rum, or did the drunkard's voice shift to something smoother, something dark and deep?

A rush of air fled my lungs when the man crowded me, nearly spilling me off my seat. He tossed the hat onto the counter and tugged the thick wool scarf away from his chin.

All the bleeding gods, *no*.

Verdant eyes held mine, so green they looked like I could step into a sprawling meadow. His tousled brown hair was dark in some strands, then almost auburn in certain light.

When I had seen him across from me during the fighting, blade in hand, his eyes were black as pitch from his own horrifying magic.

Now, he wore a smug, stupidly handsome grin on his lips when he leaned in close. "I draw the line at being called a jailer, Princess."

My future husband.

Jonas of House Eriksson.

"H-How?" The word struggled over my tongue.

"We'll need to work on your sneaking. You're quite obvious, but your lack of discretion gave us plenty of time to think up this little scheme." He chuckled and opened an arm to the ale room.

Dammit.

Every man who'd stood in my way, from the man with a matted beard that was clearly false, to the brawlers, to the sea fae who'd shifted me out of his path, pulled away shrouds and scarves to reveal faces I'd often seen wandering the corridors of the palace.

They were friends and allies of the damn prince.

I faced the aleman, still scrubbing that drinking horn.

He popped one shoulder. "Sorry, lady. You're not to be out of the gates."

"You know." Jonas leaned closer, the scent of his skin—parchment, oak, and deranged man—burned through my nose. He tugged at my false eyepatch, holding my gaze. "I thought you were supposed to be rather . . . empty. They say you're unable to feel since the battle."

On instinct, I stiffened, allowing the cold mists of my affinity to draw me back, to shield up my emotions. Difficult to do when my heart would not stop pounding.

The gods-awful prince laughed. "No, don't do that. Don't even try." He had the audacity to lean his lips close to my ear and whisper, "I've already seen the fire in your eyes."

With a flourish of his hand, the prince backed away, but boots shuffled and floorboards creaked.

"Princess Skadinia."

I closed my eyes and fought the urge to groan. Jaw tight, ire burning toward the nightmarish prince at my side, I turned on the simple stool. "Dorsan."

My grandfather's inner guard stood at the back of the alehouse, a dozen Dokkalfar royal guards in their dark blue tunics and bronze spears were positioned at his back.

There was not a line on Dorsan's pale face that hinted the man had ever laughed. Stern as marble, but loyal as the tides, Dorsan approached my side, taking hold of my arm. "Time to return, My Lady. The negotiations are set to begin."

At my other side, the prince strode past me. "See you shortly, *Wife*."

I leveled him with what I hoped was a dagger-sharp glare, allowing the elven guards to drag me from the alehouse, back to my unavoidable fate.

Back to my prince of nightmares.

CHAPTER 2
THE NIGHTMARE PRINCE

MONTHS AGO, I DID NOT EVEN KNOW ELVEN CLANS STILL EXISTED OUTSIDE OF lore. Now, I was about to vow with an elven princess who detested me.

"Couldn't have done it without you, Gavyn." I clapped the shoulder of one of the sea fae lords. Gavyn Seeker was only a few turns my senior, but had been a lord of a noble house since he was a small boy.

His curious voice that turned him into sea mist at the smallest drop of water made him built for assassinations. A mark would never see him coming.

Tonight, he was our eyes, following my sly bride from the palace to the royal township below.

Gavyn shook out the damp from his dark hair and readjusted a silk scarf over his head. His brown skin was still dripping in water from his shift. "This was more entertaining than actual noble duties. I hope the vows are equally exciting. Until tomorrow."

With a wave, Gavyn split away from our group with a crowd of sea fae, his father, and some of the burly crew from the royal ship in his wake.

Vows. I forced a smile, a skill I perfected turns ago, whenever I wanted to hide disquiet from others.

Tomorrow, I would have a wife.

One who saw me as nothing more than a brute setting out to make her life miserable.

Perhaps she wasn't entirely wrong. When I petitioned the elven king, I hadn't thought much on what his granddaughter might want. Truth be told, I hadn't thought of her much at all.

What I wanted was an end to war, a way to keep peace. When the elven tried to invade fae lands, I was desperate enough to stop it and took a magical oath that I would do anything to keep the fae realms safe.

The moment I discovered the elven created mystical familial bonds—so fierce they could not harm their kin without dreary consequences—I knew a marital vow would rid us of a threat from the Dokkalfar. With their fealty, the light elven clan would be crushed should they ever rise against us again.

Vows, a wife, were never in my plans. In truth, I purposefully avoided such a connection.

But I feared losing my people more.

Every damn kingdom in fae realms had already fought too many wars.

Once, we even battled sea fae. Nights like this where we schemed and laughed with the fae of the sea would've only ended in blood.

Those were wars of my childhood. Those were horrors that had never left me.

We had peace now, so it could be done again with elven clans. Even if it meant taking a reluctant wife kicking and screaming back to Klock-glas, our royal township.

Warmth tangled with the chilled mist with each gust of wind. The Ever Kingdom always carried rich scents of satin blooms and clean brine. Lately, I traveled to the glittering royal city of the sea fae almost as much as I spent time in my own lands.

Livia, a friend since birth and a sister in all ways but blood, was the queen of the Ever. A surprise, to be sure. Erik Bloodsinger, the king, was a prickly sort, but she'd won his heart and sealed peace between the last of the fae realms with their alliance.

I was merely doing the same with the elven clans.

"We ought to be going." Tait Heartwalker, Erik's cousin and royal grouser, pinched his herb-rolled smoke between his fingers and inspected a curious clock he pulled from his pocket. It told the clock tolls, but also warned of danger. "It's nearly time."

"Feel anything?" I asked when we began the walk to the royal coaches awaiting to drive us back to the palace. The man's magic revealed the desires of hearts. If the princess had secrets, Tait would know.

Heartwalker lifted his red-brown eyes. "She wanted to be defiant for the night."

That was . . . unexpected.

When I first caught sight of the princess's silver hair fading into the shadows of the gardens, I thought she might be running, not merely defying fate for a few tolls.

A bite of guilt dug into my chest when I settled onto the bench of a coach. Maybe I should've allowed her the moment to be free.

In truth, I thought the damn woman couldn't feel. From the word of her own people, her magic made her cold and apathetic. Nothing but fire burned in her starlight blue eyes when she realized she'd been found out.

Another surprise—I wanted to see that fire again.

Sander took the seat beside me. My twin was gentler, always feeling so fiercely and with such passion. He could've been the one to make the alliance, but how could I rob him of the chance to find a true mate, a true love with another?

I never sought to give up my heart and those plans remained unchanged.

Sander nudged my shoulder. "Last chance to decide if you see this through."

"You planning to be furious with me like our parents and every other king and queen?"

"Bloodsinger isn't furious with you."

"Only because the Ever King finds it entertaining and a way to get the elven folk out of his palace."

Sander chuckled. "I'm your brother and will be at your side, even when you're being a damn fool."

Across from us, Aleksi settled on the bench. We were not blood related, but shared cousins since his aunt and my uncle were consorts. Much like Livia, Alek had been a friend to us since birth.

"What say you, honorable Rave warrior?" I used my toe to nudge his shin.

Alek sighed, running his fingers through dark hair he typically kept braided down the center of his skull. "We are here, aren't we? What am I supposed to say at this point?"

Loyal Aleksi. Always there, even if he didn't agree with the choices.

"Although," he went on, his odd, gilded eyes pouring into me. "I've decided to stick to Rave camps and battle strategy. The way you sods are pairing off, next thing I know, I'll be vowing with an empress I never met."

"Wouldn't be so bad, Alek." Von grunted and pulled himself into the coach. His dark hair was cropped close on the sides and longer on the top, and his features were innocent—big, sad eyes and a smile that hid the true cunning he kept inside. With a sigh, he adjusted the cloak on his shoulders and sat back on the bench between Heartwalker and Alek, knocking Aleksi's knee. "I'll take an empress."

Von was half-alver, but never presented with mesmer magic. We didn't know if he would live like a mortal, or like magical blood. Not that it mattered. There were elixirs aplenty to extend mortal lives back home.

I was glad for it. Alvers like us lived centuries akin to fae, but without the aid of different magics or spell casts, our mortal friends would fade to the Otherworld too soon.

Von was older than the lot of us, and had become a playful, scheming brother of sorts to me and Sander.

"Well, both my fathers think you're mad." Alek kicked up one boot, resting it on my bench. "They even offered to keep you chained in the Northern realms until you come to your senses. I think Uncle Kase considered it."

Ah, no doubt my father would be overjoyed to lock me away until I changed my mind about this entire vow.

I folded my arms across my chest. "I'm strategic, and I think you all are jealous."

Heartwalker was the one who chuckled. "Jealous? To have a woman who knows how to slaughter men as a wife? No, Prince. This move is all yours."

"Heartwalker." I feigned a bit of stun. "Watch what you say, or I'll seat you next to Mira the entire ceremony."

Tait's face twisted into a deep frown. He said nothing and looked out the window, likely bracing for the whirlwind the youngest royal of the earth realms brought with her.

Another like-a-sister, Mira was the princess of the glamour fae—illusionists and shifters and compulsion magic—and had it in for Tait Heartwalker since the grumbly fool seemed to be the only soul in the kingdoms who was not enraptured with her.

With a jolt, the coach set off toward the palace. Simple conversation overtook the ride. I listened, sometimes chuckled, but my thoughts were lost to the stink of the alehouse, to the disguised princess who almost seemed at peace for the few moments we allowed it.

On first glance, she was unthreatening. But when the elven tried to overtake the sea fae, I fought close to her, and there was no denying the woman handled a blade as well as any Rave warrior.

"Sander." I kept my voice low, so only my brother would hear. "Do you see this as a betrayal? Tell me honestly."

He arched a brow. "Why do you think that?"

"She nearly killed you." There was the other purpose behind vowing with this princess. She had gifts and abilities strong enough they nearly killed my brother, a skilled fighter on his own.

Beneath Sander's tunic was a gnarled scar across his middle.

"Jo, I've told you my thoughts on the elven princess."

"Perhaps you are too forgiving."

"She fought to protect the king, the same we would have done." He adjusted on the bench. "You need to see the memory of it. Maj is willing—"

"I don't want to see it." My jaw pulsed with tension.

Our mother was an alver capable of borrowing, sharing, or stealing memories. Sander shared the memory of his near death with her shortly after I petitioned the Dokkalfar king. Like him, my mother insisted I ought to see it.

I couldn't. It was a nightmare I kept in my own imaginings. To see my brother truly fall, I would never be able to unsee such a thing.

"You know what it would do to me," I said, voice rough. "You already know what *not* seeing it did."

"I do, and wonder if you plan to share that part of you with the princess. She might be there when—"

"After tonight, I doubt the woman will ever willingly be alone with me to ever experience the sight."

"I think she should know about the attacks, that's all."

"Noted." I propped my chin on my fist and watched the pale buildings of larger estates and cottages pass by the nearer we came to the palace.

Sander settled back against the bench. "To answer your question, it is not a betrayal. To the princess, we were invaders. But it does not lessen my concern for you. This is no small thing, brother."

"I know what I'm doing." Confidence bled through each word with enough vigor, I nearly believed the lie.

Aleksi used the back of his knuckles to strike the top of my knee, drawing my attention toward the front drive of the sea fae palace. "There's Liv and Bloodsinger. They're not alone."

The gold of Livia's intricate crown caught the gleam of the lanterns lining the curved drive. Her dark hair was free from braids and a little feral. Like her kingdom, like she'd become.

It suited her.

Erik Bloodsinger stood beside her, an arm around her waist, clad all in black, red eyes narrowed in his typical sour expression like he despised the whole of the world save for his queen.

The sea king wasn't so wretched, not once the murderous outer layer was peeled away.

But the two faces beside them were the faces that tightened my stomach. "Daj keeps looking angrier the nearer this vow gets."

Von laughed. "I'm not sure what's worse—Kase's frown or Malin's flat expression. I can't tell what she's thinking, and that's unsettling."

True. My mother, normally vibrant, playful, and as devious as my father, wore a face as stone. Her crimson braids were tossed over one shoulder and her mouth was set—neither a frown nor a smile.

My father's countenance teetered nearer to enraged when he caught sight of the coach. Whatever soft expression he kept in the presence of Livia faded knowing I was returning. The clash of gold and green in his eyes darkened to an inky pitch as his magic took hold.

Kase Eriksson was made of darkness. To me it was home, a comfort.

Ironic that my father controlled, manipulated, and killed through the power of fear, yet his glossy black eyes were a sign of his own. I knew they fretted over these vows; this choice had unsettled my entire household.

I hated it, but they wouldn't dissuade me.

Not when it could protect them all.

"Livie." Arms outstretched, I exited the coach, ignoring the alver king and queen for a moment longer. "Why the curdled face? Has Bloodsinger become a disappointment since we left?"

Bloodsinger's lip curled, flashing the point of one of those elongated canines in his mouth. Gods, it did a heart good to irritate the Ever King.

"Seems you were successful, Prince." Erik used his head to gesture toward the side of his palace.

The small unit of elven guards stomped toward the side doors. In the front was my fiery princess, still dressed in those ridiculous clothes and boots. As though she felt my stare, her sharp eyes found me in the shadows.

Without the slightest flinch, she turned away and strode into the palace, chin lifted.

As though she no longer felt a damn thing.

Livia used the back of her hand to strike the place over my heart. "Jonas, this doesn't need to be done."

"Not you, too. I've heard much the same the entire journey from them." I gestured toward my mother and father.

They both cut their own looks my way, and I wished they hadn't.

My parents had glares that lanced to the bones. Skilled in slyness, beneath the crowns they never wore, the truth was they'd lived half their lives as cutpurses and crooks.

My father took my mother's hand, but kept his scowl on me. "Since you're back, let's get on with it."

The Ever Queen followed them into the palace, smiling and chatting with my mother as though frustration only emerged near me.

"You've had her fretting over you for weeks." Bloodsinger twirled a knife in his hand. "I dislike anyone who upsets my queen."

"Threaten your disdain all you want, Ever King, I assure you this won't be the last time I upset Livia. Or my mother and father. Been doing it for turns."

A throat cleared behind me. The old palace steward puffed out his chest near the coach, causing his silken doublet, a size too small, to stretch at the seams. "If the proceedings are to continue, I do suggest we follow the alver king and queen and be on our way."

My gut twisted. Raised with a father who could taste my fear and a mother who could rob me of any memory I tried to hide, I'd learned how to mask discomfort behind glib remarks and cavalier grins.

I hooked an arm around Sander's neck, the other around Aleksi's. "Well then, let us go and get me a wife before she runs again."

CHAPTER 3
THE MIST THIEF

"That was foolish of you." Cara draped one of my newly styled plaits over my shoulder. "What were you thinking? Ruffians, vagabonds, and the worst sort of men keep to places as that. You are fortunate we've decided to keep it from the king. Gods know, he has enough to fret about tonight than if his own kin will humiliate him."

It was not the first lecture I'd endured from the woman, nor would it be the last.

Cara had overseen my education and etiquette since my youngest turns and was made of more steel than most. Firmly devoted to propriety, she was never one to shy away from telling me if I had stepped out of line.

Tonight, it seemed less about propriety and more like she might've been truly worried over my absence.

"I wanted to be alone, Cara. Nothing more."

She let out a puff of air through her slender nose and swiped some of her pale hair back into the stern knot behind her neck.

The woman was voluptuous and lovely, in a terrifying sort of way. More than one royal guard shuddered beneath the heat of Cara's scrutiny.

"Remember to speak only when spoken to, be pleasant, and gods all, show some gratitude they are not planning to overthrow our folk. They're a frightening sort of magics."

Unbidden, my knee bounced. I scanned a small scrap of pale rice paper with a neat scrawl, a gift from the queen of the sea fae after she was informed of the pending alliance with the alvers.

Queen Livia had taken to the trouble of writing out odd names used to classify the different magics in my future clans.

It was a small thing to offer, and I suspected she would be willing to give up more, but I was keen to avoid folk most days. While in the sea fae palace, I rarely left the rooms I was afforded to use.

Still, I had studied at length the small scrap of knowledge until the edges were creased and tattered.

Alvers took their affinities from shifts in the body—the rush of blood, the race of a heart, the senses, the response to pain—and each power had strange titles.

Mediskis were the healers, able to spur the body's natural healing processes at a swifter rate.

Profetiks were otherworldly with their senses: sight, hearing, some could even taste the guilt of a lie or poison when they drew near enough.

Hypnotiks took power from the mind and thought, controlling or tricking folk with illusions. Elixists were fierce alchemists, poisoners, and potion masters.

Rifters were frightening, alvers who found power in reactions to pain. They could snap bones, slash flesh, break necks.

Then Anomali alvers took from the emotions of the heart—fear, hope, even nostalgia—but their magic was always unknown with how powerful it might be.

Almost like mine.

"Frightful." Cara clucked over my shoulder.

I folded the scrap and tucked it away, unaware she'd been reading as she finished the braid.

"They must not be so frightful if they have such allies with the other fae kingdoms," I said.

Cara frowned, like she might want to say something more, but held her tongue. It wouldn't be proper to speak ill of a future ally.

Where Cara would think the gifts of alver folk as dreary, it almost sparked a bit of hope they would not despise my own darkness as fiercely as others. Not that I would ever reveal to them the depths of my mists that could steal away lands, armies, even life.

I was to be silent and mistrusted in my new house. It would not be so different from the home I'd always known.

Gold hinges on the thick, wooden doors groaned and opened. King Eldirard entered the room. He was not my blood grandfather, but he'd raised me like I was born of his house.

When he smiled, the lines of age showed beneath the silver stubble on his strong jaw. His pale hair was smooth and long over his shoulders, kept off his brow by a bronze, spiked circlet.

Despite the annoyance of the evening, my heart leapt in relief at the sight of him.

"Skadinia. It is good to lay eyes on you."

"You as well, Grandfather." I entered the corridor at his side and tapped the herbs wrapped around his neck, frowning. "Why do you agree to wear these?"

A necklace of pungent herbs was around my own neck. A spell from the witches of the sea, a way to dull the magic in the blood.

"It eases fears, Granddaughter." He patted my cheek. "Once the alliance is signed, there will be no need for them not to trust us."

This alliance was wretched.

Dokkalfar and Ljosalfar craved alliances and deals and treaties. There was a strange draw to them, to grow more powerful through the cleverest deals. It was the way of the elven folk, and had merely become a game of who crafted the best outcomes through the centuries.

Our people were laden in tradition and trade arrangements that stretched back to the time of lore.

"I've missed you since you returned to Natthaven." I slipped my hand through his arm when he led us from the chamber and into the corridor.

"And I you." My grandfather studied my features. "You seem less in the dark."

My affinity locked me in coldness when used for greed or cruelty. Prince Arion did not invade the elven isle of Natthaven to use my ability for anything gentle.

For weeks after, I found a bit of comfort remaining in the cold of indifference. Reality was not as painful when a heart and soul could not summon a reason to care.

"I am a little better." I kept my responses stiff, desperate to keep a few barriers in place lest I break under the truth—I was terrified.

My grandfather paused before we stepped into the doorway of the great hall. "Skadinia, you are to keep any reservations for this union to yourself, understood? This is an opportunity to grow the Dokkalfar throne and strengthen our forces with other affinities. If it all goes well, everyone will get what they want."

The magic of familial bonds through elven blood was strange, but powerful.

The king winked. "Even Gerard, aggravated as he is with losing our previous alliance, sees the merit. Although, he would rather the elven claim fae realms without fae on the throne."

I arched a brow. "The king of the Ljosalfar does not have claim to any fae realm, Grandfather. This alliance is for our clan."

"It is. My line will be written in the sagas as the first to bond a kingdom of fae with elven."

I nodded in compliance. In truth, that was what Eldirard desired most—a legacy. He had never sired an heir with his many mistresses over the centuries of his life, and lost hope until he took in a girl living in the trees.

With my wretched affinity he had something clever, new, and powerful. A new chance for his line to go down in the glorious histories of our folk. Elven were a proud people, always looking for the next move to strengthen the power and legacy of the clan.

This was the reason both elven kings once desired a betrothal with me and Prince Arion. Two powerful rulers joined as one over the two clans had not been done for centuries.

Arion was stronger than his father with his affinity to summon light; he could draw enough that it burned holes in the fabric between walls and doors. The light prince could literally walk through his magic from place to place. With my darkness, our vows would've crafted an unprecedented union.

I studied the profile of my grandfather. A greedy gleam lived in his blue gaze. This new direction was perhaps more enticing to him, for there were no tales of elven clans ever uniting with other kingdoms of magics.

There was no part of me that desired this vow, but because of Eldirard, I was skilled with a blade, I could read languages in fae, mortal, and ancient elvish. I had been nurtured and fed and given a home.

I tightened my hold on his arm. "I won't disappoint you."

The sea fae palace was wide and open. Most rooms had grand, arched beams framing the ceiling, and wrought iron chandeliers speckled in moss from the damp air carried endless tallow candles with strange blue fire.

From a raised dais to one side, the Ever King and Queen stood. The sea king kept his familiar venom. His harsh, fiery eyes flashed in mistrust, but the queen held my gaze, even offered a gentle smile.

I looked away. Our brief interaction during the battles did not mean I mattered to fae folk. I'd do well to remember they were not truly pleased with me being here.

I was in this palace as a pawn of war to be played for their benefit, not mine.

As hosts of the negotiations, the sea folk would observe, but that was the extent of their role.

Attention went to the long, black oak table in the center of the hall. Blue satin ran the length, and decanters of wine and amber ale were arranged with drinking horns of all sizes.

Inside, my heart beat like it might be trying to snap free of my ribs. Outside, my face was as ice—cold and biting.

The steward ushered my grandfather to one side of the table. There, already seated, were several of his guards. Elven folk were all lean and lithe warriors. Dokkalfar were diverse in their skin tones, but most of the shadow elven boasted some shade of blue to their eyes. Some rich and royal, others like Cara, so shockingly pale it looked like the irises were frosted.

The guards rose to greet their king. Gold hilts with black onyx stones marked their blades, all symbols of the inner Natthaven court.

Differences between us and the alver clans were stark. Without the chaos of battle and the numbness of my affinity shadowing my thoughts, each opposite trait was clear.

Alvers looked mortal, their ears oddly curved. They did not keep their hair silken and long over the shoulders like elven warriors. Instead, rugged knots and braids were styled in their hair, and a few wiry beards covered chins.

Men and women stood behind the table, dressed in furs and leather, tunics without a distinct emblem, and wore scuffed, sturdy boots.

Were they guards? They seemed to be trying to look the part, but appeared more assassin than anything.

None of the strange assassin-guards were as intimidating as the gazes studying—no *memorizing*—my every movement.

The alver king and queen and the two princes.

One of their sons nearly fell beneath my blade, and now I would be vowed to the other.

The sea queen wove her fingers together, a show of nerves, or perhaps Livia felt as suffocated by the tension as me.

"King Eldirard, Skadi"—she dipped her chin toward me—"Allow me to introduce House Eriksson."

"We've met, Livie," said my nightmare prince. With his strong jaw, his chestnut hair, tied half up on the sides, he appeared so different than his ruse as a drunkard. "But I suppose she ought to meet her future in-laws."

I schooled my face into stony indifference, but faced the king and queen as though it were simply an instinct.

The king was a handsome man, but his jaw pulsed with untamed rage. His hair was dark as soil after rain and his eyes were a collision of gold and emerald, as though molten ore spilled in through one side and stained the true shade.

The queen was pale with a dust of freckles over her nose and hair like a flame. She combed her eyes over me, taking me in, a groove of concern on her brow.

Wise to be worried with a woman like me joining her house.

"Let us get this over with." The alver king's voice was rough and low. Direct, no disguising his disgust.

Doubtless they did not approve of such a bloodline as mine uniting with their precious son. I was inclined to agree.

The queen placed a hand on her husband's arm. "Have it known this was not our decision and we are against it."

My grandfather scoffed. "Alliances bring peace and power. Together, we will achieve that. Skadinia has accepted her burden, and I was under the belief your son took the burden for reasons much the same."

Burden. The title every bride yearned to be given for her vows.

"My son is being an ass." The alver king shot a glare at the prince.

I bit down against a sudden urge to snort a laugh. The outburst was hardly regal, yet entirely sincere. Perhaps this king was not so furious at me and my elven blood, and more irked at his son for causing this alliance at all.

A guard handed me to my seat, across from the prince. Gods, I hated him. He was one of the most entrancing men I'd ever seen.

After this, he would be the hero in the end. He would claim to be the bold, brave prince who kept a monster from the hands of a shared foe.

I'd known my life was fated for such a loveless, purposeful match long before fae rose against us. The only stipulation that might've kept me from Arion was if he forced me into a cold heart by using my affinity for cruelty.

I had to be free of my darkness to agree to the match with the Ljos-alfar prince.

With this alver alliance, there'd never been a choice offered to me.

Once my grandfather was seated beside me, he drummed his fingers, focus on the king. "Do your reservations stem from my grand-daughter's actions against your other son during the siege?"

I dipped my chin, awaiting their rage.

It was the queen who spoke. "It is more toward the nature of obligation, the lack of choice they seem to feel."

"Maj." The prince leaned onto the table, eyeing his mother. "We've discussed this. There were no destined vows in my future, never were. An alliance is reason enough to take them."

"Yes, I've heard your reasoning, but your heart was not the only one I was considering."

Breath froze in my lungs. My brows tugged together. Me? A woman who ought to desire my throat slit for disrupting the lives of both her sons had considered this vow might rob me of a true love match?

My grandfather chuckled. "Kind of you, Highness, but there are no suitors for Skadinia in our clans."

His laughter stung, as though the notion of anyone seeking my heart for anything other than political alliances was nonsensical.

"Prince Arion of the Ljosalfar was the only one. I found your son's offer more tempting, and there *must* be an offer." My grandfather sniffed with a bit of condescension. "Without a royal vow, elven customs do not allow the throne to pass to a lone sovereign who is not of royal blood. Skadinia is an adopted limb within my line. Without a match from a blood royal, she cannot be a lone queen of our clan and it will naturally fall to the inheritance of the light elves. I assure you, when Arion claims the power, he will be inclined to finish his quest. He will meet your shores again."

"Why was this bastard's head not taken?" asked the alver king. "The way I see it, you let him scurry away to his comfortable little palace."

A muscle jumped in my grandfather's jaw. "Battle is how an elven king ascends the throne in our culture. He failed in his battle against you, but did nothing against our laws, aggravating as it was."

Battles were more than aggravating. I hadn't expected to leave them alive.

"It's a foolish custom," the king said, voice low and sharp. "And it makes no sense why the burden was left for her to shoulder."

I studied my palms, befuddled at the sudden urge to stand beside the alver king in solidarity. *My thoughts exactly, Highness. My thoughts exactly.*

"Because she is the coveted prize. I have spoken of my granddaughter's affinity before." Eldirard sat back in the chair. "It is beautiful in many ways, but more so it is frightening, dangerous, and vicious. She could drag your household, your sons, the magic in your veins, and send them into the void of her darkness until the final wars of the gods."

Hells, I wanted the floor to split open and devour me.

"That all?" The alver king said, almost disappointed.

"Is . . . is that all?" My grandfather's forehead wrinkled in confusion. "You do not find that formidable?"

"I do. I'm merely waiting to hear why everyone speaks about the girl like she ought to be in chains."

It would be wise to keep the mask of coldness on my features, but the damn king was making it rather difficult. If he spoke again, I might leap across the table and embrace him until he went red in the face.

I expected fear from my future clan. They hardly seemed impressed by the dangers from my affinity.

Eldirard cleared his throat. "As it stands, Prince Arion is set to inherit Natthaven as the heir. If Skadinia does not have a king at her side before my death, Arion will be her king. Every elven king is considered kin to his subjects. Her affinity will be loyal to his desires."

"Seems unfair." The queen was the one who spoke. "She was adopted into your royal house, now pays a price."

"Naturally, it was not part of the plan for Arion to invade our isle and cause turmoil," Eldirard said, a little disgruntled. "Kinship bonds are part of our affinities, and Skadinia's will be yours through this vow; her power could not be used against you. The Ljosalfar will not have the warriors or strength to stand against you without our clan. I believe their king sees the greater opportunity in aligning with the fae, rather than fighting them."

"You assume he does," said the alver queen. "And we're not fae."

"Forgive me, I mean the whole of the fae realms. Your connections with all the kingdoms are expansive, and now you will have the alliance of elven. A first." The glee written in my grandfather's features was not shared by the alver folk. Eldirard sobered. "If her lack of choice is your concern, I assure you our contracts must always hold a touch of willingness, a desire to see them through, a bit of choice, or they will not seal correctly. Skadinia is here because of her desire to see her people at peace."

I studied a divot in the table. Part of it was true; I didn't want trouble for the Dokkalfar clan. Perhaps it was selfish, but I wished my heart was not the sacrifice needed to ensure such a thing. I wished this meet was an alliance founded in love, trust, and passionate anticipation.

When I dared look at the prince, his face was hardened.

There was no heart in this deal. I'd be wise to remember it.

Prince Jonas leaned forward. "The merit of the union remains, and we understand the risks of what might happen should it not proceed. Now, allow my mother and father to see your terms."

CHAPTER 4
THE NIGHTMARE PRINCE

Eldirard wore a smug kind of grin on his thin lips. From beneath his tunic, the elven king removed a gold chain. On one end was a wooden vial with gilded, painted runes on the sides.

No larger than my smallest finger, yet when the king tapped the top of the opened vial, as he pulled his finger away, a slender roll of parchment followed.

The thickness of the scroll grew the farther from the vial it became, and when removed completely, a fully formed scroll, sealed in blue wax, was delivered to my father by an elven guard.

"How the hells?" Sander leaned forward, reaching a hand for the enchanted parchment, but I pressed my fist over his heart.

I shook my head, holding him back.

With a curl to his lip, Sander slouched in his chair. There was little that could draw out my brother's petulance, but refusing to let his curiosity be free was the swiftest way to see it done.

His movement tore me from my deliberate focus and I made the mistake of looking across the table.

Gods, why did she have to look as she did—like the first crystal star in the night, an untouchable jewel.

The princess had glowing, rich skin, slightly darker than mine, and eyes so blue they nearly glowed. She was slender, but not brittle. The woman had the power of darkness. The strange murky magic that coated her palms stole lands and fierce curses.

The princess could steal entire men and armies into the void of her dark mists.

Dark mesmer—the magic of alver clans—was not a foreign notion. In truth, there weren't many alver folk I knew who didn't have some level of wickedness in their hearts. The princess was as formidable as them all, and this union was to keep her darkness from the hands of our shared enemies, nothing more.

It would make it all simpler if my damn heart didn't quicken when she looked my way and my cock would stop twitching every time she shifted, offering more glimpses of what curves she hid under that dull gown.

I didn't understand it; my body rarely flared with heat in the veins and a desire for skin to touch skin, unless a woman made it clear she wanted the same.

Never had the elven princess offered a glimpse she felt anything but repulsion for me, and here I was imagining what her bleeding hair might smell like if I leaned a little closer.

I thought I hated her a little for it.

Lust and passion were no strangers. From the first time I stole away to the grove near my palace and discovered what it felt like to settle between a pair of thighs, I delighted in warming my nights with women.

Livia and Mira called me a charming rake. Aleksi always agreed with Sander that I would father half a dozen littles with half a dozen women one day.

I wouldn't. I'd taken herbs to prevent littles since I was a lanky boy of sixteen.

Intentions were made clear whenever I took a lover for the night. Farewells and a few tender kisses were traded when it was over, and I was always left the same—knowing they tangled their bodies with mine because of my title.

Exactly as I preferred it.

Few would know me, the man. My friends, the other kings and queens of the fae realms, my brother, my parents and their guild that stood at their backs now, knew me. There was no purpose for anyone else to do the same.

Hence, the reason this vow was ideal.

A princess with her own title who cared little for me would not be searching for my heart to make her a queen. In fact, I was quite certain she was disgusted by the sight of me. She kept lifting her eyes, then promptly looking away, a grimace on her face.

After the vows, I doubted we'd have need to speak much to each other at all. She would keep her isle safe from the light clan, and my life would be mostly unchanged save for the new assurance elven armies would not come against those I loved most.

I leaned back, creating a bit more distance between us.

My father slyly handed the scroll to my mother without glancing at it. I feigned disinterest as she began to read out loud.

"For a dowry, each turn we're afforded trade supplies and ten thousand"—Maj squinted, stumbling over a new term—"juvel?"

"Our coin. Made from black gems of Natthaven. Rather valuable, I imagine, in foreign lands."

More than one of the recovering thieves behind us shifted.

Raum, the most restless cutpurse of them all, flashed his silver eyes with a greedy thrill until Niklas stopped tossing his leather pouch of— no doubt—something poisonous, and smacked his shoulder.

"No." Niklas jabbed a finger between them, voice barely over a whisper. "No moves until the deal is done."

Nik had always been like an uncle to me and Sander, studious as my brother and sly as my father. He told Raum to stop, but I had few doubts he was already thinking of a dozen ways he could make this dowry the most profitable trade in our kingdom.

The truth was everyone who'd sailed with us was here out of mere intrigue and a chance to scout the Ever Kingdom.

I was half convinced my father planned to rob Bloodsinger's treasury before the return home.

My mother read on. Dull terms about implied treaties and councils to be had with the bride's kingdom once a turn as part of the alliance. Focus waned, and I studied a chip in the table's edge for a long pause until she made a strangled sound between a grunt and a gasp.

"What is this term of dissolution if the bride is unfaithful?"

One of Eldirard's brows lifted. "Which part is unclear?"

"Well, you see, my confusion comes from the term below that states any heirs born to my son's *mistresses* would not be considered for the throne, only legitimate heirs." My mother's face was flushed. A look I knew well from the many times I'd pushed her to the limits of her patience as a boy. "Forgive me, I'm simply curious, why is it implied my son will have mistresses?"

Eldirard chuckled, like my mother was losing her mind, even made the mistake of looking to my father for support. His smile faded at once when Daj returned it with a deep-set scowl.

The princess lowered her chin until I was certain it was melded to her chest.

Eldirard cleared his throat. "Is a future king not a powerful figure? Mistresses are expected, are they not?"

"They are not." My father's fist curled over the table. He pinned me in his glare, mutely repeating his statement.

The elven king looked befuddled. "I have never known a king who does not have a mistress."

Livia snorted in disgust on the dais, whispering something to Bloodsinger. By the feral gleam in the Ever King's gaze, she likely threatened to cut off his cock should he dare do such a thing. He pressed a kiss to the side of her neck in response.

My father leaned forward, voice rough. "You do now."

With a huff, my mother went on. "We will ignore that clause and continue."

The princess watched, brow furrowed, as though she didn't quite know if she believed my mother's stance. A jab of guilt dug under my ribs. Did she anticipate women flaunted in front of her face, with no regard for her feelings or station?

My knee bounced under the table. Hadn't I anticipated doing

exactly that? Take vows, then return to life as I'd always known it, new lovers while my wife slept in the chamber beside mine.

Gods. I might very well be a piece of shit.

This was not a love match, so if she preferred to take lovers, why would I stop her?

I settled back in my chair. After the vows, I would tell her she was not expected to be lonely in some tower.

The more I paid attention to the terms of the vow contract, the more I felt like a fiend to my future bride. Terms like, no beatings that caused permanent damage, no refusals were allowed should I come to my wife for her body. I named all future littles; I approved of her hobbies and travel.

There were a few conditions on me. The vows were to be held on Natthaven, but we would live in my kingdom for ten turns, giving my new wife the opportunity to learn her husband's culture. Then, the next ten would be spent in her realms (alone or with me) for her studies to be a queen of elven.

For the first turn, we would slip into the shared lands by spending one week on the elven isle where I would be expected to report to the Dokkalfar king of my approval or disapproval of the alliance, then, the rest of the month was spent in alver lands.

I was not permitted to ignore her completely. Every full moon we were required to share a bed from dusk until dawn—for the best chance of providing Natthaven with an heir, of course—and I was to give my wife an allowance she could spend at her leisure.

What a grand alliance she was making. It was no wonder her eyes were dull and emotionless.

My shoulders slumped, each term a lash on my spine. Of the two parties, it was not me who sacrificed here.

All I wanted was safety for my people.

For the first time I considered my good intent might have caused more of a disaster in this woman's life. Then again, the same terms would be offered up to that light elven sod. He would likely hold her to each one.

When my mother finished, she rolled the scroll again, and slid it to the center of the table.

"Perhaps the king would like to read now," Eldirard said.

"My wife read it." Daj narrowed his gaze. "What more could I learn?"

"To ensure nothing was missed."

"Do you think she is incompetent?"

Gods, Daj's temper was flaring. Insult my mother and he was prone to bones and blood.

"Of course not, but . . . well, you are the king." Eldirard straightened.

A haze of black clouded over my father's eyes. Much like mine could blot out until nothing but darkness coated my gaze, so could my father.

He pointed a finger at the poised elven king. "There's something you should understand, the only reason I have my title is because I am *her* husband. She is the blood heir of our lands, and you will stop speaking down to her, or you will not leave this room in one piece."

"Daj, we're trying to stop bloodshed," Sander muttered, but the corner of his mouth twitched, holding back a grin.

"Are you able to accept *those terms*?" Daj cocked his head. "I do not know what kings are like in your land, but in ours, we do not silence our queens."

On the dais, Livia grinned with affection toward my father. She'd been raised much the same. It was all we'd known—fathers who loved our mothers—and a strange wash of shame and pride collided like a barbed knot in my chest.

Pride was in no short supply for the way my father treated my mother, the way he taught us to treat her. Yet, I'd arrived here with dismissive thoughts toward a woman I planned to give the same title— my wife.

"I accept." Eldirard sniffed. "Who will be signing? It will require a drop of blood."

Both my parents removed their hands and pulled away, their silent protest that they did not agree with any notion of an arranged vow.

Silence fell over the table until the weight of it bent my spine. This was the moment I planned for and dreaded, all at once.

Thoughts whirled, but no matter which direction they took, it all came back to the fact—Princess Skadinia had powerful magic. It would be used with abandon by the wicked sod of a prince should the shadow elven clan fall under his rule.

I stole a look at Livia. She returned it with concern, but understanding.

The Ever Queen knew I felt compelled to do this. There wasn't a better way.

I swallowed and steadied my hand. With a prick of my knife I pressed my fingertip to the parchment, adding a drop of blood to the corner, and picked up a gray goose quill. "I will sign."

My mother and father abandoned the hall the moment my blood soaked into the parchment, taking with them those who'd come to gawk at their prince as he bound himself to one woman.

The princess was taken away in the next breath by a frenzied elven woman with eyes paler than a winter frost. Only Sander, Bloodsinger, and Livia remained with me and the elven king.

Eldirard took his enchanted scroll and tucked it away beneath his fine tunic. "I see your people do not see much use in celebrating this historic alliance."

My jaw flexed. "It is not personal. This is all rather new for our clans. We do not arrange vows if we can help it."

The elven king rose, a grin of delight on his face. "Different cultures, I suppose. Elven clans value alliances, agreements, and trade like we value our own life. Our legacies are built on our expansion in power and lands."

"No doubt that is the reason the prince attacked your isle."

Eldirard frowned. "Arion came to Natthaven for Skadinia's influence, but his sights were to overtake your lands."

I looped my thumbs through my belt. "Good thing he never can now, wouldn't you say?"

There wasn't an immediate agreement, and it set my instincts on edge. Truth be told, the Dokkalfar king even shifted where he stood for a breath. "Deals and contracts are voided all the time, Prince Jonas."

Sharp dread struck like a fist to the heart. I wasn't the only one.

From the dais, Bloodsinger let out a low sort of growl. "I'd speak clearer, elven. I don't care much for what you're insinuating."

Eldirard cast a wary glance toward the sea king. "I do not mean this alliance will be voided." Once more, the elven king faced me. "So long as the prince gives my granddaughter no reason to accept another offer."

"There are no other offers." I ground my teeth. "You made that clear."

"I made it clear there was one offer."

"Prince Arion has no claim here."

The king sighed and pressed a palm to his chest. "Do not mistake me, Prince Jonas. My desire remains for Skadinia to align our lands with yours. I merely feel it is prudent to tell you that the Ljosalfar are hesitant over this new contract."

"I care nothing for their tender feelings." With a heavy step closer, I nearly stood chest to chest with the king. "They should've thought of all that when they tried to attack the sea fae and overtake earth fae lands."

"Agreed." Eldirard lowered his voice. "But be wary, Highness. They may not give up so quickly. Legacies, sagas, histories, they are what elven crave. King Gerard and his son desire to be the first house to rule both clans in centuries."

"I've signed my name in blood. Your granddaughter agreed. They have no claim on the Dokkalfar, nor fae."

"But they could, that is what I'm trying to tell you." With a knowing smile, Eldirard clapped a hand on my shoulder. "As I mentioned, every contract comes with a bit of choice. Within the first turn, should Skadinia decide she might have more peace elsewhere, she can re-enter into her betrothal with Arion."

"You're saying if the princess is miserable in our lands, she can . . . null this vow?" Sander approached my shoulder, a groove of worry over his brow.

"Within the first turn, yes. She has so few choices," the king said, "she deserves to have one. Arion knows of this clause, Prince Jonas."

"Yet you felt it wise to keep it from us."

"I made it clear, choice, desire, it was all part of this alliance. I am telling you the finer points now."

"After I signed in blood."

"I can have him killed, Prince." Bloodsinger's eyes burned like dark flames. The Ever King wasn't a man of idle threats. He meant what he said.

I held up one hand before Erik started slaughtering. "We did this to avoid bloodshed."

"Well spoken," Eldirard said with a touch of slyness in his tone. "I desire the Dokkalfar to keep this alliance. I was not under any obligation to warn you, but I am. Take that to mean something, Highness. But I would not be surprised if Arion took it upon himself to make amends with my granddaughter."

"He's not touching her." My words came rough, harsh. Gods, I hardly knew the woman, but I did not want that bastard to put his cruel hands anywhere near her.

Eldirard held up his beringed fingers. "As I said, I am hopeful you are the victor here, but they were once close, being raised together, and all. I think you are a wise man and will do what is necessary to keep Skadinia satisfied."

I wasn't certain if I'd been played or not. The Dokkalfar did not need to confess the truth, he could've watched me destroy the alliance on my own, but he spoke.

"I will take your warning in good faith, King Eldirard."

"As you should. This is all made in good faith. We all benefit from this alliance."

I cracked one knuckle, then another. "Agreed. So, I assure you, I will do all in my power to keep your granddaughter satisfied."

The king barked a laugh. "Good man. I warn you, there is more to Skadinia than you might see now. I wish you the best of luck. The Ljosalfar are my kin, so I would be required to side with them should my granddaughter return."

There was a veiled threat in his levity. When I clasped his forearm, I gave him a tight nod, a show I understood his meaning entirely.

Sander folded his arms over his chest once the king left. "What do you plan to do with all that, Jo?"

What did I plan to do? I cast a glance toward the doors where the princess was taken away. "I suppose I will need to be friendly with my future wife."

Sander chuckled. "Maybe you ought to do more. I hear a lot of men love their wives."

I backed away, my comfortable, unbothered smile in place. "Ah, unfortunately, brother, hearts were never part of this deal."

CHAPTER 5

THE MIST THIEF

THERE WAS SOMETHING PEACEFUL ABOUT THE COVES SURROUNDING THE SEA FAE palace.

Wind kissed my cheeks. I closed my eyes, breathing in the warm scents of honey blooms, like a baked sweet with an undertone of salt and rain.

It reminded me of Natthaven. Sea winds were cooler on the isle, but the towering trees caught the breeze and rained clean, spicy air across the knolls and village.

The fading isle could be summoned. It was the skill of elven folk —summoning.

My gift of darkness that could take was a mistake to many. Too much dangerous power for one soul.

I never wanted power. I still didn't.

"Am I intruding?"

A shiver danced down my spine, stiffening my body. His voice held a strange power—it chilled me from within, rendering me unmovable.

I glanced over my shoulder. There, the nightmare prince stood, engulfed by the dim lantern light spilling from the open door of the palace. From this angle, his eyes were shadowed, resembling the empty black they'd been the night we met.

I turned back to face the sea. "It is not my place to say if you are intruding or not."

My right to protest was signed away moments ago.

His slow steps scuffed over the sandy cobbles until he settled next to my shoulder. "King Eldirard is arranging for ferries to the elven isle after he draws it nearer. It's strange how it can move about."

"Hmm," was all I said. I cast a look at the prince. Tall, strong, an enemy. Why was he here?

A slice of fear cut through my middle. There was violence under the surface of this man, and once he had wanted to kill me.

"You seem afraid of me." He spoke without looking away from the sea.

"Should I be?" I wasn't certain he even heard, my voice came so soft, so distant.

The prince opened his arms and twisted side to side. "I am unarmed, Princess."

"Blades are not the only weapons."

"True." The prince hooked his thumbs into his thick leather belt. "I meant to speak to you after the alliance, but you were taken away by your lady's maid."

I didn't respond with anything more than a nod.

Cara thought it indecent for me to remain, expecting the kings to celebrate with drink and debauchery over their grand achievements. The woman was practically scandalized when my future father-in-law insisted he and his queen with their strange guards wanted to retire to their chambers.

I wasn't certain what shocked her more, the alver king's disregard toward the Dokkalfar king, or the admission as he left that the only person he cared to spend his time with was his wife.

Like she mattered.

It was . . . endearing. Strange, but endearing all the same.

I wish it would be the same for my own vow.

No, my husband was not one who would knock chests with kings at the mere inkling of offense toward his queen. I doubted he would even be irked by the idea.

I took a step back. "You are under no obligation to speak with me."

"Ah." The corner of his mouth curved into something beautifully wicked. "If that is an elven custom, it will take me some time to acclimate. Where I am from, those who are vowed speak to each other quite often. In fact, sometimes they even enjoy it."

Was he . . . teasing me?

What was this? Break down my guard before he struck?

Decisions to trust too easily spoiled my past. Pain always followed. If his plan was to find a crack, to take hold of my confidence, he would be met with formidable resistance.

I steadied my features into the frosty exterior. "I will talk if you ask it of me. Tell me what it is you would like me to say?"

Steady. Calm. Empty. He wanted his levity to be met with a cautious grin? Perhaps a flush of my cheeks, a spark of curiosity.

He would be met with none of it, for how could he break an empty heart?

The prince faced me, one elbow propped on the rail, the last remnants of his grin fading like the retreat of the tide. "What do you want to say? Surely you have a thought or two about this alliance."

"What are your thoughts?"

"I believe I asked you first."

"But I only wish to hear yours."

The prince came closer. My heartbeat quickened. Gods, I prayed he couldn't make out the thud of my pulse point.

"You're pretending to be cold, Princess. I'm not certain why?"

Teeth clenched, I fought to keep my face schooled into something so flat not even a twitch of the cheek would be noted. "You have my apologies if I've displeased you."

"And you wish to please me?"

Behind my back, I clasped my wrists, hiding the curl of my fists. "I wish to do my duty."

"Are those your true thoughts? You'll do whatever it takes?"

Another step. His shoulder brushed mine. I dug my fingernails into the skin of my palms, battling the urge to shudder from the touch.

His smirk transformed into something sly, a sneer and grin that spoke of a thousand tricks and ploys he was crafting in his mind.

"I have no thoughts." My voice was low, a soft rasp. "What would be the point?"

The more I tried to be nothing but a shell of a woman, the more the prince seemed drawn to me.

His thumb tilted my chin. The touch was warm, almost gentle, but when my eyes clashed with his, there was a darkness in his stare that lifted the hair on my arms.

"Tell me." The prince brushed his lips over my ear. "If it pleased me to have you crawl to me, to thank me for saving you from the light elven, would you do it?"

A flash of anger seared through my blood. He wouldn't bleeding dare.

Before I could stop it, the prince spun my back to the wall of the palace, and flattened his palms beside my head. His broader body made a cage around me, trapping me, blocking me.

All I could do was hold his vicious stare.

"There it is." His gaze bounced between my eyes. "The fire is in there."

"I-I don't know what you mean." Gods, my voice wouldn't stop trembling.

"How well you keep secrets, Princess. There is a stunning blaze you keep buried inside you."

"You mistook my expressions, Prince." Each word cut through my teeth like jagged glass. Harsh, annoyed, and riddled in emotion I did not want him to catch. "If I looked your way it was nothing more than memorizing the face of my future. I am in no place to oppose your alliance."

"Liar."

Arrogant bastard. The ruse grew too difficult to hold up, and my eyes narrowed. "What would you have me say? You wish for my compliance, you shall have it. I have no move to make, so that is what you will receive from me."

"Here I thought I was getting a wife, not a captive."

"Gods." Unbidden, my palms shoved against his chest. It only made him chuckle again, and the heat of frustration boiled in my blood. "What else am I but a captive? I know why you are doing this."

"Oh, and why is that?"

"You took an oath riddled in deep magic that compels you to protect your people, and I am the one you must bind to soothe that need."

The prince's eyes widened. "I did not realize you knew of the oath."

"I've heard all the gossip in this palace. Tell me, do you crave the glory of being the hero, Prince?"

His grin twisted into something vicious. "That's exactly it. You've unraveled everything there is to know about why I am here, Princess. Now, why don't you tell me why you agreed if it is so repulsive?"

The way he looked at me, it was as though he saw the truth—I would do nearly anything to keep my fate untangled from Arion. Steeling against him, I straightened my shoulders. "Vows are all we must give each other. It is better not to think too much on it, wouldn't you say?"

"I'm inclined to agree."

I dipped my chin in a stiff nod. "Good. You'll get a silent, docile wife who cannot harm your people. You've no need for anything more, so do not strive to find it."

I thought he might be angry at my outburst. Instead, he gripped my jaw, drawing me close enough I could make out a faint scar just over the bridge of his nose.

"Wise to set out expectations, so let me tell you what you can antici-pate, *Wife*: expect to interact with folk who do not fear darkness."

He crowded me, as though he wanted me to cower beneath his nearness.

I had few choices in the match, but for a moment I chose defiance.

Chin lifted, I pressed closer, my body aligned with his, shoulders to hips. His eyes flashed, and I took a bit of satisfaction knowing I claimed back a bit of power.

"And what do I get from you, *Husband*? Your undying love and the whole of your heart?"

"Since it sounds so disgusting to you, you'll be pleased to know my heart is not part of the negotiations. This alliance achieves your desires, and now I have found what *I* truly desire."

I swallowed. "And . . . what is that?"

His white grin flashed in the night. "To unravel you piece by piece, until the flame inside you scorches through this façade you keep. Until that fire is mine every bleeding day."

My lip curled. "You do not offer your heart, so expect the same from me."

"As long as I get your fire. It speaks to me." The tip of his nose brushed over my cheek. "So, I plan to make it *mine*."

CHAPTER 6
THE MIST THIEF

On Natthaven, the shadow elven had grown to fear me.

Declarations of the power held by the adopted heir of the king were shoved down the throats of my own people so deep they could hardly speak to me.

I was feared, viewed as different and dangerous, but it was a trepidation in which I'd grown accustomed.

When the sloop docked on the dark shoreline of the isle the morning of the vows, I hadn't realized how fiercely I'd missed the familiarity of my homeland.

I would only get to revel in it for one more night before being shipped away to a distant kingdom.

In the prince's land, did rivers line stone cottages with quaint black moss and golden clay? Were houses made of dry wood and brittle foundations? Did roads weave through endless forests and meadows and swamps, or were lands flat and dull?

Scents of boiled red pheasant would not permeate the corridors of his palace with rosemary and savory juices.

The squalls on his shorelines would not taste of the sweet salt and spice from the far seas. Night market chimes and chatter would be replaced with foreign words, ale, and strange, rounded ears of the patrons.

I closed my eyes, drawing in a sharp breath, once, twice, again and again until the ache in my lungs retreated beneath an unreadable expression.

Shouts from the sloop's crew shook me from my thoughts. Two thick-armed men dropped an anchor. Ships and skiffs nearby did the same. Crewmen shuffled about, directing the small row boats to be lowered into the tides for the passengers to load.

Elven folk had returned to Natthaven with my grandfather, even Cara had gone ahead to prepare for the ceremony.

I was left to be surrounded by the strange, feral guards of alvers.

I had not seen the prince since our interaction after the alliance. Part of me wished to see him again, to read his eyes as though they might reveal his cruel intent. Another part of me was uneasy around the scrutiny of his people and would prefer if the prince escorted me himself.

I was a traitor to my own dignity for such a thought, but like the fear of me in my own lands, the cunning, annoying presence of the prince was becoming familiar.

"My elven." Knee deep in the vibrant blue of Natthaven's shores, one of the alver guards held out a hand. Tall and lithe with cropped dark hair. Older than me by turns, but there was still an innocence to his features.

"Your elven?"

"What should I say?" he asked. "I was told most royal folk prefer titles. Never was terribly skilled with them, I'm afraid."

Not skilled with titles? "What do you call your prince then?"

His mouth quirked. "Depends which one we're discussing here. Sander is normally pest, thinker, or little ass. Jonas, well, he's always just little ass."

I looked over my shoulder, half expecting some sort of horrid reprimand to fall down on the man for speaking so informally—so *disrespectful*—about his royals.

No one took notice.

I leaned closer, whispering, "What do you call your king and queen?"

"Mal, mostly for the queen. For Kase, he's simply Kase, but if I want to especially irritate him, I'll call him King." The guard laughed. "What title should I be saying for you?"

Grandfather would be livid if I did not insist on something regal. "Skadi will do."

"Simple enough." He cleared his throat, straightened his shoulders toward the shore and wiggled his fingers. "Let us go, then, Skadi."

I took his hand and hopped down into the tides. The guard kept hold on me while elven warriors and the sailors built a line to pass supplies from the boats to the shore.

"What title should I know you by?" I inspected his informal attire. Brutal, lined in knives, but like alver guards last night, he bore no emblems or formal uniform.

"Ash," he said. "Just Ash."

"You are an inner guard, Ash?"

"Yeah." He spoke like he didn't believe his own voice. "Yeah, you could say that. Sure."

"Then I suppose I will see much more of you when we return to Kloshglas."

Ash chuckled. "Klockglas. You'll see some of me. I do often spend time in the fae kingdoms of the South."

"Oh?" From maps provided to me by the Ever Queen, I understood there were four main territories of the earth fae lands. My new home would be on the eastern coastline. Strange to have a dedicated inner guard travel to neighboring kingdoms. "Are you more of an ambassador?"

"Gods, we haven't had any of those for turns. No, my wife is a lady of a lower court among the glamour fae."

"And the king simply allows one of his inner guards to leave for such a stretch of time?"

Ash didn't answer for a breath, taking a pause to see to it I did not stumble as I stepped onto the dark sand of the shore. "To be honest, I never really thought to ask."

No permission from his royals? No contracts between courts to craft similar alliances for a warrior and a noblewoman in another kingdom?

"May I ask, are you an alver? I understand there are mortals who live in your realms, and forgive me, I don't know how to tell the difference."

Ash grinned. "Draw blood on an alver and it'll smell a lot like piss and rotting plums."

My nose wrinkled. Memories of fetid scents during the battle were there, but I assumed it was all the death from the fallen warriors.

"I am an alver," Ash went on, "what we call a Rifter."

All gods. The sort who reveled in pain and broken bodies. What a pity, he seemed so . . . kind.

"From the look of fright in your eyes, I'm guessing you've heard a thing or two about Rifter folk." Ash shouldered a satchel from one of the stacks of supplies. "I won't lie, I could break you if I wanted, Princess. I could sense where it would hurt the most. But I've no need, and I have a feeling you're going to unsettle my little ass of a prince. I look forward to watching it."

A strange, choked sort of laugh slipped through. "I don't know about that, but I am grateful you have no plans to break me."

"From what I hear you could just eat me with your mesmer."

"Mesmer? That is what you lot call your affinities, yes? You don't seem uneasy at the thought of mine."

"Should I be?"

I didn't have time to respond before Cara shouted my name, waving her hands as she approached. Clad in a simple dress, Cara had her smock tied around her waist and her light hair braided in a crown over her head.

With a hesitant glance toward Ash, she stepped between us. "I will escort the princess from here."

"Join us if you wish," Ash said, "but I'm to see that she safely reaches her room."

Cara took Ash in from his head to his boots. "We're on elven lands. She is perfectly safe with her folk."

Not always.

The kindness of Ash's face faded into something more cunning, something reminiscent of the prince's sneer.

"I'm certain she is." He slipped the satchel over his head, settling it on one of his shoulders, then leaned in so his face was close to Cara's. "I'm still going to see her safely there. Prince's orders."

With a sniff, Cara stepped in front of us.

Ash opened an arm, mutely signaling me to walk ahead.

"You call your prince an ass, yet follow his order without wavering." I bit down on my cheek to keep the smile from cracking.

Ash winked. "Only the orders I want. This one seemed important to him, so at your service I'll be until the vows."

I hated how the notion of holding any sort of importance to the prince of nightmares fluttered in my chest.

It felt like turns had gone by since I'd been in my own rooms. The royal chamber was arranged in a wing of four sections. A washroom, the bedchamber, a sitting room with a black marble inglenook, and a tea room I'd transformed into a small library.

The moment Cara left me to my own thoughts, I clutched a tattered leather-bound book of fables and fae tales I read as a child when I wasn't convinced fae folk even existed.

My fingertips traced the gilded symbols on the front cover describing the stories inside. Legends like the Skald who fell in love with a forest nymph, and when an envious troll discovered their affair, the troll was given a talisman from one of the trickster gods to transform the Skald into soil to be pounded beneath his feet for all time.

Pages crinkled as I flipped through the tale to the faded end. I smiled, resting my palm over a drawing of two towering trees.

Heartbroken, the nymph sacrificed her heart to the goddess of lovers and vows, and was transformed into a beautiful white aspen tree. From the Skald's cursed soil, a new towering oak sprouted with the soul of the

Skald within, and tangled its roots with the nymph aspen. There they grew together for centuries to come.

A tale of sacrifice and unfailing love.

Once, I believed such a thing to be possible. Now, it was nothing but a thing of folklore.

I gently closed the tome and hugged it to my chest, peering over the balcony.

Trees on the jagged hills were thick and lush, tangled in great bowers across the forests and pathways that wove this way and that over the isle. Boughs were threaded like intricate threads of a weaver's web.

Blossoms from hedges below carried honey smooth scents with each kiss of the breeze. Buried in the silken shadows of the morning mists were flickers of gold from sun wings welcoming the dawn.

The insects were curious little things and suspicious of the unfamiliar. Faint glimmers cascaded down Natthaven's hillsides like tiny flickers of a candle. Doubtless the tiny beasts were uncertain what to do with so many fae folk on the isle.

Scorch marks still marred some of the trees black from fires of battle that waged not so many weeks ago.

A knock on the door sounded. One of the palace guards slipped inside the room. Behind him, two maids carried in a glittering silver gown.

The guard cleared his throat. "Highness, the alver prince dismissed the maidens who were to assist you in preparing for the vows, but asked you be tended to with the aid of ladies of his choosing."

"Pardon? His choosing?" Cara was likely furious if the prince made a request for anyone other than her and maids she plucked from the palace halls.

"Yes, My Lady." The guard lifted his nose. "His thoughts were along the lines of putting you at ease by those who might proclaim his attributes to you. And, well, they have come to you."

CHAPTER 7
THE MIST THIEF

THE EVER QUEEN STRODE PAST THE GUARD AND GAVE ME A SMALL SMILE. "Hello, Skadi. I hope you don't mind, but it is customary in our lands for fellow royals to aid fellow royals. We thought we could help you dress."

Queen Livia had deep blue eyes and her long, dark hair flowed in a loose braid over her shoulder. The gown she wore reminded me of the tides with vibrant layers of different shades of green and blue.

The door had started to close again, but was practically kicked open by two other fae women in silk gowns. One woman had rings pierced along her tapered ears like mine, the other wore a single spike in her only ear.

"If you think I'm not going to take this opportunity to meet her properly, you're sorely mistaken. I'm Krasmira." The taller fae leaned against the edge of the vanity table, a sort of smirk on her mouth. "Most folk call me Mira."

I held her gaze, uncertain if her grin was meant to be friendly, or if she was plotting something more sinister. Mira was taller than the Ever Queen, with amber eyes like the sap on the trees in the wood. A bit of mahogany deepened the brown of her hair when the fading sunlight caught the braids.

"Mira is the heir of the Southern fae realms," Livia offered. "She also grew up with Jonas."

Mira's grin widened. "You realize you're getting an utter fiend for a husband."

Panic throttled my throat. Gods, her smile was one of delight. So, my fears were confirmed. The fae folk would take pleasure from my suffering.

"Mir." Livia frowned. "You've got her thinking Jo is some sort of brute."

"Oh, gods. I didn't mean he was a cruel fiend. Just a loveable sod who is the most cunning of tricksters. Many bouts of frustration in my childhood came at the hands of Jonas Eriksson."

"Skadi." Livia went on, shaking her head. "You've met Celine Tide-caller, yes?"

"We have crossed paths in your palace," was all I said.

The sea fae woman with the spike in her ear flicked her fingers, but did not smile like the Ever Queen. "He's not cruel, elven. You can stop looking like you're about to get your throat slit."

Livia closed her eyes. "Perhaps this was a bad idea."

Mira waved her hands. "Allow us to start again. All we wanted was to know you a little better. Jonas is part of us, so that now includes you."

"Is she still iced over?" Celine was horrid at whispering, but the way she leaned in to the Ever Queen, voice low and husky, she made an attempt to be sly.

Mira tilted her head, fiddling with the end of her long braid. "I heard your magic dims your emotions. True?"

I nodded and avoided their gazes. "It is worse if I use my affinity for cruel reasons."

Mira nudged my shoulder. "You won't be treated or used cruelly by Jonas. Not like that light elven sod."

Part of me yearned to believe her, but she was fae, a royal. They all wanted this alliance to keep threats from the elven away from their lands.

"I wouldn't lie," Mira went on, as though reading my thoughts. "If Jonas was a bastard who took delight in harming the hearts of women, I assure you, I'd hide you away after I buried him with his own cock shoved down his throat."

"Gods, Mir." Livia laughed as though such talk was practically expected.

"Don't let Livie fool you, she'd be there with me."

"Whether you believe us or not," Livia said, working on securing one of the ribbons on my underskirts, "you are vowing with one of the most vicious, protective, and loyal hearts in our lands."

"Forgive me for believing otherwise," I said. "I have heard folk call him a nightmare prince."

Mira snorted. "Oh, that's because of his mesmer magic. Not because he is a nightmare. Well, not always."

"You recall the guide I gave you of the alver magics?" Livia looked at me in the mirror. "Jonas is an Anomali. Everyone in the royal household is, actually. His ability is fueled by creating the emotion of intense fear of an individual mind. What might frighten me, wouldn't frighten you. His magic knows that."

All gods.

"Sander, his twin, is similar," Mira explained, wholly focused on securing a blue jade pin into my hair. "But he uses pleasant memories and twists them into something horrific. Together the twins can manipulate minds into a bit of maddening terror where folk no longer know what is real. They're both a good tangle of their mother and father."

"What do the king and queen do?"

"The alver queen steals memories." Celine leaned forward, grinning like a wolf. "She can make folk forget how to breathe."

"She's quite lovely, though," Livia said with a warning look at the sea fae.

"Uncle Kase—the king, I mean—uses fear," Mira said. "It's fascinating. Anything that is a fear of someone he can grant it. Think of it—most folk fear dying, right? So he can kill with it."

I blanched. "Truly?"

Livia clicked her tongue, glaring at her fellow royal. "They do not use their abilities unless threatened, like all of us."

"Right, of course. They're lovely, Princess. A little broody and tricky at times, but lovely," Mira said quickly.

Discomposed as I was, the conversation was becoming easier. "Elven have simple summoning affinities; they are powerful but normally peaceful. Ljosalfar summon light and fire through the smallest gleam or flame. Dokkalfar are known to summon healing. But I take. My affinity does not summon or give, it steals and destroys."

There was a drawn pause for a breath, and I wished I had not spoken. I gave up too much, and I did not truly know anyone in this room.

Not really.

For a time we were quiet. The women painted my lips in a rosy shade, braided small strands of my hair, and smoothed the gown I was to don.

Mira nudged my shoulder, a signal to stand for the dress. "You're a different sort of elven. Maybe that's something you have in common with the prince and his house. They are all different."

Strange, but there was a bit of comfort considering they might call me one of their Anomalies, only elven.

The three women set about telling me secrets of the prince—he enjoyed carving wood into little shapes, he preferred being out of doors, he had a silver tongue that charmed the surliest of folk.

"Jonas is the man who will laugh away his frustrations and fears instead of admitting to them," Mira said. "My father does the same, and it's aggravating."

"I am certain even if the prince wished to confess unease, it would not be said to me."

Livia frowned in the mirror, but said nothing, merely finished settling the silver chain around my braids.

"You have a lifetime to find out, I suppose." Mira helped me fasten the back of my gown. "This is stunning, by the way. Are these crystals?"

She pointed at the bodice coated in glimmering gems along the bust, designed to appear like branches of a tree.

"They are called heart glass. Traditional stones used for Dokkalfar vows. It is said a man will see the joy in his bride's heart on their vows."

"Rather romantic." Livia beamed at me, like she wanted me to feel some sort of gladness.

For others, perhaps. I asked that no heart glass be on my gown. Like my other requests, it was ignored, another slight to remind me my heart was cold and darkened by cruel magic. It was a subtle way for my people to show my new husband the truth of his bride.

My folk were brilliant at never allowing me to forget who I was.

When Livia tucked a woven band over the crown of my head, she lowered her voice. "Skadi, battles are behind us. I know this vow was brought for a purpose, but it does not need to be a wretched thing."

"I was always destined for arranged vows, Queen. I hold no ire and no joy for this day. It merely is."

"I admit, I did not see Jonas gaining the title of husband, at least not so soon." Livia placed her hands on my shoulders. "But I have known him all my life, and he will never harm you."

My jaw tightened. "I harmed his brother."

"He does not do this because of Sander. This isn't some grand scheme of revenge. He wishes to keep your folk and ours safe."

"From me."

Livia shook her head. "No. From Arion and any more feckless schemes he might make to overthrow fae and elven lands."

I almost believed her.

"Beautiful things can come from arranged vows." Mira pressed a hand to her heart and bowed at the waist. "Me, for example."

I arched a brow. "Your folk?"

"Yes." Without a word, Mira helped herself to a rouge lip stain in front of me and dabbed her own lips in the mirror. "My mother and father were arranged to stop wars, curses, and all manner of mayhem turns ago."

Curious. "I suppose heirs are produced even without affection."

"Oh, I assure you, my parents are affectionate. Ridiculously so. They're beautifully devoted to each other. Love came, even with arranged vows."

"Could be you, elven." Celine didn't look at me, her gaze was trained on a loose bead on her own gown.

Mira nodded. "Celine would know all about romance—"

"Earth fae." The sea fae snapped her head up. "Don't speak it."

"What? Speak of your new lover?" Mira wiggled her brow. "Why? All I want to know is every bleeding detail, is it so much to ask? What has it been like with such a burly man in your bed?"

Red flushed Celine's dark skin, but she faced Livia. "Why do you bring her?"

The Ever Queen laughed. "Because Mira has ways to get folk talking."

"I do. I am the Ever King's favorite besides you, Liv."

I almost grinned, almost wanted to join in the taunts. The Ever King had no care for much of anyone beyond his queen.

Celine flattened her palms on the vanity table, sneering at the fae princess like a challenge. "What would happen if I turned it on you, earth fae? You've looked more than once at Heartwalker."

Mira heaved a sigh. "My greatest failure. Where I have befriended the wicked Ever King, alas, his cousin is as hardened as stone. I fear I may be forced to concede."

I studied my fingers, a curl to my lips. "You could always draw a blade against him. Before you know it, you might be taking vows."

The room hushed, and I bit the tip of my tongue until the heat of blood filled my mouth. Gods, why did I speak?

Then, they laughed. Even Celine.

"You might be onto something, Skadi." Mira held up her hands as though displaying a thought in the air. "How to snare a husband—threaten to kill him."

This was odd. Not . . . horrible, but odd.

And it ended too soon. A heavy knock came to the door with a deep, urgent voice of the guard, insisting it was time to find our places.

The vows were about to begin.

CHAPTER 8
THE NIGHTMARE PRINCE

THE ELVEN PALACE WAS FILLED WITH GUESTS AND ROYALS FROM ACROSS THE kingdoms, but familiar voices were drawing too close to my dressing chamber.

"Although, I'm thrilled you've finally sought me out first, I must ask if we've thought this through?"

I let out a long sigh as the door opened with a crash against the wall. My father filled the doorway, clad all in black as though this were an ordinary day. He had hold of the arm of King Ari, Mira's father.

The two kings were vastly opposite.

Where Kase Eriksson was dark, Ari was bright. Daj did not speak much, and opted to be a silent, broody observer in most settings. Ari reveled in chatter and levity and busy words.

My father nudged Ari's shoulder. "Just use that mouth of yours and speak some bleeding sense into him."

I returned an exasperated look. "Really, Daj?"

My father said nothing, merely pointed a finger at me, a silent threat to comply and allow him to carry out his new scheme.

The door slammed behind him, leaving me alone with King Ari.

"Jonas."

"Ari."

The king adjusted a black circlet of raven wings over his golden hair. "How long do you think we must remain in here until he's convinced I've endowed you with my immense wisdom? I need your father to believe I've done it, for he has never openly asked for my input, although we all know he craves it."

I laced the front of my tunic and puffed a rogue strand of my dark hair off my brow. "I'm curious what made him seek you out. Are you the distraction while he arranges a kidnapping to steal me away?"

"I believe that might've been his first plan but your mother stopped him."

Gods.

With a sigh, Ari came to my side. "He wishes me to speak to you, hoping I talk you out of this decision since I also took vows of convenience. He's merely worried for you, and in his frenzy, has obviously overlooked a gaping flaw in his plan."

"What's that?"

"I am madly in love with my wife." Ari clapped me on the shoulder. "Your father knows this, *you* know this."

"I've grown up retching at the sight of you being odiously in love, Ari. This will not be the same."

The king hesitated. "But it wasn't always that way. We were tossed into a circumstance that forced us to be near each other. To learn of each other. To feel something more. You made this choice, and your intentions are good, but is that where it ends?"

"This isn't about love, this is about peace. Don't mistake me, I told the elven king I would see to it the princess is content, but this is larger than any one person. I don't want another war, Ari."

"I understand all that, I do. But the question remains: will you not try to make this something greater? Why can love not be part of it?"

To keep the princess content enough she did not wish to entertain the notion of Arion, was all I had planned beyond this day. I did not need to love her to do it.

In my silence, Ari gripped my shoulder. Like the other kings of the earth fae realms, Ari had been a second father to me and Sander. A man of jests and taunts, but in this moment he was wholly sincere.

"Happiness is all your mother and father want for you." He gave my arm a slight shake. "That is all any of us want. If there is no hope that it may come from this decision, don't tell him, but I am keen to share your father's worries."

I'd always been the feckless prince, the rake who bedded women well, but never asked for more.

Skadinia did not care for me, and I had no desire to care for her. We could find a bit of comfort around each other, perhaps, but to want more would be reckless.

I'd tried to demand it of myself over and over the whole of the morning.

But . . . I was the fool who'd stepped close to her on that damn shore last night. My hands touched her warm skin. Then I saw the hidden fire in those crystalline eyes, and the craving to have another dose would not leave.

It damn near tortured me.

"Happiness or not, I am seeing this through, Ari."

"Then I suppose it is time for you to absorb my stunning advice on how to make the most of it."

"There isn't much time—"

"Hush and listen. You'll be inspired soon enough." The king held up three fingers. "You do not know each other well, but find something that brightens her days. No matter what it is, seek to grant her that, simply to watch the joy fill her eyes." He waggled his second finger. "Give her your trust in her strengths, her ideas, and learn to trust her with yourself."

"What do you mean?"

Ari smiled. "Those secrets you think we don't know are in there— they should belong to her now."

The king would be disappointed, but I would never let her in on the weakest part of me. I hardly accepted the notion of Sander and my mother and father knowing.

"And finally, work at the first two every day until she is the one you want at your side on a battlefield."

Unexpected. "How is that important?"

Ari leaned a bit closer. "In that moment, when she is the only one you want standing with you against a foe, that is when you will know you've fallen in love with your wife."

My family was waiting in the corridor.

Ari followed me and glared at my father. "You seem to have forgotten the last twenty turns of my adoration toward my wife. She'll be horridly offended you think I'd carry any regrets. I plan to tell her, you shadowy sod."

My father merely grunted and turned away from his fellow king.

This was one final, desperate attempt to put a halt to this alliance.

Ari let out a long breath and took my mother's hand, pressing a kiss to the top. "Have it be known, I imparted my majestic words of advice, and I believe we still have vows to attend. Don't look at me like that." He glanced at my father again. "He is a grown man, what would you have me do? Chain him to the floor?"

Daj folded his arms over his chest. "I'm not above it."

My mother stood at my father's shoulder. A beautiful queen, but vicious in her own right. Her hair was braided around a jagged black circlet, and her bright eyes looked wet with worry.

My mother squeezed Ari's arm in thanks before the fae king went to find his own family.

She took my hand. "I have no more words to offer, just make certain you do this for the right reasons, Jonas."

I wrapped my arms around her slender shoulders. My mother was fierce and gentle, as cunning as my father, but she was not so reluctant to reveal her tenderness. "I don't know what else to tell you. I know this is my mark."

"This is your life, not a heist."

I stepped back. "You both taught us how to feel out a step in a plan and never act until you knew the move was sure. This is not a scheme, but it is what I feel is the right move to take."

A head shorter than me, my mother had to tilt her chin to meet my gaze. "Then we stand at your back and follow your lead. You have us."

Sander leaned against the wall, flipping through a thin book that looked like short tales of elven lore. "Mira insists she's never going to forgive you for choosing me to stand at your shoulder."

"As much as I love my Mira, I refuse to stand through this day without my brother." I nudged his ribs. "We share such a similar face, perhaps we can swap if I become a coward."

Sander scoffed, but there was a shadow of words unsaid in his gaze. Like he might want to offer to take my place.

Wouldn't happen. I had vowed to defend the fae lands, sealed in a spell cast, and I would be the one to see it through today.

I adjusted the polished leather belt around my waist. Everything was finely made from my tunic to the laces on my boots. The title of prince was mine by birth, but my upbringing was hardly regal, not the way I was certain my bride was raised.

Unwelcome apprehension needled into my belly like barbed rope. Would she be miserable in such a court?

Back home, finery was overlooked, prestige and propriety were dull, and I misplaced my official crown over two turns ago. I rarely looked like a prince and never thought much of it until now a woman I was forcing into our world might find it all . . . awful.

"Where are your thoughts?" Sander stepped in front of me, a furrow to his brow.

I forced a smile and patted his cheek, too rough, as we always did. "With the elven wine. I've heard a great deal about its taste and potency. Let us hope old Eldirard has overindulged tonight."

Sander slapped the book closed and tucked it under one arm. "I will stand at your side today. Although, after it's over, I have things I've been learning about the elven folk and—"

"Later." I shoved his head. "Gods, can you *not* read about something for one day."

"That would be an awful day." He pounded his fist against my shoulder, took my mother's arm, and left me with my father.

Silence was thick and potent. At long last, I squared to him. "Daj, I never wanted to disappoint you."

"You never have." His voice was the low, dark rasp that once told me tales until I fell asleep as a boy. He blinked, clearing his eyes of the darkness of his mesmer and stood so our chests touched. "But hear me—you'll be faithful, Jonas. Don't you dare dishonor your wife. She is your choice, no matter what has brought you together. You will respect her as that choice, understand me?"

Good hells, there was a desperation buried in Kase Eriksson's tone I'd never heard before. "Daj, this isn't exactly a traditional vow. She may never allow me to touch her."

"I suppose that is a problem you'll need to solve." He cupped the back of my head and drew my brow to his. "You do make me proud. Now meet your mark; I will see you out there."

CHAPTER 9
THE MIST THIEF

THE LAST TIME I WAS IN THE FESTIVAL COURTYARD, BLOOD AND SMOKE FILLED the air. Half the trees were burning along the portions of the towers. With the way the courtyard had been dressed for the vows, I would never guess battles were fought not so long ago.

Walls made of polished black stones were draped in blue and silver satins with the seal of the shadow elven clan. Natthaven used a rune meaning wisdom and honor wrapped in black ribbons settled over the top of crossed arrows. Iron sconces held black candles to light the yard when dark fell.

Sunlight broke across the stones, threading skeins of gold and red over the pale woven rugs that were arranged between long, moss coated benches where folk were seated.

In the front row, Princess Mira and Celine were seated with other heirs and noble sea fae. I recognized some faces from the sea fae palace and the battle. Folk who came against us with blades now were arranged and prepared to watch one of their beloved princes vow with an enemy.

My grandfather was seated atop a dais draped in black satin.

His beringed fingers curled over the clawed arms of his seat. Two guards held silver spears. Dorsan was on Grandfather's left. Stoic and unreadable.

When the guard on the king's right shifted, revealing his features, my heart stopped. Cian. Slender and tall, he kept his russet hair braided behind his neck.

Young to be one of the king's guards, only thirty turns, a decade my senior. There was something about the coldness in his bright eyes my grandfather revered, like he knew there was a viciousness in Cian that could be utilized as a threat to enemies.

But the king knew of my discomfort around the man. Wasn't today meant to bury the anger of battles?

I drew in a sharp breath and scurried away from the diaphanous shades when Cian glanced toward the covered bower.

Would he mock me in front of the fae? Stand as a voice to show my new folk the truth of their formidable war prize—a weak woman who was more terrified of her power than they were?

I peered to the other side of the courtyard. The alver king and queen were seated on an opposite dais next to every other king and queen of the fae—ten seats in total with the inclusion of the Ever King and Queen.

The prince's mother and father said nothing to me during the negotiations, but their faces were not so tormented as they'd appeared last night.

The king had his fingers laced with the queen's and used both their linked fists to prop his chin, as though he merely wanted her skin on his. The queen even laughed with one of the others who looked a great deal like Mira.

She seemed happy enough.

Heat skirted across my middle, toward my heart. I glanced down at the heart glass on my bodice. *Dammit.* Whatever magic was said to reveal the heart was burning in a brilliant glow, doubtless something to do with the anticipation of my impending vow.

The glass was revealing I felt more than I wanted to let on.

After a few deep breaths, the beads returned to the clear, sparkling hue.

The sound of crinkling parchment drew my attention to the back of the tent. My breath caught. A sealed missive slid beneath the tent, a starlight wax seal over the back. Written on the king's pale rose parchment from the palace studies.

My mouth curved in the corner. Grandfather was not a man of many declarations of affection, but I would revel in his assurances now.

With my thumb, I broke the seal, and froze. This was not from the king.

He will never truly accept what you are. You do not belong with his folk.

I crumpled the parchment and rushed for the flap of the tent, peering out. No one was there save a few patrolling guards keeping watch on the vows. Who would write such a thing? It was as though they could read my every fear of this new alliance.

The prince did not know every dreary truth about me. I doubted he would have much interest in my presence beyond the obligations of the alliance. There was no reason to fret over secrets of the past being discovered.

I slipped back into the tent, a hand pressed to my heart. One deep breath through my nose, then another, until my pulse ceased pounding.

A soft lyre began to play. The shades parted. I dropped the disorienting anonymous note. Clearly, there were some who did not agree with my grandfather's alliance. This was nothing but a weak strike at unraveling a chance to end battles.

I would not allow cowardly words to stop this chance for the Dokkalfar to have protected shores. Personal misery be damned. I would endure a man who despised me as a wife if it kept my folk safe.

It was time.

The parchment crumbled beneath my foot. My skin prickled like a dozen drops of hot rain cascaded over my arms and legs. Once more, I shook out my hands. For the Dokkalfar, for Natthaven, I would see this through.

Gowns and leather rustled and groaned when folk stood once I stepped into the sun.

Heart in my throat, I fisted my hands by my sides and strode toward an arched bower at the end of the woven rugs. Damp leaves, herbs, silken petals, and copper juvel coins landed at the hem of my gown with each step.

Traditional elven vows made a bride stand alone while folk tossed symbols of her home and past at her feet as she walked toward her future.

I kept my eyes schooled on the designs in the rugs—stars and moons, runes and swords. Until I made my way past Grandfather's dais and he cleared his throat. I swallowed and lifted my chin.

Breath stuttered in my chest.

By the hells, it was true—my new prince was a fiend. The sinking sunlight burned at his back, casting his darkly clad shoulders in flames, like he was my beautiful destruction preparing to devour me.

The prince had his deep chestnut hair tied off his face, and a dark steel blade tethered to his waist. In all our acquaintance, this moment he truly appeared as a delectable villain from one of the folktales on my shelves.

His twin stood at his back in the traditional role of a friend or relative standing in wait to welcome a new member of the house. There wasn't anger or rage in his brother's eyes. On the contrary, the second prince looked about the beginnings of the ceremony with utter fascination.

I dared not look to the other dais, dared not face the long row of fae royals, and kept my focus ahead.

Jonas Eriksson. His name tumbled about in my skull, as though my mind could not be convinced he was my future. Foe, defeater, now husband.

A muscle ticked in his jaw. The gleam of his rich green eyes never wavered when he held out a hand. Rough calluses collided with my palms after our fingers curled together, and the subtle squeeze he offered splashed my insides with a strange sense of calm.

The instant I faced him, an elven speaker—a man who devoted his life to speaking with the gods in the hillside chantry—began reciting vows in elder elvish.

"I have no idea what is being said."

The prince's whisper startled me from the haze of the moment.

"Oh." I kept my voice hushed. "He's . . . he's speaking of the honor it brings a woman to join with a new house. Now, he describes the duties the vowed must accept."

"Hmm. What sort of duties?"

His eyes were rife in mischief, like he wanted to spar with me. So be it.

"Duties like a husband's requirement to tend to a bride's every whim."

"Tell me more about these whims."

I cast a glance at the speaker who was wholly uninterested in our quiet chatter. "He is saying desires such as solitude for reading are of utmost importance. To better a bride's mind for her husband, of course."

"Naturally."

"And long baths, so her beauty never fades. For her husband's benefit."

"A grand benefit."

"Also, there is a duty to ensure her need for delicacies is satisfied, lest she grow temperamental and sour toward her husband."

Jonas leaned in, his lips close to my ear. "Tell me about these *delicacies*."

Gods, had his voice always been so silken? Heat dripped in my belly. I was a weak woman and could not even rise to the challenge of unsettling this man before such a simple word burned through my veins in a strange collision of disquiet and desire.

"Delicacies like sweet cakes, obviously."

"Foolish of me to consider anything else."

"Honey filled, with a bit of spiced cream to be exact."

Jonas's mouth split into a grin, the dangerous sort, like he was head first in this game of unraveling the other, and planned to rise victorious in the end.

Before he could respond, the speaker cleared his throat, annoyed. Cupped in his palms was a wooden bowl filled with blue stain. The speaker soaked a finger in the color. "You are to be marked as bonded in this life and the journey into the Otherworld."

Jonas watched as the tops of my palms were painted in runes of honor and respect and fealty. Next, my brow.

The speaker faced the prince and did the same.

"Bonds and vows may now be sealed with the kiss. As the gods kissed barren earth to sprout new life, you now begin your united paths."

The world around me blurred. I knew this moment would come, by the hells, by the laws of Natthaven, he could command any piece of me now as my husband. I should not be so startled at the notion of a kiss.

I took a bit of pleasure when the prince hesitated for half a breath, like he might be as unsteady as me. Dithering did not last long. Jonas cupped a hand behind my neck and tugged my mouth to his.

Tight lips met the softness of his. His second palm cupped under my jaw, drawing our bodies closer.

Little by little, my lips parted. I shuddered when my mouth moved with his, longer than the uncomfortable, forced kiss I imagined. This was maddeningly slow, as though the prince wanted to take his time, memorizing the way my mouth fitted to his.

The tip of his tongue touched the edge of my lips and my knees stumbled. One of my palms pressed over his heart before I could recoil, and I should've. I ought to have pushed away, kept carefully boarded barriers in place. I ought to curse him for his devious success at clawing his way through.

I could not think of anywhere I would rather be.

The prince tasted like the morning—crisp and cool—and something horrid was happening. Somewhere deep in the marrow new, relentless hunger bloomed into a craze for more. Such a meager taste of the man would not be enough.

Jonas pulled back. His eyes were darker, like a night forest, and kicked down to the glass over my heart. The smile curved over his mouth held more viciousness than tenderness. "There's my fire."

Beautiful gold burned over my bodice. Damn the hells. Everyone would see the evidence that my blood rushed from the prince's touch.

"I was told of those clever little stones. It seems, wife, your heart is racing. Is that all for me? You're not so aloof as you let on, are you?"

Damn bastard.

I narrowed my gaze. If he wished this to be nothing more than a game, I now had our entire lives to play.

"You think you're clever?"

"Every day."

"All right, you might've discovered I am not so lost in the remnants of my affinity, but hear this, *Husband*"—I followed his lead and whispered near to his odd, rounded ear. There was a spark of delight when he drew in a rough breath— "I promise you, if I burn, so will you."

The green of his eyes brightened. "I can hardly stand the wait."

CHAPTER 10
THE NIGHTMARE PRINCE

ELDIRARD OVERINDULGED ON ELVEN WINE. SWEET AND THICK, LIKE SATIN ON the tongue, an opposite flavor from the harsh, burning taste of alver brän ale.

I rolled a crystal flute between my fingers, watching the burgundy drink swirl about. Would Skadi retch with brän, hate it, favor it? Would she come to love anything in Klockglas more than elven lands?

I snorted and took another sip. What good was it to fret over such things? The moment we were declared vowed, elven women pulled her away from me—to dress her in something more sensible, I was told.

Now for all the revelry surrounding us, I had not spoken two words to my wife. Another rough chuckle slid from my throat.

"These are warm." Mira leaned forward and touched a clay bowl filled with pale pebbles that looked as though flames were trapped inside.

"I read about these." Sander plucked one. "Everlast stones, I think they're called. A guard said it was a gift from the light elves."

I bristled. There was nothing I wanted from that clan. They could fade away into the far seas and never return for all I cared.

"Light elven use light and flame, and if I'm right, they can trap light

71

in these stones that never fades." Sander studied one of the stones. "These are their most common trade item. Useful, I think."

The table descended into a few touches to the stones to test if they were truly warm like a distant flame. I lost interest and took another drink of wine.

The Ever King sat across the table from me, a look of befuddlement on his face. "Is this how fae vows are, love? If so, I don't care for them and I plan to make ours much better."

"You're taking vows, Bloodsinger?" My voice was darkened with drink. "I hadn't heard."

"It's a recent discussion." Livia draped an arm over her mate's shoulder, tracing one of the scars on the side of his neck. "It's not sea fae culture, so I told him we didn't need them, but—"

"I want them." Erik pressed a kiss to her palm. "Every damn way to be bonded with you, I want it, love. But not like this." The king lifted his own drink and used it to gesture at me. "You'll be properly placed on my lap through the whole of it."

"Is it proper to have a bride on your lap the whole time, Blood-singer?" Sander leaned back in his chair, laughing.

The king's crimson eyes flashed. "When your bride is my queen, there is no other way to see it done, Prince."

Livia rolled her eyes, but kissed Erik's jawline.

Mira leaned onto her elbows over the table, her attention on the somber features of the king's cousin. "What of you, Hearttalker?"

"*Heart. Walker.* And what?" Tait had the same red in his eyes as Bloodsinger, but they darkened when he faced the princess.

"Would you carry your woman around like the king during your vows?"

Tait frowned. "I wouldn't vow."

"You might change your mind if—"

"No." His voice was cutting and final.

Mira cursed under her breath, muttered a few words like *fool* and *sod*, then abandoned the table until she joined a crew of Rave, the warriors of the fae kingdoms.

She didn't look back to notice that Heartwalker tracked every step of her retreat.

Aleksi pounded his drinking horn on the table. "Strange, but I have to agree with Bloodsinger, Jo."

The sea king narrowed his eyes. "There are times you don't agree with me?"

I tossed back the last of my wine. "What are you trying to say, Alek?"

"You should be with your wife during the vow feast."

The great hall of the elven palace was aglow with endless torches and sconces with flickering candles. Tables lined the edges, holding noble folk of Natthaven, Rave warriors, noble houses from the Ever Kingdom, and the royals of our lands.

In the center, couples danced to the beat of drums and curved harps. Servants traipsed between the crowds filling wine and ale for guests. It was a revel of note to celebrate a bride and groom.

It merely seemed the only two who had not interacted were the actual bride and groom.

Starlight hair gleamed from across the hall. Godsdammit. The sensible gown she'd abandoned the courtyard to don was made of blue fabrics, delicate enough the slightest breeze rustled the skirt like sea waves. The neckline was carved out down to her smooth stomach, revealing the sun-darkened tint of her skin and side swells of her breasts.

To make her all the more alluring, coils of designs peeked out across her flesh. Was it paint for the ceremony? An elven tradition? Or had my apprehensive bride inked places of her skin like I'd done with mine?

My depraved mind drifted to the unwelcome desire to peel back more of that gown to see more of those delicate designs.

Bleeding hells. This was meant to be the end, a vow to secure peace, then we could live our lives by all other means quite separate.

Buried in the corners of her full lips was a secret smile, pleading to break free should someone be clever enough to draw it out. Would her laugh be like a song or soft as a whisper? A courtier from one of the fae kingdoms dipped his chin, drawing her attention.

Beneath the table, a fist curled over my knee. I did not blink as she tipped the crystal flute to those sweet lips, listening as the bastard told her what was likely a dull, arrogant tale.

He looked to be from one of Mira's forest courts where revelry was as common as breathing, and skill with a blade was a foreign notion.

What a sod.

Until he waved his hands with a new bit of exuberance and my wife closed her eyes, jolting like he might strike her.

Dark heat gathered like a knot of jagged iron in my chest. She flinched and I wanted to know why.

A desire for violence burned in my veins, swift and fierce. Wicked dealings were no strangers in my world, but the onslaught of this was a cheap strike from behind, claiming all my rational thought.

I rose from my seat, burdened with a new starvation for answers that twisted low in my gut. I didn't look anywhere but at the tension in her jaw, the expression that hinted her thoughts had drifted somewhere drearier.

Conversation stalled when I shoved through some of the elven and fae, some addressed me regally, others congratulated me on my vows. I ignored it all and gripped the top of the fae's shoulder.

He startled. "Oh. Prince Jonas, I was telling the princess of the similarities of the forests of Natthaven to Southern . . ."

He winced, words dying, when I dug my fingertips into the meat of his shoulder.

I pinned him in a grin that was more or less a snarl. "You've made my wife uncomfortable and have not taken a pause in your tale to take note. Step. Back."

He twisted his features in horror, murmured a swift apology, and bowed away from the conversation. Others had taken a cue and gave more space for me to face my wife.

A flush darkened the slender bridge of her nose and cheeks. "What are you doing?"

Wine loosened my tongue. "Protecting what is mine."

"By humiliating me?" Skadi's brilliant eyes shadowed with a touch of her own darkness.

If she hoped it would deter me, she would be disappointed—her villainy only drew me in more.

"I am not trying to draw you in," she said, voice a low hiss.

"Did I speak all that out loud?"

She ignored me and set her full lips in a tight line, then leaned in. Gods, she smelled of candied pomes and ripe berries. I tilted my face, yearning to bury my damn nose in her hair.

Skadi sniffed my skin, then nudged me back, brow arched. "How much wine have you had?"

"A bit."

"Elvish?"

"It's delicious. Have you ever tried it?"

She let out a groan and took hold of my arm. The way she positioned us, it would look as though the bride had lovingly linked arms with her groom.

Clever, wife.

"Where are you taking me?"

"To our chamber."

"Excellent choice." I stumbled through the doorway.

Skadi's arm went around my waist and I was certain I would be satisfied if her fingers became stitched to my body. "Elvish wine is known to fuel boldness and bravery, but too much and it makes men like you—who already think a great deal of themselves—reckless and stupid."

True enough, my head was heavy with grand gestures and declarations I planned to speak against her glistening skin tonight.

When we rounded the corner, I shifted and pinned her back to the wall. Skadi drew in a sharp breath. Good hells, I could listen to the sound again and again, preferably with her body beneath mine, her claws leaving marks on my back.

My grip went to her throat, not enough to hurt, merely a way to touch her, hold her. "That fae did not touch you, but I saw your eyes, your reaction. Someone has touched you and not kindly." I tugged on her bottom lip with my thumb. "I'll be needing a name."

"What? Why would I tell you anything? Especially when you don't even know what you're doing right now?"

"I know exactly what I am doing." My eyes felt heavy. I wanted to fall into bed, her arms and legs tangled with mine, and sleep until the next sunset. "If he is still breathing, I would like to change that, Wife."

Skadi's eyes widened. Why did I never consider the dangers of vowing with such a beautiful creature?

Silver rings lined the edges of her ears, all the way to the narrow point. Her fingers were much the same. Firelight gleamed over her eyes, and I took a pause to consider the blue. Brighter than a deep sea, but not so pale they looked like a summer sky. They were like sapphires with shattered silver in the center.

She wanted her fire to remain doused, little did she know her husband had plans to fan the flames until we were both set ablaze.

Then my forehead fell to her shoulder.

Voices surrounded me, spoken as though a thick door muffled the sound. Someone nudged me forward. Were my feet moving? Air shifted, cooler than the corridor, there was softer light.

"All hells you're enormous."

I was tossed backward onto something soft and cushioned.

I laughed. "In more than one place."

Skadi's soft features hovered close to mine, as though she had me pinned on my back. Was she straddling me? Bleeding gods, I was a lucky bastard.

Until she shifted away and something soft was placed behind my head. "Spoken like a man truly trying to compensate."

"Only you . . . will know from . . . now on, I suppose."

Cool air struck my feet. Where were my boots? Next, a weight of fur tickled beneath my chin. Words were a challenge, too muddled to speak.

But I remained lucid enough to catch a soft sigh, then, "Such an alluring nightmare."

CHAPTER 11
THE NIGHTMARE PRINCE

Sunlight was absolute shit.

Horrid and unfeeling, it sliced through my eyes like a molten stoker fresh from the fire. One arm fell over my eyes, but the weight of it added a pounding rush of blood to my skull.

Another groan, and I rolled onto my shoulder, cursing when whatever held me off the floor failed me, and I landed face down on a scratchy, woven rug. "Damn the gods."

Eyes half opened, I padded around until I found purchase on a table's edge that felt sturdy enough and heaved myself onto my knees. I hooded my eyes with my hands to keep the light from attacking again, and peered about.

I was in a sitting room of sorts. Gold filigree edged a dark inglenook. There were shelves with scattered books, some in stacks, others flipped onto their sides. The narrow bench seat where I slept was half covered in a fur cloak.

Atop the table was a tin of water and a few crushed herbs.

"Take them."

I whirled around, the movement sending nauseous waves through my insides and my head spinning.

Skadi, dressed in a simple slate gown, strode into the room, three thick tomes cradled in her arms. She added the books to a sturdy satchel on the floor, and once she stood, pointed at the herbs. "Take them, or you'll likely retch on the sea."

The sea?

Skadi folded her arms over her chest. "Are you prepared at all? The ships will be setting sail before the noon sun."

She spun around and kept stacking books and furs and what appeared to be diverse gowns for all seasons.

Gods. We were to sail home. With my wife.

I was vowed. A man with a household of his own. "The vows."

I fell back to the rug, the heels of my hands dug into my eyes, and another groan broke free.

"Ah, did your disappointment still rise with the sun?"

With a slight lift to my palms, I glared at her. "You twist my words."

She shook her head and went back to her preparations.

Bile teased the back of my throat. A few deep breaths through my nose, and I sat up, slowly staggering to my feet. Gods, I smelled like I'd rolled in a goat pen—sweat and leather and old drink. Careful not to stumble, I took the herbs and added them to the water, tilting the tonic onto my tongue in one swallow.

"That's gods-awful." I pinched the bridge of my nose.

"Perhaps, but it acts swiftly against a spinning head and belly."

"An elven trick?"

Skadi paused, smoothing a rabbit hide over the top of one pouch. "A me trick, I suppose."

She strode back into the bedchamber. I rubbed the back of my neck, following. My tunic was askew, my feet bare, I was certain my hair was standing on end. Hardly the vision a woman would want to greet with the dawn.

"A bit of a healer, are you?"

Her eyes lifted from the disheveled quilts over the grand canopied bed. "From age six to eight I learned to survive on my own, Prince. I'm certain you find that rather beneath you, but one learns tonics swiftly when seasons bring about illness. It is nothing but a mix of tidebane root that soothes upset bellies and sjal vine—a leaf native to Natthaven —that soothes the deepest aches of the skull."

I knew Skadi was not Eldirard's blood, but I never thought long on her life before the king brought her into the palace.

If I was to entice her to keep choosing this alliance for a turn, I was off to a piss-poor start.

"I, uh, I'll just clean myself up before I embarrass you further with my appearance." My fingers tapped the thick frame around the door. "I didn't make an utter fool of myself—or you—last night, did I?"

For half a breath Skadi almost seemed stunned by the question. She folded a linen shift and shook her head. "No. I managed to remove you from the hall before shame befell us."

"And I, we . . . I wasn't untoward, or—"

"Other than the moment you made maddening love to me? No, you slept quite soundly."

I coughed, hand to my throat as though it might steady the thrum of my pulse. "What did you say?"

One corner of Skadi's mouth twitched. She kept folding night shifts.

My shoulders slumped with relief. There was my fire. "You're mocking me. Well played."

"Never fear, Prince." Skadi strode to the doorway to the sitting room, glancing over her shoulder. "You didn't bed the beast."

A touch of bitterness wrapped the term and it turned my stomach over again. Is that how she thought I viewed her?

"I won't be long," I said, pausing halfway into the wide washroom. "Oh, and Skadi." When she met my gaze, I forced a weak smile. "I do not see surviving in the streets as beneath me. My folk did much the same. Look at that, Wife, we have so much in common already."

I closed the door, relishing in the puzzled furrow to her brow.

Sea fae would ferry the earth fae and alvers home. The magic in their voices was the only power capable of diving vessels beneath the tides like a bowing whale before we slipped through the watery borders and surfaced back in earth realms where fae and alvers made their kingdoms.

Natthaven was a fading isle. A place from myths and old lore. To fade and appear in different seas was a strange magic, one Skadi tried to engage the night we fought against each other.

The strain to pull away the whole of her land into her darkness was too fierce. It was the move that made her vulnerable for the strike of my mesmer, the burn of waking nightmares I shoved into her mind.

On the docks, I blinked against the sun. "Why did the isle not fade for you that night?"

Skadi hesitated. "It stopped speaking to me."

"What do you mean?"

"Natthaven has a magic all its own." She turned, taking in the dark trees coating the hillsides. From the shore, the peaks of the palace carved through the trees like spears. "Grandfather taught me, the affinity of the Norns flows through the soil. Fate is felt, and the isle will help those it trusts to meet their fate."

"So, you believe it was fate that brought us here since the isle did not bow to you?"

"I think it's nothing but a story to tell a curious girl so she respects the land. The only fate there that night was you arriving when I was utterly exhausted."

Something about her tone made me wonder if she spoke more to convince me, or herself.

King Eldirard positioned his isle on the edges of the Ever Kingdom and the far seas, open waters leading to lands I did not know.

As part of the treaty, Bloodsinger insisted the king keep the isle within sight until the vows; keep enemies close. Now, with the alliance secured, the elven king would be free to shift his lands out of the sights of sea fae if he desired.

By the water's edge Eldirard beamed like a man long starved who'd been given a feast. He bid farewell to the folk boarding the ships.

Celine Tidecaller had her crew loading their decks with belongings for Mira's clans. Bloodsinger and his dark Ever Ship were anchored nearest to the shore and would take the Night Folk fae, Livia's people. In truth, the sea king and queen would likely remain in the Northern realms for a week or so. They always did.

Cerulean sails hoisted along a ship with a narrow hull were positioned nearest to our dock. Gavyn was Celine's brother and had been tasked with sailing our clan home.

A hand struck my shoulder. Aleksi, clad in his Rave tunic and sword, tugged me against his chest, clapping me on the back. "I'm bidding you farewell and good luck."

"I have no need of it. I'm already the grandest husband in all the lands."

Aleksi stepped back and glanced over one of my shoulders where Skadi remained stoic and distant. "How was last night?"

"What sort of man do you take me for? It's improper to share the secrets of a bedchamber."

"The way you stumbled from the hall, I wasn't certain if you'd make it to your room, or if she'd kill you for being such a fool along the way."

"Elven wine is ruthless," I said with a shrug.

"No jests, Jo—how are you with all this?"

Moments from the previous night were lost in a drunken fog. Bits and pieces of anger, a compulsion to get to Skadi's side, and whispered words I could not recall before I fell into nothingness. I could tell Alek nothing had changed. I could tell him I felt little, but it wouldn't be entirely true.

I didn't understand it, but somewhere inside was the phantom tug of a possessive need to be nearer to the woman. To only her.

Never had I desired one woman. After turns of bedding many, I convinced my own heart it was not made to settle on one.

Now I couldn't get her damn face from my mind.

I gave him a quicksilver grin. "I survived my first night as a vowed man, and she didn't murder me out of annoyance. We will survive at least one more."

Aleksi's smile didn't reach his eyes. "Don't be a sod and you might survive longer."

Farewells between the fae kingdoms were rife in fanfare and mourning, as though we would not see each other numerous times through the seasons. Kings and queens—the men and women forever embedded in my life—all offered their well wishes to Skadi.

My wife was a cunning sneak, a beautiful trickster. Clearly, the woman knew how to mask her unease.

With each word offered to her from the kings, queens, and courtiers, welcoming her to the fae lands, Skadi would dip her chin politely. She would paste on a proper smile. She'd even take a hand or two. But where she thought no one would notice, a finger would flick by her side, or her cheek would sink inward, as though she were gnawing on it.

The other kingdoms were making efforts to welcome a new princess, but she'd yet to be alone with my mother and father.

Kase and Malin Eriksson loved fiercely, but they were a suspicious pair, always seeking out that cruel ulterior motive in those they did not know. No mistake, my folk would lurk in the shadows until they'd observed long enough to emerge.

Bells rang from the ships. I blew out a breath and went to her side. "It's time."

A lance of pain dimmed her eyes. Skadi looked once more behind us as though memorizing the trees, the sea mists, and the thatched rooftops of the palace.

I shouldered one of her satchels, feeling a great deal like a villain in her life. "We'll return soon."

"No matter." She cleared her throat and faced the sea. "This was part of the expectations. Shall we go?"

I offered a curt nod and walked with her down the docks to the small row boats that would take us to Gavyn's ship, while elven guards kept three paces behind. Eldirard awaited us with the same two guards who'd stood beside him on the dais during the vows.

The king wore a fur-lined cloak on his shoulders that winged out when he opened his arms wide.

"Ah, Skadinia, how lonely these corridors will be without you." The king pressed a kiss to her brow. "But be well in your new lands, keep to our agreements, and write to me often, child."

She embraced her grandfather.

Eldirard looked to me. "You are pleased, I hope, Prince Jonas?"

"Time will tell."

The king's face fell. "Was my granddaughter not pleasing?"

Shameful gazes pointed at Skadi boiled in my brain, and the same unsettling need to step in front of her, a shield against her own folk, caused my body to hum in overheated irritation.

"Time will tell," I went on, "for I do not yet know if my wife is pleased. Is that not the way of things? A satisfied wife makes for a pleasant life? If she is pleased, then I will be."

One of the guards chuckled like it was a ridiculous notion. A man with young features and a smugness that left me rather inclined to strike his jaw.

Skadi looked away, fingers tangled. Not so long ago she was standing toe to toe with me, taunting me, the fire in her eyes my new obsession. This man's mockery doused it.

I rather hated him. "What is your name? I don't believe I've been introduced."

The guard straightened. "Cian of House Aeburg."

"Ah. And tell me, Cian of House Aeburg, what did you find amusing about my wife's satisfaction?"

Cian's lip twitched. He looked at Skadi, but I took a step to the side, blocking his view.

"No offense meant, Prince Jonas. I simply hope you understand the darkness in our beloved princess. It is difficult to please."

"Darkness, you say?"

"Jonas." Skadi's fingertips touched my arm.

I didn't look back.

For me, mesmer magic was cold, like icy water replaced my blood. Sander described his as a roar of wind in his chest. When I blackened out the whites of my eyes the world looked as though the sun hid behind thick clouds.

My arm slipped around Skadi's waist, tucking her against my side. "I suppose it is a good thing she goes to a realm of nightmares then. She'll fit right in." Without brightening my gaze, I looked to the elven king. "We'll return to fulfill our obligations of the alliance."

Eldirard swallowed. "Of course. Dorsan will accompany you as the representative for my court."

The second guard with stern features sharp enough to cut glass stepped forward, a pack of belongings strapped to his back. The same man who'd come to gather my runaway bride at the tavern.

"He will be welcome, so long as he is not foolish enough to insult my wife, no matter how *subtle*." My teeth flashed at Cian. "You see, I have a terrible time forgetting such things, then I'm nothing but poor company."

Skadi stiffened against my side, but said nothing as she bid her grandfather another swift farewell.

Together, we stepped into the small row boat with a stone-faced Dorsan.

Once we were far enough from shore, I held Skadi's chin between my thumb and finger, drawing her face close. "Angry with me?"

"Yes."

I hummed, blinking until the darkness of my mesmer faded from my eyes. "I hope you'll forgive me."

"All so you can do the next infuriating thing?"

"I guarantee it."

She pinched her lips and shifted on the bench, barring me out.

I propped my elbows onto the edge of the boat and pointed my face toward the sunlight. "By the way, that was the first time you've called me by my name. I look forward to hearing it again and again, perhaps more breathless next time."

Skadi's toes struck the side of my shin. I jolted in a bit of stun, then laughed, rubbing a hand over the spot.

There was my fire.

CHAPTER 12
THE MIST THIEF

From the black helm, Celine's nobleman brother shouted commands for his crew to aid the alver passengers on their land.

Sea fae could dive the ships through a watery barrier to earth fae realms. It was the reason Arion attacked the sea realms first, the hope being that by conquering the Ever Kingdom, it would open the way to the other fae and alver lands.

I looked back at the dark strip of a current that marked the barrier. Once it had been violent and crushing, filled with a spell to divide the fae folk. As a show of good faith, my affinity had stolen the maelstrom away, leaving gentle seas, smooth enough even mortals could journey between earth and sea fae realms.

Gentle as it was, it still felt as though worlds now stood between me and Natthaven.

Gavyn Seeker nodded a curt greeting my way once he returned his grip to the helm.

Tall, with rich brown skin, dark hair and eyes, the man was a lord over one of the noble houses in the Ever Kingdom and spent more time in his own territory. I did not know him as well as others.

Unfamiliar shores came into view through soupy mists. My insides fluttered against my heart. What would I find in my new lands? I no longer knew what to anticipate. Already, these vows were not going according to plan. Where I imagined indifference, I could not stop thinking of the actions of my damn husband.

Even as drunken as Jonas was in the hall, there was a deliciously sincere threat in his voice when he asked for a name to slaughter.

Then with his sharp words toward Cian . . .

I curled my fingers back into fists. No one had stood for me in such a way.

Jonas, without a pause, pulled me behind him and showed his own darkness. Like mine was welcome, even . . . admired. My head was spinning in the oddities of the damn man. The only reason we were vowed was fear of my affinity.

Why would he defend it, encourage it, welcome it?

The ship shuddered when Gavyn dropped his anchor, knocking me against the rail.

"Gods, Gavyn. Were you trying to toss us overboard?" Jonas's shout reached the upper deck, as though he knew his features consumed my thoughts.

"Take your complaints elsewhere, Prince," the sea fae returned. "I am not a passenger ship. In fact, I am too noble blooded for this. It's insulting."

"You're a snob."

Gavyn laughed. "I am that too."

Air was heavy and wet with a coming storm. Each breeze carried salt and smoke and damp wood from the dark edges of a shoreline.

The Eastern shores of the earth realms were not mountainous but for a few foggy peaks in the distance. In the haze of the sea spray, outlines of townships revealed most of the trade had to be placed directly on the sea front.

Alver lands were made of longhouses and tenements on the edges of narrow, serpentine roads that disappeared into the mists.

Stomach in knots, I made my way to the stairs leading to the main deck.

"Best of luck, Princess." Gavyn leaned onto his forearms between the handles of his helm. "Don't kill each other. We're tired of fighting."

Before I could respond, one of his crewmen lifted me onto the gangplank leading to a wide dock below.

Crooked shops with slanted rooftops were made of three to four levels. Tenements lined the roads with green and orange moss spotted laths. Some roads were cobbled, others were made of mud and clay, but even this early in the morning, all were stuffed with hawkers and traders.

"Rather different than Natthaven, Lady Skadinia." Dorsan, one hand on the dark pommel of his elven sword, took in the port of the land with a wrinkle to his nose.

"It is." One corner of my mouth curved. "Perhaps different will be interesting."

Unflappable most days, Dorsan's grimace deepened. "It does not seem altogether . . . *tidy.*"

Inner roads on Natthaven were made from polished stones and homes were pleasantly whimsical. Forests were lush with meadows of silken blossoms and the Night Market was rife in sweets and sugared scents, not this new air of brine and smoke.

Alver lands seemed to keep a chaotic sort of order. Dark and mysterious, the kingdom did not gleam with pleasant greetings. No. Alver lands came with jagged edges and sharp teeth.

Laughter and taunts rolled over the dock. I drew in a sharp breath when the silver eyed guard shoved the king—the damn king—in the shoulder, mocking like he might toss Jonas's father into the water.

In Natthaven, such a thing would be cause for the rack.

Here, the king merely muttered something that had the silver-eyed man laughing, the sort where his head fell back with utter glee.

"How was the journey for you, Princess?"

A familiar face approached. Not the prince, but his brother. The one who nearly met the gods by my blade.

I froze.

The second prince smirked. "Ah. I get it. I'm all healed up, swear it. I'm not going to toss you into the sea."

"Sander is annoyingly logical." A deep, throaty whisper blew against my ear. Jonas drew his face alongside my cheek. One tilt to my head and my lips might brush his. "My brother let bygones be bygones the next morning, Fire."

Fire. I forced a scowl at the ridiculous name, hoping he would not catch the flush in my cheeks.

"It was pleasant enough," was the only answer I could give.

"Good. Welcome to the royal city of Klockglas. Thoughts?" The gleam in Jonas's eyes was filled with true pride as he took in his homeland.

Until he looked at me. Buried beneath his arrogance and delight was something uncertain. As though he might truly care for my approval. Like he wanted me to see a home as much as him.

To buoy up my new husband wasn't an expectation. I could tell him his lands were strange and uninviting, but a cinch tightened in my chest, cracking the shield against this land, this man.

"It's beautifully mysterious."

Jonas's grin widened. "You can't see from here, but there are groves and forests and old ruins not more than a few lengths away. Then other trade markets in other townships, of course. Oh, and the hunt arena hosts a days' long festival at the end of the frosts. I think you'd find it exciting."

I took a step closer to his side. "Perhaps someone could show me about."

"I will." Jonas readjusted the pack on his shoulder, holding out a hand for me to take. "There are better ways to move about Klockglas, you see. I'd hate for you to be shown wrong."

For a heartbeat, I hesitated, then slipped my palm into his. Unbidden, my top teeth dug into my bottom lip.

His delight was contagious. The prince did not see the crooked stoops or the unsteady structures. He merely saw home.

My new home.

CHAPTER 13
THE MIST THIEF

WE STEPPED OFF THE DOCK ONTO THE DAMP COBBLES OF A WIDE ROAD. A slender hand shot out and took hold of the prince's arm before I even realized a woman was there.

"Well, this must be her."

Jonas's expression turned smug. "Why so sour, Friggy? Miss us?"

The woman was dressed in a pale tunic and oversized trousers, kept a sliver of wood between her teeth and tilted her head to reveal her eyes hidden beneath the brim of a straw hat.

"The day I miss you is the day the gods come to claim me as their mistress."

"Don't sell yourself short, Frigg." Sander shoved past us, his own shoulders lined in satchels, and tapped the brim of the woman's hat. "It could happen."

Frigg shot a glare at the other prince and tore off her hat to readjust it. She was bony in her features, sharp cheeks, and a narrow nose. But there was a rugged loveliness about the woman. Long corn silk hair braided over her shoulders, pink lips, and sharp blue eyes.

She seemed familiar—*comfortable*—with the prince. I hated how some part of me cared to know if she was a lover.

What would it matter if she was? Heartache would follow if I fell into those verdant eyes, the sly jests off his tongue, if I started to believe Jonas Eriksson had any plans to cherish me.

"What brings you down to the shore?" Jonas asked Frigg. "Thought you'd be helping your maj with her orders."

A bit of pride brightened Frigg's eyes. "I was until I saw the ship. So, you going to introduce me or what?"

The woman returned her scrutiny to me.

"Not sure I should subject her to the likes of you," said Jonas.

"You're an ass."

I looked away. "Folk keep calling you that."

Jonas merely laughed. "Frigg Hob, meet Princess Skadinia of Natthaven. My wife."

"Skadi." I swallowed and held out a hand. Frigg glanced at it, pausing long enough, I wondered if I'd caused offense. In the next breath, she clasped my forearm, like we were warrior maidens together.

"Can't believe you're vowed." She shook her head. "Best of luck, Princess. He's a ridiculous amount of work."

"Jakoby, look, they're back." A woman with satin black hair stepped onto the stoop of a stone shop with a roof that tilted one way while the walls leaned another.

Frigg snorted a laugh. "Ah, you've been spotted. Hold tight, Princess. My mother hasn't stopped talking about this since the announcement was made. She won't admit it, but she wanted to be the one to make your dress. Been studying elven fashions as best she can."

A woman here wanted to make a gown for me? She knew nothing about me save for the truth that I was positioned on the opposing side of a battle.

"Inge, my love." Jonas opened his arms.

With her skirt gathered in her hands, Frigg's mother laughed, then wrapped the prince in her arms that barely reached around his broad body. "A vowed man? Can't believe it."

"Maj." Frigg plucked the sliver of wood from her teeth. "Meet Jonas's wife—Skadi."

"All gods. An elven princess." Inge waved her hand stiffly by her side. "Jakoby. Jak. Come here."

"My sweet, I'm clearly coming." A lanky man sauntered toward the docks, a paper smoke between his teeth, and dark hair tucked behind his ears beneath a napless cap. The man had a devious sort of glint to his dark eyes, but it softened when he pressed a kiss to Frigg's brow.

"Well, well." He spoke around the paper smoke. "Wasn't a big jest, and the boy brought home a wife."

"Princess, these are my parents, Inge and Jakoby Hob." Frigg gestured at them, as though putting her mother and father on display. "Like I said, Maj would fall into the Otherworld if you'd let her make you a dress."

"I'd be bleeding honored. The way the elven use real gold in their threads." Inge practically hummed. "Stunning."

I returned a cautious smile, uncertain what to say or what to approve here. Jakoby clasped Jonas's arm in a greeting.

"Hob." Jonas grinned. "Before we left, I heard you and old Hervor had a falling out."

The man frowned. "Is that what he's saying? I ought to rob him blind. Gods, it's been so long since I've been on a good heist."

"Herv would take to knives if you try it."

Frigg's father scoffed. "What sort of cutthroat do you take me for, boy? A slob?"

Jonas laughed, and I felt as though my world had been turned upside down. Cutthroats, heists. What was this place?

"Oh, let it be." Inge kissed her husband's cheek. "You'll need to forgive Jak, Princess. He takes it rather personally if someone does not praise my every piece."

"Hervor damn near insulted you, sweet." Jakoby drew a long puff of his smoke.

Jonas rolled his eyes and shook his head. "We ought to be on our way. Inge." The prince waited until the woman met his gaze. "My wife won't ask for it, so just make her the dress. I'll send you the penge for payment tomorrow."

"Best of luck, Princess," Frigg called after us when Jonas urged us down the path. "He really is a horrid amount of work!"

She snickered with a bit of wickedness when the prince shot a crude gesture back at her without turning around.

Dorsan kept a pace behind us, hand never falling from the hilt of his blade, but his gaze kept watch on the few towers near the gates.

Men leaned out the windows, less formal than the elven guard, more from curiosity. They murmured to their watch partners, some gnawing on strips of jerky or roots, then pointed down at the road.

I felt like a damn spectacle.

Near the gates to the inner town were three black coaches with silver edging along the side panels.

"Seems my family has abandoned us." Jonas propped his hands on his waist as the first coach peeled away into the crowds.

A crack of leather lurched the second coach forward.

"Jonas. This one's open." A thick-necked man stood beside the door.

He wasn't alone. The man with silver eyes who'd been taunting the alver king winked and spun a knife in each hand with unnerving precision.

The prince tossed the packs on his shoulders into the cab. "I don't believe you've met any of the Kryv yet. Dorsan, if you see them lurking, I assure you they aren't here for assassinations."

"Unless that was our plan," the man with knives said. "Keep you comfortable all your life, then strike."

I laced my fingers in front of my body. "The Kryv? Is that what you call the guard?"

"No." Jonas let his thumbs hook around the top of his belt. "The Kryv are a guild, so I suppose they might be comparable to inner circles of other kingdoms."

"Only a little more wretched." The man winked and tucked his knives into sheaths on his thighs.

"I don't understand."

Jonas folded his arms over his chest. "When my father greets the Otherworld, he will not wish to be remembered as a king. In fact, he'd come back through the gates to slit our throats if we try. He will want to be remembered as a thief, scoundrel, and guild lead of the Kryv."

I scoffed, as though it were a jest, but I was the only one. "You speak true?"

The silver-eyed man leaned a shoulder against the side of the coach. "We don't jest about our glorious past of heists and schemes, lovey."

"This sod is Raum," Jonas said, clapping him on the shoulder, then turning to the brute of muscle and leather "And this berserker, here, is Lynx."

The other man dipped his chin and murmured a soft, "Princess."

"You'll see the Kryv about. Ignore their poor manners and watch your jewels."

"How dare you." Raum pressed a hand to his chest, disgust curled on his lip. "I won't be thieving from the princess." He turned to me. "Not unless she deserves it."

I cracked a knuckle, wholly unsettled.

Jonas did not hold the same disquiet, merely chuckled, then held out a hand for me. Warmth from his palms scorched under the chill of my fingertips.

The dark centers of his eyes flared as he handed me into the coach and heat flooded my veins. For a pause, we merely stood there, nose to nose.

Gods, what the hells was wrong with me?

I shook away the prickle of his touch and stepped into the coach. He was not going to love me. In truth, it was a bit puzzling that my new husband did not still wish me dead.

Violence was in his blood—I witnessed it firsthand during the battle.

"You killed him." The prince hovered over me, eyes black as the wing of a raven. His palms clasped my head and when the cold filled my skull, all I heard were my own screams as the nightmares flooded my mind.

Knives slashing my grandfather's chest while he sobbed for the pain to end.

Cold hands shouting at me to cut out the darkness, then a lithe body rewarding me by pinning my hands over my head and telling me he would love me as he thrust too hard.

A woman who kissed me goodnight while a tall man blew out a small

flame, leaving promises of swimming in the morning. But their smiles faded to
lifeless eyes and cold flesh beside me as fists pounded at the door, there to take
me away.

"Where did your thoughts go? Raum won't truly rob you."

I jumped when fingers tapped the top of my palm. The prince pulled his hand away and took his place on the opposite bench in the coach.

"It's just been a long journey," I lied.

Once Dorsan was seated on the driver's bench of the coach, Raum clapped on the side, and the charge lurched forward.

My spine was straight, stiff, senses at the ready for an attack from this lawless sort of kingdom at any moment.

Jonas slumped against the back of the bench. "How do you wish to spend your first night here?"

I folded my hands in my lap, watching the crooked walls of shops shift to stone walls. "I am accustomed to being solitary. If you have somewhere else to go, someone else to be with, I understand."

"I won't deny, I enjoy the hint of jealousy in your tone."

My mouth pinched when I met his gaze. "I think you are hoping to hear jealousy. I am not blinded to your attractive . . ." Good hells, I cut off my words before I made an utter fool of myself.

It was too late.

"Attractive, you say?" Jonas leaned forward. With such a small space, it was simple enough to draw his face close, his breath warm on my lips with each word. "Think my bed will be filled tonight? Think my hands will be caressing a woman's skin?"

He was goading me.

"It certainly will give me freedom to do as *I* wish."

"Oh? And what is that?"

The damn prince did not pull back. His nearness was made worse when he tilted his terribly beautiful face, as though he might align our mouths.

"I suppose you can wonder while you are tangled with your lover."

Jonas studied me for a drawn pause. "Who should I take as a lover?"

His hand fell to my knee, thumb rubbing slow, tight circles over my skirt.

94

"Frigg is rather lovely."

His mouth twitched, his hand eased up my leg. "She is."

"And she seems fond of you, so simple enough. Perhaps she is already your lover."

"She is not, and there are a few problems with your choice of woman." Jonas's wicked fingers dug into my upper thigh, voice a low rasp. "Frigg has been a friend since birth and doesn't much care for cock. Prefers women, you see."

He kept his hand climbing. I bit down on the tip of my tongue to keep in a gasp of pleasure when the prince curled his palm around my hip, yanking me forward to the edge of the bench.

The angle of his knees forced mine to split. One of his legs was positioned between my thighs, and bunches of my gown furled around him. My knee was nearly nuzzling his length.

I glanced down to see how near, once, twice. Shame heated my face and I forced my attention to the top of the coach.

Jonas held me in a way that my body tangled around him as much as possible without straddling his lap.

I was a weak woman, for I wasn't certain I'd mind if I did.

"I'll rephrase my previous question." The prince spoke with a deep silky darkness, so near to my parted lips the heat of every word brushed over my tongue. "Would it bother you if I spent my time with other women?"

"No."

"If you care so little, I wonder why your skin is flushed, Wife."

"I'm merely annoyed by your nearness."

He returned a wolfish grin. "Ah, see, I thought you might've imagined being the one in my bed. It is a marvelous thought, you ought to give it a go."

"Only in my nightmares." The lie felt heavy with each word.

"But they would be such satisfying nightmares." The prince leaned forward. "And I think you are lying."

He gripped a handful of my gown, like he might lift it, baring my thighs to him.

I didn't push him away.

My voice was ragged, too low, too soft. "I will not tell you to do otherwise. Your folk even made it clear we were not bound to fidelity. Perhaps I'll do the same."

Rough breaths made the prince's shoulders rise and fall with a bit of strain. "If you're trying to get under my skin, you're succeeding. The notion of you being seen by anyone else has me feeling rather violent."

He couldn't mean it. It didn't fit the reality I'd shaped for this vow.

One corner of my lip curled. "Are you saying you want to reap the benefits of your claim on me, Prince?"

"My wants must come second." He tilted his head. "Until you want the same, my hand will be my lover."

"I don't believe you."

"I don't blame you."

Jonas's palm drifted up my spine, slow and sensual, the tips of his fingers memorizing each pearl button on my gown. This close, my breasts brushed against his chest.

Perhaps it was imagined, but a flash of dark ink seemed to spill into his eyes, and a strange rumble rolled from his throat on his next draw of air.

"I will do what I can to prove it to you," Jonas said.

"You are not obligated to me but on the full moon. I am not here to disrupt your existence. I am simply your wife."

Jonas dragged the tip of his nose across my cheek. I fisted my palms over my knees.

When he spoke, his lips grazed my ear. "Yes you are, Fire."

Need throbbed between my thighs, and for a fleeting moment, I imagined his mouth on my neck, the hand on my spine unfastening those buttons.

Before I could rationalize through the haze, I let my knees widen a bit more, and nudged forward until the point of his knee added friction and pressure to the ache of my core. Jonas moaned and turned his face against me, his teeth nipped at one of the rings in my ear.

The coach shuddered to a halt, nearly spilling me off the last bit of the bench.

Jonas pulled away, blinking like he'd been tossed into the shadows of want as much as me. When movement from the front rocked the coach, I hurried to smooth out my skirts and return to my stiff, distant position on my seat, head turned away from my husband.

In another heartbeat, Dorsan wrenched open the door. "We've arrived, My Lady."

CHAPTER 14
THE MIST THIEF

I COULD NOT BE NEAR MY NIGHTMARE PRINCE. WHAT A FITTING NAME. HE WAS A stunning terror that kept infecting my mind, my heart, until I lost my bearings. Until I could not return to the safety of my strategic plans.

Dorsan held out an arm for me to place my palm, formal and frigid.

We were here to represent the poise of the Dokkalfar clans. In truth, in my new home, it seemed snobbish regality was the interloper.

Laughter and curses and foul jests rolled through the crowds outside the palace.

Jonas's mother was positioned in front of a man who kept tossing a leather pouch back and forth in his rune-inked fingers. The queen shoved his shoulder, and he did much the same, even tousling her hair until the king stepped between them.

They laughed.

There wasn't malice in their movements.

My stomach tightened until bile rose in my throat. How was I to do this? All my life, tutors guided me in etiquette aimed for royal condescension.

Here, it was hard to make out who held a title and who didn't.

"My Lady?" Dorsan pressed. "Is there something the matter?"

"Everything." I kept a distance from the unloading. No one seemed

98

to notice. Not yet. "I was not the princess the Dokkalfar desired, always falling short of the expectations. Now, I do not know how to be . . . this."

Alvers seemed a touch uncouth, but also free.

Dorsan never broke his stern observance. "You will learn their ways. You must. This is your place now."

My place. I felt as though I had no place.

Royals were meant to be dignified. They were the figureheads of the kingdoms, never faltering. Cara would be horrified to see a queen tossing a roll of furs over her shoulder, or a king speaking with those unloading their coaches like they were his equal.

My grandfather would be ashamed, but I envied them.

I closed my eyes until the jagged tension eased in my chest. "Klockglas. This is Klockglas."

"The Black Palace is what we call it."

Hair raised on the back of my neck when *his* voice brushed against my ear again.

"I have studied maps of your lands. I thought the royal house was in Klockglas."

"It is." Jonas came to my side. "But the Black Palace is the whole of this hill. It's practically a town all its own."

Behind the portcullis folk walked the grounds. Courtiers in woolen tunics and dresses. Some with long bows and spears. There were a few guards with red cloaks, the only hint of a uniform at all.

Towers with sharp spires topped the palace and sliced through fading wisps of the chill like gnarled fingers. Black stone and dark wood shaped the walls. From what I could count, the palace was made of four levels.

Lancet windows boasted the only color. Stained in paintings of white blooms and vines on some, others depicted ravens in flight or moonless nights.

"Thoughts, Wife?" Much the same as the shore, a sliver of vulnerability broke his tone. He wanted me to delight in his home.

"It is the most expansive royal grounds I've seen. Greater than Natthaven's courtyards."

"Truly a marvel, My Lord." Dorsan dipped his chin, playing his role well. The slight twitch to his nose, I wasn't so certain my fellow elven spoke true.

But Jonas smiled, pleased, and for a fleeting moment I did not feel so out of place.

Mutely, Jonas led us forward. Crowds moved to various areas of the outer yards and entrances. There was no true formal reception, but beneath the smoke in the air was a savory scent of spices and herbs.

The front entrance of the Black Palace was enormous. A domed ceiling so high, voices and steps echoed through the corridors like haunts in the night. Panels on the walls were made of cold stone and the same dark wood from the outer walls.

Shelves and tables aligned the corridors, most topped with colorful glass, blades, or oblong wooden figurines of wolves or birds that seemed a little childish.

Folk rushed to and fro. On first glance, the inner halls seemed chaotic, but the more I stepped into the palace, the more it was clear each member of the royal staff knew exactly where they were to be. No one accidentally collided with anyone else.

Some servants, without even looking up, rolled over their shoulder to the other side of a hall, avoiding clashing with another.

A sort of wild dance.

"Should you need anything and I am not there, palace staff wear blue leather bands on one wrist," Jonas explained.

"Not a certain attire?"

"You'll come to realize the king and queen have a great distaste for stripping folk of their choices. Even with what they wear. They compromised for bands on the wrist."

I had a thought to argue it was readily accepted that a royal household would be dressed in a unified style, but the prince would understand such things were common. He had seen Natthaven's palace, the blue and silver tunics of our guards and servants. Even the guards who accompanied the other fae realms were marked in different styles and emblems.

"No set attire and you do not call them servants?"

"Maj prefers staff. They work for pay, for increases, and only do tasks like tending the grounds, preparing meals, or upkeeping the palace."

"Who turns your beds or draws a bath?"

Jonas lifted his hands. "These are rather skilled in more than one way, but I find the simplest task I've encountered has been turning down my own bed."

I almost laughed. "So no courtiers? No ladies in waiting?"

Jonas hesitated near a wide staircase. "I know you are accustomed to such things. If you require ladies, I'm certain we can find some. They won't know what to do, but they'll try. Or perhaps Eldirard could send your lady to you and—"

"No." Before I realized, my hand fell to his arm. "Gods, the idea of Cara here is frightening. She will be in a constant state of gasping and pleading to the gods to deliver us from such an uncivilized land."

"My Lady," Dorsan warned.

I covered my mouth with one hand. "I . . . that's not what . . . I didn't mean to insinuate your folk are uncivilized."

"Pity." Jonas flashed his white smile. "We've worked hard to be the feral kingdom. My father will be wholly disappointed you see him as kingly in the slightest."

Instead of shirking away my arm, Jonas folded my hand between his elbow, and began up the staircase.

"I like it." My voice was low, soft, meant for the prince alone.

"Like what?"

"Your feral kingdom."

The same heat from the coach flashed in his eyes, and instead of fearing it now, I thought I might want it to swallow me whole.

An open corridor on the third level was empty but for a few tables with fiery blooms and willow branches to add color. Overhead, chandeliers with tallow candles cast eerie shadows against the corners.

"This is my wing—our wing," Jonas said, voice rough. "Dorsan, my good fellow." The prince spoke with such forced propriety, I could not swallow the laugh. He gripped my guard's arm and aimed him toward an arched doorway. "I had this chamber arranged just for you. Has a washroom and study for when you tire of following the princess around."

A furrow gathered over Dorsan's porcelain brow. "My Lord, it is my duty."

"Does duty not get rather tiresome? I assure you, here, you will not be maimed should you wish to leave her with others from time to time. I won't even tell Eldirard. Go now. Go, see if it is to your liking."

Dorsan shifted, pale from uncertainty. To my grandfather, the prince's word would supersede my own, but he seemed wary to leave my side.

"Go, Dorsan," I said. "We are in the same wing."

With a stiff bow, the guard retreated through the doorway. Alone, Jonas took hold of my hand. Twenty paces from Dorsan's chamber were two new doors, separated by a mere arm's length.

"Your chamber," he said, opening one side. "It is still under some work, but you have a sitting room and bedchamber. Afraid the washroom is only on my side, but you have the largest window and—"

"You redesigned your bedchamber?"

Jonas halted in the doorway. "I wasn't certain how fiercely you might wish to murder me, so I thought you might prefer your own space."

A strange, natural grin tugged at my lips. How long had it been since I smiled in earnest?

"Probably wise. You are irksome and I do like to murder irksome things." Chin lifted, I strode past the prince.

"Noted, Wife." Jonas left the door open, but followed me into the room.

The smell of freshly dyed rugs and lacquered wood perfumed the air. Blue and silver, like colors of Natthaven, were strewn over thick, wood floorboards. A half-built hearth was in one corner. Gray stones were stacked neatly on the floor, and when it was finished, the open nook would be large enough I could step inside.

Wooden chairs padded in wiry furs were positioned around a table with clay cups and a crystal ewer—almost like the flutes and decanters of Natthaven. As promised, a reaching, arched window let in the pale light. Below my side of the chamber was a garden. Tangles of green briars and pale blossoms were kept in rows of neat hedges and shrubs. Orderly and opposite from most of the kingdom.

"I love gardens," I whispered, pressing one palm to the bubbled glass.

"While you were at the sea fae palace, Liv mentioned you enjoyed the gardens there. Fortunately, I do as well, so my wing overlooks them."

"But you didn't keep the window."

"I have a smaller one." Jonas glanced at his boots and set the satchel he'd shouldered on one of the chairs.

Gods, he tried to make me comfortable even before the vows.

In the bedchamber, a polished bed of cherry wood was draped in a thick quilt of fur and a blue, woven duvet. The mattress was fuller than mine back in Natthaven, and stacks of pillows were disorderly against the headboard, with more in neat piles on the floor.

"I didn't know your preferences, so you can arrange your space as you please." Jonas leaned one shoulder against the doorframe.

My furnishings back home were fine enough, but simple. Alver clans did not display refinement, but the prince had clearly strived to drape the chamber in elegance.

He cleared his throat and took a step back. "Your belongings will be here soon. In advance, forgive the vulgarity of whoever brings them. Take the night to get settled. There will be a feast in the coming days to welcome you after the full moon."

Gods, the full moon was in only two days. Grandfather added the stipulation we were to share a bed each full moon with intention, but his insistence to have the vows so near the next moon likely had as much intention to draw us close in haste as anything.

I cleared my throat. "What is feast attire for alvers?"

"Attire?" The prince hooked his thumbs in his belt. "Don't arrive naked, I suppose. I already made my sentiments on others seeing you known."

My heart jumped. "This informality will take some getting used to. I don't want to . . . overdress or seem as if I'm not trying to conform to your folk. I never want to offend."

Hells, I hadn't meant for the words to spill out, a sieve of insecurities and fears that couldn't be held back any longer. I turned my back toward the door, feigning interest in the runes etched into one of the bedposts.

"Skadinia—"

"Skadi." My name trembled over my lips. "I hate Skadinia."

My breath caught when Jonas dragged his knuckles along the back of my arm. He crowded me from behind. With slow hands, the prince slid my hair off the curve of my neck.

"Skadi." His breath heated the bare skin of my shoulder. "I am not ignorant to how drastically your world has changed by vowing with me. You have no reason to believe me, but I truly only want you to find some peace here."

"Why?" I spun around, my body aligned to his. "We fought against each other. You could make my life miserable for what I did to your brother."

"I could." Jonas pinched my chin in his fingers. "But I have no desire to make you miserable."

"Your folk know what I am. How will they ever see anything more?"

"And what are you?"

I hesitated. "A weapon. A bit of monstrous darkness."

On my final word, Jonas coated his eyes with glossy black. Such a shift from his bright green was startling.

His palm cupped the side of my face, his body pressed me into the post of the bed. "Then *be* monstrous, Wife. If that is what you are, that is what I want you to be."

My fingers dug into his waist. Gods. He was so close, so hard against me. Never had I craved a touch so fiercely.

My husband refused to indulge. As though, all at once Jonas realized what position we'd taken, he pulled away.

In two blinks, his eyes drifted back to his normal shade. "Trust me, be you, Skadi—just you—and that will be enough."

I did not have time to respond, to argue, or to truly absorb his meaning, before the prince insisted he was expected somewhere else, and would see me in a few tolls—I took that as their marks of time.

When the door gently closed in his wake, I pressed a hand to my rapid heart, letting my eyes close.

I vowed to burn the man, but he was a force, and I was in the path of destruction, unwilling to save myself.

The prince's vow of vulgarity being delivered with my belongings was not exaggerated. A gruff man appeared with Ash, cursing the younger man—something about his large feet—and shoving into the chamber without a warning.

"Hello again, Skadi." Ash clung to one side of a trunk handle and used his chin to nod a greeting.

I smiled, catching sight of a round-faced fae woman with a swollen belly behind them.

With a grunt and declaration such things ought to be tossed into the sea, the brisk, surly man and Ash dropped the trunk. With the sleeve of his dark tunic, Ash wiped his brow. "Skadi this is my wife, Lady Shelba of the Court of Serpents—a glamour fae court located in the Southern realms."

Shelba had sharply tapered ears and eyes that were round and owlish. She bent at the knee, dipping her chin. "Princess."

"Pleasure to meet you," I said. "Thank you for bringing this."

"Next thing you know, I'll be cookin' right beside Ylva." The brutish man poked Ash in the chest. "I'm no cook and no delivery boy."

Ash rolled his eyes. "Forgive Osta, Princess. He's not the most personable sod of the Falkyns."

"Falkyn?"

"Only the fiercest guild in the kingdom." Osta smacked Ash against the chest. "Not like these Kryv. Lost your touch boy, heard you comin' from across the damn hall."

My eyes bulged. Ash was one of these . . . thieves-turned-inner guard? "Kryv?"

"Since I was a little boy." His eyes burned with a touch of pride. "My sister is as well."

"And the . . . Falkyn guild is like the Kryv?"

Osta blew out his lips. "Except sharper, fiercer, and deadlier in all ways."

"All right, you old sod." Ash clapped the man on the shoulder. "Falkyns are simply another guild, Skadi. Led by an Elixist and his wife —our lie taster. I'm sure you'll cross paths eventually."

Ash spoke with a clear attempt to make this kingdom of trickster guilds more innocent than was true, but I glanced at his wife who mouthed *smugglers* as though it was nothing to fret about.

"I see." I clasped my hands in front of my body. "Well, thank you for bringing the trunk."

"I'm sure more will arrive tonight and through the morning." Ash led his wife and Osta toward the door. "Sleep well, Princess. Welcome to Klockglas."

I did not trust my voice, and bid them a silent farewell. Once the door was closed, I scrambled for the trunk. My night shifts, day gowns, a few formal silks. Nothing was missing, and a bite of shame tugged at my heart.

Alver folk had dreary affinities, they did not seem altogether honest, but no one had mistreated me. They'd all been kind enough. Even my nightmare prince.

Brine coated my skin from the journey. I took to washing in the bedchamber, using a small wooden basin and soft linen until my skin pinked from the scrubbing.

Jonas vowed I could have the night to settle, undisturbed. As promised, the room was quiet, the only hint someone had entered as I washed was a tray of pale cheeses and brown rolls with honey, and placed on one of the chairs was a parchment wrapped box, my name printed on the side.

Inside was a small wooden box engraved in stars and moons of Natthaven. Perhaps a gift from the vows? I opened the lid and lost my grip at once.

The box clattered to the floor. My stomach cinched. Who would send such a thing?

Vicious pins stabbed the wings, the head, the middle, and every thin leg of a gentle sun wing. The creatures were unthreatening, they offered guidance in the wood if their trust was earned. As a child, facing the wilds of Natthaven alone, sun wings protected me.

This was a small, unassuming act to some, but to me, this was a betrayal of their trust. I would never display such a cruelty.

My fingers trembled when I plucked a rolled piece of parchment that had spilled from the box. A simple message, but it raised the hair on my neck.

A small token of home, so you never forget where you belong.

CHAPTER 15
THE MIST THIEF

Dew drops gleamed like crystals on silken black leaves. The blooms were strange, a vibrant lavender on dark stems.

Fae foliage was the same as elven, yet a world all its own. Roses and lilies were there, but rows of gnarled, stubby trees were mingled with hedges of fiery leaves and branches.

I pulled back the woolen hood of my cloak and leaned forward to smell the center. It smelled like smooth honey, a scent that lingered in the back of my throat until I tasted it.

After the disturbing gift, sleep abandoned me shortly before dawn.

My rooms remained askew, and my thoughts would not stop racing through the events of last night. I reasoned the sun wing was a misplaced attempt by someone on Natthaven to keep me connected to elven culture. I burned the box in the fire of the inglenook in the great hall before leaving for the gardens.

It was peaceful here, and there was a bit of heady relief knowing my new lands were not so horrid.

In truth, it seemed even my new husband was not the fiend I imagined.

His words last night would not bleeding leave me. *Just you.* A soft plea to be myself, the woman I kept locked in my heart, hidden beneath pious indifference and regal air.

Jonas spoke like he wanted to know me and I couldn't understand it. What the prince didn't know was the Skadi he wanted me to show was a ridiculously hopeful and romantic woman to the core.

I blamed my fluttering heart on the tales I'd read since childhood, books I still had not managed to locate since arriving. Romantic stories of long quests for love, desperate acts to save the beloved from danger.

Deep in the secret corners of my heart, there was always a piece that dreamed I'd look down from a tower window to see my good, honorable prince storming the gates to reach me.

A man who risked body and soul because of his unyielding love and devotion.

I abandoned the flower vines and continued strolling through the gardens. There was a reason such tales were kept between parchment pages. They were not real.

Dorsan had waited for me outside my chamber before the sunrise. My guard did not press on the contents of the box I'd burned in the flame, and now kept a healthy distance as I turned down stone pathways, admiring and gawking at strange trees and blooms.

By now, morning mists had lifted and the sunlight chased away the last drops of dew on the gardens. Still lovely, but not as quiet.

More than one servant—*staff*—had taken to pruning and yanking noxious thistles before the heat of the day grew too fierce. I sat atop a stone bench and observed the bustle inside the open doors of the cooking wing.

A sharp looking woman barked orders. Her hair was tied back with a blue kerchief and one hand kept hold of a knobby walking stick.

Men, women, girls, and boys raced about. Some stacked wooden crates, tossing out roots and garden spoils. Others carried thick wooden trays of unbaked breads.

Alvers worked like an army in the throes of battle. Curses, ramming into shoulders, shouts and insults, some elbows striking noses so blood spilled. But more enjoyable was the way, even in the chaos, folk seemed happy.

They smiled, they didn't glance over their shoulders for a rogue royal or sharp-tongued steward entering to berate them.

"Alver lands are strange, are they not, Dorsan?"

The guard sniffed and lifted his chin. "I am not in a place to make such a declaration, My Lady. For now, I will agree these lands are different from Natthaven."

"I rather like them." The truth was soft and sincere.

"Well, they are your lands. It would be prudent for you to like them."

I wanted to roll my eyes. So stern, so unruffled.

"I won't be making them again." A voice thick with smoke insisted.

"Ah, Ylva my love, yes you will."

My heart stopped. His voice was a flame, me the moth, and I could not help but be drawn toward it.

There, amidst the battle of the cooking room, Jonas shoved between the surly head cook and a few other staff.

Clad in dark clothes with a black steel sword on his waist, the prince looked like a villain from those childhood books—only now, the villain intrigued the princess a little more than the hero.

"Took nearly two tolls." Ylva clapped her walking stick on the floor.

"But it was at my request, and I am your favorite, for I repay my deals." The prince's grin was sly as a snake about to strike.

Little by little, Ylva the cook cracked. Her thin lips lifted. She patted Jonas's cheek and chuckled. "Aye, that you do, boy. I'll need you to pay old Pucey a visit."

Jonas clicked his tongue. "Still giving you trouble?"

"Always. Make him piss from his nightmares."

Jonas bowed at the waist and turned into the gardens. The tips of my fingers tingled in a bit of anticipation, as though they wanted to reach for him.

In the prince's hand was a wooden plate covered in a linen.

"Wife." Jonas tipped his chin. "Good morning. Enjoying the gardens?"

I stood and kept my tone tepid. "Very much."

"I intended to bring this to you in your room, but I caught sight of you in the window." The prince removed the linen, revealing a small cake the size of my palm, and on the top was a layer of cream dusted with cinnamon coils.

"What is it?"

Jonas held out the plate. "Honey filled with spiced cream. As you ordered."

By the hells, he remembered? I'd spoken the words during our vows as a jest, a way to unsettle him.

"You look a little confused." Jonas stepped closer, lifted one hand, and placed the plate in my palm. "It is meant to be eaten. Ylva might bury you under the palace if you don't at least taste it. Poor old girl added an early morning to her day to fill the cakes."

My lips parted and closed like a fish out of water. Fitting. Dead trout always died with an open mouth, and a wide-eyed look of stun. No mistake, I looked the same now.

"Why?" was the wonderfully cunning reply I mustered.

Jonas arched a brow. "You said you liked them. I'm not sure they'll taste like elven cakes, but they smell delightful, and if you don't start eating it, I will."

What game was this?

I swallowed and lifted the cake to my mouth. Sweet cream melted on my tongue. Honey oozed out with the bite and tangled with the soft cake. A sigh slid through my lips before I could stop it.

Jonas smirked, rather pleased with himself. He spun back toward the cooking room. "Success, Ylva."

My cheeks heated. I didn't realize the woman had been standing in the doorway holding her walking stick in front of her body, watching and waiting.

I offered my best smile, but feared it came out more like a sneer.

Another bite and another, until my stomach protested the sweetness with half the cake left. "You may need to finish it for me."

Jonas took the plate from my hand and pinched off messy pieces. "Now you know I eat like a little who has not learned to control his hands."

"This was . . . thoughtful of you."

The prince simply shrugged and placed the plate on the stone bench when he finished.

"What will you want from me in return?" I lifted my chin, terrified for the response.

"What do you mean?"

"This was generous. I should repay the favor."

"It was a cake, Fire."

That damn name. "Most would expect such gestures be repaid."

"Like a transaction."

"Well, yes."

"How shall you repay me then? Shall I request my favorite meals made by your hands?"

"They will be scorched and horrid, but if it is your desire . . ."

"So compliant." The prince met my eyes like he could see through the façade. "It was a cake, Princess. A way to bring a bit of familiarity on your first morning here. Nothing more."

I snorted. "I've learned there is always something more expected."

Jonas let out a sigh. "I should've anticipated you'd make this difficult. I'm not certain you trust your own hands not to be plotting something against you."

"I'm not being difficult." My voice was strained. "But when folk try to embrace the little elven monster there is something expected in return."

"Stop calling yourself such things."

"Is it not true?"

"I do not see you as a monster. I see you as my wife."

"But not really." What was it about this man that flared a dormant temper and a reckless tongue? No doubt, he enjoyed it.

"What are you insinuating?"

"I have not come to you as a wife since we took vows." The moment the words spilled out, I wanted to snatch them back and sink into the cold nothingness of my own magic.

Jonas towered over me, a dark gleam of something heated in his eyes. "You mean my bed?"

"It is an expectation." Gods, why was I even bringing attention to such a thing when the full moon was tomorrow and we would have no choice but to sleep beside each other? It was his nearness. It unsettled me, cracked more hysterics, and a bit of fear that loosened my tongue. "Unless you find me unappealing."

"Ah, there is so much wrong with those words." Jonas lowered his voice. "You still fear me, and I don't want my wife to look at me like I might slit her throat as she comes."

His voice shuddered through my chest when he spoke. "Well, that isn't realistic anyway since I've never . . . done *that*."

"Done what? Bedded someone?"

"I have, but have not . . ." I clamped my mouth closed, cursing myself for allowing this talk to go on.

"Been able to come?" Jonas's mouth twitched.

"Hush. Don't be vile."

"It's too late to stop. I would be delighted to make you come under my hands, my tongue, or on my cock."

Horrid, vicious, awful man. "Says every overly ambitious fool."

"You'd come and . . . you'd *love it*!" Now it was the prince whose voice grew in defensive retorts.

"We'll see."

"Yes. Yes, we will. Soon." He jabbed a finger toward me. "The corridors of this palace will be filled with cries of my name from your lips."

Bleeding gods.

"Wonderful." I tossed my hands up. "Something to look forward to."

"Can't wait," he snapped.

"Good."

"Upon your word, *Wife*."

Relent, give him the last damn word. Leave. Turn and bleeding leave.

"I'm going to go now."

"Do as you please, Fire." The prince folded his arms over his chest.

"Gods, you're aggravating."

"I'm aware."

"Do you ever let people have the final word?"

Jonas bared his teeth. "Never."

With a huff, I spun on my heel and nearly crumbled from horror.

A dozen paces away, amidst a small crowd who'd witnessed the pathetic, bawdy argument with the prince were the damn king and queen.

Jonas's mother had her vibrant hair in loose braids and wore a simple tunic and trousers. His father was clad in black and whispered something to his wife, the slightest grin on his mouth. They were surrounded by their guard, most of whom chuckled, their eyes locked on me.

"If you're wondering if they heard, they did." Jonas's lips brushed against my ear. "A deal has been made here, a challenge has been leveled, and half the palace heard it. Best for us to see it through."

What they all must've thought of me. "I would like to sink into the pits of the hells."

"Ah, don't do that. How will you scream my name when you let me touch you?"

I spun on him. "And what if I always refuse? Will you force it?"

"Never." Jonas's eyes shadowed. "Not even tomorrow. As I told you, my hand and I will become very well acquainted." The prince backed away. "I think, dear wife, we've had a rather successful first morning in our new home. Glad everyone could enjoy it with us."

I wanted to either strike his smug face or burrow into his arms until I was pulled away from the scrutiny of the gardens.

The prince allowed neither, simply brushed his knuckles across my cheek, then strode back to the cooking rooms, his gait a little haughtier than before. As though he believed he won this day.

Only my first morning, and I knew I would not be able to withstand my damn husband.

CHAPTER 16
THE NIGHTMARE PRINCE

"No matter how much you glare at the moon, it's not going to shrink." Sander had his boots kicked up on the narrow desk tucked against a wall in my chamber.

A few scrolls about Rave recruitments from Klockglas were there, some weapon reports from our black steel smiths, and some fury blades the Night Folk First Knight supplied for me.

By the frost seasons I would be traveling across the realms, inventorying our Rave armies.

It was aggravating to know one soul in this damn palace would revel in the idea of me being gone, sleeping in cold tents, surrounded by brash, smelly warriors—my wife.

No mistake, those weeks would be Skadi's most cherished.

I scowled at the rising moon once more like it had wronged me greatly and deserved to meet the ax for it.

"Quite a show you gave the morning crowds." Sander tried again, a grin that looked a little too devious for my mood on his horrid face. It wasn't that horrid of a face since it looked a great deal like mine, but still awful in this moment.

"Why are you here?"

"I'm always here."

"You're not helping."

"I'm not here to help. I've been helping you all day. Which"—Sander kicked his feet off the desk and righted in the creaky chair—"by the way, fascinates me. You have focused with such intensity on this project of yours, yet look like this now."

"You're right. I ought to stop the construction of it immediately."

"I didn't say that. I'm just curious why you are doing it at all?"

"I don't know." I peered down at the drawings of the plans for the empty room, a project I began to fashion in my head the day after the vows.

To spite me, my fiery princess would likely burn it.

My frown deepened and I hated it. Never before had I scowled so often and so skillfully, certainly not when I knew I would not be spending my night alone.

Before this alliance I strived to keep most of my nights filled with warmth and feminine whispers. Trouble was the woman I had no choice but to sleep beside tonight spent her days dancing between the notion of ignoring or stabbing me.

In the distance, a heavy clock toll boomed the time.

Sander chuckled and rose from his chair. "My cue to leave. Maj wanted me to remind you not to be an ass. Daj wanted me to remind you he expects you probably will be."

Gods knew my brother was trying.

"I'll manage to make them both unspeakably proud, I'm sure."

Sander laughed, but stalled when he opened the door. "Hello, Princess. Ah, that is an interesting tale, I think you'll like it better than your company tonight."

Forget his attempts to lighten the tension, I was going to kill my brother. My parents only needed one son, after all.

Sander must've sensed my scathing murder plot because he had the gall to grin, wave, and wink at me before he slipped around my wife standing in the doorway.

Gods, why did she have to be even a little bit beautiful?

Her hair hung in a long braid over her shoulder. It was the color of starlight, but deeper than only silver—sometimes when the light struck just right there was a flash of amethyst, blue, or pale gold in her hair. Secret shades, much like the secrets she kept tucked away in those eyes.

She was draped in a silken robe, nothing covering her feet, and tucked under her arm was a thick, black leather book with yellowed pages.

Over her head, Dorsan met my gaze. "As stated in the alliance of Dokkalfar and alver, the princess Skadinia and Prince Jonas shall share a chamber each full moon. The alliance clearly states a bed will be shared."

"What?" I pressed a palm to my chest. "You mean I can't ravish my wife on the floor? Perhaps the chair? I've been rather inclined to try a position involving my desk."

Dorsan's smooth, unruffled demeanor nearly shifted in a bit of shock. Damn, it was close. I would get him eventually.

My wife, on the other hand, looked properly scandalized. Lips parted, eyes wide, I did enjoy that rosy flush that always took the tips of her ears.

The elven guard cleared his throat and backed away. "Until dawn, then."

"Unless we do not feel like emerging after all the lovemaking it seems we will be doing, Dorsan." Skadi did not flinch, not the slightest twitch of her lips as she spoke and entered the room.

I nearly choked on my own breath. Her smug little smirk flooded my veins with heat—annoyance or something else, I wasn't certain—but she looked fiercely pleased with herself when she strode toward my desk, her imposing book in hand.

The guard seemed a touch paler when he closed the door.

I clicked the lock and faced the . . . *aggravating* creature invading my bedchamber. "Well played, Wife."

"You are not the only one who can unsettle the nerves." The spine of the book crackled when she opened the pages to a previously marked place. "In fact, much of my existence unsettles folk."

She wasn't wrong.

The woman shook my steady footing often, but I did not think it was the same way she meant. Apprehensive glances followed her aplenty. Not only here, but I noted much the same on Natthaven.

What was I supposed to do now? I was no stranger to sleeping with a woman, but I was a stranger to sleeping with a woman in my bed.

I took lovers anywhere but here—not in my room.

It was too close, too personal. It opened hope for expectations I never intended to deliver.

"Do you plan to sit over there all night?" I asked when silence went on too long.

"You heard Dorsan." Skadi didn't look up from the page. "I must *sleep* beside you. So, I believe you already have your answer. When it is time to sleep, we will sleep. Until then, I'll remain here. It is a long book though. Could be some time."

Another frown. Soon, my mouth would be horribly set in a downward turn.

She wanted to play indifferent, and I would be happy to test her tolerance. "If I'm right, that is the saga of the seven raven brothers?"

Skadi nodded. "And the golden maiden. A fae tale I haven't read before, but it's adequately interesting for now."

I unlaced the front of my tunic. "It's a romantic tale."

"Hmm."

"About a fated love that emerges between the maid and one of the brothers."

"I assumed that was the design of the story."

I yanked my tunic over my head. Skadi tried to hide it, but she looked. She swallowed a little harder and nearly pinned her nose to the pages. "Are you going to sleep now?"

"No." I strode across the room. "I plan to wash while you read."

"Good." She said, voice strained. "You look rather . . . unkempt."

Did I? With a discreet sniff under my arm, I settled that the work on the upper room earlier had left a bit of a smell behind.

Perhaps I ought to leave the day on my skin, let her breathe it in all night.

Instead, I tossed my tunic on the floor, landing it a few paces from her feet.

She wrinkled her nose, but it seemed intentional, like she wanted me to believe she found me utterly repulsive.

Fine. Let the games begin, Fire.

The door to the washroom was on her opposite side, and when I reached it, she shifted, barring her shoulders against me, actively not looking at me. If I had to guess, her cheeks might have some of that rosy heat in them.

"I won't be long."

"Take your time. I have plenty of pages."

I was about to commit a travesty greater than murder according to my brother. Wasn't my fault. I was the villain in her eyes and had no choice but to rise to the occasion.

"She chooses the last brother, by the way." I clapped the frame of the doorway. "The weakest. Her belief in his heart and strength transforms him into the fiercest warrior and he goes on to win back the kingdom in the end."

Skadi whirled around, my fire alight in those fierce blue eyes. "I . . . I just got to her interactions with the first brother and . . . I hadn't gotten there yet!"

"Oh, apologies." I shrugged. "Well, I saved you some time."

I closed the door in the same moment she let out a strangled shriek. I chuckled, back against the opposite side. The dance between indifference and murder continued, and if I was still breathing at dawn, the night could be claimed as a success.

When I stepped back into the room, Skadi had taken the place in my bed nearest to the wall. She was curled up beneath the quilts, back facing me.

I dragged a hand through my damp hair, shaking a few drops free from the strands, and made my way to her side.

Her eyes were clenched unnaturally and her breaths were too forced. She was awake.

"This is my side."

Skadi cracked an eye. "I suppose you'll need to take the other side. This is also the side on which I sleep."

"It's my bed."

"I thought everything was meant to be ours."

The thud of my pulse filled my ears. "Scoot over, Fire. Or I sleep on top of you."

This damn woman merely hugged my pillow—mine—a little more in her arms and nestled deeper in the bed.

"All right."

I tossed away the quilts, ignoring the way my bleeding cock twitched at the sight of her in the green sleep shift, much too diaphanous for my thoughts not to wander to how soft her skin looked, how her body would fit so well beneath mine.

Dammit. I needed to keep focused.

Skadi propped onto one elbow, readying to battle, no doubt, but she wouldn't get the opportunity.

I scooped her up beneath her knees, taking her into my arms. She squirmed and shoved against me. "Put me down. I was sleeping!"

"Hmm. You'll sleep better over here." I tossed her to the other side of the bed.

Skadi let out a cry of surprise when she plopped onto the edge of the mattress. I took my place under the quilts.

"So warm." I tucked my pillow against me, breathing it in. "Smells perfect too. Many thanks."

Those flames in her eyes were going to devour me. Part of me hoped they would.

"You are a brute."

"I'm rather protective about my side of the bed." I brushed my fingers over her face. "Now, hush. It's time to sleep."

Skadi jerked her head away, sitting up. Wrong move. Unless it was planned, then, well played. One of her thin shoulder straps slid down her arms. The tattoos I noticed on the night of our vows curled around her skin in beautiful filigree and vines of blossoms. They seemed to curl around her breasts, her ribs, likely down her stomach.

Gods, I adjusted to hide the rush of blood between my legs.

Without a word, I made the foolish misstep of sliding the strap back on her shoulder.

Skadi smirked. "Do you enjoy my attire, Husband?"

"Not at all." I didn't look at her and rolled onto my stomach.

I shuddered when her fingertips started to trace the crossed blades inked on my back. Skadi pressed her body against my arm. The warmth of her skin, the way she smelled like the spiced icing she loved so much, tangled my mind in a fog.

"Are you certain?" Her voice was low, almost needy. "It is the perfect dress for a man's hands to handle."

This was a game, I could see it. Raised by crooks and schemers, I'd do well to keep sight of my mark.

In one swift motion, I released my pillow and managed to roll my bride half under me. Her eyes went wide, but there wasn't fear there. Perhaps it was the same stun I felt from how easily we fit each other this way.

I stared down at her, my fingertips tracing the lines of her throat. "Do you want me to handle you, Fire?" The tip of my nose followed where I touched. Skadi's breaths sharpened when my lips ran across her jaw. "I'd be happy to. Want me to undress you?"

I tugged the strap of her shift off her shoulder again.

"That . . . isn't necessary." She shifted, her thigh rubbing across my cock. Gods, she'd feel the need there.

This was a dangerous play—one where I might cause more harm to myself in the end. "So certain?" I let my hand fall to her leg. "I could make good on my promise to have you screaming in pleasure."

A soft whimper spilled over her lips. She desired a piece of me, and hated it. I knew the feeling.

"We . . . it is expected."

I arched my hips against her just enough to add pressure to her own. "It is."

Skadi's shoulders rose with rough gasps. Gods, she was stunning and I feared if I allowed it—if she allowed it—I might find too much comfort with her wrapped up in my arms this way.

"We could do all of it, Fire."

"If . . . we could just . . . get it over with."

"True. I could start with my fingers, slow and gentle, just enough to get you ready for my cock."

My hand drifted higher, nearly falling into the heat of her center. Skadi dragged the tip of her tongue over her lips. She didn't want to enjoy my touch, but she was bending beneath it.

"I could do it all." I leaned close, hovering my mouth over hers. "But I'm rather tired. Sleep well."

I planted a quick kiss to the tip of her nose and rolled back to my side of the bed, pillow smashed under my body again.

Skadi's breath shuddered. It only lasted a moment before she grunted in frustration, made certain her feet kicked my hip once or twice as she readjusted on the bed. The woman moved with enough force she rocked the entire structure. Intentional, no doubt.

When she finally settled was the moment I allowed myself a look.

"What did you do? Build a nest?"

Skadi had aligned two long pillows on the edge of the bed, like a wall between her and the door, and the quilts gathered nearly over her entire head.

"Go to sleep, Prince."

"Is this how you sleep?"

"Yes."

"Why?"

"Well, I do not have my regular spot, do I?"

I chuckled. "You didn't build your nest on this side."

"I hate the door!" Skadi tossed the quilt off her head as she shouted the truth. A shadow crossed her eyes, like she wished she could take the words back. "Never mind."

"Why do you hate the door?"

"Good night."

"Skadi—"

"Gods." She tossed the quilt back again. "Because when I was a little girl, stealing food to stay alive before my grandfather found me, I had to barricade my door at night from fear the royal guards would barge in and take me to a young house. Those are work houses among the Ljos-alfar clan. Is that an adequate reply? I like to sleep as far from the door as I can or I tend to have nightmares, so prepare yourself. I am told I thrash."

She covered her head again and went still.

I could not find the words. I laid back, eyes schooled on the rafters overhead. When I was convinced Skadi was asleep in her tangle of quilts, I eased off the bed and went to her side, gently nudging her toward the middle. She sighed and wrapped her arms around my pillow once again, nuzzling her face into the surface.

I took the side nearest to the door and watched her lashes flutter through her dreams—perhaps nightmares I unknowingly forced her to face.

Those I understood more than she would ever know.

I reached out and brushed a lock of hair off her brow before rolling onto my shoulder, facing away from the peace on her features.

Well, I would make my father proud—I was an absolute ass.

CHAPTER 17
THE NIGHTMARE PRINCE

I DID NOT SEE MUCH OF THE PRINCESS IN THE COMING DAYS AFTER OUR FULL moon night.

Before the sun rose each morning, I left my side of our divided chamber for the upper corridor, sometimes pausing to wonder if she still slept or if she rose with the dawn. She spent most of her days in her chamber, even taking meals alone.

One of the few times we'd crossed paths was when I delivered a missive from the elven king. She'd offered a brisk thanks, but when I returned to retrieve her response, it had been placed outside her door.

Tonight would be different. A week since the vows, there was a feast to honor the alliance our way. More ale, rowdy chatter, and simplicity. Dorsan insisted the princess would attend for it would be improper to refuse.

I didn't see how, but I took it to mean I would be beside my wife after days of clear avoidance.

I let my head fall back against the wall.

Damn her.

Damn me.

The night of the full moon with her body close to mine, her scent all

over my bed, turned into something dark and greedy, like I might suffo-
cate on my own desire if I did not touch her, hold her, *taste* her.

"Done for now." Von smacked my arm. "He's out here, Sander.
Doing nothing while we work."

My brother emerged from the empty room, wiping a bead of sweat
off his brows, and closed the door at his back.

"Sander won't do it, so I decided to become princely and order you
about, Von."

"Give it a try." Von rubbed his neck where runes were tattooed on
the sides. "I'm older, more cunning, and will promptly ignore you."

"Do you have a key for the lock?" Sander asked.

"What would be the point?" I tapped the latch. "Everyone in this
place can pick a lock in their sleep."

The benefit of living amongst those of questionable moral character
meant it was never impossible to gain access to anything. A benefit, but
when I hoped to keep a private project private, it proved difficult.

"We forgot some." Von had his hands in his dark hair, re-braiding
the longer, center strands out of his eyes, and used his stubbled chin to
point to a stack of dusty books.

Dammit. I plucked them off the floor, studying the top cover. Blue
leather with gold filigree embossed on the corners. A saga of the
wandering maiden who was kidnapped by a troll king and dragged to
his underground world.

Opposites. Forced together. The maiden soon came to love the troll
king and his dreary world, so much she gave up her upper lands and
placed her heart in one of the troll king's chests in his treasury.

His, for all time.

With a sigh, I shouldered into the darkened room.

Dust and the smell of old parchment burned my lungs with each
breath. It was a corpse of a room. Tattered draperies blotted out the
sunset. Linen covered sitting chairs that would need new padding and
furs were shoved to the sides, and in the center endless piles of supplies
for the empty shelves were stacked and orderly thanks to Sander and his
focus.

I added the stack of children's folk tales to the chaos, then returned to the corridor.

"Jonas." Von leaned a shoulder against the wall. "Where are your thoughts? You look miserable. Quite unlike you, my friend. Was your moonlit night so terrible? Not compatible in bed?"

"Not miserable. Hungry." I used the back of my hand to strike his chest, laughing to hide the disquiet in my blood. "And you know we did nothing but sleep, stop trying to imagine anything else."

"I do not imagine you in bed, you ass. That would ruin any pleasure I hope to find in my own."

"Ah, did you decide to speak to Brunhild other than thanking her for the food she serves?" Sander asked. "If you never say more, she'll never know you wish to eat more than her wine rolls."

"Gods, Sander." Von studied my brother like he had never seen him before. "Sometimes you say things that make you more of a sod than Jonas."

"Because I enjoy reading, you all think I am some innocent babe. Von, you live with Niklas Tjuv, the least innocent of us."

Von chuckled. "True."

Niklas and his wife, Junius, had territories in the northern provinces. Former smugglers (who were still prone to smuggle) and guild leads of the Falkyns.

Niklas was the most scholarly soul I knew. When we visited their province as boys, Von and I would race through the streets while Sander and Nik read the days away, then tested each other's knowledge about different mesmers or cultures of fae folk.

"So what is all this, Jonas?" Von asked when we made our way down the darkened corridor. "What's the ploy?"

"Not every step is a mark."

"I'd believe that except here, we scheme." Von winked. "Tell me about her. She's why we are here behaving like gentlemen, right?"

What the hells was I to say? Should I admit how it felt damn near impossible to keep my distance from her after a mere week? How somehow the bleeding woman sparked heat in my blood?

In my bed, she'd left me in an inferno.

To get close again would simply be another dose of this new, unwelcome obsession.

"Damn." Von's voice snapped me from my melancholy. "I've never seen you so out of sorts. I think I might be in love with your new bride if she has done this to you."

I narrowed my gaze, and it only made both Sander and Von laugh.

"She is a piece in a game, much the same as me," I insisted. "Nothing more."

"A game you arranged." Von quickened his step and followed me around a corner. "Now, I have to wonder if you added stakes greater than you anticipated."

"There are no stakes other than peace for the fae realms and sea folk against the elven. What other stakes matter?"

"Stakes of the heart, Jonas." Von cuffed the back of my head.

"Those are not on the table."

"Then what is the purpose of this little secret project for the princess?"

Sander said nothing, but came to my side, the same furrow of concern he had the day of the vows written on his face.

"It's nothing but a bit of advice from Ari about adding joy to her days." I looked at each of them once before going on. "It's nothing more than trying to make a piss-poor situation more tolerable."

The trouble was I didn't think there was nearly as much misery returning home with a wife as I anticipated.

Von sobered. "I don't think it is a bad thing, Jonas. I was glad when you asked for our help with all this."

"Von, your tender heart is showing." I knocked his shoulder as I strode past. "Don't read so much into it. You're as romantic in the eyes as Mira."

"Well, she might have a point."

"I have a request," Sander interjected.

"What?" I spun around, walking backward to look at my brother.

"Find a way to make my new sister not look at me like I'm going to attack in the night. You've told her, right? You've let her know I don't hold ill feelings that I was wounded?"

"Probably thinks you're embarrassed by the scar." Von gingerly patted Sander's ribs where Skadi's knife had lodged into his innards during the battle.

He shook his head. "Not in the least, she was the better fighter of us. The woman is fearsome with a blade."

It was a strange feeling, the pain of nearly losing Sander to the Otherworld was there, but now it was edged in a bit of pride that Skadi was a damn warrior beneath her stoicism and mild temperament.

"Jonas, she knows, right?"

These bouts of drifting thoughts needed to end. "I might've mentioned it."

Sander frowned. "I'll speak to her."

"Don't corner her and demand friendship, Sander." I hooked an arm around his neck, squeezing him against my side as we descended the tower staircase that led back to my wing. "Give her time to get her bearings."

"Well, I think she is searching for them. I do hope she finds them soon." Von went still at the bottom of the stairs, eyes straight ahead. "She's mystifying, isn't she?"

A strange stutter stilled my breath. Skadi was in her doorway, one hand behind her back, glancing in the opposite direction.

"She is." I wasn't certain if I was the one who spoke or one of the others.

Like a fist rammed through my middle, I could've doubled over from the sight of her. Hair spilled down her back in loose waves. Delicate braids crowned the top of her head, and woven around them was a small silver chain. The dress she wore was a shade of green like sea foam and moss that split high enough on her leg I could see the smooth shade of her soft, sun-toasted skin.

The scrape of our boots from stone steps to wooden floors drew her attention.

"Oh." She straightened and drew in a sharp breath. "I was looking for a ser—staff."

"Jonas." Sander elbowed me. "She's speaking to you."

I cleared my throat and stepped forward. "Ah, they're likely down-stairs finishing with the feast. What is it you need, Fire?"

Skadi's cheeks pinked. "Oh. I suppose I could ask Dorsan, but . . . he will likely die of impropriety."

"We can't have that. You have your husband and two sometimes-dependable men at your disposal."

"Von Grym." Without waiting for me, Von shoved his way toward us. "It is a pleasure to meet you at last, Princess. I was at the vows—"

"And negotiations," Skadi whispered. "You stood in the back behind the king and queen."

Von looked delighted. "I was there, more out of curiosity than any real purpose."

"He's still finding his purpose in most things." I nudged him back. "What do you need?"

"Oh, nothing. Never mind. I'll manage fine."

"Don't do that." I stepped closer, voice low.

"I am doing nothing."

"You're retreating, trying not to ask of me, trying to convince your-self I have no interest in your wellbeing."

"I saw how you handled me in your bed, Husband."

The corner of my mouth lifted. "Were you left unsatisfied?"

"You know the answer to that."

"I will die of shame should I leave you in such a state again."

She scoffed. "I doubt that very much."

"Well, let me try now. I'll ask again, what is it you need?"

Skadi dragged her bottom lip between her teeth, and all at once, I wanted to do the same. She leaned closer, the sugar scent of her hair under my nose. Her voice was low, rife in embarrassment. "I cannot fasten my gown."

"I'd be honored to help." Von lifted a hand, laughing when my fist struck his chest.

"Go clean yourself or Brunhild will avoid you all evening."

Sander, the good brother he was, kept a hand on Von's arm, guiding them past the door. "Lady Skadi." He dipped his chin awkwardly. "I don't hate you, you know."

I groaned. "Gods, Sander. We just talked about this."

"What?" He kept his pace, merely spoke over his shoulder. "I don't. In fact, I'd love to spar again. You are better with a short blade."

I stepped forward, guiding Skadi into her room, and slammed the door behind us. "Apologies for them. They are fools."

Skadi held a touch of defiance, or perhaps fear, in her taut jaw. "Does he mock me?"

"Sander?" I glanced at the door for a breath. "No. Not at all. He was just spewing your accolades at the way you use a weapon, but is rather concerned you will never want to know him."

"He . . . wants to know me?"

Did I desire her to be close with my brother? Did I want the folk I loved best stepping over boundaries I thought we'd keep?

Then again, the people in my life held no sense of boundaries.

I clasped my hands behind my back. "He does. But who you come to know here will be left to you. Now, let us see this dress."

I opened my palms, dancing my fingers.

Skadi hesitated, then slowly turned in front of her mirror. She gathered her hair over one shoulder, exposing the flesh of her back to me. Lies of boundaries, peace treaties, and duty could spill over my tongue all damn day.

Nothing readied me for being dumbstruck by my unwitting wife.

"The buttons"—Skadi arched a hand over her shoulder, pawing at the top of the gown—"there are too many."

"I see why you use ladies. Forgive us, we are made of more men here, and my mother finds more comfort in trousers."

Once I aligned behind her, Skadi lifted her piercing blue eyes to mine in the glass. I was glad for the position; she wouldn't see the tremble to my fingers.

What the hells was wrong with me? I had a fair bit of practice with women's laces and buttons, now I could not steady my hands.

My knuckles brushed along the heat of her skin at the first three. Her breath was sharp, her skin rose like a cool breeze kissed her spine. A reaction of disgust . . . or something else?

"You have ink designs. I noticed them at the vows."

All down her spine, tattoos made a coiling pattern of blossoms on vines.

"Yes." Her voice was soft, a little breathless. "I noticed yours as well." She looked at me again, less uncertain now, almost a smile on her full lips. "Any meaning behind them?"

"The two crossed blades on my back are made of black steel, symbols of our court. On my chest I keep the Kryv motto and emblems of those I love."

"What is the motto?"

"Fight to the end." I struggled with two more buttons, biting back a moan each time my fingers brushed over her skin. "It means to keep battling until victory or the Otherworld, but do not let enemies take you. No matter who or what it is."

"Hmm." Skadi smoothed her palms over the green satin of her gown.

Head down, I kept the mirror in the corner of one eye. "You disapprove of us?"

"No."

Another button, another gasp when I intentionally traced the line of one of her stars. I leaned in, whispering, "Liar."

For a moment, Skadi's lashes fluttered. She swallowed and steeled her features. "I don't disapprove. I'm merely curious how a kingdom thrives if its folk are constantly thieving."

"Valid question." I took a step closer. "Most people have quite honest trades and our days are rather dull. Thieving was simply once the only way to survive before House Eriksson was on the throne. Mesmer was hunted and used, forcing them into the underbelly."

"Magic was hunted?"

"Fiercely, often by other alvers in power. They were tyrants and folk suffered. The only way to live was to fight for survival, which led to less reputable ways to make a living. But the guilds are family. They're loyal to the end."

My thumb brushed over the back of her neck. Skadi shuddered. Her steps shifted, and she leaned into me a little more.

I secured the final clasp between her shoulder blades but didn't pull away. I rested my brow on the side of her head, slowly allowing my hands to slide over her shoulders, down her arms, falling to her waist.

"And . . ." She drew in a sharp breath when one of my palms slid across her middle. "And what of the king and queen?"

"The most crooked of us all." Good hells, my voice was thick and rough, like sand lined my throat. My fingers ghosted across her ribs, drawing higher, higher. Blood heated, I looked back to the mirror.

Skadi's eyes were blown wide. One hand was curled in a fist at her side the other reached back, holding my hip, as though she needed purchase to stand.

"Do we frighten you?" I brushed my lips over the slope of her neck.

"I . . . could ask the same of you."

I paused over her pulse point, pressing a gentle kiss there, then looked back into the glass. "You terrify me, but I doubt it is in the way you think."

"Then explain," she whispered.

I would not survive this woman. Something had rotted out my resolve, something dangerous had overtaken my rational thoughts. She consumed me—actions, thoughts, fears, desire—they now belonged to her, and I did not think she understood how much stunning chaos she was causing in my life.

She was destroying me, moment by moment.

My palm glided between her rising breasts, resting over her heart. The beat was erratic, fierce, heavy. I pressed her into me. "Because this frenzy in your heart has made mine do the same."

A soft *gods* fell over her tongue.

Skadi let her eyes close, but rested her palm over my wrist, then nimbly guided my hand to one side, until I covered her breast.

A rough, agonized sound tore from my chest. I let my forehead fall to her shoulder, tightening my grip, and kneaded the shape of her. I encircled her waist with my other arm and pressed a kiss to the sliver of flesh on her shoulder.

Skadi tilted her head, granting me access to her neck. "Jonas."

Gods, to hear my name on her lips. My smile lifted against her skin. "I promised the next time would be breathless."

Skadi's heel stomped on my toe. I laughed, my teeth nipping at the silver ring pierced in her ear. She moaned and stumbled, one hand bracing on the edge of the vanity in front of her mirror. Gods, the desire to lift her skirt and keep her bent over like this made my cock twitch.

I spun her around. Her lips parted in stun. One breath, two, and I crashed my mouth to hers.

Skadi stuttered through the kiss at first. I demanded more, my tongue against the seam of her mouth. She tasted like fresh rain.

Another heartbeat, and Skadi ceased her stun and kissed me back.

I leveraged her onto the table of the vanity, stepping between her knees. Her body was lean and trembling, the layered skirt lifted over her smooth legs.

A new want and need filled my chest. One that was like sharp claws desperate to hook into her flesh and keep her tethered to me always. There was a thought for her freshly styled waves, but passion won out, and I tangled my fingers in her long hair, soft as silk.

Skadi hissed into my mouth when I tugged on her roots.

My mouth abandoned her lips. She let her head fall back, baring her throat, when I sucked and kissed my way down her neck.

Behind my thighs, Skadi hooked her ankles and yanked me closer.

"You are wicked, Wife." I tugged her sleeve over her shoulder.

"And you're horrid." She held the back of my head.

With her sleeve askew, more of her breast swelled free. On the underside, a bit of the ink she promised was there peeked through, but that wasn't all.

I pulled back, the tip of my thumb ran over the raised flesh, gnarled and taut beneath a piece of her tattooed skin.

Upon my touch, Skadi went stiff as stone. She pulled away, her arms abandoning me, and covered her body. In haste, she fixed her sleeve, avoiding my gaze. "That went too far. We . . . we don't want to be late."

"You have scars."

"Many people do." She slipped on a black pair of leather ankle boots.

My teeth ground together. "I know what knife scars look like, Skadi."

"How happy for you."

Damn woman. I turned her around. "You flinch. You hide scars beneath ink. Who has harmed you?"

"It is of no consequence to you." She ran her fingers through her hair, desperately trying to smooth out the waves.

"No consequence?" Heat of anger burned behind my eyes. I fought to keep the rage of mesmer from dimming the color.

"It is nothing," she repeated, "and not anything so horrible like I'm sure you're thinking."

"I'm thinking you have scars you've intentionally covered because you do not wish to see them. Scars like that usually come with some sort of pain. Who. Did. It?"

She straightened, eyes ablaze. "Why would I tell you anything? It does not matter."

In three strides I had her pressed against me again. "You are my wife."

"And you do not want me!" Skadi shirked me off. "Not *me*. Yes, we are vowed. Yes, I have a woman's body. Yes, I am here with the title of your wife. But do not pretend all that automatically brings true affection for the heart. You said so yourself, hearts are not part of the alliance. So do not pretend there is any care to know the tale behind a scar."

"You don't—"

"No!" Tears glazed her eyes. "I don't want this."

"Don't want what?"

"Whatever happened here." Her hand gestured between us. "I won't."

"Why? What if this doesn't need to be nothing?"

"It *must*. I have no desire to draw close to you." Her voice cracked. "Don't pretend you do. I beg of you to respect me enough not to play games."

"I am not playing."

"You are born of thieves; tricks and games make up your people by your own word." She retreated again, eyes dull, intentionally shutting me out. "All I am to you is a dark, dangerous elf you were forced to muzzle for the sake of all fae folk."

Her voice was raised, almost frantic, but there was a brokenness to it.

"That's all you see with me? That's all you want?" I asked, voice sharp. "To be indifferent strangers who are vowed?"

Skadi sighed. "It is always the same, Prince. Intrigue, maybe a bit of attraction, until the truth of the brutality within is seen and cannot be unseen. Save yourself some time and live your life as if I were not here. That is how I will live mine. We should do our duty, nothing more."

It stung, more than I anticipated. What she meant was she did not want to grow closer with me. Odd how positions had shifted. I went into these vows without much thought on connection or emotions. Now, she rejected mine, and I felt the scar of it in my chest.

I flourished my hand in a mock sort of bow, and stepped for the door. "As you wish, *Wife*. Should I return to take you to the hall, or would my presence be too disconcerting?"

Her face pinched, her voice softened. "If it is all right, perhaps I should not attend tonight. Unless you command it."

"I think I'll put my tyranny to rest for the night. Do as you please." I wrenched the door open in time to catch sight of Frigg's long braid and Sander's messy hair fade around the corner, their voices hissing and screeching like two hogs caught out of their pen.

How much had they heard? Asses.

I slammed the door to Skadi's room the same moment Dorsan emerged in his finely spun elven tunic and blade. The only hint of emotion came when he lifted his brows.

"Your lady has chosen not to attend the feast. Remain here should she need you." I said nothing more before storming into my own chamber, locking the door at my back.

CHAPTER 18
THE MIST THIEF

Something struck my door, rattling the hinges. I jolted up in my bed, positioned to reach for the small paring knife I'd taken from one of the meal trays sent to my room. To remain unarmed as I slept never settled well. Even back home, I kept a blade nearby.

The door didn't rattle again, but raised voices filled the corridor.

Outside was still lost to the satin black of night. I blinked through the lingering fatigue and slipped a woolen cloak over my shoulders, peeking out into the corridor.

Jonas was strapping a dagger to his belt, but had a hooded cloak over his shoulders, speaking frantically to Sander and Von as they left the prince's side of the chamber.

My husband glanced toward my door, catching my gaze. "Stay put," he said.

"What's going on?" I hugged the edge of the door. There was pain in their features.

With the way I shouted at him earlier and demanded he leave, the prince did not need to speak to me, but he strode to my side.

"Something has happened at the home of one of the guards of the palace. Some sort of illness has taken to him and his wife and caused violent delirium. We're going to help if we can, even if it's tending to his littles."

Young ones. "May I come?"

"No, Skadi. I don't know what it is, and—"

"I could look after the littles." I dipped back into the room and returned with one of the only fae tales I had, a thick book with bright paintings on the pages. "I could keep them distracted."

"I don't want you getting ill."

"I'll stay back. I . . . please, I want to help."

I did want to help. There was a soft place in my soul I kept for young ones who might be frightened and alone. But another piece of me yearned for a chance to show my new clan I was not a creature who wanted to bring them harm.

Jonas closed his eyes with a sigh. "All right. But if I say to return to the palace, you must return."

"Agreed."

Jonas roused Dorsan, insistent my guard could keep watch over my back while the prince aided the ill household.

The longhouse was situated on the edge of the palace grounds, tucked between tall aspens with pens for hogs and goats. It was a fine estate and proof of the generosity of the royal house to those they trusted.

Folk in night shifts, some darkly clad guards, and men and women with baskets filled with vials and pouches, were scattered throughout the yard. Fires roared, burning linens and stuffed toys.

All gods. What sort of illness was this?

"Skadi." Jonas brushed his knuckles along my arm. "The littles are there."

Three young ones sat beside a stack of damp straw, a small hound pup in the tallest child's arms. Thin blankets wrapped their shoulders, their feet were bare, and matching golden hair was on end.

A woman in a blue cloak crouched, urging the children to take something from a vial.

"Stay back?" Jonas asked it like a question, a request.

I nodded, clutching the book to my chest. When the prince turned toward the chaotic longhouse, unbidden, I snagged a hold of his wrist. "Take care."

No snide comments left his tongue, there was nothing worth jesting over in a moment as this. He left me with a slight nod, accepted a cloth mask from Von, and hurried toward the longhouse.

Dorsan kept a distant but stern presence when I approached the children with a bit of nerves. The woman was urging the smallest girl to take a sip of whatever was in the glass vial. The child whimpered for her mother, and her skinny brother kept glaring at the woman like she might be intending to poison his sister.

"Silvery." A second girl, a little older than the crying child, lifted her big eyes, pointing at me.

I touched the line of elven silver rings in my ear. Dokkalfar silver reacted to moonlight, and sparkled like gemstones. "Do you like it?"

The girl had red rimmed eyes and damp cheeks, but she nodded with a bashful smile.

I knelt beside the woman trying to aid the young ones. In a few swift motions, I removed a few of the rings and held them in my open palm. "I think they would look beautiful on you."

The small one hiccupped and dared follow her sister's movements as she drifted nearer to the glimmering silver.

I smiled when she bit into one of the linen blankets, sucking on the corner, but hesitantly joined her sister, watching the rings shine.

"Would you like one?"

The older girl let out a little gasp, but nodded.

"I shall make you a deal then." I cast a look at the woman. She was not behaving cruelly with the littles, and I suspected whatever was in that vial had a touch of magic to protect the young ones against illness. "This tonic is here to help you all stay strong."

The woman hurriedly nodded when I looked to her for confirmation.

I smiled back at the young ones. "If you will take it, I will show you how to wear elven silver. They say it has a bit of magic from the gods of the night within it. Whenever you feel alone in the dark, they will always shine brightly, reminding you that you're not alone."

There was suspicion in the children's gazes when the tonic woman nudged closer. It took a bit more coercing, and a few more rings added to the trove of rewards on my palm, but soon each young one had a dose of the tonic in their bellies.

Sniffles and silent tears remained, but a few curious smiles broke out when I was careful to hook the elven silver around their curved ears. They did not have holes in their lobes, but I managed to fashion some of the rings into bracelets with long blades of grass with the promise to return with chains or twine soon.

"Thank you," the woman whispered. "It's an elixir to stave off fierce disease. Since we don't know what it is, it's the best prevention we have."

"What are the symptoms?"

The woman glanced over her shoulder, a shudder rolling through her body. "Thrashing, and shouting. They're delirious. Screaming in pain. It is as though something is rotting them from the inside out."

There were toxins that could cause a mind to go rabid in the deep wood of the fading isle. I wondered if alver lands had something much the same.

"Not even Niklas has found a tonic to stop it," the woman went on, "and he has been here since before midday."

"Is this Niklas a healer?"

"An Elixist, the lead of the Falkyn guild, and brilliant with his mesmer."

The Falkyn guild, the smugglers.

I looked at the longhouse. Distant shouts were there. Folk kept bringing things from inside and tossing them into the pyre. A smuggler, but it seemed the alver clans trusted him as their hope for this house.

"Meriba." A woman raced for us, a man with a russet beard holding a bundled child in his arms at her back.

I tried not to stare, but the woman had odd eyes, green so bright they almost glowed and the dark center was sliced through like a cat's.

"Lady Tova."

The woman adjusted a leather satchel on her shoulder. "We've talked about lady, Meri. Call Bard lord all you wish, he loves a good preen, but not me. Can Kåre remain with you? Boy won't sleep without one of us lately."

"Of course." Meriba took the small boy from—I assumed—his father's arms.

"We'll be back . . . when we're back." The cat-eyed woman studied me for a long breath, then rushed toward the longhouse.

"Have you met Tova and Lord Bard?" the woman asked. "He's one of the queen's brothers."

Gods, they were part of the royal house.

"Tova is one of the king's Kryv. And this boy"—Meriba bounced the sleeping child who couldn't have been more than three turns—"is the cleverest thief in the making. He'd take to your silver like these littles."

She chuckled and settled on the grass with the young one, humming a gentle folk tune.

I drifted toward the other children. The boy was clearly the eldest, maybe around eight turns.

"You've been brave while caring for your sisters. What is your name?"

"Pavva."

I opened the thick bindings on the book of fables. "Do your sisters enjoy stories, Pavva?"

He glanced at the pages, using the back of his hand to wipe beneath his nose, and nodded.

"Do you read?"

Again, the boy nodded.

"Would you like to read to them, or should I?"

Pavva hesitated, then pointed to me, and nestled beside his young sisters.

The smallest girl held up her new grass bracelet. "Wook, Pav."

Her brother smiled and tapped the gleaming silver ring on the end, then let the girl snuggle close to his side with her damp blanket.

Once the littles were tucked close, I began to read the first fable. A tale of a poor farmer who stumbled upon the three Norns at the base of the tree of the gods. To keep him from telling other mortals how to find them, the Norns offered the traveler a gift—the opportunity to rule over every land, to have every eye turned to him until the final war of the gods.

"What the traveler forgot," I said, a low, eerie timbre to my tone, "was the Norns are often the trickiest of the gods."

The littles forgot to weep, they forgot to be afraid. All three had scooted closer, eyes rapt with intrigue.

"Can you guess what the truth of his reward became?"

"A king?"

"A god?"

I shook my head. "Those Norns wove their threads, changing his fate, until he became a gleaming star in the heavens. For they kept their word—every eye turned to behold him in the night sky, and he was above all the lands. It is a lesson to us all, to never think we can outsmart our own fate. The Norns do not take kindly to those who think they know better."

I tickled the smallest girl's chin until she giggled.

Even Pavva smiled.

"Fire."

I startled and wheeled around. My weary husband stood five paces away. The linen mask was tugged off his chin, his hair was damp with sweat, and there was a heaviness in his gaze.

The littles greeted the prince. Jonas winked at them, but faced me again in the next breath.

"Pavva, your turn to read."

The boy seemed to understand and took the book from my hands, ruffling through the various tales until he and his sisters settled on one.

I hugged my middle and stepped beside the prince. "Is it well now?"

Jonas dropped his chin. "No. They've been forced into a mesmer sleep with elixirs. It will slow the spread of whatever this disease is, but I don't know if they will wake before we find a cure."

One palm covered my mouth, a new ache in my heart for three young ones who did not know their world teetered on the edge of pain.

"I've known Teodor and Annetta since I was ten turns."

"I am sorry." Without thought, I slipped my fingers around his and squeezed. "They sound honorable, and I pray the gods bring them healing."

"I hope you're right."

"What about the littles?"

Jonas lifted his eyes, darkened with his frightening mesmer. "Annetta's sister lives in the province of Furen, a township on the other side of the kingdom. Word has been sent and I've no doubt she'll be here by the afternoon. She and her husband are good folk; they'll take the young ones while we care for Teo and Nettie."

We were not a love match, but there was a sharp pain in my chest seeing the prince without the gleam of taunts in his eyes. I wanted to ease it from him, and I did not understand it.

"What do you need me to do?"

Jonas forced a smile and tilted my chin with his thumb. "Return to the palace, get some rest. There is nothing more to do."

"I . . . if I can help you . . . I would like to."

"Your generosity is stunning, Fire, but there is nothing. We do not know what took them, so until we do, I want you nowhere near here. Dorsan." The prince turned away from me. "Take your lady back to the palace, please."

My guard stepped to my side without a word.

I let my shoulders slouch when Jonas returned to the crowds near the longhouse. The woman with the tonics offered me a sad smile, as though telling me she would look after the young ones who were snickering as they read fanciful tales.

People were scattered across the palace gates and walls. Curious staff and folk who lived on the grounds, wanting to know what had become of one of their own. Dorsan kept a pace ahead of me, one hand on my arm until we reached my chamber.

"You were regal tonight, My Lady."

"Pardon?"

Dorsan remained stiff and stalwart. "Your actions to assist where you could, to provide comfort—even to young subjects—is what a leader ought to do."

He closed my door, leaving me aghast. Dokkalfar never acknowledged my position as heir to the shadow elven throne. They were too busy being leery.

I stripped the cloak from my shoulders, sweaty though I had done nothing more than tend to heartbroken littles, and went to the window. My thoughts were with three children I'd just met and a prince who tried to conceal his pain, but the shadows of his magic always gave him up.

A few clock rounds ago, I told Jonas Eriksson I did not want to be more than our duty. As he said after the negotiation, hearts were not part of this agreement, yet I could not help but feel the weight of worry. How long would he remain out there, clearing out a house, risking his own health with whatever wretched disease had taken an innocent man and woman?

A sliver of dawn was rising in the distance by the time I forced my body to climb back into the bed, tuck under the quilts, and close my eyes. When my cheek pressed against the down pillow, a rough scratch of parchment rubbed against my skin.

My heart stopped. Another wax sealed missive with my name was laid over my pillow. It had not been there when I left the room.

Fingers shaking, I tore the seal.

My blood froze with each word.

They will blame you for this night, and what is to come with the dawn. It is the only way to get you free of here and back to those who understand exactly what you are.

Look for me when he falls.

CHAPTER 19
THE MIST THIEF

I POUNDED ON DORSAN'S DOOR, THE THREAT CRINKLED IN MY GRIP. THERE WAS no longer any room to consider the strange happenings were mere coincidence.

The missive at the vows, the slaughtered sun wing, made it clear Dorsan and I were not the lone elven here.

My guard wrenched open the door, blade half in his sheath, his tunic untucked. "Princess, what is it?"

"This is not the first strange note. What am I to make of this?"

Dorsan blinked when I shoved the parchment into his hand. "This is not the first?" In a frenzy, I repeated the note at the vows, and the gift. Dorsan's jaw tightened. "You must take this to the king and queen. I will join you."

I fastened the robe over my shift and hurried after the guard, only pausing to inquire of a maid polishing frames of paintings in the lower corridor where we could find the king and queen.

"They've returned just now. Such a pity." The woman shook her head. "They've gathered with the princes and some other folk for a bit of a meal. Cook Ylva demanded it after the night they've had."

I didn't pause to offer thanks before rushing toward the great hall, dread I couldn't explain tight in my belly.

Two men in hoods and dark cloaks stood near the doors, the strange palace guards who always looked frightening more than regal. They watched me run through the doorway into the hall. The king and queen were there as promised, Jonas's mother had her head rested against the king's shoulder, her eyes closed.

Raum, Ash, and the woman with cat eyes and her husband were seated on long benches. The man with runes inked on his fingers I'd seen on the day we arrived kept flipping through a strange book with Prince Sander. Jonas took a place next to Von Grym. The prince had his brow propped onto his fists, as though he could not peel his gaze from the table.

"Come to dine, lovey?" Raum's silver eyes found me first as staff from the cooking rooms slipped around me in the doorway.

They set to work placing trays of breads and cheeses, plates of berries and ewers of ale in the center of the table. Each seat was given a cup of what looked to be herbs for the steaming tins at their sides. Doubtless some sort of mesmer tea.

Jonas lifted his chin after Raum spoke. "Skadi?"

I didn't respond. My attention was drawn to dark berries on the tray. The outer skin glistened as though soaked in a glaze, but the pockets of seeds on the top were white as pearls. Sweet venom.

The shrubs grew in the wood of Natthaven, the berries sweet and used for delicate cakes and thick syrups in the palace. Rare and only expert hands sought to cook with sweet venom, for any touch of the stem, leaves, or greenery was toxic to the mind. An unstoppable poison that made the victim . . .

Damn the hells. It caused violent convulsions until their hearts gave out.

What was an elven berry doing here?

"Where did you get those?" I pointed at the venomous berry, voice sharp.

The woman from the cooking rooms paused. "They were arranged, I thought it was for the morning meal."

They will blame you.

Look for me when he falls.

All gods, no.

Jonas lifted a brow, befuddled, and reached for the tin of herbs at his side.

"Jonas! Stop." Frigid damp coated my palms. The mists of my affinity flowed like diaphanous ribbons off my palms.

Several of those who were seated jumped back when the darkness wrapped around the prince's settings—the herbs, the drinking horn near his plate, the tin with steaming water. All of it faded into nothing.

I tossed my palms aside, and from a cloud of darkness, every piece I'd stolen clattered over the stone floors of the hall.

I rushed to the mess of plates and food. "Bleeding hells."

"What is it?" Jonas crouched by my side, everyone from the table at his back.

I used my robe to cover my fingers and pinched some of the leafy herbs, crushed to appear as a fresh tea. "This is called sweet venom. It grows on Natthaven and it's deadly."

Someone gasped in the hall.

Jonas's jaw flexed. "How did you know?"

"I . . . I received a note that told me to"—blood drained from my face —"someone told me they'd be there when *he* fell. Gods, I think someone was coming for me."

I abandoned the mess and sprinted for the door, thoughts in a fog.

"Skadi! Wait." Jonas followed me up the staircase toward our wing, taking the stairs two at a time.

I didn't stop. My side of the chamber was empty. There was no one in the wardrobe, no one waiting to tear me away inside the sitting room.

"Will you tell me what is going on?" Jonas bent to the floor when I peered under the bed.

"I don't know, but . . ." Words died when I peered out the window.

There, tucked beside the blossom coated archway that led into the gardens was a man crouched near a hedge, uncoiling what looked like a rope. I could not see his face beneath a woolen cowl, but he did not appear to be one of the gardeners.

"There." I pointed through the glass. "Gods, he's there."

Jonas looked to where I pointed. He took out the dagger on his belt and went for the door.

"No." I scrambled after him. "He could hurt you."

Jonas spun on me in the doorway. "The only one who will be hurting is him. Stay here."

"Are you mad? I'm coming to see—"

"You will stay here." The prince startled me by tugging me to his chest. "I do not know who he is, but he is no friend of yours and he will not come near you." The prince faced my guard. "Am I clear?"

Dorsan lifted his chin. "Yes, Highness."

Heated anger flooded my face. "You do not get to put your neck at risk and demand I sit back to watch. Don't walk away . . . Jonas Eriksson, stop. Damn you!"

My protests were wholly ignored as the prince disappeared down the staircase. When I tried to follow, Dorsan held out an arm. "I agree with the prince. Do not put yourself at risk, or it will put him at risk if he is distracted by keeping you safe."

"What says he will need to? I know how to lift a blade," I gritted through my teeth.

"Not today you don't, My Lady."

When Dorsan positioned himself in front of me, I let out a hiss. "If I would not stain my soul by harming you, I would devour you in darkness, Dorsan of House Nardin!"

"Understood." He didn't move in the slightest.

I slammed the door and ran for the window. With care, I cracked the pane just enough to hear, but the day was silent beneath the morning breeze.

In a breath, anger bled to fear, then to a bit of awe.

They moved like a looming shadow. Without rustling a single hedge, a hooded man—from his build and height I took him as Von— slipped unseen onto the path where the assailant might try to flee. From another corner Sander and the man who'd been reading at the table drew nearer, both crouched low. Darkness rolled over the cobblestones like a murky flood, but I didn't know who controlled it.

My heart stuttered when Jonas materialized at the front of the archway.

Jonas's voice was low, deep, a barbed threat. "Looking for someone?"

The invader startled, but with hardly a pause, he reached for a knife on his leg and had it launched at Jonas in the next breath. My prince ducked and the assassin took the moment to flee past him.

He did not get far.

The blade Jonas carried flew after the man, and dug deep into the attacker's thigh. He cried out in pain, stumbling.

"You've nowhere to go," Jonas said with raw hate when more of his people slipped into sight along the edges of the garden.

The attacker tossed back his hood. His hair was pale and silken, ears pointed sharply.

A Ljosalfar elven.

He spun toward the window of my chamber. "He deserved to have you! Forgive me. I tried to save you before you destroy us all."

The alvers closed in, but the elven man freed a wretched sort of laugh, like he was delirious with glee, and sprinted forward.

"Stop him!" Jonas shouted, and tried to meet the man's pace.

It was over so swiftly. I winced and clenched my eyes when the elven raced with all his strength straight into a pillar with a jagged, wrought iron sconce on the side. The points pierced through his chest, his throat, impaling him with a wet, strangled gasp.

Bile teased the back of my throat. Blood fountained over the stones of the pillar and the elven's body convulsed for one breath, then another, until he went still.

Dead.

CHAPTER 20

THE NIGHTMARE PRINCE

MY MOTHER COULD SEE THE FINAL MEMORIES OF THE DEAD WHEN A BIT OF BONE was crushed onto her tongue.

There wasn't a true reason to read the dead elven's memory—most of us had been there for it—but perhaps there would be enough for my mother's mesmer to see his actions just before his demise.

I paced behind the garden bench where the queen sat, eyes closed, still as the stone beneath her.

After a moment, my mother shook her head. "He does not agree with the alliance. His thoughts kept repeating that the princess belonged to his clan."

"How long has he been following her?"

"Since the vows. He caused the chaos of the night to give him a chance to slip into the palace. All of us had toxins in our tea, and it was his warped plan to take back the princess."

Niklas tucked his herbal reference tome under his arm, cracking each knuckle just below the rune tattoos across his fingers.

He lifted a glass vial filled with the black leaves of the elven plant. "I'd like to study this. It's a poison I do not know, but seems we have need of its antidote for Teo and Nettie. Your wife had beautifully quick thinking today."

Skadi. I stopped pacing. When my gaze lifted to the window of her chamber, the bright shade of her hair stepped back from the glass pane.

Wicked, beautiful, befuddling woman.

Last night she'd shouted at me that she had no desire to know me, to care for me, to want me. Next, she was drying tears of littles, reading them fae tales, then saving my ass with the magic she feared.

Now, again it seemed, she had little desire to speak to me. I'd gone to her after the elven died, but Dorsan emerged, stating he would confirm if the man was Ljosalfar, a familiar face, or if he had any insight on behalf of the princess.

Someone tried to send me to the Otherworld to get to Skadi.

The truth of it brought a fierce panic and commanded my every step afterward and brought the realization that I would stand against a blade to keep her with me.

The frightening part was my fear ran deeper than merely caring for the wellbeing of an innocent woman. It transformed into something darker, something brutal, where the compulsion to pluck the bones from the sod's body took hold, until I feared I might lash against someone I loved should they stand in my way.

It made little sense, it was reckless, and the sentiment was not returned.

"Jonas." My mother rested her palm on my arm. "His mind felt a great deal like a man lost to a twisted belief. He believed to his soul that this alliance was temporary; he merely wanted to hurry it along."

"A zealot." Sander leaned against the wall of the palace, face hard. "You heard what he shouted. He thought this was saving the elven people."

My mother played with the end of her messy braid. "I will see to it the Dokkalfar king hears of this, and understands that if he knows of how this happened, any alliance he thought he had is over."

"I am not sending her back." My fists curled at my sides.

"Did I say that?" My mother narrowed her eyes. "What I am wondering is why you are here, and not speaking to *your wife* about all this?"

"She does not wish to speak to me."

"How do you know?"

"She sent Dorsan to speak on her behalf."

My mother clicked her tongue and shook her head. "Such a pity."

"What? If you have something to say, Maj, say it."

"It's nothing." My mother strode past me, aiming for the open entrance. "I just never took you for a coward."

The queen was gone before I could return any sort of protest.

I frowned. It wasn't cowardice, I was granting her desires; surely that was the honorable thing to do. Still, I turned on my heel and made my way toward the entrance to our wing. Perhaps it would be wise to see that she was not entirely unsettled by this ordeal.

Not to mention, I'd yet to thank her for saving my neck.

Much the same as before, Dorsan stepped into the hall when I went to Skadi's door. "I need to speak to her."

"I do not think the—"

"Pardon me." I shoved around the guard. "I need to speak to my wife."

Truth be told, the man didn't put up much protest when I slipped into the room. Either the guard did not feel he could overrule the word of a prince, or he agreed with me.

Skadi was seated in one of the chairs near her half-built inglenook, knees touched against her chest, her eyes vacant and aimed at the threads of the rug beneath her. When I approached, she jostled from her seat and stepped around the chair, like a damn shield between us.

"Is everything dealt with?" She curled her fingers over the back of the chair.

I paused in front of the seat. "We believe he was convinced this alliance would be the downfall of your people. I don't know why, nor where he planned to take you."

"He was of the light elven," she whispered. "I don't know if it is hard to guess."

"Do you believe Prince Arion was behind it?" There was the condition of the alliance where Skadi could choose the wretched prince within the first turn. This could've been an attempt to frighten her into his arms.

"Doubtful," she said. "The prince is a fool, but this would be an act of war and he lost many men in the battle. He's not strong enough to bring another one. Yet."

I did not revel in her last word. My fingers dug into my palms when I curled my fists. "Then this sod acted on his own."

"It is possible. Many Ljosalfar adore Arion. They might think he was slighted." Skadi took a step for the bedchamber. "Thank you for telling me."

She was trying to distance us.

"You saved me," I said. "I have not thanked you."

"Well, we're square, I suppose." Skadi tucked a lock of her hair behind one ear. "You didn't slit my throat for nearly killing your brother."

I folded my arms over my chest, biting back the words I truly wanted to speak. "I know this was likely upsetting for you. Are you all right?"

A crack of vulnerability sliced through the mask she tried to hold in place. "I am sorry for you and your people. Destruction follows me like a curse. Because of me being here, three littles could lose their mother and father—"

"Skadi, that is not your doing at all."

"I did not poison them, but my presence brought their pain. You and people you love nearly died."

"And you saved all of us." I drew closer. "Skadi, we aren't afraid of you."

"You have not seen the true dangers of my affinity."

"And you have not seen all of mine, something else we have in common, Wife."

Skadi returned a hesitant sort of smile, one that barely curled the corners of her lips.

Hells, I wanted to go to her, offer a bit of comfort, but I held back.

Since that bastard was spotted in the gardens, since a gleam of terror had flashed through Skadi's eyes, I wanted nothing more than to ensure it never returned.

The strange possessiveness burned in my chest, I merely refused to reveal it. What would be the point? Not even a day before, her senti-ments were clear—she did not want to know me above our duty.

With a reluctant step, I returned to the corridor. "Well, I am glad this day did not end with royal funeral pyres. I will leave you to do as you wish, merely wanted to make sure you were well and tell you what we learned. Do not blame yourself for Annetta and Teodor. As always, should you need anything, I am not far."

Distance was likely for the best. Already I was growing too vulner-able with her, and that was the trouble. For the first time, I wanted to.

CHAPTER 21
THE MIST THIEF

Jonas kept his word. I saw little of the prince in the days after the Ljosalfar attack. The only sign he remained in the palace came from the sound of his door opening and closing, his steps on the stone staircase that took him to some mysterious place I dared not investigate.

My nights were haunted with dreams of me never reaching the great hall in time to stop Jonas from drinking the sweet venom leaves.

Each morning I woke drenched in sweat, gasping, with a damn near insatiable desire to pound on his door, all to ensure my husband was alive.

For his sake, it was better to stay away. Those I let inside my soul never made it out the same. There was something that twisted them into darker pieces of themselves.

And some never made it out alive.

Near the window, I stirred a tin of herbal tea aimlessly. My quill had paused on the parchment. I'd yet to hear from my grandfather about the attack, so I began a missive describing the event.

Whenever I attempted to write how close the prince and his folk came to ingesting the sweet venom, the ink blotted and I couldn't go on. And when the sun rose today, I admitted a truth I'd dared not face—I missed the prince.

I rather enjoyed the heat he brought to my blood, a reminder I hadn't forgotten how to feel. I missed his snide looks, his cunning grin. I even missed his overuse of the name *Fire*.

My self-imposed exile was dull and loathsome. To make it all worse, I'd yet to recover my trunks of books and had given them up for misplaced or left behind on Natthaven.

The three tales I'd packed in my personal satchel had long since been read, and there was little else for me to do but write letters.

Now, with Jonas plaguing my mind, I could not even do that.

My forehead fell to the edge of the table. I was a damn fool.

"Lady Skadinia." Dorsan entered without a knock. "You have a visitor."

I snapped my head off the desk, swatting at the parchment sticking to my skin, and spun in my chair.

A woman in a woolen dress and curled hair tied behind her head followed him into the room. She faced Dorsan and returned a wobbly bow. "Thanks, my good man."

Dorsan sniffed, his sharp features furrowed. Alver folk befuddled him as much as me.

Once he was gone, the woman faced me, a crooked grin on her full lips. "Remember me?"

I tilted my head. She looked familiar. "Lady Frigg."

"Lady?" She made a sound like a gag. "I'm no lady. Frigg will do just fine. I've come at the order of the queen. She wants you out of the palace."

My throat tightened.

"Oh, gods." Frigg held up her hands. "Not like that. I just mean, Mal is fully aware you're rotting away in here, and she asked me to take you around to get some air, maybe some sunlight. Or do you shadow folk not like the sun?"

"The queen asked of me?"

"Yes?" Frigg spoke the word like she wasn't certain if she should respond. "Think she's starting to get a little worried about you. So, can you tolerate the light?"

"Uh, we like sunlight fine," I said. "Dokkalfar summon healing from

155

blood or foliage, but we are named shadow elven because most of our plants and herbs bloom in the moonlight. It is when summoning is strongest."

"Huh. Interesting. Sander mentioned something of the sort earlier."

"The prince is learning about Dokkalfar?"

"Trust me, Princess, he's been fascinated by elven culture since the battle."

I was glad Prince Sander did not harbor resentment, but I could not cease with the hope that his brother might do the same and ignore my demands, see through the lies, and barge into my room. Possibly put his hands on my skin again.

Frigg scratched her head. She truly was lovely. Without her straw hat, her light hair was full and wavy and her features were fair save for a few freckles on her nose.

She swung her hands by her sides. "The queen asked me since, if you recall, my maj was seeing to it you had a gown. It's ready, so Malin figured it might be a good opportunity for you to see a bit more of Klockglas."

An unmistakable thrill rushed in my blood.

Frigg must've seen the shift in my features for her grin widened. "I swear, there've been no sightings of murderous elven."

I swallowed. "How are those littles?"

"With their aunt in Furen. Fed, clothed, and a little heartbroken they can't be with their mother and father. But they are resilient. No matter what fate rests in the hands of the wicked Norns for Nettie and Teo, the littles will be well looked after."

She spoke in a way to ease my guilt. In my mind, I knew I could not have foreseen such an attack, but I still held a cruel ache of guilt over Pavva and his sisters.

I reached into a wooden box near the side of my bed and removed three chains. "Do you suppose someone could help me post these? I gave them some elven silver and promised to send them chains so they could wear them."

Frigg placed the chains into a small pouch on her thin belt. "I'll see it done. Shall we go?"

There was merit to learning the land, and it was gods-awful dull in this room.

"Yes." I forced a smile and took hold of a thin, diaphanous cloak from the wardrobe, wrapping it around my shoulders. "I am beginning to rot."

"Does he just follow you around?"

I bit down a laugh and looked over my shoulder. At the end of the market road, Dorsan still strolled along, a satin wrapped gown draped over his arms, casting dubious looks at the merchant stands.

Frigg's mother had to have a bit of magic. The gown was stunning. Simple enough to be worn on any occasion, but when the light struck it seemed made of shattered stars. Fit for a royal ball.

Dorsan paused when one of the merchants stopped to gawk at him, eyeing his weapon belt and the gown in hand, like my guard might have a few more hidden valuables tucked out of sight.

"It is his duty to look after me," I said.

"Well, his duty is annoying."

My smile widened as I tipped my head and bit into the end of a cream roll. The stand had been the first stop on the market path, and Frigg insisted it was a coveted sweet of the region.

We ended up going back for three more when the berry filling made me nearly sob with delight. I licked my thumb and tucked the parchment wrapping into the satin coin purse on my belt.

The Klockglas market was boisterous and filled with scents of leather, smoke, and fish. Vendors bartered from windows of their crooked shops, or from behind rolling carts with canvas tops.

Knives adorned everyone, even the littles ran about armed and wild.

I tried to guess who was alver and mortal—their ears were the same —but it was impossible.

There were fae here, mostly sea fae with their golden skin, bright eyes, and fluttery voices. Since sea fae were the only ones capable of ferrying people from the earth realms to the Ever Kingdom, many had taken up residences throughout the different earth fae realms.

Frigg tore off down a cobbled path leading deeper into the township.

Homes were made of small cottages or longhouses. Most had goats or hogs behind rickety fences. Some were larger estates with small gardens.

I paused at a totem made of black granite. A remembrance totem. Names were etched into the stone and at the bottom were crossed blades with the saying of the Kryv: *Fight to the end.*

"How do these lands seem . . . so loyal when it is made of self-proclaimed crooks?"

Frigg's face pinched like she was confused. "Because we are willing to reach into our depravity to protect our own. We will place goodness aside and be the worst sort of folk should our people be threatened."

It was frightening and beautiful all at once.

"Come on." Frigg linked her arm with mine again. "We ought to be returning before dark. Dockers and such get rowdy at taverns, and brän has a way of making folk forget their better qualities."

The road cut down the back side of the slope, lined in more trees that weren't seen from the shore. Along the edges of the path, thick trunks twisted and tangled together like a ballroom of giants. Limbs with thick oak leaves crafted a canopy overhead that only let in a few beams of pale sunlight.

The air was cooler and fresher, like damp soil and moss rather than the heavy salted winds near the shore.

Frigg chatted about life in Klockglas, how most folk were good and honorable unless they were crossed, then they would plot against you to get even. "The king and queen view the consequences of disputes a little differently than other kingdoms."

"Different how?"

"Well, if someone finds their goat missing, only to turn up at another house, they can cry thief and bring a fine or punishment upon their neighbor. Or it can be handled another way."

"Like what?"

A dark gleam flashed in Frigg's eyes. "The one who was robbed can craft a heist against the first thief. Bring evidence you were wronged, and you are free to restore your belongings *with* interest."

"Meaning?"

"The heist better make off with not only the goat that was stolen, but some penge coin or a few hens. No killing is allowed, no blood is to be drawn. Stealth is the key. If successful, the royal house will give the second thief a banner stating ownership of the entire haul."

It seemed like madness. "What's to stop the first thief from retaliating?"

"The banner." Frigg paused at a small, wooden gate that led to the back paths toward the Black Palace. "If the first thief chooses to retaliate they do so knowing the Kryv and the Black Palace will make their own moves against them. No one wants to go against the royal house."

"How did they come up with such laws?"

"I think the way the king and queen see it is if you are foolish enough to thieve and get caught, you earn what's coming to you. And if you're even more foolish to thieve, get caught, then have your haul and more taken in return, they find you embarrassing and stand against you."

"And does it work?"

Frigg nodded, balancing on a fallen log on the side of the path as she walked. "There is actually very little crime here. Squabbles, sure. You heard my own father do the same."

"Well, your father doesn't seem the type who'd get caught."

Frigg's palm pressed to her heart. "Good hells, that was awfully nice of you to say."

Her eyes burned in sincerity, as though I'd stumped her with such utter praise she didn't know what to make of it.

What a strange place this was. Schemes were dealt with greater schemes, and honor was brought to house names by who pulled off the cleverest moves.

I kept close to her pace until we rounded a bend, and my blood turned to ice. Even Frigg let out a gasp of surprise.

On foot, four men approached from some of the lower townships that speckled the hillside of the palace. Silver-eyed Raum stood next to a man with wavy red hair who held the hand of another man with a scar through his brow.

I didn't pay them much mind; I was too lost on the sharp, shadowed stare of the form in the middle.

The alver king stopped where the paths converged, practically drinking me in with his dark gaze.

"Ah, hello." Raum waved. "Didn't see you, which never happens. I see everything."

"Profetik," Frigg whispered, as if sensing my confusion. "Heightened senses."

Gods, could he really see anything? Through clothing? I folded my arms over my chest, and Raum laughed, muttering something to the king I couldn't make out.

The king took a step forward, shifting a few rolls of parchment between his hands. He stood nearly two heads taller than me, black coated him from shoulder to toe, and his dark chestnut hair was kept tied at the sides, but a little tousled—like his sons'.

What was I to say? Should I say anything? Was I to bow? Did I hold out a hand?

All my body managed to do was tremble like a damn hummingbird when he stopped three paces away.

Say something. Anything would be better than this . . . silence.

Frigg took a step closer to my side. "Maj made her a gown."

The king glanced at the woman, his expression unchanged. "Good." His voice was a rasp, deep and dark. It faded and he returned again to his scrutiny of me. Surely he must expect me to speak.

"We've all been rather keen to thank you for stopping us from dying by tea. It would've been a horribly embarrassing way to greet the gods after all the bloodier things we've done," said Raum.

"No thanks needed." Gods, my voice trembled. "Forgive me for being distant, I . . . I haven't been feeling well."

Raum laughed and nudged the king's arm. "More like she's avoiding Jonas."

Cold damp coated my palms with a flush of embarrassment. No, no, gods, no.

My affinity often presented when I was discomposed, like it wanted to tear me away into the mists to hide me. To show it here, in front of the king, might be seen as a threat.

I clutched my skirt, willing the frigid magic to fade. "I apologize for being so absent."

The king took another step toward me, glancing at my palms. Did he see the darkness? Was he threatened?

When he lifted his chin again, his expression was softer. "You've my thanks for your quick thinking. Saved my family."

I froze. "Of course, sire"

"Has he mistreated you?"

"Pardon?"

"My son. Has he mistreated you?"

"No, Highness."

The king grimaced for a breath, then took a step away. "Good."

Without another word, he continued down the path, toward the main township.

"Isak." The redhead paused by my side, a hand to his chest. "Good t-t-to finally meet you." His stammer was heavy, but he spoke with confidence and gestured at the other man. "Fiske. My husband."

Fiske nodded a greeting.

I thought I might've smiled, but in truth I still reeled from the strange interaction with the alver king.

Once Fiske and Isak followed the king, Raum leaned in, a playful glint in his pale eyes. "Steady on, Princess. I think your fears are showing."

With a wink, he followed the others.

Frigg snickered and threaded her arm through mine again. "Breathe. You survived a Kase stare."

"I thought he was looking straight through me."

"Oh, in a way, he was. Don't worry, you've won over the king."

I pressed my palms to my cheeks, hoping to cool the flush in my skin. "That was me winning him over?"

"No, that was done when you snatched poison out of their hands. Right then, he was proving it. He gave you a look of concern, inquired on your happiness with Jonas. All signs Kase cares. The way he looked at you though, something in your fears must've spoken to him."

"My fears?" Thoughts spun wildly. What fears was I holding? Fear of the king, of alvers, of my own affinity. My heart dropped. I'd thought of the prince and the way I feared drawing close to him. "He can truly read them?"

"Feels them, tastes them, I don't really know. He can use our fears against us, or in your case, likely read your heart a bit. We keep our true fears in our hearts, after all."

Good hells.

"Come on. Don't worry so much about folk despising you here. We don't." Frigg tugged on my arm, urging me toward the back courtyard of the palace.

Voices from the bustle inside the palace walls filtered down the path. The day was surprising. A day where no one cast me wary glances, where I laughed with another woman almost like we might be friends, and through it all I forgot to be on my guard.

I forgot to hide away and keep the distance I demanded of my prince.

"You ever going to talk to Jonas again?"

I coughed against a rough swallow and met Frigg's gaze. "Pardon?"

She sighed and paused inside the gates. "We know you fools argued before the attack, but I thought with you being a damn warrior maiden and saving his ass, you lot might've cleared the air, but you're not talking. I can't figure it out. He's like my annoying younger brother, but Skadi, he is one of the best men I know."

"Why do you say this?"

"Because you have a look on your face that I noticed the first time you stepped foot on Klockglas. It's how you looked at him, and I'd take a guess you're thinking of him now."

My shoulders slumped in defeat. "Before I was tossed into alver clans, I was quite skilled at hiding my expressions."

She chuckled. "We have ways to pull out the truth here, I suppose."

"I told the prince it was better if we kept a distance and didn't make this more than duty."

"Gods, that sounds miserable."

I winced. There was a festering absence I noticed when the prince was not close, and I did not understand how—through all my attempts to shield against him—the man still managed to sink his claws into me from the first kiss.

"He is merely honoring my request."

"Well change your request." Frigg's brows flicked twice. "He's been sulking as much as you, so I'd say Jonas would be more than willing to shave some of that distance away."

What if this doesn't need to be nothing? The prince had asked the question before the attack, and I rejected it. No one looked deeper than the affinity in my veins, but what if Jonas meant what he said?

Risk was there. To trust another with a piece of my heart was a chance I never wanted to take. Not again.

With a sigh, I made my way toward the gardens. "You might be right, I—"

My voice cut off. In front of the door that would take me to the staircase of our wing, my nightmare prince stood with his back to me.

He wasn't alone.

Head lowered, I could just make out a woman with her hands on his chest, her body close. Jonas shifted, and I noted the way her fingers fell to his belt without shame.

Gods. I asked for distance, but I did not anticipate the man flaunting his lovers for all to see.

The ache in my heart took me from behind, sharper than I imagined, and hot like a molten spear. I wanted to fade, to forget, to hide in the coldness of apathy. My affinity would shield me for a time, but the deepest indifference required cruel acts.

But there were other ways.

I spun on Frigg before she reached the top. "Actually, I have one more request, if you're willing."

She canted her head. "What's that?"

"You mentioned these taverns. I hear all the time of alver revelry. Care to join me?"

"Oh, I don't know, Princess." Frigg glanced over her shoulder. "It might be best to do so with your hus—"

"Suit yourself." I drifted around her side. "I'll have Dorsan take me. Thank you for today, it was wonderful."

"Now wait a damn moment." She took hold of my arm again. "If you're determined to try brän and not wait for the prince, I'll be required to go with you. It's a fool's choice to toss back that ale without a Klockglas native looking out for you. And as a woman who enjoys a fair amount of revelry, I should tell you, I think this is a reckless idea."

CHAPTER 22
THE NIGHTMARE PRINCE

BLOOD WAS EVERYWHERE. HOT AND FETID, MORE THAN ONE MEMBER OF THE cooking staff had to leave the rooms to breathe in fresher air.

Being an alver, I was rather accustomed to the cloying scent of the mesmer in my blood, but some never seemed to grow a stomach for it.

I didn't have time for this. There was still work to be done in the upper room. Sander and Von were up there, but I was compelled to be part of every damn step, and I didn't want to peel back those thoughts to understand why.

Intolerable thoughts of her blue eyes and the way she leaned into my touch before her mind told her to hide away had kept my mind wandering while shaping one of the shelves.

The woman was torture.

Our shared touches, our kisses, they were a siren's call, and I could not escape the pull to more with my wife. But fate was cruel and she would rather keep to her chamber than risk the sight of me.

Since the attack, my mood had grown sour and wretched. Part of me wondered if Sander had rocked the shelf on purpose all to get my grumbling ass out of the room.

The gash on my finger bled like it was fatal, but was slowly clotting with Ylva's pastes she kept in the cooking room for the staff who grew too lax with their chopping knives.

Hands padded across my back. Gentle, feminine. My skin raised in deeper annoyance, and it festered in my chest.

"Are you well now, Prince Jonas?"

"Fine." I tightened the bloody bandaged tighter around my hand.

"Here." Another woman named Runi approached with a new linen. She kept a hand over her nose, blocking the smell. "Ylva demands you keep it fresh. You know better than to argue, and I think she's trying to get you out of her kitchen with your stink."

I gave a nod of thanks and took the clean bandage, peeling the old off my torn flesh. Runi was pleasant enough. Once we took a bit of pleasure from each other in the stables, but she was not under any illusions our time was anything deeper.

Runi was not the problem.

Oldun, new to the staff of the palace, would not step away. Where I would move, so would Oldun.

"Let me help you."

I pulled away. "I'm fine. Thank you."

Oldun ignored the request, feigning concern over my hand, and used the moment to press against me. Her eyes were big and hazy with desire. Once, I might've enjoyed it, might've taken her somewhere where we'd both give in to lust.

Now, I could not rid my thoughts of a woman who did not want me.

With care, I nudged her back. "All thanks, ladies. I think I'll be good to return now."

Oldun's fingertips lingered too long on my wrapped palm, unbothered by the smell. "Would you want company?"

"No." My tone came out harsher than intended.

"I don't understand."

"I plan to leave here without company. Is that better?" Gods, I was an ass.

"Do I not please you?" Oldun's eyes were wide, almost hurt.

My grousing was not her fault. I let out a sigh. "I am vowed."

Oldun covered a laugh with her palm. Even Runi snickered.

"Forgive me, Prince Jonas." Again, the woman took hold of my arm. "But we all know the circumstances. It's not a typical vow."

"Oh? Did I not take a wife? I don't believe you were there, but I was, and I recall vows much like anyone else would take."

Oldun tilted her head, looking at me like I was an exasperating child. "Everyone knows you don't speak to the elven. She does not leave her room."

"I think you speak of things you don't understand."

"Oldun." Runi tried to reach for the other woman. "Leave it be."

"It is admirable that you try to be a husband." Oldun did not pull away, even stepped closer. "Surely you've been . . . lonely."

She had the gall to touch the front of my belt.

I gripped her wrist, pulling her hand aside briskly. "Do not place your hands on me again."

"Who does then?" Oldun bit down on her bottom lip. "Surely not the elven, we all heard how it is, and she is a fool not to join you in your bed."

Mesmer clouded my eyes. I took a bit of delight in the wash of fear paling Oldun's features. "Do not speak poorly of my wife."

"Jonas. Gods, there you are. What the hells are you . . ." Von's voice faded, but he made his way through the cooking rooms and cut an arm between me and Oldun. He shot a look my way. "Step back."

I bared my teeth, but blinked until the blur of darkness faded from my eyes. I shoved around them and made no attempts to greet a soul until I slammed the door behind me in the half-constructed room in the upper corridor.

Sander sat on the floor, legs outstretched, with a book of elvish plants and herbs open on his lap. "What's wrong with you?"

"Seems one of the women in the cooking rooms thought she had a right to my bed, and did not believe me when I said she didn't."

"Hmm." My brother didn't look up from the pages. "You could've."

"Could've what?"

"You could've returned with her. Could've taken her to wherever you do bed women. No one on Natthaven would be able to speak against you."

I drew to a halt, my hand hovering over the handle of a wood scraper. "Is that how highly you think of me?"

"You vowed with Skadi to bring peace, didn't you? You fear war, it eats at you, haunts your dreams."

"Shut up, brother." I took up the tool and returned to the damn shelf that should've been finished by now.

Sander chuckled, slapping the pages closed. "Isn't that why you took vows? More than that spell you absorbed to keep the sea and earth realms safe, it is the fear of war and battle that led you to vow with the princess."

"What does it matter?"

"Nowhere in that reason does it say you must not live your life as you did." He let out a long breath. "So, you could've gone with the woman."

I yanked the book from his hands, using the spine to point at him. "Stop telling me to betray my wife. What's gotten into you?"

"Is it a betrayal? Your negotiations do not speak of fidelity, they do not speak of love." Sander folded his arms over his chest. "Unless those pieces are becoming rather important to you."

I blew shavings off the surface in an angry breath. "Why don't you speak a little plainer. What are you getting at?"

"You want to care about her; I think you already do. I think something about her speaks to you."

"I think you are wrong." There could be no caring for my wife, not in that way. "I told her when we first arrived, I would not have other lovers. I gave her my word."

"And what did she say?"

"That she did not believe me."

Sander hesitated. "Jo, why have you never wanted to love anyone?"

"I love plenty."

"You know what I mean. You never wanted to take vows."

"Circumstances changed."

"I know," he said. "Now you have taken them, and you look miserable because the wife you claim not to care for isn't speaking to you."

"It is aggravating, that's all." I flicked dust off my trousers. "I hoped we might be amicable."

"Why aren't you?"

"Because she does not want it!" I closed my eyes, drawing my pulse to a calm. "She told me she does not want to make this more than a duty. She does not want to know me."

"That was the argument the other night?"

"Yes, and I am trying to honor her desire, but . . ." I let the words die. They were sharp and sour on my tongue.

"But you want it differently?"

I dropped the shaver and rubbed a thumb over a bloody spot on the bandage. "I don't know. Gods, she's awful. Wretched. I cannot get her out of my head. I think she's cast a damn spell on me."

Sander grinned. "I think that is how it feels at the beginning of the fall, you bastard."

I did not dignify that with a response. Sander didn't press, merely took up his book again. After a time, Von returned.

"Well, I think you properly annoyed Oldun." He folded his arms over his chest.

"Ah, Oldun." Sander shook his head. "Heard chatter that she has a wager on being the first to bed you after the vows."

Anger pooled tight in my gut. I was nothing but a conquest, and I hated how it had been acceptable for me all these turns. Strange how a vow, a new circumstance, left me realizing I never wanted that with Skadi.

If ever she wanted me for more, I never wanted her to feel like it did not matter, like she was merely a body.

Gods, what was the bleeding woman doing to me?

"What upset you?" Von's mouth was set into a tight line. "I've never seen you draw mesmer like that."

"She insulted Skadi."

"Should've known." Von took up a cloth and settled in to finish staining the edges of another wall of shelves. "Makes a bit more sense then."

"Don't start. Sander already tried."

"Tried what? To tell you that you're falling for your wife?"

Sander and Von laughed at their own stupidity.

"You're both bleeding fools."

I wasn't certain how long we remained silent, surrounded by the scent of wood and dust, but by the time a voice called out from the lower corridors, my spine ached, and I would likely need a fresh bandage.

"Is that . . ." I abandoned my tools and hurried down the staircase toward our chambers. "Dorsan?"

The elven guard looked like a knight from a fae tale, his fist on my door. Boots polished like the gleam of a raven's wing, a fur cloak over his shoulders, his tunic starched and stiff.

"Forgive me, Highness." He dropped his hand and squared his shoulders to me. "I have been sent by the Lady Frigg to fetch you."

"What's wrong?"

Dorsan flinched, a crack in his marble flesh. "It involves the Princess Skadinia."

"I figured, man. Where is she?"

The elven lowered his voice. "There is a disruption at one of your taverns. My Lady was introduced to alver wine, and I'm afraid it has not taken to her well."

"Skadi had tavern brän?"

"That's not ideal." Von groaned at my back. I hadn't realized he and my brother had followed.

"Yes." Dorsan's voice was steady and flat, but his bright eyes gave up his discontent. "You see, after she indulged, My Lady confessed why she did not wish to return to the palace after the Lady Frigg took her through the townships. She apparently grew rather emotional—strange for her—when she saw you with your mistress. Now, to avoid embarrassment for both Natthaven and your house, I hope you—"

"My mistress?" *Dammit.* Skadi likely saw Oldun touching me. I dug the heels of my palms into my eyes. "I do not have a mistress, you sod, and she is not an embarrassment to any house. Show me what tavern she's in. Now."

CHAPTER 23
THE MIST THIEF

Brän was rather disgusting.

I could not stop drinking it. Once it burned through the ache in my chest, peeling away memories of Jonas entangled with others, I poured horn after horn.

Somewhere in the haze of my mind, I knew this was my doing. I laughed and tipped a horn back. Pain always seemed to come from my own hands.

The tavern was lively. Rawhide drums pounded in one corner, a skald stood on a stool chanting fanciful tales to the crowds. The laths reeked of sweat and bile, but most of my senses were dulled from the beautiful, *beautiful*, disgusting brän.

"Princess, I think that's enough." For the third time, Frigg tried to pry the horn from my fingers.

"I thought you wanted me to enjoy Klosh . . . Klockglas." I snickered and tried to tip the drink to my lips.

Damn Frigg got the drop on me and snatched the horn when I let my second hand fall away.

"Look, I'm not here to unravel whatever this is"—Frigg gestured to me—"but I think you might feel better once you return to the Black Palace, sleep, then speak to Jonas."

I blew out my lips, rising when the drums took on a different tune. "I don't want to speak to him."

"Skadi, where are you going . . . wait, *Skadi.*"

Frigg hissed when I turned away from our small corner and approached a long, heavy oak table filled with men of all kinds—brutish and wild, long and lean, some with knives on their belts, others with sharp, handsome features.

Not the strong angles of Jonas's face, but they'd do.

I nestled between the shoulders of two men and slapped my palm onto the table. "Hello, alver clans." I flashed a grin. "Have you ever met an elf?"

A few rumbles rolled down the table.

"No, sweet. Can't say I have." Three seats down, a man with a beard braided down to his heart winked. Handsome enough, but there was more of a natural brutality in his eyes than my prince's.

A shudder danced up my arms. I'd be wise to step back.

Instead, I drifted down the table, running my fingertips over his shoulders. "Now . . . now you have."

"You're the princess they brought back to the palace?"

I snorted and took a swig from his drinking horn. "A little pet."

"Hmm. Not satisfied with our prince, sweet? Or is the bed too crowded?" His hand slid around my waist.

The urge to pull back caused me to stumble. He mistook my retreat as drunken steps. Against his chest, I could breathe him in. All wrong. He smelled all wrong. Sweat and ale, leather and wood. Not the smoke and heat and forest pine of Jonas.

"I better go."

"Ah, don't go." He drew me back to the table. "As you said, we've never seen an elven. Music is bright, you are beautiful, show us an elven dance."

Before I could follow my steps, I was atop the table. Cheers and chants shouted for the elven princess. Drums thudded like blood in my skull.

"Skadinia." Frigg tried to shove through. Most of the men were on their feet now, shouldering her out.

They cheered for me. For me. In this moment I wasn't the creature of darkness, I wasn't a weapon used for battles. I wasn't the desire of the Ljosalfar to use against elven and fae.

For now, I felt desired.

"There is one dance."

More whoops and hollers followed, men with too much brän in their bellies cheered for me to show them. I spun around once, my skirt flaring.

"Show us, sweet." The brute shouted again.

I forced a grin, shoving thoughts of battles, enemies, and old betrothals far from my thoughts.

Elven dances were graceful, not a match for the rapid tune of the drums and clasp, but I rose onto my toes, one hand clutching the skirt of my gown, all the same.

I dipped and spun, arms out like a partner led me across the table. Pain was there, dulled to be sure, but still a hot ache needling into my heart. To see Jonas with the woman took me like a strike to the chest. Ruthless and fierce, I could not breathe.

Feeling was the trouble.

At the end of battles, I thought he was a fiend. Then we spoke without bloodshed between us, without the dull fade of my affinity numbing my soul. He was . . . infuriatingly beautiful.

Our vows, gods, the kiss. It was like a fire erupted in my blood.

I spun around faster, head reeling, toes slipping.

The feast afterward, the way he'd peeled me away, demanded to know if I'd ever been harmed, even lost in his own cups. Truth be told, I wasn't certain he even remembered.

Faster. Faster. The room tilted.

My chamber. To feel his hands against my body, his mouth against my flesh, was burned in my bones. Never had I desired another in such a way. To claim his weight over me, arms and legs tangled, was a craving I never anticipated.

Faster. Faster.

Arms caught me around the middle, drawing me to an abrupt halt, and tugged me off the table.

I blinked. Every wall was a maelstrom of haze and fog, but two vicious green eyes pinned me in place.

I snickered and arched into him. "Hello, Husband. I am becoming . . . becoming more alver . . . alverish."

"Shame. I prefer you exactly as you are." Jonas steadied me around the waist amidst protests and groans from my ale-riddled audience. "Time to come home."

"No." I weakly shoved against his shoulder. "I think I'll stay."

Across the tavern, Frigg devoured her thumbnail, standing between Sander, Von, and—*gods*—Dorsan.

"Skadi." Jonas's voice was against my ear. "We're leaving."

"She doesn't want to leave, My Prince." One of the brutes from the table rose.

Jonas sneered at the man. "Sit down, Balki."

Balki was undeterred. In my haze, I did not understand how he managed it, but somehow he reeled around the prince and had me pressed against his chest.

"It's not fair if the sweet doesn't get what she wants. Said she wanted to spend a night with me. You find beds aplenty, Prince. I say let your new princess do the same."

I didn't want his bed. Gods, I did not want any bed but my own.

"From what we heard, even the elven folk tried to snatch her back."

My throat tightened. I did not want this man touching me. He spoke so callously about the attack of the elven assassin, as though his attempts to take me back had not nearly slaughtered the royal house.

"Careful, Balki," Jonas's dark voice followed. "You're crossing a dangerous line."

"It's not a love match." Balki laughed. "Don't let your pride keep our sweet from taking the best of what Klockglas has to offer."

In my mind, I tried to shove away from the bulky chest, but I wasn't certain if my limbs were working quite right.

Not that it mattered. In another heartbeat, I was yanked out of the brute's arms, and handed over to Frigg. She held me close, like a friend who might sincerely be afraid for me, but I was lost to the commotion near the table.

Balki, large as he was, was screaming on his knees.

Black, inky veins covered his face, splitting off from his eyes, his nose, down his neck. Jonas circled the man, spinning a knife in one hand, but when he turned his face toward me his beautiful eyes were endless pools of black.

Jonas stepped behind Balki and hooked his arm around the brute's throat, pressing the point of the knife under the man's chin. "Tell me again, Balki. What right do you think you have to put your filthy hands on my wife?"

"N-None. Stop, please."

Jonas teased the tip of the dagger against Balki's cheek, slowly dragging it across his face. "Are you seeing what I'll do if you touch her again? Creative, don't you think? I hear you can live for quite some time with innards spilled in such a way."

"Jo." Sander warned.

Jonas blinked, clearing the darkness from his gaze. With his knee he nudged Balki onto the tavern floorboards and stepped over him, making certain his boot kicked his ribs as he did.

The veins were fading in Balki's face when the prince crouched. "Mistake my wife for yours again and I'll kill you. Understand?"

All Balki did was nod and murmur a swift *yes*.

With a white smile, as though nothing had happened, Jonas strode to me. "Time to go, Fire."

"No." I was still wobbly, but I shook my head. "After what . . . you did? Why—"

A shriek burst over my lips. The room flipped, top over bottom. My feet were in the air, my face was tucked against the small of Jonas's back.

"Put . . . put me down." I pounded my fists against his hips, I doubted he felt it at all through his damn muscle. "Jonas Eriksson!"

"I do enjoy my full name from your lips," he retorted, shoving through the crowds. "But I'm afraid your cries will need to wait until later."

Bastard. I might've shouted it, I wasn't certain. At this angle, blood rushed to my head and I could hardly focus on the floorboards. In the next breath, cool air struck my cheeks. Jonas didn't return me to the ground.

"Put me down." I cried out, and soon regretted it. Once more my world tilted and my head moved slower, like a rolling tide. The moment my feet touched the cold cobblestones, I began to fall over.

Jonas caught me around the waist, holding me to his chest.

This close, I saw the sweat on his brow, I saw the fury in his eyes.

"You're deranged and . . . beautiful." I stumbled over the words, my body falling into his. "I think I hate you for it."

"Hate me then." Jonas brushed hair from my eyes. "But do it safely in our rooms."

Our rooms. *His* room. Perhaps he'd just come from his bed, from her arms. I shoved against his chest.

"No." I swatted his hand away. "No. I thought I was free to do as I pleased. Or am I to be your shackled prisoner while you do whatever you want with anyone you like?"

Jonas moved so swiftly, I gasped when his hand gripped my chin, drawing our lips close.

"You are my wife," he breathed against my mouth, a slight curl to his lips. "If you'd like me to tie you up, all you must do is ask."

The ground rolled as waves on the sea.

"You did not keep your word."

The scrape of his stubble ran along my cheek. "If I broke my word, why does it matter if you do not want me?"

Vision grew blurry, my legs felt like brittle straw, unable to bear my weight. Somehow Jonas must've predicted the collapse, for when my knees gave out his arms were there to scoop me up.

My cheek fell to his heart, the steady thrum of the cadence a lullaby in the fog.

"It matters," I said, breathless and distant, "because I do want you, but I know you will never truly want me."

White hot agony lined every side of my head. Something damp and cold covered my brow to my nose, smelling like cloying mint and rosemary. I cracked one eye. A pale linen was over my face, but I could not pull it away, my hands felt weighed down by a thousand stones.

Bit by bit my mind drifted between syrupy haze and the chirps of morning birds outside. Soft quilts cushioned my heavy limbs. If only I could cease the screech of my skull.

With a heavy groan, I swung one hand to my face and peeled back the pungent linen. Gods, what a mistake. I recoiled from the light like it was daggers to my eyes.

Someone chuckled. "Brän is not to be trifled with. It is a friend in one gulp, then a foe in the next."

I spread my fingers, squinting against the villainous sunlight to find a woman seated in a chair five paces beside my bed. Slender, with fair skin and freckled cheeks. Her vibrant hair was braided loosely over one shoulder, and reminded me of a sunset before a sea storm.

"Highness." The title came out so softly, I wasn't certain I spoke at all.

Jonas's mother smirked and leaned back in her chair. "I would ask you how you are this morning, but I can plainly see you are moments from begging the gods to open the gates of the Otherworld."

My heart stuttered. Gods, no—did she see the state of me last night? Moments were wrapped in murky nothingness. I recalled laughter, drums, the wretchedly sour taste of the biting drink.

Safe arms.

Mossy eyes.

A heartbeat lullaby.

Jonas.

By the hells, the prince had carried me out of the tavern, home to the palace, a shame on his house, his folk, on my people.

I wanted more than the Otherworld to swallow me up, I wanted my mists to devour me, locking me away in whatever void they originated.

"Here." Queen Malin plucked a steaming tin mug off a table and forced one of my leaden hands to encircle it. "Drink this. Within another toll, you'll feel like you can stand again."

I winced, forcing myself to slide up in bed and rest against the headboard.

Gods, how I must've looked. Hair was wild over my brow, stuck to my face. Doubtless whatever kohl had lined my eyes last night was smeared over my cheeks. Smoke and ale stained my skin, and now the damn queen was nursing her feckless daughter-in-law back to health.

I took a sip, the only way I could honor her in the moment, and coughed. Sharp herbs—parsley and wormroot, garlic and salt—coiled in a jolt of something like cinders in the back of my throat.

True to the queen's word, the sting of sunlight had already dulled.

I cupped the tin in my lap, staring at the murky liquid. "I beg your forgiveness, Highness. My behavior has shamed your house, and I would not blame you if you wish to return me to—"

"You're not going back to Natthaven." Malin crossed one leg, still grinning. "And you've shamed no one. Elven are rather inclined to propriety, aren't they?"

I blinked once, twice. "Yes. Etiquette and expectations were in every lesson."

"Well, we're rather terrible at it. Frankly, I haven't laughed as hard as I did last night in weeks, and gods, after the dreary that has been here these last days, we've needed it." The queen snickered and slumped in her chair. "Jonas came home, all red in the face, you in his arms, humming and trying to lick his damn neck."

I was going to retch. "I beg your pardon, My Lady. If I behaved out of sorts—"

"That's one way to describe it. Truly made our night." The queen looked around the room, even plucked a porcelain vase I'd brought from home off the table to inspect it. "Frigg informed us what led to the tavern."

I rubbed my brow. "I don't know why I had such a reaction."

"Oh, I have a few ideas." Malin returned the vase to the table and looked back at me. "You certainly left an impact. Sander and Kase had to chase off Balki again this morning. After his head cleared, he still felt rather entitled to the elven princess."

"All gods."

"Seemed to think you were unhappy with us here and wanted to take you for himself. I think Sander did well enough shifting his memory of it into something terrifying, but if you'd like I could take the memory altogether."

A memory thief. Part of me didn't think it was possible to have such an affinity. The potential to be cruel with such magic didn't fit the playful gleam in the queen's strange golden green eyes.

"No, thank you." I dipped my chin. "This was brought by my choices, so I must live with the consequences."

The whole of this conversation was puzzling. The only thing that seemed to be disappointing to Queen Malin was she wasn't present during the chaos.

"We received a missive from King Eldirard last night." The queen's grin faded. "He insisted your clan will investigate if the light elven prince had anything to do with the assassin. He also provided a few herbs that should aid Niklas in battling the spread of poison for Teo and Nettie."

Relief was sharp enough it robbed my breath. "Thank the gods."

"Well, thank them if you must, but I'm rather perturbed they let it happen to begin with," Malin said in a huff. "Teodor and Annetta didn't deserve what happened."

"They didn't," I said, voice small. "I hate that it was done to get to me."

The queen waved her hand, as though dismissing the notion. "It was a wretched distraction to plant the poison in our cooking rooms, but the only thing that angers me about that sod is I couldn't kill him myself. It is not on you." Malin rolled a silver ring with four runes etched into the surface around her center finger. "Eldirard was gracious with the herbs, but believes since this alliance is historical, there is likely to be naysayers."

"He did not offer more protections for the palace? I thought . . . well, I imagined he would offer a stronger show of support."

"The king spoke a great deal about our mesmer, and seemed to believe it was formidable against elven powers, then insisted you were protection enough."

I tangled my fingers in the quilts, a barb of hurt in my chest. To even offer Dokkalfar support would be an act of good faith in the alliance. My grandfather seemed to consider the act something expected, an act that could have killed Jonas, his family.

He did not react in the way I thought an ally should, and it would likely not give my new clan much confidence in our people. "I am sorry for the troubles all this has brought to your house."

"Well, that is the final apology I'll hear." Malin rose and brushed her hand over a dark pair of trousers. "It is not you who brings troubles, and I hope you have not taken offense to us keeping a distance from you. We wanted to give you time with all this." She waved her hands about. "I know it is jarring, but if you're ready, I hope you will start moving about the palace, meeting some more folk."

"I saw much of the town yesterday."

"That is a start. But here, I believe you hide away in these rooms. We don't bite." The queen offered a playful smirk. "Well, I cannot promise anything with Raum around."

A soft chuckle rolled from my chest.

"Many of us spar once a week," Malin told me. "You know, to let out some unused mesmer and aggression. We have plans to do so today after mid-meal. I hope you'll join us." She moved toward the doorway, but paused, pointing to the tin. "Drink it all. I promise it helps."

Perhaps I could still blame the brän in my brain, for the next question came before I could stop it. "Queen Malin, why are you being kind to me?"

"Do you not trust it?"

"I feel you are sincere." Suspicious as I was, the conversation with the queen felt . . . light when it ought to have been riddled in disappointment. "But that is what has me surprised."

"You are my son's wife. You are part of our house now, would you like me to be cruel?"

"No." I drummed my fingers alongside the tin mug. "But after all I have done—"

"What have you done?" Malin narrowed her eyes. "Yes, you fought against my sons and the sea fae whose queen I see as a daughter. But all that pales next to what else I know about you—a woman who protected her only family in a battle, a woman who saved mine from an attack we did not see."

Silence gathered like a storm, hot and sticky, the sort that left residue on the skin. Malin returned to the bed and sat on the edge.

"You think I should hate you for what happened with Sander. My son nearly died." Her voice was small, pain was there. "It is a truth no mother should ever face. We have lost many in our life, but I cannot lose my men—my trio, I call them." The queen smiled. "I was furious when I found out. I wanted war, and I hate war."

"What has changed?"

"Sander showed me that day." The queen tapped the side of her head.

"You stole his memory?"

"No. My mesmer can take or share. He shared it with me." The queen let out a trembling breath. "Gods, it was agonizing to watch him fall, but I am keen enough to see you were protecting Eldirard. I heard you apologize for the blade that struck Sander, and I know a look of desperation when I see one. You did not want to be there. Not like the light elves."

My jaw worked. "I did not want battle. It felt like an invasion."

"I know. Every kingdom in the fae realms knows. Perhaps if Sander had not survived, this conversation would be different, but battles have ended and I still have both my sons. Now, we have you."

She spoke like I was truly a piece of their house, not a political pawn.

Malin rose again and went to the door. "When the tonic has worked its magic—and it is mesmer filled—come down and spar with us. That memory gave up your little trick. Everyone has been mightily curious to see it again."

The corner of my mouth twitched. "Are you certain everyone would care to see me? I embarrassed your son last night."

Malin laughed. "Ah, Skadi, why do you think we have Elixist tonics so readily available? I assure you, Jonas has done his fair share of tavern table dancing."

CHAPTER 24
THE NIGHTMARE PRINCE

Old courtyards of the Black Palace had been made into soft lawns and sparring fields. Speckled across the field were folk from the inner palace, a few Kryv, and townsfolk who enjoyed working sore muscles through a match of mesmer or blades.

My uncle Bard grunted and let out a curse when I slammed his back to the grass, breaths heavy, blade at his throat. He tried to break free, but the shield strapped to my arm kept him locked in defeat.

Bard let his arms fall to the side in surrender. "Gods, I concede. Unless I'm allowed to snap a few fingers."

Strange how he'd vowed with Tova, a Mediski alver who healed. Bard was a Rifter like Ash. Should he desire it, he could snap my spine.

"Only if you want me to haunt Kåre with nightmares so you never sleep again."

"Brutal, Jo. You'd do such a thing to your young, innocent cousin?"

"No. I'm not that diabolical yet." One palm clasped with his, I tugged him to his feet.

We'd long since stripped our tunics. Smudges of dirt and streaks from the green grass painted our skin across shoulders, spines, and chests.

My mother stood next to Junius Tjuv from the Falkyns, the wife of

Niklas and a Profetik who could taste lies. Junie tied back her long, black braids and wiped a towel over the heat on her dark skin, laughing as Niklas and Raum were nearing a standstill.

Raum could see Nik's moves before the Elixist could even reach for one of his endless powders of fire or poison. Now, they were locked in a dance of equal skill with the blade.

Von sparred with Isak and Fiske. Even without mesmer Von knew his way around a blade and managed to knock one of Fiske's daggers from his grip. To the far side of the field, Daj's eyes were blackened like night, and Tova was retreating, cursing at him when dark skeins of shadows wrapped around her ankles.

Buckets of water for drinking or washing were lined across the grass. I splashed my face once, then tilted water into my mouth, soothing the burn in my throat.

When I traveled to other kingdoms to spend time with Aleksi, or Mira, or Livia, these were the days I missed from home. Everyone laughing. Everyone safe.

I wanted Skadi to be part of it, and I could not deduce why. More like I did not want to face why. All night her words would not leave me. *You will never truly want me.*

If only she knew she was a poison in my veins and I wanted to drown in it.

Skadi's words crawled under my skin like burrowing pests I could not shake. The pain in her eyes when she looked at me was a wound placed there long ago by the thoughts she spoke in her mind, with words spoken by others.

How often was she brought low and put in her place to keep silent?

I ought to have realized it at the first true conversation we had, when she told me her wants and desires did not matter any longer.

They mattered to me.

"Ah, hello, lovey." Raum's cheerful taunt drew me back to the moment.

He spun a dagger in his fingers and beamed at the gate to the field. I turned and choked on the gulp of water, spilling it down my chin. Skadi with Dorsan at her back filled the space. Tight silver braids fell from a knot on the top of her head, revealing the soft edges of her face, the string of piercings in her pointed ears.

Free of her elaborate gowns, her curves were defined by a black tunic, vambraces on her slender arms, and a thick belt with a bronze elven blade.

She was indescribable.

Her bright eyes found me. I watched her shoulders rise in a deep breath, then fall again upon her first step onto the field. Dorsan looked about with a hand on his blade like we might pounce.

Two paces away, I reeled through what I might say. Last night seemed to crack something inside me. She likely didn't recall, but there would be no going back to where I'd been with her. Not after her admission that she wanted me too.

I parted my lips to stammer out anything but was knocked in the shoulder.

Sander shoved past me. "You're here to spar? Finally. I summon a rematch."

Skadi's eyes were wide, hesitant, her hackles visibly raised.

"Sander." I tugged on his shoulder, drawing him back. "Stop pushing her to adore you."

He shirked me off and took out his own sword. "What do you say, sister?"

The slightest hint of a smirk teased her full lips. She withdrew her own blade. "Will your ego recover if you lose a second time?"

Jeers and laughter rose, some taunted Sander, others demanded Skadi humble the prince with less near-death this time. Her cheeks were flushed with a bit of mortification, no doubt, but she squared against Sander.

"What are the rules?" She took a step to one side; Sander took a step in the opposite direction. "Blades alone? Or affinities?"

My brother blackened his eyes. "Oh, I want you to show them what you can do. Make them ease up on me. I even wager, not one soul on this field could defeat you. Hear that, you sods?" Sander spun around, glaring at everyone. "You'll see how I was brought down."

"Remember though." I sat on the edge of the water table. "I was not, brother."

Sander jabbed his practice sword my way, glaring.

"Hardly a comparable moment." Skadi said over her shoulder. "I was exhausted."

I scoffed. "And you think I was energized?"

"Much more than me."

"Hmm. When you finish with my brother, perhaps we'll see about that, Fire."

Skadi returned a smug look, then rolled her blade in her hand. "Ready?"

"Truthfully?" Sander shook his head. "No."

He lunged.

Skadi blocked Sander's strike aimed at her leg and kicked at his thigh. He rolled over his shoulder and swung at her spine. The bronze of her dulled blade blocked. She parried. He cut at her ribs.

The more she fought the more her eyes brightened like a dying star. She dodged, struck, jabbed. The woman was a damn sight and I could not look away.

Kryv and townsfolk paused to watch, some even passing over copper penge coin, placing barters on who'd walk away victorious.

Sander's black steel collided with Skadi's bronze between their faces.

He darkened his eyes again and said with a snarl, "Show them."

Her arms shuddered under the pressure of his hold, a look of uncertainty on her features.

After a drawn pause, Skadi swiftly shifted one of her hands. With the slightest touch across the guard of Sander's sword, the blade was swallowed in a wave of dark mists. With the blade faded from his grip, Sander stumbled forward.

She promptly pulled her blade away. If she hadn't, with their position, their nearness, Sander would've landed on the point. Even with a dull sparring sword, it would ache and bruise. In a true battle, with the position, it would've run him through.

But . . . possibly not intentionally.

Mists still hovered at my brother's back. Skadi spun on her heel, racing around him, and reached into her darkness. From the cloud of her affinity, she pulled the black steel blade free.

Breaths heavy, Sander opened his arms. "See! How the hells do you win when she can pluck your damn blades from your hand?"

"Was that how it happened?" I hadn't meant to shout the question. But when gazes fell on me, I pressed again. "Was that what happened?"

"Not exactly." Sander wiped sweat off his brow with the back of his hand. "But close. I told you brother, I recalled an apology whispered in my ear."

"I've offered to show you, son," my mother called from across the field.

I refused to watch the memory. To watch Sander nearly bleed out once before was one time too many. I had no plans to relive the experience. My folk were never one to push, but my mother had tried to show me the memory many times once I announced I'd been granted permission from Eldirard.

Skadi gathered the two swords, avoiding my attention.

"Is that how it went?" My voice was edged in grit.

"It was my fault your brother was wounded. Don't mistake it for anything else."

"Was it intentional?"

Skadi rubbed a hand on the back of her neck. "I wanted to remove the threat—the blade—but . . . I didn't intend for him to fall into the knife. You all kept coming after that. I felt I had no choice but to use my affinity against you."

Her darkness had stolen my blade much the same as she'd done just now. Hells, she had even swallowed Aleksi whole, tossing him across the palace room. But she never tried to kill us. It was as she said, more like she wanted to disarm us.

Sander's wound was a damn accident?

Her hands were forced to fight. Skadi feared her own magic, she never wished to use it for cruelty, and she hadn't wanted to kill any of us even though we invaded her palace.

Heat from desire for more of her dug deeper.

I cleared my throat and took hold of her hand, curling her slender fingers around the hilt. "I believe I demanded a rematch as well, Wife."

Dorsan cleared his throat. "Forgive me, My Lord. It ought to be known, the princess should not engage her affinity much more in aggressive acts such as sparring and battle."

A little of Skadi's starlight gleam left her eyes. "He's probably right."

"Why?"

"You've seen why," she said, voice soft. "I cannot—should not—step into the dark too long when the intent is to overpower, cause pain, or defeat another. I grow cold and become . . ."

I lifted her chin with my thumb. "Become what?"

She hesitated. "Heartless. A bit of a monster."

Only when her power was questioned did the fire douse in her gaze. While using it, with Sander practically boasting about her ability, Skadi damn near beamed with pride.

I brushed my mouth against her ear. "Then be monstrous, Wife."

Skadi drew in a sharp breath.

"No one is intending to hurt anyone today," I went on, "other than your feelings, perhaps. I plan to best you, so prepare to weep in your defeat."

Soon enough, her lips parted in a grin. "I hope you've said your farewells, Husband."

"Farewells?"

"You won't be showing your face in front of anyone for at least a week once I am through with you."

CHAPTER 25
THE NIGHTMARE PRINCE

Skadi was wholly irritating.

On the fifth set, I landed twenty paces away, skin cold from the lingering mists as they faded into nothing, breath knocked from my chest.

Hands in the air, I closed my eyes. "No more. Gods, no more."

I hadn't even landed a decent strike and had sparred since I was old enough to hold a knife. I was not the only one. Von held a cold herb press to his brow after landing on his head.

Isak's mesmer was cruel and dreary. He could blind the mind into darkness. Skadi half-swallowed him in her affinity before he came close, his legs visible, head in the mist, until he kicked viciously enough she released him.

Tova abandoned the field, insisting she had to see to Kåre.

Junius laughed and declared she was not mad enough to face the woman.

Fiske was a Hypnotik, he could bleeding see flashes of future moments, and Skadi still leveled him after she'd feigned a need for reprieve, then kicked out his ankles and let her mist toss his sword beyond the gates of the field.

"All right, lovey." Raum spun a dagger in one hand, a short blade in the other. "Shall we?"

Skadi crouched, taking note of Niklas prowling on the opposite side of her, and Lynx and his thick body on the other. Three on one. For the first time, Skadi seemed uncertain.

I slunk to where the defeated were lined near the water, licking my wounds.

Sander propped his chin on his fist, studying the set up. "If Lynx can get behind her, he could calm her to sleep."

Another Hypnotik, the man could soothe the mind so fiercely, his victims fell asleep before he robbed or slaughtered them, depending on the scheme.

"It'll take Nik tossing some fire powders. Maybe venom clouds to choke her a bit." Von offered, no doubt, seeing the potential marks. "Distract her, you know?"

"She might mist them away before they even fall," Fiske grumbled, wiggling his fingers.

"Raum could see her moves and maybe stop her." Sander shook his head. "Ack, doesn't seem likely. May the gods bless their souls."

I grinned, sitting on the grass, and let my head fall back against the leg of the table. *Come on, Fire.*

Smugglers, thieves, warriors, the three men were not simple foes. Raum snapped his teeth once, then threw his dagger toward Skadi's heart. It wasn't to strike her, the way they closed in, it was clearly a distraction.

Skadi closed her darkness around the blade, and had to spin quickly to block Lynx's strike with his sword. He tried to swipe at her head, likely planning to use mesmer, but she spun away. Niklas was there to meet her.

Sly and vicious, Niklas had coated his palms in one of his elixirs. In most spars, he tossed things. With this, he had another trick—he wanted to touch Skadi. Incapacitate her, perhaps? Did he have something that could block her power like the herbs she'd worn during the negotiations?

Sander and Nik had read more than anyone on elven folk, it was possible.

"Forgive me, Princess," Niklas said as he attempted to close his hand around Skadi's wrist.

Her face burned with levity, free and bright. "No. Forgive me."

Niklas disappeared in the next breath.

Von sat straighter. "Where the hells did he go? Usually there's another cloud of her magic."

"She's holding him." Three hells, she was utterly mesmerizing. "Her affinity works like a door opening and closing if she desires. Whatever void is in her magic, Niklas is being held there."

"I mean, she'll let him go, right?"

I chuckled. "We'll see."

Skadi was laughing with joy, not villainy. It was the first time I'd seen her so alive. I glared at Dorsan who looked on at his princess with a bit of befuddlement.

Raum curled his lip. "Tricky, tricky, little princess. But can your darkness match darkness?"

The sparring field descended into shadows. I clambered to my knees, noting where my mother stood, five paces behind my wife. Her hand was outstretched toward walls of shadows surrounding Raum and Skadi.

Von clapped and laughed.

"Skadi!" I called out. "At your back."

"Traitor!" Sander shoved me away.

My fire spun around and let out a sharp shriek. From the wall of shadows, my father took my mother's hand, emerging from the darkness. More than Daj stepped through—Tova had returned, Bard, Hanna, who was Ash's younger sister, and Junie who kept her eyes to the sky, a little frantic to see her husband again.

Surrounded, exhausted, Skadi held up her palms, and let her blade fall.

In the same moment, her mists opened beyond Daj's shadow wall and Niklas fell to the lawn with a grunt.

It took a moment before he shot to his feet. "Bleeding *brilliant*! Gods, I have so many questions. So. Many. Damn questions."

I strode across the field to the fading ring of darkness.

Shadow walking as a boy was my favorite part of my father's mesmer. Fueled by a certain vow with my mother known as alver vows, my father's magic could reach out and find his wife, shape a wall of shadows, then bring him and anyone with a fear to wherever my mother was waiting.

Skadi never saw them coming.

She laced her fingers behind her head, breathless. "You . . . you have darkness too, Highness?"

My father leveled me in a glare. "Have you not explained about titles?"

"Apologies, Daj." I clasped my hands behind my waist. "My father adores being called Wondrous King or Glorious Majesty only."

Daj opened his palm and before I could move, one of his ribbons of darkness curled around my ankle, ripping my feet out from under me.

Fear of looking foolish. Well, he dug deep into my adolescence to find that one.

I coughed when I flattened on the grass, but was lucid enough to hear him grumble, "We should've had daughters."

More than one boot nudged my leg as my folk, those who'd raised me, loved me, trained me, merely laughed at my defeat. A shadow passed over my face. Skadi's braids fell across her shoulder when she held out a hand and heaved me back to my feet.

Chest to chest, I studied her. Dirt and sweat coated her skin, but my fire was there in her eyes, blazing. "You are beautifully terrifying. Do you feel the emptiness?"

"No." Skadi stared at her palms. "Strange. I learned the blade back home, but rarely was allowed to use my affinity." She hesitated. "The coldness is strongest when I steal anything through greed, pain, hate, battle. In those moments people fear me, and it is as though my affinity turns beastly from their apprehension and makes me care nothing about them."

"But you wanted to defeat us here," I said, voice low. There was something off about the consequence of coldness, it didn't settle right in my blood. "You laughed, you . . . looked happy."

"I don't understand it," she admitted.

"I have a theory." Sander shoved between us, his logic in full view. "There are consequences to all magics, right? What if yours is tangled with intention. The more brutal the act, the more your affinity pulls you in?"

Or what if folk had merely convinced her she was horrid?

Skadi considered the idea. "Could be. I didn't start feeling cold on Natthaven until Arion and his supporters ensnared the Ever Queen and wanted me to harm her."

"The light elf sees you as a weapon," Sander said. "He would use you for his own cruel ambitions, but you pay the consequence. Dark acts would change any heart."

"It's interesting to think about," Skadi admitted.

Sander tapped his chin. "I'll read up on it and let you know what I find."

"I already have a shipment of new writings from the Ever Kingdom on the way," Niklas said.

My mother sighed. "An honest shipment, Nik? Peace with sea fae is still rather new."

"Why does everyone assume every shipment is smuggled?"

"You're a wise man." Maj rolled her eyes. "You tell us."

Niklas waved her away and hooked an arm around Sander's neck, already lost in their theories.

"Would you like to know something baffling, Husband?" Skadi said, back toward me, watching them go.

"I love to be baffled."

"We are to go to Natthaven next week, and I . . . almost wish we weren't." Skadi paused for a breath. "I think I might miss your lands, your folk, and I hardly know them. I have never felt so accepted, I suppose."

"You're not a creature to them, Fire." I stepped close to Skadi. "They are not studying your affinity because they fear you."

"My people fear me. It is strange to be around those who don't, even if they should."

"Welcome to the Black Palace." My mother strode past, a devious glint in her eyes. "We all embraced our darkness long ago. It is home now."

Alone, Skadi seemed completely confused.

"What my mother meant is you will never be shunned because of magic you never had a choice in receiving." I tucked a lock of her hair behind her ear. "We know it is not the power that makes a monster, it is the heart. There is nothing wrong with your heart, Fire."

"Do you mean what you say?"

"Every word."

Skadi fiddled with a ring on her finger. "You do not know how much that matters to me."

I took one of her hands and squeezed. "The alliance was not because I feared *you*, Skadi. I feared the light elves and how they would use you."

"Arion and his court were always fascinated by my affinity once it was made known." She shook her head. "I tried to be good as a girl, obedient, docile. I knew what people believed me to be, I knew the fear of me. It is rather lonely."

I cupped one side of her face. "Now you have vowed into the most meddlesome house in the fae realms. You won't even know they are there, yet they will know everything about you."

"I don't think I will mind."

My smile faded. "About last night—"

"Please." She turned away. "I can't bring it up without wanting to fade away from embarrassment."

"You were upset because you saw a woman with me." I nudged her arm, turning her back into me. "Before all this, I did not refuse lovers often."

"You don't need to explain yourself."

"I want to." I took her hand and rubbed a thumb over her knuckles. "There were still some who believed I would be the same, but I made it clear I would not betray you."

Skadi shook her head. "I hardly know what to make of you some-times. You are a strange man, Jonas Eriksson."

"Better than being dull and uninteresting."

She arched into me, like she might be leaning in to kiss me, but changed her mind at the last moment. Skadi stepped back, chuckling nervously. "I, uh, I should wash. I'm filthy."

She was stunning to me.

"As you wish, Wife." I placed a hand on the small of her back. "That, I can do for you while I hide away, ashamed at being bested again."

"I warned you."

I smiled, a little softer. "Trust me, I will never forget what you have done to me today."

I patted Kjettil on the shoulder after he finished helping fill the deep wash basin with steaming water. The man had a toothy smile, one tapered fae ear, one with the alver curve, and no one truly knew what sort of magic lived in the man's blood.

He never gave it up, and we stopped asking.

"For the lady?" he asked.

"This is for the lady."

Kjettil lifted a wooden box from one of the washroom cupboards. "Petals and herbs and pink salts. No idea what they do but they smell rather nice. Hear the ladies enjoy them."

I took the box, all at once realizing this was a first for me.

Preparing this room.

In my chamber.

For a woman.

Part of me felt like a bastard for being so disconnected to others, another part was alarmed at the delight that Skadi was the only one.

Alas, a first meant I was vastly out of my comfort with such things as how many dried petals or fragrant salts ought to be added to water.

By the end the surface was floating in dark bloody red petals and the water looked a little milky.

A tentative knock rapped on the door. Skadi poked her head inside, hair loose, a lavender silk robe around her shoulders.

She was beautiful. A vision in the dark, and the way she kept glancing at the ground I doubted she heard it often.

"I can't take my eyes off you."

A cautious smile curved over her lips. "I hope it's not because there is something on my face."

"No. I find you beautiful, Fire." I rubbed the back of my neck, turning away. "Anyway, water's ready. Might be too hot, maybe filled with unknown foliage. Likely all of it, but should wash well enough."

Skadi sat on the stone edge, dragging her fingers through the petals. She demurely peered over her shoulder. "It's perfect."

I swallowed through a scratch, returned the wooden box to the cupboard, and stepped toward the door. "I will be out here if you need anything."

A bridge of pink brightened her cheeks. She nodded.

I faced the door before I embarrassed myself by giving up my half hard cock. Gods, it was as if I was unacquainted with a woman. No. I was unacquainted by this insatiable, near obsession with my reluctant wife.

"Jonas."

My name on her tongue was soft as a night breeze, almost reverent, maybe a little frightened. It burned through my veins like an inferno.

Hand still tight on the door latch, I kept my back to her. "Yes?"

"I do need to ask your forgiveness for last night."

"There is no need." I faced her. "If you think I have not overindulged on brän more than once, you're quite mistaken."

Skadi hugged her middle. "You carried me home."

Home.

Another step closer. "I am your husband. It will always be an honor to carry you should you stumble."

She tangled her fingers in the tie of her robe. "Why do you say such things when you did not want a wife?"

One final stride closed the space between us. I dragged my knuckles across her cheek. "I petitioned your grandfather for vows in a political alliance, true. But you must stop pretending nothing has changed."

"Has it changed? Are we not still pieces in an alliance?"

"A great deal has changed. My loyalty is not to an alliance." I brought my hands to her face. "It is to you. I *want* you."

I kissed her. My tongue slid across the seam of her lips until she parted them and let me taste her. One hand went to her waist, drawing her against my chest, the other held the back of her head.

Skadi arched her hips into mine, moaning and rubbing over my swollen length. Gods, I would not last long if she kept doing that. She stumbled backward, striking the edge of the washbasin, and sat on the wide ledge.

"Jonas," Skadi breathed against my lips. "I am still filthy."

"Sorry." Our brows touched. "I lost my head. I'll leave you to it."

Before I could leave, Skadi grabbed my arm. Her eyes were dark with a new sort of desire. Her breaths heavy. "I . . . might need . . . help getting in. I'd hate to slip, after all."

"Wouldn't want that." My voice was stupidly rough, as though I swallowed sand.

Skadi stood, her breasts pressed to my chest.

With painfully slow fingers she unlaced the tie of her robe. I let out a strangled gasp, holding her waist when she deftly shrugged her shoulders free.

Gods, bared to me, I could hardly form a thought.

Ink coiled in beautiful vines and pale blossoms wrapped around her ribs, beneath her breasts, ending in the center of her chest. I pressed a soft kiss to the petals over her heart. There was roughened skin there, but her scars would be explained when she wanted.

If she wanted.

She shifted her hips side to side until the robe pooled around her feet.

I drank her in, all soft curves and edges. I kissed her sweetly, dragging my teeth along her bottom lip when I pulled back. "You rob me of breath, Fire."

She smiled, holding out a hand.

Body ablaze, I helped her step over the ledge, watched her sink beneath the petals, then knelt beside the edge.

Skadi looked at me through heavy lashes. "Husband?"

"Wife?"

"I very much want you to kiss me again."

My mouth twisted into a half grin. "With pleasure."

Then I crushed her mouth with mine.

CHAPTER 26
THE MIST THIEF

THE CLACK OF TEETH AND FRENZY OF LIPS CAUSED A MOAN TO BREAK FROM MY throat. Jonas speared his fingers through my hair and tilted my head. My lips parted, and his tongue slid against mine in slow, masterful strokes. He tasted like cool spice, mint, and fire.

This was never meant to draw out heat in the blood, aches in the belly, a need in my heart I'd buried so long ago. Jonas was a fiend, and I did not stand a chance against him. Those eyes, bright and playful, but under all that was something like pain. As though my husband had his own secrets.

His hands were kind, gentle, demanding. His words were brazen and sweet.

A formidable foe, but the way he kissed me like he might never have another chance felt like standing on a battlefield, watching my destruction come nearer and nearer, until I released my weapons and joined the enemy.

He leaned over the edge of the basin, the sleeves of his tunic already soaked. I snickered against his mouth when he slipped, one arm falling beneath the water to steady himself.

"I'm trying to figure out why you are out there and I am in here."

The green of his eyes had gone dark, not only from his magic. With one hand, Jonas tugged his tunic over his head, tossing it in a heap to the side.

The Kryv motto was placed below his collar and other symbols were inked down his ribs. Too many to ask about now.

"You should never have been so beautiful." I swiped my tongue over my lips. "It makes you rather difficult to resist."

Jonas flashed his teeth. "Then you've discovered my greatest scheme—become irresistible to my wife."

Without removing his trousers, as though he could not wait any longer to have his mouth on me again, Jonas stepped into the bath.

The prince knelt between my thighs, his bare chest warm against my breasts. Skin to skin, tightened my nipples. He groaned, and I took it on my tongue for myself.

Jonas held one hand on the back of my head, tilting my face to one side, and pressing kisses along my throat, my shoulder. He bit the ridge of my collar, licked the fragrant water off my skin. A choked breath slid between my teeth when his lips sealed around one nipple.

I whimpered, cradling his head against my chest, bucking my hips until water sloshed onto the stone floor.

Jonas took the peak between his teeth, grinning as he swiped his tongue back and forth, his hand covered the other side. I tugged at his hair, his shoulders.

No mistake, marks would mar his skin in the morning. His legs settled between my thighs, and the pressure of him pooled heat in my core. I groaned unashamed and let my knees fall open, thudding against the edges of the basin.

Jonas kissed the swell of my breast once more, then pulled back, voice low. "You need more, Fire. Will you let me touch you?"

Words turned to nonsense on my lips. In the end I simply nodded.

A deep rumble of a growl rolled from his chest.

Jonas shifted on his knees and nudged his thigh against my center, moving it enough the friction drew out a breathy whimper from my throat.

A beautiful fog clouded my thoughts when he kept one palm over my breast, pinching and rolling the peak between his fingers.

I arched my back, wanting more. I wasn't certain I would ever get enough. Jonas lifted his eyes, dark and hungry, and I could not recall a time when anyone had looked at me with such need and desire. A look of fiction, the sort I read about in tales with fanciful romance and grand heroes.

Now, it belonged to me from a dark prince of nightmares.

Kisses speckled my chest and his other hand slipped beneath the water's surface, gliding over my stomach, my hips, until the tips of his fingers teased the ache in my core. Gentle and slow, agonizingly so, Jonas circled his fingers over my slit.

He never looked away.

Breaths heavy, lips parted, we shared gasp after gasp as he kneaded my skin, claimed my body with his hands.

The callus of his thumb added friction and pressure to my core. I rocked my hips into his hand, unable to stop, as sensation built in the lower half of my belly. He was vicious. The touch drew out the ache, but he never soothed it, leaving me on the precipice.

Jonas tilted his head, his tongue running along the slope of my neck. "More, Fire?"

"Gods . . ." A sharp breath stole my words when he dipped one finger inside my core, then retreated. I gritted my teeth, fingers digging into his arms. "Yes. More, Jonas."

He hummed. "That does it. You are the only one who may speak my name from now on. It is too intoxicating on your tongue to be said by anyone else."

The prince returned one finger into my entrance, then another, filling me, stretching me. The sensation was a spark of heat that jolted up my spine.

With a sharp draw of air, I snapped up, my brow pressed against Jonas's shoulder. He held the back of my head, and never stopped his destruction.

He pumped his fingers, curling them in the right moments, stretching them in the next. My head was lost in a fog of him—pine and leather—my body no longer was mine. I could not draw in a deep breath and let out rough gasps against his chest. Hands traveled, unable to stop moving over his chest, the edges of the basin, his shoulders, back, head.

Jonas's wicked fingers brought me to the ledge. One more step and I would fall into pieces. His thumb pressed against the apex of my thighs.

I shattered. Heat rolled up from my toes, through my chest, to my skull. One wave after the other left me locked in a bit of madness I didn't expect. Cries of his name—as he promised—tangled with the frenzy of water sloshing over stones and skin.

I writhed and gasped and tried to mute noises. Jonas took them as his own when his mouth covered mine, tongues and teeth, he held me through the fall.

When he pulled back, I finally breathed again. "So that's what it feels like?"

"With you? Yes."

I would never get enough of his touch.

The green of his eyes was clouded with passion and need. Every limb was heavy, as though my veins were filled with wet sand. Hazy from release, I traced the bottom edge of his lip.

His fingers still remained inside me. When I tried to shift back, Jonas curled a hand around my waist under the water. "Can you stand for a moment?"

I didn't think I would ever be able to move again, but nodded.

His hand remained between my legs; I bit down onto my inner cheek, still throbbing from my own release. The sensation of his fingers was almost too much. Jonas kept his hand in place until I wobbled on my weak legs, water dripping down my naked skin.

Only when we were out of the water did he remove his hand. Jonas helped leverage me back into the warmth of the bath.

Hovered over me, Jonas's mouth curved into a wicked smirk. My eyes widened in a delirious stun when he took those two fingers that touched so well and placed them in his mouth. He sucked the taste of me off the tips, then slammed his mouth to mine, kissing me deeper than before.

"Didn't want the water to wash away a single drop of you."

Gods, I was at risk with this man. Any more of him, and I might fall, heart outstretched like a supplicant, an offering for him to take.

I slumped back against the edge of the bath, still trembling from the shock of pleasure he drew out from my body. My fingers went to his soaked trousers, strained from his own desire. "Now you."

Jonas gripped my wrist, and lifted my palm to his lips, shaking his head. "Let me give you this, Skadi. Just you."

My brow arched. "Why?"

Jonas kissed the tip of my nose, dropping his forehead to mine. "You spoke once like you would always be a sort of transaction to me. You're not."

The tears were unnecessary, but the bastards came all the same.

My entire existence was a barter. Be it for what my title brought for a man regarding the claim on Natthaven, or what my affinity could offer those who claimed me as theirs. I was always a piece in another plan.

Grandfather loved me, but it did not diminish that there was purpose in his moves regarding my life.

Jonas kissed my forehead, whispering against my skin, "Tonight was simply me wanting to please my wife."

"What if I want to touch you?"

His eyes flashed. "I hope there will be many more opportunities."

He meant what he said. Jonas didn't leave me, nor did he try to claim his own pleasure, as though mine was enough for him. Wet trousers and all, he remained, washing my skin, following sometimes with kisses.

Jonas settled on the ledge of the basin behind me. My elbows were propped on his knees while he rubbed cleansing oils in my hair, sometimes pausing simply to trace the point of my ear, or press a kiss to the top of my head.

We talked. We *laughed*.

He told me about ruins in the forest they called Jagged Grove, how he played there as a boy.

I told him of Stärnskott, a show of bursting stars over Natthaven each week. How there was a secret spot where I would watch the event.

The prince admitted he grew queasy watching the butchering of a kill after a hunt, but he never told anyone, convinced they would start slaughtering deer and foxes at his feet.

I admitted there was a savory cake Cara and my grandfather thought I loved, but actually couldn't stomach.

"Why eat it?" He braided the ends of my damp hair.

"They spend time making something they think I love, and I don't have the heart to tell them otherwise."

Jonas chuckled and kissed the top of my head again. "You are all soft inside."

"Not a monster?"

Jonas stilled for a breath, then leaned forward, drawing his cheek alongside mine. "Be kind, be gentle, and be monstrous. I will want you every way."

Bleeding gods.

His presence was calming, a little too much for somewhere through our chatter, my eyes closed. The heat from the water, the stroke of his hands, lulled me off to nearly falling asleep. I startled when his knuckles touched my cheek.

"Skadi," Jonas whispered. "Your skin is going to wrinkle away, and the water is getting cold."

I jolted awake, mumbling slurred apologies. Somewhere in my haze, I took note that the prince was now in dry trousers. His top remained bare, and I was glad for it. His warmth cocooned me when I stepped out of the tub and leaned against his skin while he wrapped me up in the robe again.

Jonas lifted me, the way he'd done after the tavern.

I snickered. "I can walk."

"You're tired."

I was. Seemed days with laughter and pleasure were as lively as running without pause.

"The moon isn't full, but . . ." Jonas paused in his chamber. "Will you stay with me tonight?"

"I"—a yawn slipped out— "could muster energy for you."

"Good to know, but I plan to let you sleep. I simply don't want you anywhere else but beside me. Afraid I'm growing needy, Wife."

It was new and a little wonderful to be needed.

I settled under the heavy furs and quilts of his wide bed (he placed me on the side away from the door) and rolled onto my shoulder, facing him.

A single lantern flickered dimly, casting a warm glow over his face. I rested a palm against the stubble on his chin, and draped my leg over his hip.

Jonas let an arm fall over my waist, drawing me close. It wasn't long before the slow, steady hum of his heartbeat lulled me into safe, peaceful sleep.

CHAPTER 27
THE MIST THIEF

THE FIRST GLIMMERS OF A PALE DAWN BROKE THROUGH THE NARROW WINDOW IN Jonas's chamber, a reminder he'd given up his cherished view for a stranger.

Most mornings were cool in Klockglas. Air from the sea and drafty corridors in the palace ensured the chill dug into the skin until fires were lit and mists faded into daylight.

My body felt like it was already roasting beside an inglenook. Damp clung to my skin and everything had gone muggy beneath the quilts. I blinked sleep from my eyes and my heart fluttered.

Jonas's bed. I was in Jonas's bed. Dressed in my robe with nothing else beneath it.

My stomach swooped in delightful waves when I rolled over, but dropped at the sight of him.

Still sleeping, Jonas's skin was flushed, soaked in sweat, and his body kept twitching. Soft words spilled over his lips, desperate sounds, like he might be pleading with someone.

"Jonas." I touched his shoulder and nearly recoiled from the heat. He was burning with fever. How? He'd gone to sleep with smiles and good health.

I pressed the back of my hand to his brow, dabbing at the damp. He winced and shuddered.

"Jonas." When I touched his cheek, his stronger grip snatched my wrist, dragging me over the top of him when he rolled onto his back.

I let out a shriek when his eyes snapped open. Black as the deepest sea, empty and ominous with his mesmer. I didn't have a frightening thought, so where was the nightmare?

"Don't." The word was rough, broken. "Don't touch her."

"Jonas." I clasped his face. "Can you hear me? It's Skadi."

His features pinched, but the darkness of his eyes looked straight through me. "Let her go."

Gods. He wasn't truly awake.

Panic tangled in my throat when all at once his hands fell away, and he went still. Those haunting black eyes remained pinned on the ceiling. His chest hardly rose in a breath.

"Jonas!" I shook him. Nothing. "Gods, wake up." One palm patted his burning cheek. My voice cracked. "Please, wake up. Dammit."

He was deathly still, but his skin burned. Healers. He needed a healer. One of the Mediskis.

I tumbled from the bed, tripping on the edge of the quilt, but hastened to my feet and sprinted from his chamber.

"Dorsan!" I pounded on my guard's door, frantically closing my robe. "Dorsan, wake up!"

Dorsan opened the door in a frenzy, hair askew, and topless. The most disheveled I'd ever seen the man.

"There's something terribly wrong with the prince. He's . . . he's ill, or . . . I don't know. Go fetch a Mediski alver, a Mediski."

Dorsan might've held a bit of resentment for being the guard charged with stepping into a new kingdom, but he was loyal to the marrow. No hesitation, not even a moment's pause to dress, he nodded and hurried down the corridor.

Before he rounded the corner, another man nearly crashed into him.

"Sander."

The second prince was breathless, his own eyes darkened, and his steps were swift. "Where's Jonas?"

"He's in there, something . . . something's wrong."

207

Sander explained nothing and shoved into his brother's room. As though he knew what to expect, the second prince clambered onto the bed and started shredding quilts off his brother's overheated body. "Come on, Jo, snap the hells out of it."

"What's happening?"

Sander didn't stop working, keeping a thin linen over Jonas, and rushed to a small bowl with cool water for washing the face and hands. He dipped a small cloth inside.

"Can you get me more of these?" He looked to me. "It helps to cool him."

Hands trembling, I followed Sander's orders, soaking linen cloths and helping arrange them on Jonas's head, neck, and arms.

"Sander." My voice quivered. "What's happening to him?"

His brother sat back on his knees, lifting his ominous dark gaze to me. "Jonas is sometimes attacked by his own mesmer."

"What!"

"He gets trapped in a deep fear that becomes a nightmare, then burns as a fever."

Unknowingly, I curled a hand around my husband's limp palm. "Is it . . . dangerous?"

"Yes. If we do not cool him, it's possible he won't be free of the attack."

My stomach bottomed out. "How did you know?"

"I sensed it. Our mesmer connects when we want it to, but I like to think this connection comes simply because we're brothers."

"What do you need me to do?"

"Did anything happen last night out of the ordinary? Did he seem different?"

Good hells.

"Um . . ." There was no time to be demure, not if Jonas would suffer. "We bathed together and I stayed here."

Sander nodded. "Makes a bit of sense then."

"Did I cause this? I wouldn't hurt him."

To see a genuine, kind grin on the prince's face when his eyes were so eerie was unsettling. "You did nothing wrong, Skadi. The nightmare is of you, so it makes sense. He only succumbs to this when he is truly terrified someone he cares about is being harmed."

I could not summon the words. Jonas had pleaded to someone. Whatever was happening in his head involved me.

My hold tightened on his hand. "You know what to do though?"

"We do. It was terrifying the first time. Jonas's emotions fuel his mesmer at times to the point his body cannot release it, so it attacks him. He doesn't like people knowing, not even the other royals know this happens."

My teeth clenched. I brushed my fingertips over his brow, helpless. He was bleeding trapped in a wretched nightmare and could not escape.

"How do we help him?"

"With this."

I reeled around as the queen, wrapped in a sleeping robe much like mine, raced across the room, worry in her eyes, the king at her back. In Malin's hands was a vial of a murky liquid.

The queen came to where I stood at the side of the bed and knelt over the mattress. She handed the king the vial without a word, like they simply knew their parts to play.

Kase pressed a hand against Jonas's cheek and tipped the vial to his son's lips. The king was quiet, somber, but I did not need his magic to see the fear in his eyes or the soft way he whispered, "Break free of it, boy."

Malin rested a hand to Jonas's brow. She closed her eyes. After a horrid pause, the queen began to smile here and there, even chuckle.

"Maj is drawing happy memories forward," Sander said, not looking away from Jonas, but it was clear the explanation was for me. "Helps combat the terror until the elixir brings a dreamless sleep."

I pressed my back against the wall, steering clear while they brought him back to me. Dorsan, still tunic-less, stood in the doorway, stern and stiff. I waved my hand, mutely dismissing him.

He didn't move.

"There we go," Malin whispered and moved aside.

I let out a rough breath. Jonas's eyes were now closed and his chest was rising in slow, steady breaths again. Nothing more than a peaceful sleep.

"I'll send for some herbs to work the fever." Malin squeezed Kase's arm. The king had not stopped watching his son's features once.

Upon his wife's touch, he seemed to realize the fear had passed, and backed off the mattress. "Will you look after him while we gather the herbs?"

"Skadi?" Sander's eyes were once more the brighter shade of green, lighter than Jonas's but still as piercing.

"Sorry, what?"

"Will you watch him?" the king asked again, his voice a rough rasp.

"Yes." I stepped to the edge of the bed, nodding frantically. "I won't leave him."

Malin rested a hand on my shoulder. "The fever usually burns out within a day. He should be more like himself by tonight."

"He wasn't long into it," Sander said. "Good thing Skadi was here."

A bit of the heat of Jonas's fever burned in my face. Sander was laughing, taunting me in front of their parents, but it was much like they did with everyone.

It was a bit of belonging.

I shot him a narrow look, then sat on the edge of the bed, listening to the soft laughter as they quit the room to gather the needed herbs.

"Is he well, My Lady?" Dorsan asked.

I dragged my fingertips down Jonas's cheek, his features softened and peaceful. Without looking at the guard, I nodded. "He will be. Thank you for helping, Dorsan."

"I merely summoned the king and queen."

"And it was helpful. Go back to sleep if you wish. I won't be going anywhere."

The whole of the day folk came and went through Jonas's room. Niklas made certain I had more elixirs on hand if the mesmer attacked again.

Tova brought her son who had drawn a few scratchy pictures he wanted his older cousin to hang on his walls.

Most who visited thought Jonas was merely prone to fevers. Sander spoke true, my husband did not share the true cause beyond those friends and family closest to him.

When Frigg and Von joined Sander, the three didn't leave. They ate mid-meal with me, told childhood stories of Jonas and his rather zealous opinion of his whittling abilities.

"All those oblong wooden creatures you've seen about the palace are his creations since childhood." Frigg popped a square of pale cheese on her tongue, grinning. "They're all just out of proportion and crooked, but Mal loved them and it went straight to his head."

We played a few rounds of an alver game with paper cards and wooden dice, but the trio still remained.

I plucked one of the books I still had and read some elven folklore out loud.

Von slumped back in a chair, hands laced over his belly, eyes closed. Sander was enraptured by each fable, and Frigg sent for more food until the woman from the cooking rooms told her she could use her damn feet and get it herself.

I snickered at that. The notion of servants (or staff) being ordered about so much they snapped at my grandfather would shock the whole of Natthaven.

The three left before the nightly meal, insisting they'd check back in the morning. Sander told me if I needed to sleep without interruption, if Jonas didn't wake, he would come sleep in his chamber.

Uneaten herring and bitter herbs remained on a plate by the time the sun dimmed to evening.

"A kingdom of caves and tunnels," I read out loud in the bed. One palm rested on Jonas's brow, playing with his hair. "A world unsuitable for such a maid. But when her father vowed war against the troll king, his daughter, lovely and gentle, took up her lover's blade and leveled it at her own neck. Between two great armies, between enemies and worlds, she stood steady as a great oak. She vowed her heart to the soul of her troll mate or vowed death should her people come against them."

I smiled, studying the painting on the thick pages. A woman surrounded in light holding a narrow blade to her neck, eyes pointed to the skies as though imploring the gods for help.

My blood rushed to my head when my palm was taken from his hair and pressed to full, dry lips.

"What happened next?" Jonas's voice was rough, weary.

"All gods." The myth of the troll king and his bride fell off my lap. I choked his neck with my arms. "You're awake."

Jonas coughed, running a hand down my spine. "Not for long if I cannot breathe."

"Sorry." I pulled back, palms on his cheeks. "I should . . . let me get your mother and father, they—"

"Skadi." Jonas tugged on my hand. "Stay. For now, just . . . stay."

I slipped beside him, rolling over to face him. "How do you feel?"

"Like I have been tossed into the sea again and again from a very high cliff." Jonas's eyes were burdened and shadowed.

My chin trembled. "It was terrifying, Jonas. I didn't know what was happening."

His face sobered. "I'm sorry. I should've told you about the fevers. Sander told me I should, but I thought with more peace, fears might lessen and they wouldn't be severe."

"What causes them?"

"I do." He rubbed one thumb over his forehead, as though soothing an ache.

"What do you mean?"

Jonas took a moment to speak. "Ever since I was a boy, my mesmer would craft nightmares of horrible ways I would lose people I love. During childhood wars, the nightmares started to overtake me. I do not know how to manage the fear of loss, Skadi, so I keep it buried until it cracks through."

"Sander said it has something to do with your emotions. He spoke as though there wasn't much known about the fevers? Has this happened to anyone else?"

"Not that we know of, but Anomali alvers always have unknown mesmer." Jonas stopped rubbing. "On the first, it was my father who sensed the attack of fear. The fevers stem from the truest fears of my heart which stems from the idea of losing the people I love. I wish I could . . . feel less, I suppose."

By the gods, the man could swell my heart and shatter it all at once. His fear came because he loved folk too damn much.

"How old were you when they began?"

"Almost ten. It was during a battle with sea fae before we were allies. I dreamt I lost my parents. I've had smaller bouts of the fever here and there. Any woman I care about who gives birth, nightmares of the worst happening will follow. Once Frigg caught a blood illness that Mediskis couldn't heal. Nearly lost her to the Otherworld and I fevered even after Niklas and other Elixists found the right tonic to cure her."

"Sander said there have been fierce fevers like . . . last night."

Jonas nodded. "One was months ago when Livia was taken by Bloodsinger."

I sat up. "Taken? What do you mean?"

"Don't you know how they began? He bleeding kidnapped her when the sea fae returned."

"You speak of the same Ever Queen whose eyes light at the very sight of her king?"

"Love comes in the strangest of circumstances, doesn't it?" Jonas laughed, but it was laden in exhaustion. "I thought she was dead, then Aleksi disappeared while searching for her. I've told you, they are like another brother and sister to me. That fever was fierce, but shorter than most. It was as if my mind knew I needed to get my ass back to searching for their sakes."

I settled beside him again. "Were there others?"

"A little over a month ago. It was the fear of losing Sander."

I winced. "Caused by my hand."

"No." He pressed a palm to my cheek. "It is caused by me. I do not face these fears. I bury them so far away, they fester and overtake me."

"You can tell them to me if you want. I won't tell another soul."

He scoffed. "Will you not think me a weak, trembling babe, terrified of what *could* be, not what is?"

I leaned closer, dragging my nose alongside his cheek. "Not if you don't think me weak for my fears. I told you I did not want to know you, Jonas Eriksson. But it was a lie because I am afraid."

"Of what?"

I swallowed, clearing tension in my throat. "If I know you, I've no doubt my heart will be utterly yours to break."

A muscle pulsed in his jaw. Jonas leaned forward and kissed me sweetly, letting his forehead rest against mine. "If given such a gift, what a fool I would be to handle it so carelessly as to let it break."

What he did not realize is he already held it, and it was terrifying.

The last time shattered me, broken pieces were still visible, but Jonas had pummeled through the walls with more than words. Unlike moments in the past, his actions were imprinted in my mind.

"You are soft inside," I whispered.

"Not a nightmare?"

I smiled, drawing my mouth closer to his, using the words he'd spoken against me yesterday. "Be gentle, be kind, and be nightmarish. I will want you every way."

Jonas kissed me, slow and deep. His lips were dry from the fever, but demanding and gentle all at once. I dug my fingers through his hair, tugging at the roots. This was a kiss with time to spare, no need to rush, no need for frenzy.

It was the sort of kiss where two hearts knew there would be another, and another, and another.

My fingertips traced the edge of his jaw. "What do you fear now that torments you so?"

He pulled back, drawing my cheek to his heart. "You. It took me so fiercely; it was so real."

I drew small circles over his chest. "What was it about?"

"Arion came for you. He hurt you, kept you in chains, and you . . . you were calling for me. I couldn't reach you, so they kept hurting you until you didn't move anymore."

For a long moment, I didn't know what to say. I rolled over his hard body, and propped my chin on the tops of my hands over his chest.

"I am not laughing at you and you're not weak." I lifted his palm and placed it over the thrum of my heart. "This is what is real. Arion cannot touch me unless the alliance is broken. I have no plans to break it, do you?"

Jonas ran his other hand along my spine. "No, Fire."

"The nightmare was terribly unrealistic, would you like to know why?"

"Why is that?"

"Because if I were to be taken from you, after being here even this short while, I would be as monstrous as I ever was until I found you again."

I kissed him before he could speak. I kissed him for the surprising truth of each word. I kissed him for the knowledge that this arranged vow of ours had become a refuge from our nightmares.

CHAPTER 28
THE MIST THIEF

THERE WAS A SHIFT AFTER THE MESMER FEVER. AS THOUGH A NEW SORT OF trust had formed between me and my nightmare prince.

I joined the alvers at meals, interacting with the guilds, learning more of their customs and histories. Jonas spent most mornings with Von and Sander working in upper corridors. A rope was kept over the stairwells as a clear sign only the trio was welcome.

Someday, perhaps, he'd tell me what went on up there, instead of kissing me until I forgot to care.

His kiss became a part of my dreams. His touch a craving. More than trust, the fevers and our intimate bath, pulled back pieces of my new husband I didn't want to see before. The man knew how to threaten and frighten, he knew how to kill well enough, but I was beginning to see the heart his fellow royals and friends kept insisting was inside.

Jonas was gentle with the staff, well-loved by the household of the palace.

He treated his mother with the highest esteem, always seeing to it she was seated before him and speaking with her with levity but respect.

The prince did the same for brisk Ylva, for women and men in the township or dockyards. He cared for his people, even those he did not know well.

But by the hells, the man knew how to irritate.

I thought he took a bit of pleasure in trying to flush my face in annoyance. Last night, I'd nearly tossed him into my affinity when he tried to spoil the ending of yet another book.

Sander saved the tale, and practically tackled his brother for the sheer audacity of it, then stood watch by my door until I sent the signal I'd finished the story.

Jonas rejoined me on my side of the bedchamber, begging for my forgiveness. His consuming mouth, the taste of his tongue against mine, the touch of his wicked hands teasing my body, earned him the invitation to stay at my side.

He held me close, stroking my hair, merely listening while I repeated how the tale impacted me even though he already knew the ending.

I studied my features in the mirror of the vanity. My fingertips touched my lips, still swollen from when he'd kissed me after the morning meal before setting off to his mysterious room in the upper levels.

In the past, my heart led me astray. Most of my people thought me to be cold and unfeeling. There was a bit of truth to it, for I'd learned soon enough it was better to freeze the heart than feel the agony of it breaking.

Unbidden, my nightmare prince was claiming the heart I vowed never to give, and I thought he might be giving his.

Dorsan entered my chamber, a piece of parchment in his hand. "Forgive the interruption, My Lady. You've received a missive from Natthaven."

My stomach dipped. Since the Ljosalfar rogue tried to slaughter Jonas and his household, correspondence was typically kept between king and king. Or so I was told. My grandfather had not offered any word to me on Gerard or Arion.

I made quick work of schooling my curiosity and held out my hand. "Thank you, Dorsan." A quick scan of the missive gave up the author. "Oh, it's from Cara."

Stern as my lady had been, Cara was a constant in my life, and there were days I missed her haughty words and huffs when folk did not live up to her opinions of propriety.

Lady Skadinia—

I write to you with some trepidation. This inquiry borders on inde-cent, and I beg your forgiveness, but I do hope you'll soothe this woman's mind.

His Highness, King Gerard, and the Crown Prince Arion, were present in the palace these last days. I was troubled to learn of the attack from the rogue Ljosalfar, but am relieved to hear of your safety.

It is this topic which brings this letter. Although, the Ljosalfar appeared regretful for the attack, their belief is that your safety would be better suited with your own folk. Your new vow was enough of a concern, the disgraced prince approached me to hear of your wellbeing. He was quite remorseful for his part in pushing you toward this alliance. He insisted he intended to prove his contrite heart in the hopes you might choose him again before the turn is finished, per the alliance condition.

I am not prone to palace gossip, but I had to ask. It was confirmed this alliance can be returned to the Ljosalfar should you be dissatisfied with your new husband within the first turn.

Due to this, I would urge you to respond and tell me if you find a degree of peace in alver lands. I am hopeful you do, for my heart remains soured toward the Crown Prince at this time. Do not think little of me for speaking so plainly.

I will watch for your reply, and do hope the feral prince is doing what he should to keep you content. I have no doubt he would not want to lose the prestige of this alliance either.

Your lady,

Cara

Return to a betrothal with Arion? I knew if I had not agreed to the alliance with Jonas, my only choice would be to secure the legacy of the unification of the two elven clans with Arion.

But I was vowed now; my choice was made.

"Dorsan, may I ask you something?"

"Of course, My Lady."

I hesitated. "Do you know anything about a condition of the alliance that states I might return to an agreement with the Ljosalfar prince?"

Dorsan clasped his hands behind his back. "I believe it is a standard condition to allow you a voice in your household. Should you be discontented with your new vow within the first turn, as I understand, you may choose to realign the two clans of elven. Either legacy is satisfactory for the king."

Breath tightened in my throat. "So, if Jonas is not pleasing, it will be left to me to rescind the vow?"

"I believe so."

Skin heated under my collar. "No doubt, the alver prince would want to do all he could to keep me content."

Dorsan's mouth tightened. "I imagine the prince would."

"Thank you, Dorsan." I flashed him a bright smile to hide the shock of pain in my heart. "I think I'll go to the gardens. If you don't mind, I would like to spend the afternoon alone."

The guard frowned, but after a long pause, dipped his chin and abandoned the room.

I clutched my fist around the missive and for the first time since I took vows felt the first frost of my affinity numb a bit of my heart.

I desired to be anywhere but here.

Gods, was I still so bleeding desperate for my heart to be cherished that I'd been duped by another man?

Tears burned behind my eyes. I would not live a ruse, but I would not return to Arion.

Jonas, even if his motivations were to keep me blissfully content, was kinder than the Ljosalfar prince. My observations of him and his people were fair, light, and laden in mutual respect.

Maybe we would not develop a love match—not like I'd hoped—but I would strive to keep similar respect between us. Only after I soothed my cracking heart and gathered my thoughts on how to speak to him about what I knew.

Reckless. Stupid.

My bruised heart had fit the prince inside so well; he filled the spaces that were left in pain from old words and actions. I'd let him in, let him touch me, hold me. We burned through a fever together, laughed, and teased.

But he'd done it to keep his new wife appeased and an alliance strong.

Perhaps, I could settle for friendship. I could not so easily dismiss how much I'd come to care for the prince, and if it was not as lovers, I could not deny the desire to still find a place in his life.

Still, the tears came. I hurriedly entered the stables on the other end of the gardens and started to prepare a bridle on the head of a palace mare.

"Skadi?" From one of the stalls a face too similar to my nightmare prince peered out.

"Prince." I dipped my chin when Sander approached, a thin ledger tucked under his arm.

"What's the matter?" Sander leaned a shoulder against one of the stall posts, studying me.

I forced a grin. "Nothing."

"Not sure you realize, but you're part of a household of schemers trained to spot tells and lies written on the face."

I blinked rapidly, desperate to bury the emotion, and pulled myself onto the back of the horse.

Sander gripped the bridle. "Did Jonas do something to distress you? He does mean well, I promise, but sometimes speaks before he thinks."

"No. Of course not." I prayed he could not hear the tremble in my voice. "I simply received some unsavory news from home. Nothing so wretched to fret over, merely upsetting. I wanted to be alone for a moment."

The prince glanced toward the open door to the stables. "I don't know if that's wise, not after the elven—"

"Have you forgotten that I can devour men, Prince? If another Ljos-alfar attacked me, he would fall into the Nothing for eternity."

Sander eyed me with what seemed sincere concern. "Skadi, Jonas is my brother, but you're my sister now. If something is troubling you, I'm known to be a decent listener."

"Thank you, but I'll return shortly." I sat straighter. "I simply must gather my thoughts before I speak to him now that I know the truth."

"Truth about what?"

Dammit. My mind was reeling too swiftly that my words were too free. "I am told Arion still vies for my affection and your brother will try to keep it. I never wanted to be a prize, Sander. I simply wanted a home."

"I don't know what you're talking about, but you do have a home here." My brother-in-law released the bridle. "If you think Jonas does not care for you, forgive me, but you're wrong. His mesmer attacked him over thoughts of you. That affection cannot be fabricated."

My pulse thudded in my ears. All at once, the conversation and stable were too suffocating. "Are you going to prevent me from riding? It was a calming activity for me on Natthaven."

Sander's jaw went taut, but he stepped aside. "No. This family will never hold you prisoner."

His words held meaning, a bit of a veiled promise that might lend way to hope. I gave him a nod of thanks and nudged the mare toward the back wood beyond the palace gates.

When trees blotted out the sun, a new tear fell. I swiped it away in a rush. What the hells was wrong with me? The prince had never offered his heart and instead promised the opposite. There was no reason to take offense to his kindness, despite the motivations.

Was there anything wrong about taking pleasure from each other? Our hearts would remain our own, but we were husband and wife.

Perhaps, we could come to an agreement of friendly interactions, with a bit more if desired.

An ache burned in my chest. Truth be told, I wasn't certain I could remain close to Jonas Eriksson and keep my heart safe.

Better to return to duty and distance.

The decision was wrong, and felt horrid in my mind.

Sander had more reason to despise me and bring me misery than anyone, but he offered up a truth about my husband's nightmares.

Jonas only fevered with fears of losing those he cherished.

Dammit. I did not know what to think.

Near a dark pond, I slid off the horse and allowed her time to drink. After a few gentle strokes to her neck, I left the mare and wandered along the water's edge. Trees were tall and made of dark trunks and limbs. The wood did not smell of blossoms and sweet honey like on Natthaven. Here, it was like clean mist.

I'd felt accepted here, valued. Now my mind battled to convince me it was all a ruse to meet the condition of the alliance.

The horse whinnied across the pond, plodding her hooves with impatience. No wonder. Through the gaps in the branches, a tumult of darkened clouds rolled across the sky. I let out a sigh. If I wished to beat the storm, I would need to confront the prince sooner than later.

I kept walking around the pond, already halfway back, but on my next step, the ground gave out and I fell into nothing but empty black.

CHAPTER 29
THE NIGHTMARE PRINCE

"HAVE YOU SEEN THE PRINCESS?" I TOOK HOLD OF A GARDENER'S ARM.

The man wiped damp off his long hair from the rain. "No, can't say I have."

Skadi was not in her side of the chamber, not in the great hall, nor the gardens. Dorsan was nowhere to be found, and there was a heat in my blood that something was not right. I strode toward the front of the palace.

Heavy sheets of rain pounded against the glass panes of every window and dark skies let out the anger of the gods with booming thunder.

I took a few steps up a spiral staircase until I could peer out one of the lancet windows. Only some of the staff raced across the front drive of the grounds, seeking refuge from the storm.

Where the hells was my wife?

A side door crashed open. Sander was soaked from his pale tunic to his hair, slicked to his brow from the storm.

And he wasn't alone. Dorsan wiped his eyes free of water.

"Jonas." Sander lengthened his strides. "Did Skadi return?"

"Return from where? I've been looking for her."

"Dammit." Sander dragged his hand over his soaked hair. "She left at least three clock tolls ago a little upset."

Dorsan stepped forward. "I might know why. She inquired on the condition of the alliance where she was given the choice to return to her former betrothal. She mentioned something about it being prudent for you, Prince Jonas, to keep her comfortable in that time, and she left shortly after."

"I met her in the stables during my inventory," Sander explained. "Now it makes a bit more sense. I think she's under the belief you might be showing her affection merely to keep her from Arion. She said something about not wanting to be a prize."

Bleeding hells. "And you let her leave during a storm?"

Sander's fist shoved against my chest, eyes narrowed. "I'm not an imbecile. It wasn't raining at the time, but I wasn't going to chain her to a post when she insisted she wanted a bit of time to think on her own."

Shit. Shit. Shit.

"All right, we need to find her. The storm might have her trapped out there." I looked to the elven guard. "Dorsan how well do you ride?"

"Impeccably, sire."

"Then prepare horses. I'll get others to start the search."

Sander followed Dorsan back into the storm. I rushed deeper into the palace. A panic took hold deep in my chest, making breath difficult to draw. Not unexpected, not after the ferocity of the mesmer fever. Images of Skadi trapped, sobbing, hurt, flashed through my mind until my movements were made on instinct.

I never wanted this, but it couldn't be denied—I'd fallen for my wife, and I could not lose her.

"Anything?" My voice roared over the rage of the storm, aimed at a copse of evergreens.

"Not yet," Raum shouted back. He urged his horse forward, deeper into the wood of Jagged Grove.

Skadi, where the hells are you? I kicked my heels against my own gelding and tugged the woolen hood over my eyes to keep the rain off.

It was rather pointless.

Gusts of wind and rain lashed against our faces, slowing our pace, and dimming our vision. A dozen riders joined me into the trees, my father and his guild included. Raum's uncanny sight gave us a chance at spotting her, but my father's mesmer to sense individual fear would hopefully catch hold soon.

"Skadi!" Von shouted against the wind.

More joined. Back and forth we called for her, but only angry skies responded.

Black spilled into my gaze, my skin felt too flushed for the chill of the air. Not here. Gods, when fear grew too swiftly, my mesmer turned inward, feasting on my own despair until fevers took hold again.

"Jonas." My father rode to my side. "You need to fight it."

"I'm trying," I gritted out through my teeth.

He used his chin to point toward the wetlands. "This way."

"You feel something?"

"It's faint."

I didn't bleeding care and forced my horse deeper into the wood.

"Ahead!" Raum shouted.

Ten breaths, fifteen, and a frightened snort came from shadows. One of the palace mares paced between trees, terrified of the wind and rain, and without a rider.

Ash was the first to reach the creature, clicking his tongue, and taking hold of the bridle until the mare settled.

"Jonas." Sander brought his horse beside mine. "This area is filled with burrows. Troll folk enjoy the ponds."

True enough. Mira's kingdom had a great many faeish creatures and troll folk were some. They traveled between the kingdoms in underground burrows that were deep and damn near impossible to escape alone.

Most did not find our lands appealing with the chill and the mists, but King Ari would send missives through the burrows with the troll folk when he wanted to irritate my father by tilling up our land.

I kicked my horse, urging him forward, until the pond came into view. Mud and tall reeds shrouded the sides, but there were mounds from old burrows all around the banks. If someone—a foreign elven princess, perhaps—did not know what to look for, the burrows would be easy enough to fall into.

I slid off the back of my horse and sprinted for one of the mounds, looking for an opening. "Skadi!"

Please be here.

The storm wasn't letting up, and the thought of her being lost in the grove through the night brought bile to my throat.

"There is more fear than ours here."

I hadn't realized my father was on foot. He looked side to side, no doubt trying to find the source of his mesmer. *Our fear.* It was Kase Eriksson's subtle way of admitting the household of the Black Palace cared for Skadi.

When my father gestured to one of the mounds on the other side of the pond, I didn't wait before running across the slick, mossy soil. A sunken bit of earth revealed an opening. Water cascaded along the edges, clods of thick mud falling inside.

Careful not to sink into the tunnel, I moved gently to the edge and peered in. "Skadi?"

Nothing.

Damn the hells. "Skadi, are you there? Answer me."

"She's there." Raum hovered over my shoulder, his silver eyes bright with his mesmer. "Caught sight of her dress in the dark. She's around a bend. Not sure she can hear you with all this." The Kryv waved his palms about, gesturing at the storm.

I cursed and started to leverage my legs over the sides.

"Jonas," My father snapped. "These tunnels are prone to cave-ins."

"Then be ready to pull us out," I shot back. "I'm not leaving her down there, and nor would you if this was Maj."

He could not argue the truth of it. With a rough wave of his hand, the king called for ropes and spades we carried in saddle packs, he called for everyone to be ready to dig us out if the Norns chose to bury us inside.

226

I slipped into the tunnel. Raum guided me with my hand and foot placements until swampy earth touched my boots.

Heavy falls of soil and rain already coated my face and shoulders. Another breath and a wrapped torch fell into the hole. I caught hold of the handle, then a thick leather satchel with the flint inside.

Elixirs always coated our torches, keeping them flammable even in storms. It wasn't long before a spark caught hold and ignited the wide tunnel in a golden beam.

Long, claw marks marred the thick walls from the trolls. Based on the roots and narrowing corners, this burrow hadn't been claimed in a turn or two.

"Skadi!"

A sharp draw of breath drew me to a rounded alcove in the tunnel.

"Gods." I rammed the handle of the torch into soft soil and knelt in the alcove.

Skadi was there, soaked through her gown. Her silver hair was crusted over her brow and the blue of her eyes was dim. She hugged her knees to her chest, shivering in the cold.

"Fire." I reached out a hand. "Come on. Let me get you home."

A gleam of brighter blue flashed in her eyes. She furrowed her brow. "Jonas?"

Her affinity. Good hells, she'd been trying to fade into the numbness of her mist. It was no wonder Daj couldn't sense her fear until we drew so close; she was concealing it.

I rested a hand on her knee.

Skadi jolted and in another moment flung her arms around my neck. "*Jonas.* I tried to pull the walls apart, I tried to get out, but it started crumbling. I . . . thought it might bury me. I couldn't get out."

I held her close against my chest, stroking the back of her hair. "It's all right, Fire. We found you."

Skadi's shoulders shook, from the cold or emotion, I didn't know. She didn't release my neck when I scooped her up and made our way back to the opening. Raum caught sight of us before we were beneath the hole and summoned the ropes.

Violent shudders rolled through Skadi's frigid limbs when I secured a loop under her legs and placed her palms around the rope.

"Can you hold it?"

She lifted her weary eyes, water from the surface still spilled around us, but she nodded.

I pressed a kiss to the center of her brow, knowing she'd left the palace in distress, knowing it would have broken me if she had never returned. With a tug on the rope, the others lifted her from the tunnel.

Skadi was already draped in a thick woolen cloak by the time I was pulled out. I leveraged her onto my horse between my arms, and made certain her face was shielded. She nestled against me.

"A little longer, Fire," I whispered.

"I . . . hate . . . that I've caused . . . more trouble," she said through the chatter of her teeth.

"Hells, woman, I hope you never stop." I tightened one arm around her waist, holding her closer. "Life would officially be dull without you."

I thought she might've chuckled—or perhaps another shiver—but she went quiet, keeping her cheek against my heart the entire journey back to the palace.

CHAPTER 30
THE MIST THIEF

I WOKE WRAPPED IN ENDLESS FURS. ALL NIGHT THE CHILL FROM THE STORM seemed to have seeped into my bones.

A flutter raced through my heart when I looked to the side and found Jonas asleep in a chair, his chin propped onto the claw of his hand, his neck angled in a way that seemed horridly unpleasant.

My body ached, my head still pounded from the time spent in the thick darkness and cold of that burrow, but Elixist tonics had halted any fevers and chills from taking hold. I slipped out of the bed and tried to cover the prince with a fur without waking him.

Jonas snapped his eyes open. "You're awake." He scrubbed a hand over his face and sat straighter. "How do you feel?"

"I'm fine."

Jonas reached out and traced the edge of my jaw with his fingertips.

Gods, he was beautiful. The draw to fall deeper into my nightmare prince was worse than before. The man scoured a forest for me, never stopping until he found me, then risked his own neck sliding into an abandoned burrow, set to flood or fall apart if the storm had worsened.

"You should get some better sleep," I whispered. "I will not be going to the Otherworld or lonesome rides anytime soon, Husband."

It was an attempt to keep my tone light, but Jonas didn't grin.

229

Instead, he rose, and gave up his seat to me. I had no time to protest before the prince was on one knee, my hands clasped in his.

"There is something I must say if you are feeling well enough. I know why you left the palace yesterday, and I know how much this will pain you to hear."

He paused, and I could not breathe.

I steeled myself for his words. It would hurt, but I had already decided before the burrow, Jonas Eriksson was my choice. Be it friendship, lovers, accomplices in some tricky scheme, I wanted this life more than I would ever want Arion.

"You must know that you are wrong, Wife."

I cocked my head. "Wrong?"

"Horribly." The prince tightened his hold on my hands. "I know you believe it is impossible, and frankly, I was beginning to think the same, but you're wrong. I won't bring it up again after today, and swear to never tell another soul about your folly."

A smile twitched in the corner of my mouth. "What are you talking about?"

His jaw flexed. In the next breath, Jonas cupped the back of my head and pulled my lips to his.

This kiss was not like the others. It was fierce and gentle, slow and hurried. Jonas kissed me like he wanted to leave the memory of it on my lips until I met the Otherworld.

By the time he broke away, I could hardly draw in a deep enough breath.

"What was that?" I whispered.

"The condition in the alliance is shit, Skadi." He pressed his brow to mine. "I mean, it's not if that is truly your choice, but I swear to you—gods—I swear, I am not playing some sort of game here. I do not spend my time with you to trick you into believing something that is not true." Jonas pressed a kiss to the place behind my ear. "I do not say I want you in a jest." One of his hands abandoned mine and glided up my thigh. "I do not touch you out of obligation."

I shuddered beneath his hands.

"I assumed you knew the conditions." Jonas lifted his head.

"Eldirard mentioned it after the signing, but after what Arion did, I did not think it would ever matter. I did not anticipate caring, Skadi, I won't lie to you. But I knew I would still never treat you so horribly you would wish to return to that bastard."

I rubbed my thumb over his knuckles on the hand holding mine. "I didn't know of the condition. When I received Cara's missive, I didn't know what to even think."

"You thought I have been merely trying to keep you at ease this whole time?"

My chin dropped. "You would not be the first to speak sweet words to gain my compliance."

In the next breath, Jonas pulled me against him, a new sort of fury in his eyes. "And if you would give me a damn name, I would leave a path of their entrails on the ground for doing so. My actions with you are not a ruse, Skadi."

"Here, we scheme," I whispered. "I have heard such words more than once in these walls."

"You are not a scheme." Jonas pulled back and removed a vial of something murky from his tunic. "I do not know what has happened in the past to leave you convinced I could never care for you, but I will not demand you merely believe my words. I'd like to also show you."

"What is that?"

"My nightmare." Jonas swallowed. "My mother shares memories in a variety of ways. I gave her my memory of the fever, and I want you to see it."

My fingers trembled when I took the vial. Jonas didn't look away when I tipped the liquid memory to my lips, he didn't look away when shadows filled my mind like ash.

It was a strange setting. Almost Natthaven, with touches of the Black Palace, and much like a dream would create. My stomach cinched at the screams. Anguished sobs of pain and desperate pleas rattled against the shadows of the nightmare.

To witness it through Jonas's perspective was odd and unsettling. Panic thrummed in my blood. Fear came so fierce it doubled me over. In the dream shadows flung at me from all sides, trying to fight me off, trying to pull me back.

I cursed and fought until the corridors shifted to an open, dark cavern.

A gasp slid from my throat. In the center of the cavern was me, naked and chained to the ground. Deep, bloody lashes adorned my skin. Endless strikes from familiar hands added new wounds.

Faces came into focus—Arion, Eldirard, Dorsan, even Cian—all struck at me, cursing me, shouting that I was unworthy to live.

"Skadi!" Jonas's voice was loud and soft all at once. A cry given in his own mind, but witnessing it this way, I could hear it rattle to my soul. He struggled against unseen tethers, pleaded with shadows. "Leave her."

Over and over the prince shouted for them to stop, offering himself in my place. My pulse raced with his, a feeling of affection, of loyalty, of desire collided with the fear of losing it all until a final lash fell and the dream form of me no longer cried out.

Pain lanced through my belly when the realization that he'd failed to protect me took hold.

Through a rush of wind, the walls faded, and the nightmare began again, a constant cycle of wretched helplessness and fear.

The memory of the nightmare faded halfway through a second round of the vision.

My shoulders slumped and tears heated down my cheeks. Jonas remained on his knees, focused on our clasped hands.

With a gentle brush of my fingertips, I urged the prince to look at me. Torment lived in his eyes, and a need to take it away bloomed in my chest. "Forgive me for running from you before speaking to you."

Jonas dropped his chin. "Run if you must clear your head, but always return to me. When I learned of the possibility you could return to your former betrothal, I merely decided I would offer you a safe home. I did not anticipate getting close to you. But it all changed the moment you kissed me for the first time."

I snorted. "No, you were the one who absolutely kissed me at the vows."

"I believe it was you. I saw those stones glowing, and I'm surprised you did not kiss me before that old bore finished his confusing speech."

A laugh broke free, wet and tight with emotion. I used the heel of my hand to wipe a stray tear. "You are an arrogant sod. I had no desire to kiss you in that moment."

"Because your heart was racing and you knew I would destroy you with passion and longing if you did. It's all right, Wife. You are safe to admit it now."

"I admit nothing."

"You should."

"Why?"

Jonas leaned closer, hovering his mouth over mine. "For I might do things to make your heart race again."

I kissed him sweetly. "You are unexpected, Jonas Eriksson."

"Trust me, Skadi Naganeen . . . Eriksson, you are as well."

"You just gave me your house name." My thumb tugged on his bottom lip.

"Do you want it?"

A strange heat built in my chest. I had felt wholly accepted by the alver clans after the sparring, but this truth went deeper—they were mine and I was theirs. Always.

I offered a brief, jerky sort of nod, then kissed Jonas in response instead of words. I kissed him, held him, trusted him.

No man who was indifferent about his bride would be so tortured at the notion of losing her.

Fears faded. We would always be an alliance to the outside, but in this moment, I dared hope that we were falling deeper into something more.

CHAPTER 31
THE NIGHTMARE PRINCE

I LIFTED ONE OF THE BOOKS FROM THE TRUNK RAUM AND LYNX STOLE FROM Skadi the day of our arrival.

A night of nightmares, recovering from fevers, and a hunt through a storm put us days behind. There was a bit of guilt from watching Skadi re-read tomes or wander about the royal study looking for anything more entertaining than alver lines and mesmer histories.

I inspected one of the colorful elven books, red leather with gold lettering and pastel paintings inside. "She brought more of these tales than she did gowns."

"I respect that," Sander said, adding a bit of white stain to a chip in one of the shelves.

The corner of my mouth twitched, recalling how long I listened to the gentle whisper of her voice while she read of the elven king and the fair maiden bride. A tale of cruel hearts being soothed by the goodness of love.

In the end, the maiden gave her life for her king before her own people could destroy him. Lost in grief, he offered his heartsblood to the land and from the soil sprouted a tree with golden leaves, the shade of his lover's hair.

An everlasting symbol of the woman he loved, the king was buried under its leaves when he went to find her in the Otherworld.

Skadi had hugged the book to her breast when she finished the story last night, a whimsical smile on her face. I was captivated in her passion, but had no retort other than she read me a damn tragedy and I wanted the ending changed.

"It is about true love," she said. "The tree roots ran so deep in his kingdom, it would never fall, and they lived together in the gods' hall."

I kissed the tip of her nose. "I would've preferred she tell her people to go to the hells instead of being a martyr, that's all I'm saying."

Skadi had rolled her eyes and nestled against my chest. "Maybe she should've, but it was still a declaration of her love, you snob."

Von cursed, tripping over a stack of books, and drew me back to the present moment. "Remind me again why you had me drag half of Nik's library here?"

"First, Nik has a ridiculously expansive library and won't miss them. Second, she didn't bring enough to fill the shelves. Thought maybe she'd like to read a few more fae tales from the dregs."

Von said nothing, simply pinched his mouth tight and shared a stupidly sly look with Sander.

"What?" I offered a narrow gaze. "You think she'll despise it, don't you? Gods, I ought to have thought of something more tangible. Blood-singer gives Liv jewelry. Daj gives Maj notes." I slumped in a chair, tossing the book back into the pile. "My gift is a mountain of fables."

Sander and Von didn't return to their secret glances. The bastards merely burst out in laughter, like I'd told some grand jest I didn't even know.

Damn sods.

Another hand cuffed the back of my head.

"Godsdammit, does everyone in this kingdom strike the royals?" I spun around as two men brought in another trunk. "Isak. I expected it of Fiske, but not you."

"You'll survive. This is h-heavy, m-m-my sobbing p-prince." Isak's red hair was braided and smoothed tonight, not the typical mess from his cowl.

Fiske peered over the top of the trunk, his dark eyes pinned on me. "We'll just drop it here."

Sander protested, insisting it could damage the books, and joined in lowering it to the wide, blue rug.

"Good man." I pressed a hand on Fiske's muscular back. "This is the last one?"

"Yes." He stretched one arm across his chest. "And a certain elven princess has been asking around for a certain prince."

"You told her I'd be along shortly, right?" Sander said without a pause.

"She would never seek you out over me." I palmed his face and shoved him to the side, stomach in knots. "Let's get these put up, and I guess we'll see if I know what the hells I'm doing."

"This is a good move, Jo." Von added two books to the shelf.

"Stop worrying, you sod." Sander shot me a glare. "You're quivering more than Mira when she's overly excited about something."

I shook out my hands. "You're right. This is fine. It will be fine."

This would be a disaster.

The lot of us huddled around the closed door, silent gazes on the delicate blossoms Frigg's mother painted on the frame.

"It's good, right?" I rested my hands on my hips.

"Gods." Von peeled away from the group. "Come on. Let's see if Jonas can find his balls to go show his bride what he's done."

Once the others left the corridor, Sander came to my side. "You're welcome for what I did."

"What?"

"Had I not sacrificed myself upon her sword, *risked* my very life, you might never have found love. I hope you name your first child after me."

I laughed, but sobered quickly. "I don't know what I'm doing, Sander."

"Keep not knowing then; it seems to be working."

"How is it even possible to feel so differently after so short a time?"

"Because you have found a woman who burned through those shields you like to keep with your companions. She was not even trying. That is how you know—at least I think so—it is a bond worth keeping."

"Jonas?" Skadi's voice echoed up the stairwell. "Are you up there? Von told me to find you."

Sander left with a cheeky kind of grin, his muffled voice followed in the stairwell, likely as he passed her. My heart swelled when she came into sight.

Gods, she was beautiful.

Since the burrow, we'd spent little time away from each other. Once, I imagined spending my days with one woman would grow tiresome and aggravating.

I now woke each day with her as my first thought.

The piercings she kept in her ears always gleamed like crystals in the light, and the silver rings on her fingers did the same. She had her hair pulled high today, like on the sparring field, but her flowing dress revealed more of her shoulders, some of the coils of her secret ink spilled from the sides.

Skadi looked to the tall, arched ceilings, the stained images on the windows. "What is this corridor?"

I blew out a long breath. "It was empty, but it isn't now."

Gods, I sounded like a fool.

One of her brows lifted. "All right. Why so skittish?"

"I'm absolutely not skittish."

"Like a frightened pup."

I took hold of her hand and smashed her against me. "You could've at least called me a frightened wolf or something fearsome." At the door, I hesitated. "I need you to know, I stole from you."

"What?"

"It was for good reason." I nudged the door open, drawing us into the open room. "You did not lose your endless trunks of books, Fire."

Skadi's eyes popped. Slowly she unlaced her fingers with mine and took cautious steps into the open space. Once an old study, the room had been neglected over the turns.

Shelves had been refastened to walls, the broken stones in the old inglenook replaced. New draperies sewn by Inge were in Natthaven blue and silver. Images of Klockglas flowers and ravens lined the molding at the top of the walls, the only symbols of unity between worlds. The rest of the hanging tapestries were commissioned with the help of Dorsan's knowledge of popular elven symbols—stars and moons, blades and dark mountains.

Books were orderly along the shelves. Some with spines facing out, others on their sides in stacks. Fur lined chairs surrounded a low, black-wood table with imported elven wine in a carafe.

The chandelier was the most challenging. I didn't want the bulky wrought iron like most of the palace. I wanted something more Skadi—like starlight. Glass and crystal glistened in the beams of sunlight through the windows, painting the rugs in prisms of color.

I thought it turned out as well as it could've, but she wasn't saying anything.

I cleared my throat. "Niklas worked with Dorsan to make the incense smell a little like Natthaven." Silence. "Look, I am sorry for keeping your books from you, I realize now, I could've built all this without the actual books. I just thought in a strange place you might want a spot of your own that reminded you of home, but if—"

I coughed when a force struck me in the chest.

Skadi clung to me, shoulders trembling. For a moment, I didn't know what to do with my hands, hovering them to my sides. After a pause, I held the back of her head and wrapped the other arm around her waist.

"Fire." I whispered against her ear. "You have me standing on knives here. Do you hate it or is this—"

"I love it, you fool." She tilted her chin, laughing, but tears rimmed her eyes. "This is where you've been going? This is what you were doing that night I . . . shouted at you. But you kept working on it, even after."

I brushed away a tear with my thumb. "I did not want to be a husband with conditions. I'd be a rather ignorant sod if I did not take into account that your life had been completely upended that night. You had no reason to trust me, no reason to think I cared at all."

She swallowed and turned back into the room, taking it in. "But why do all this? I feel rather undeserving of it."

I pinched some of her wavy hair between my fingers. "I disagree. You never left my side during the mesmer fever, and you did not need to do that. You've made a guild of thieves that helped raise me love you better. You dance on tavern tables, how many princesses can say that?"

She snorted, but faced me after a moment. Her palms trapped the sides of my face. "Thank you, I am at a loss for words. No one has ever done something like this for me."

Whatever retort I planned to make hinting that there were no husbands like me was drowned when she kissed me.

We stumbled against the doorframe. Her lips parted, her tongue brushed mine. I tugged on her hair, tilting her face for the angle I desired most. Fingers curled around my tunic as though she might want to tear it down the middle.

In a frenzy of breaths, I spun her around, pressing her back to the wall. Skadi let out a heated moan when I took hold of one of her legs and wrapped it around my waist, arching my hips against her core.

"Jonas." Skadi breathed against my lips.

"Fire?"

"I don't want you to have another lover."

Did she still believe such a thing? "Woman, I have no one—"

"I meant this." She pressed a kiss to my palm, smirking. "You said it would be your only lover until I gave the word."

Skadi took my hand, placing it under the hem of her gown on the heat of her bare thigh. I let out a rough breath when she guided my hand higher and higher, toward her center.

She dragged her teeth along my ear, drawing the lobe between her lips for a breath, then whispered, "I'm giving the word."

CHAPTER 32
THE MIST THIEF

THE VERDANT SHADE OF JONAS'S EYES SHADOWED. HE PRESSED HIS BROW TO mine, lips parted. Two fingers ran along my drenched slit.

My head fell back and I rocked against Jonas's hand, gasping when he curled his fingers inside me. Jonas cupped the back of my neck and pulled my lips to his. Whimpers and small breaths slid from my throat the more he worked his fingers in and out.

With cruel torture, Jonas circled his thumb over the sensitive place at the apex of my core. My cries grew louder, palms smacked against the door. Doubtless they echoed down the stone staircase.

Brow furrowed, I tucked my face against his neck as he worked, tormented, and loved me with his wicked hand. My breath panted against his throat until the thin glass shield shattered low in my belly.

I sobbed his name, arms around his shoulders, keeping me upright. Jonas held me tightly, working the last heated drops of my pleasure. My body went limp.

"I will never get enough of your sounds, Fire." He pulled his hand away from between my thighs and sucked one finger into his mouth. "Or your taste."

Jonas placed the other finger against my lips. All hells, my knees weakened when my own tongue wrapped around the tip, tasting myself on his skin.

A low rumble rolled from his chest. He kissed me. Hard. Never breaking away, Jonas padded around until he found the latch. The door gave way and tossed us, stumbling, into the corridor.

Again, my body struck the wall. Jonas flattened a palm by my head, his hardness pressing into me. I slid a palm down his stomach, cupping the thickness of his length over his trousers. He moaned and dragged his teeth down the slope of my throat.

Jonas hissed in a bit of pain when I nudged the tips of my fingers down the front of his trousers. "Too much." He shook his head, taking hold of my wrist. "I'll spill all over you."

Without a word, Jonas took my hand and raced us down the staircase and toward his room. He did not wait to open his door before pressing my front to the wall. I gasped. My eyes rolled back when he skirted his hand up my ribs, cupping the underside of one breast while running his hips along my backside until I thought I might come undone all over again.

A door opened, but a low gasp followed. Over my shoulder I caught sight of Dorsan slamming his door closed.

Jonas laughed when a flush crept up my neck. "I think we've shocked your proper guard."

I spun around, taking his face in my hands and backing into his chamber. "I don't care."

Jonas kicked his door closed and devoured my mouth, all tongue and desperation. Hands tore at clothes like we had no time left. His belt went first, next his boots. My dress was yanked over my head, the under shift next, nearly tripping me as I went.

Jonas paused at the bed and drank in my naked body. One palm slid between my breasts, resting over my heart. "You are everything, Fire. Perfect. I would not change a hair on your head."

"You're not here to make me cry with sweet words, Husband."

"I'll make you scream then, Wife."

"See that you do."

"I will."

I bit down on his bottom lip. "Give me the last word. At least once."

Jonas kissed me, silencing his words, until he whispered, "Never."

With one elegant motion, Jonas had his tunic tossed aside.

I kissed the inked symbols over his skin and worked his trousers over his hips until his cock sprang out. I swallowed. He was thick and hard. My insides swooped in anticipation. No, he was not my first, but in some ways he was—a first to care, a first to see me, a first to want me as I am.

Jonas scooped under my thighs, lifting me off the floor, and tossed me onto the bed. I shrieked when he reared over me, palms by my head. He kissed me sweetly, the tip of his tongue running along the edge of my bottom lip, my jaw, my neck. He kissed and licked his way to the swell of one breast, then closed his lips around the peak.

I bowed off the bed, grasping at the quilts for any sort of anchor.

When my head steadied, I reached between us, curling my fingers around his thick length. Jonas tightened his mouth over my nipple, moaning almost like he was in agony.

"I've never allowed myself to believe this could be more than a physical release," he said, dragging his lips across my throat. "You've changed everything."

"Why did you never love, Jonas?" My words were breathless, hardly there as I stroked his velvet skin.

"Because I was waiting for you, Fire." Jonas gently pinched my nipple, tugging.

I couldn't draw a deep enough breath, let alone address the vague confession. I didn't want to read more into it, but my heart pounded in my ribs—I thought my husband might be falling much like me.

With slow kisses, Jonas worked his way back to my mouth. His hips settled between my thighs, and I moaned, seeking the pressure, though it seemed too much, too fierce.

It was as though the surface of my flesh was set ablaze. Heat pooled between my legs, throbbing and pulsing until I wanted to scream with need.

For a moment Jonas lifted his head, face flushed, breaths heavy, and held my gaze, perhaps looking for any hint I wanted him to stop. My fingers traced along the muscle and strength corded across his chest, shoulders, the strong curve of his neck. I wanted to touch every divot, kiss every surface.

"Where is my fire in those eyes?" he whispered. "We need not—"

"No." I touched his lips. "Last time . . . last time we touched, the fever came. I don't want the same to take you again. It was horrid to see you suffer in such a way."

Jonas cupped the side of my face, pressing a kiss to the corner of my mouth. He held his mouth there, words warm on my skin. "I've never had the same mesmer attack twice. I don't understand it. Seems to burn out, then those dreams merely become a nightmare from the Mare demons."

"I don't want you to have those either."

"Can't be helped. I broke my last defense against you, Fire," he said. "I've nestled you beside any soul that matters to me. Once you're there, it's for good. Don't ask me to let you go."

"Wouldn't dream of it."

"Good."

I rolled my eyes. Naked and wanting, I refused to get into a battle of final words. I tilted my head and kissed him, silencing that horridly beautiful tongue of his.

Jonas dragged his nose alongside one breast. "I want to taste your skin again."

"Please." I cried out, trembling under his larger form when his tongue lapped at the hardened point of my breast. He rocked his hips against my aching center. A frantic need, an obsession to join with him in every way took hold.

"Jonas," I breathed out in a rough gasp. What was I trying to even say? I shook my head and simply blurted, "I need you."

He lifted his head from my chest, tugging at my nipple with his teeth before releasing me. "Open these pretty thighs for me."

With one hand, he pushed one of my knees to the side, spreading me out beneath him. His fiery eyes roved over my body, head to foot, stalling between my legs.

Jonas used both thumbs to run along both sides of my slickened core. "So perfect. I want every bleeding piece of you."

"Yet I'm still waiting for you to take one."

He chuckled. "Ah, be careful what you ask for, Wife."

The silky darkness of his voice rumbled through my bones, my blood, to my very soul.

The tip of his tongue slipped out, wetting his lips, as he watched me recline on my elbows and slowly let my knees drop to the sides. If he had not proven his gentle hands and words time and again, I might shudder in fear at the way Jonas looked at me, the way he hovered over me, like he had every plan to destroy me before sunrise.

Gods, I hoped he did.

Jonas fitted his hips between my thighs. Unable to stop, my body snapped in an arch to feel him, to kill any distance between us, and guided the crown of his length to the heat of my slit.

In a painfully sensual crawl, he nudged into my dripping center, but when he was met with resistance, he hesitated. "Skadi, I know you said this was not a first, but . . ."

I shook my head. "It's just been some time."

He lifted more, watching where we were connected. "Tell me if I hurt you, yes?"

"It doesn't hurt." I moaned and wriggled beneath him, as though to prove it. "You're . . . you're indescribable. Please, Jonas."

As though something snapped, Jonas let out a rough breath and rolled his hips in a quick thrust. He sank into me, tip to hilt.

"All right?" he rasped.

I nodded, digging my fingernails into his hips. Jonas set the rhythm; slow to build, but it wasn't long before our pace quickened to a frenzied rush, and the slap of skin against skin echoed through his bedchamber.

When he pressed his body down, I arched up, like we were hoping to dissolve into each other. His length filled me, consumed me, and every thrust sent bright shocks of tantalizing pleasure surging through my veins.

"You're mine," he gritted out. Jonas bit down on my bottom lip, quickening his thrusts. "Gods, I am so glad you're mine."

Our breaths, our heat, the rush of our bodies, it all burned together until a tremble of delicious warmth flowed from my skull to my belly; like molten ore, it spilled between us until I shattered.

I cried out his name. My claws left red scratches across his arms as I lost control.

"Jonas. Yes, there." My body squirmed and writhed. "There, gods, deeper."

His breaths were ragged pants. Jonas leveraged onto his knees and tugged my hips up and toward him. I sobbed in pleasure at the new depth, the new invasion.

What little control he had left snapped. He pounded into me, wringing out every last piece of my release until his body shuddered. His face heated in a beautiful twist of pleasure as his release poured into me in hot bursts.

My husband slumped forward, his palms flattened beside my head, holding him over me. Silence surrounded us save for the rough gasps we shared.

When he pulled away, Jonas kept his hand over my entrance, and whispered, "Don't lose a drop yet. I want to be dripping from you into tomorrow, Wife."

"Good hells." I closed my eyes, moaning under his touch. "Where do you think of your words?"

"It comes naturally, only for you."

Once Jonas was satisfied I would never be able to forget what went on here tonight, he settled beside me. Our arms were tangled, our legs threaded like a woven tapestry. We held onto each other like the darkness of the fading sun might tear us apart.

I could feel the heat of his stare for a few breaths before he traced the curve of my nose, my lips.

"Where are your thoughts?" I asked.

Jonas stopped tracing my profile, dropped his arm around my belly, and hooked one of his legs around mine, pulling me close. He nuzzled his face in my hair. "I don't want to say the wrong things."

My pulse thudded. To me, my body would never recover from being loved by Jonas Eriksson. Was it not the same for him?

"Might as well tell me."

His fingers drew small circles over my belly. "I'm . . . overwhelmed by you."

"I don't understand."

Jonas sighed and propped his chin on a curled fist, looking down at me. "I've had lovers, Skadi, and I'd be a liar if I said my body did not enjoy it."

"Do you think I hold it against you? I don't."

"Good." He kissed my shoulder, but concern was still written in his features. "I was a fool and thought this would be much the same, but it was something else entirely. It was like a first. I have never, *never*, felt the way I did just now, like my blood was going to burn out of my veins." He shook his head, chuckling, and returned his face to the curve of my neck. "My words aren't making sense."

I tightened my hold on his body, blinking my burning eyes toward the rafters overhead. "I understand. The feeling was the same."

He smiled against my skin and held me tighter.

When his breaths turned soft and his body relaxed with sleep, I pressed a kiss to his forehead. "I love you too."

CHAPTER 33
THE MIST THIEF

My knees were tucked against my chest, a woven wrap was around my shoulders, and half-eaten on a plate on the table was a honey cake with spiced cream.

The morning stole Jonas away with his mother, Sander, and most of the Kryv to see to a shipment from the Southern shores. I woke to a note on his pillow and a bawdy list of all the things my nightmare planned to do to me once he returned.

Tomorrow we would leave for our first visit back to Natthaven.

I would miss the laughter, the chaos, the moments where it was so simple to forget we even had royal duties. Still, I did look forward to introducing Jonas to the isle in a different light other than battle.

All week my body ached for more of the man. No mistake, I would never sleep soundly again if he were not curled around me. My core throbbed merely thinking of the wonderfully torturous ways Jonas Eriksson used his tongue, the way he twisted me up and commanded my body until I felt like I would split in two from heated pleasure.

I blew out a breath, rubbing the flush of heat off my neck, and forced my focus on the pages. The tale was a fae saga. A symbol of Mira's realms was embossed on the parchment, then again Von gave up they'd spent the first week of our tentative vow gathering tales from across the fae realms.

I had Night Folk stories, sea fae legends, twisted stories of fate from the Western lands. The tale in my hands spoke of two boys who grew as brothers and took different titles—a lord of heart and a lord of war.

It was an eerie tale, one of fate, betrayal, and the love of a woman.

The tale ended with a curse delivered from the lord of hearts over the lord of war. The warlord was forced to wander the lands, poisoning and twisting loyalty of the people until they took to battle—father against son, wife against husband—while he searched for his lost lover.

There was something about the story that felt almost too real to be myth. Brutal and a little tragic, still I could not stop reading.

Until the door kicked open with a soft curse.

The book tumbled to the ground, and I nearly spilled over with it. The alver king filled the doorway, utterly transfixed on a stack of sealed missives in his hands. He would squint one eye, then switch to the other, studying the symbols printed on the front, curse again, and do the same with the next one.

I wasn't certain he even knew I was there.

Jonas's father was broad and tall like his sons, and on my first glance at him in the negotiations, I thought him to be a cruel man. He did not smile, and seemed ready to lash out if too many folk spoke to him at once.

Time in Klockglas proved otherwise.

True, the king did not chatter endlessly, he observed. Quiet and stoic, but there was no denying a light filled his eyes at the sight of his queen and his sons and those he considered his family.

He did not raise his voice or his hands.

I took him to be a man who merely watched the world around him, a gentle shadow.

"Highness, good morning."

Kase looked up from the missives. "Didn't realize you were here. And stop calling me Highness, girl."

Much like his temperament, if I had not observed his words in these weeks, I might tremble beneath his gritty, deep voice.

He spoke like that to everyone.

"I feel strange calling you by a given name, so what would you have me call you? Father-in-law?"

"Bit of a mouthful." He stepped into the room, making his way to the desk near the window. "Call me whatever you like."

"Except royal titles."

Kase jabbed the air with the missives. "Exactly."

I clasped my hands behind my back, pulse racing. "Would it be strange if I called you Daj? My own is dead."

The king stalled his hand from placing the missives on the desk. For a breath, he didn't move, and I wanted to flee. What a foolish thing to say. It was not as though I was some beloved child of his, not like his sons.

Yes, we got on all right. Yes, he had given thanks for aiding Jonas during the mesmer fever, but . . .

"I like that," he said, voice rough. "That'll do fine."

A small smile curved in the corner of my mouth.

"Unfortunately, I have been charged as the post deliverer today." The king lifted the missives. "One has an elven symbol, so I think it is addressed to you."

He thought? I went to the desk and rifled through the stack. One was to me from Natthaven, another from the Ever Queen, but the rest were not mine.

With a touch of hesitation, I handed the other letters back to the king. "Um, these are for others."

He took them back without a pause. "Not my fault. I've said countless times, I am the last sod in this palace who ought to be delivering official missives."

Could the king not read? "I-I can tell you to whom they're addressed. If you'd like."

"Certainly would save some time."

One by one, I told him the names. Kase arranged them in a way that seemed like he was assigning a name with the position he was holding it in his hand.

Most were for him and the queen, some for the palace staff and the inner circle of Kryv. Jonas received one from a man named Silas, who Kase told me was the fate king in the westernmost region.

"Silas helped Jonas through the fae battles when he was a boy. They've been close ever since." Kase tucked the remaining notes by his side. "I can read, if you're wondering."

"Oh." What was I supposed to say? "Good."

The king scoffed. "Malin calls them dancing words. Everything shuffles about, so it takes me much longer to read a simple note."

"Oh. Now, I see why the queen read the vow alliance." I smiled, a bloom of respect for the queen taking hold. She had made no great to-do about it, had never ruffled under my grandfather's scrutiny, merely took a burden away from her husband without a word.

"My sons began reading official documents likely much younger than the other heirs, but they were all fools today, leaving me to handle the post. As if they don't even know me."

Doubtless because the Black Palace would not require a staff to do such a menial chore, the royal house saw to their own post.

I chuckled. "Well, I am here now if they do the same on the next post."

The king dipped his chin, but hesitated at the door. "Once, I would've been ashamed to ever admit that. I would hide it. There are some things that don't need to be hidden."

I fiddled my fingers by my sides, unsettled. "I feel like you're telling me something."

"Have you ever enjoyed your power?"

Not the question I expected. Words fumbled over my tongue. "I, well, I suppose I enjoyed the day we all sparred."

"Was that the first time you ever used it for entertainment?"

"It isn't a lovely magic."

"Why? Because that is all you've been told your entire life?" The king stepped back into the room. "Has anyone *not* feared those thieving mists of yours?"

"Not until . . ." My voice faded and an unwelcome sting of emotion burned behind my eyes.

"Not until when?"

I held the king's stare. "Jonas. The vows. I thought he wanted to chain me like Arion, but something he said as we were leaving made me think differently."

I suppose it is a good thing she goes to a realm of nightmares then. She'll fit right in.

Perhaps it was that moment when my heart cracked and let in my nightmare prince little by little.

Kase set the missives down, destroying his carefully placed order, and perched on the arm of one of the chairs. "Look, girl, when words and fear are pushed into your mind over and over, it becomes a truth. Magic might even shift to fit the words. Sometimes it causes our true selves to retreat to some dark place inside us."

"You sound like you speak from experience."

The king gave nothing up, simply stood again and strode for the door. "Follow me. Others might fear your power, but as it happens, I have need of darkness such as yours."

"Where are we going?" I knew better to refuse a king and followed him into the corridor.

On the final step before landing on Jonas's wing, the king paused, a crooked, sly grin on his mouth. "You're about to become a true thief."

CHAPTER 34
THE MIST THIEF

"Highness . . . sorry." I swallowed when Kase shot me a darkened look. The king was crouched on a stone ledge that ran below the eaves, wide enough for a man to walk carefully along the edge without spilling off the side. I was still at least fifteen paces away, trapped on one of the heavy beams. "I don't know if this is right. Maybe if I knew a little more of why we were doing this."

"In schemes you get to know when it's time for your mark, lovey," Raum said, crouched below us in one of the palace alcoves, a cowl over his head. "We've all jobs to do, and it's not your turn yet."

If I did not know Raum was there, I would never have seen him.

Kase used his mesmer magic to thicken shadows, creating deep empty holes in the rafters, corners, gabled windows.

I clawed along the thick rafter, sprawled out on my belly, loose trousers borrowed from Jonas's wardrobe on my waist. Every pace or so, I'd embrace the wooden beam, convinced I was about to tumble, then wait dozens of moments to catch my breath.

The Kryv who were summoned to whatever scheme the king was plotting moved like wraiths dancing across the ceilings. Steps so light, they never seemed to touch. Dressed all in black, when they drifted into the king's shadows, they disappeared into nothingness.

Once in Natthaven, an elven troop of court performers danced and leapt across the great hall. Acrobats swung from satin ropes, flipping and twisting.

The Kryv and the alver king moved with more skill than them.

Lynx tugged my own dark hood over my bright hair.

He held a finger to his lips. "Feather steps, just like we showed you."

Good hells, they couldn't expect me to walk on this beam.

"Feather steps." I clenched my eyes, clinging to the thick wood. "You mean the slow walk you taught me for mere *moments*!"

"That's the one."

"No." I shook my head briskly. "No, no. I think, it's best to leave you lot to whatever this is."

"A heist." From the back, Isak peered out beneath his hood.

"You're afraid, girl." Kase didn't turn around.

"Oh, I don't think you need fear magic to know that."

"I thought you were a feral child."

I huffed. "Turns ago. I'm rather out of practice."

"Turns are merely passing time," Lynx said, voice low. "Once wild, you're always a little wild."

He placed a hand on my shoulder and gestured toward the lot of them, toward a damn king robbing his own palace.

The bite of fear all at once eased, like a slow bleed, a soothing sort of comfort filled my heart. A bit of trust. This was Jonas's father, these were members of the inner court who'd helped raise him. How foolish it was of me to think they would let me fall.

No doubt, Raum was on the ground for that very risk. Stupid of me. Of course, he would catch me should I stumble.

I blew out a long breath, gave Lynx a quick nod of thanks, and leveraged to standing. Arms out to balance my steps, I walked—heel to toe— across the beam.

But with each step, the fear returned. Chaotic thoughts strengthened the more I imagined my neck snapping and bones splitting through the skin should I fall.

I wobbled on the beam, nearly shrieking, but in the next breath, a hand pulled on my wrist. Kase tugged me onto the wide ledge that wrapped around the top of every wall in the palace.

"Well done." He grinned through the shadow of his cowl.

"Thank you. I was so certain at first, then lost confidence rather quickly."

"Because Lynx's mesmer wore off the more distance you put between you."

I shot a look over my shoulder. Lynx waved his meaty fingers with a bit of smugness.

He could calm the mind. He'd chased away my fears and I hadn't realized.

Damn alvers.

"Skadi." The king faced me. "Are you ready for your mark?"

I kept one hand hooked over a narrow beam above my head and carefully lowered to a crouch next to Kase. Below was a wide, circular hall. Two guards in dark tunics with a pair of blades each, stood watch on a set of heavy, black oak doors.

My mark. All the king explained was they would need my help getting through the doors. I thought I might have to steal a lock perhaps, but there was nothing said about guards.

"What am I supposed to do?" I whispered, breaths too heavy to be sly. There would be few doubts who had become the weaker part of this ploy.

"There is something important I need to retrieve in that room."

"Then why not simply go inside? You are the king." My palms grew sweaty. I looked over my shoulder. "I know you hate to admit such a thing, but you do have a voice of authority in this palace."

"I'm aware," he said, a jest in his dark voice. "Trouble is one voice has more influence on those sods down there. They're rather inclined to listen to my wife."

"The queen!" My voice was small, but squeaked and cracked. "We're scheming against the queen?"

"You say it like it's a bad thing." Kase shifted slightly, making room for me to see the doors a little more. "Whatever Malin has in there she has kept from me with intention, and I cannot let that stand."

Jonas's father or his mother. Would I die by my deepest fears or forget how to bleeding exist? Perhaps the queen would have a bit of mercy on me and let me keep my memory on how to breathe.

The king let out another chuckle, shaking his head. "You're worrying for nothing."

"Nothing?" Another squeak. "I'm *stealing* from the queen."

"No. I am stealing from the queen. You are removing the guards. Ready?"

"I-I don't know."

"Perfect. It's best to act without overthinking too much."

Before another protest, darkness coated the hallway. Like the walls wept in black ink, sunlight was blotted out, gray stone was soaked in his mesmer.

Somewhere in the shadows I could've sworn one of the guards muttered something like *not again*.

"Go, go." Kase handed me a rope they'd fastened earlier to the rafter, and spilled it over the edge.

Leather gloves with the fingers cut out covered my hands, sturdy enough I could grip the rope, but slick enough scaling down was hardly a trial. The moment my boots struck the stone floor, Raum was there, holding tightly to my wrists, guiding me through the suffocating dark without trouble.

When we reached the doors, a hazy image of the two guards revealed they'd retrieved their blades and shuffled in front of the doorway. They'd literally chained their damn arms to the door.

"Ah, they're growing rather clever," Raum whispered. "All right, lovey, we need them gone. They're not going to go down without a fight."

"He's the king." I didn't understand this.

Raum beamed. "What does that have to do with anything? Take them for us, won't you?"

My mists. They wanted me to swallow the guards. It was cruel. They were only doing their duty.

I'd kept my affinity doused here, only showing a bit during the spar, but everyone had used their magics then. Still, the staff of the palace didn't look at me in horror. They didn't fear me. I was merely the elven princess who loved honey cakes.

Already, I could feel the urge to fall into the shields of apathy. Fearful glances and painful words would not touch me there.

"Skadi." Kase was there. I hadn't even heard him approach. "Pieces of you do not need to be hidden."

Cold bloomed over my palms. Mists mingled in the shadows of fear. My affinity wrapped around my arms like iridescent snakes.

With slow, careful motions I raised my hands. "If the queen takes my memory, tell Jonas he was a good husband while it lasted."

"I'll pass on the word."

I wasn't cruel. I wasn't going to hurt them. I was merely taking them away for a bit. I wasn't cruel. I wasn't monstrous.

Eyes closed, I repeated the thoughts over and over in my mind. A battle between falling into the icy indifference—to hide—and standing boldly beside a strange group of royal thieves who did not flinch beside the power in my blood.

The more my mists crept forward, the more shadows retreated. When the darkness of the king thinned, the guards lifted their chins.

One of the men crossed his sword over his chest. "No. Not this time, Kase. We're under strict orders not to move."

"I admit, I'm impressed by all this new boldness," the king said in a voice so easy he almost sounded bored. There was a strange sort of confidence in his tone, like he wanted them to be at ease, but in truth he had them exactly where he wanted them.

"Wearing talismans to ward off mesmer," Raum murmured. "That's a Niklas addition. Our Falkyn has switched sides."

"Think I can't touch you because she *poached* the Elixist?"

"Not this turn." The guard stiffened.

Gods, he'd done this more than once.

The king laughed—it wasn't kind, more a deranged sort of delight. "But we've made a few changes ourselves."

With a gesture, the king summoned me forward. It took a few breaths of the guards gawking at the mists spilling from my palms before they realized.

"No." One guard tried to unfasten the tether linking him to the doorway. "No, dammit."

A skein of mist curled around his shoulders and pulled him toward nothingness. Terror was there, but also a bit of annoyance that they'd been duped.

I wanted to shout apologies, but bit them back, realizing the curses of the guards were aimed at the Kryv, even toward the king. Words like *shameless bastard, didn't fight fair,* all manner of insults that faded until both guards were engulfed in my magic.

Whenever I held matter in the Nothing, my blood grew heavy. The urge to toss them aside, or fade them into oblivion was there.

I blew out a few breaths, concentrating on merely keeping them tucked in darkness.

On lonely days in my childhood, I learned to play games in my chambers. Mists would gather items in my room, then toss them, striking a mark on the wall to practice my aim and speed.

Sometimes I would practice holding them, like a rain-filled cloud waiting to burst. I focused on those moments, those days.

The king signaled to his men with his hand. Isak moved forward, knelt at the lock, and with impossibly swift motions had a whalebone pick clicking the lock free.

"All right?" Kase asked as Lynx and Raum tugged the heavy doors open.

I nodded. "They're still there."

"I know. They're both a little terrified. Serves the bastards right for siding with—"

"With *whom*, Kase Eriksson?"

I did not think the alver king was a man taken by surprise often, but at the voice, his eyes went wide and he spun around.

There, standing in the middle of a narrow room with towering walls of shelves was the damn queen. Malin had her crimson hair a little tousled over her shoulders, a dark cloak shielded her body, and her mouth was pinched in a tight line.

All around were shelves of scrolls, pouches of coin, fine jade, gold. Good hells, this was the treasury safehold.

Kase cursed. "How?"

Malin took a step to one side. "Do you know me at all?"

"I know you inside and out, Mallie." Kase stepped in the opposite direction.

"Then you know I'm not above corrupting your crew." She glared at Raum. "You don't even remember it, of course. Very clever plan, though."

"Mal, you didn't." Raum let his mouth part in stun. "You took the scheme from me?"

"Oh, I did." She snickered. "Right out of your thoughts."

Raum jabbed a finger at me. "And this is exactly why we don't share moves in a scheme, not when traitors steal the memory of the plan from your mind. We only worked it out this morning, Mal!"

"And your love of embraces did not serve you when you bid us farewell."

Raum gasped in a bit of horror. "You violated my mind when I was showing *affection*. Devious and inspiring."

Kase looked utterly perturbed. "You took Niklas from us this turn."

"Oh, I took him. He made those talismans mere weeks after last turn's attempt." Malin narrowed her eyes. "How dare you put poor Skadi in such a position."

"How dare I? I think that's envy in your tone, Mal. Annoyed you didn't ask her first?"

I still didn't fully know what to make of this. The king and queen practically prowled each other like they were about to engage in battle. They spoke harshly, but they both seemed to be biting back grins.

"Skadi." Malin looked over Kase's shoulder. "You can let them go. Poor Rolo and Borg. They'll never trust you again, Kase."

All the king did was shrug.

I swallowed and imagined the coldness around me splitting, like an unstitched seam. The two guards fell the short distance, landing in a heap on the floor. They groaned and muttered about how they wanted to be reassigned as they staggered back to their feet.

I anticipated their fear, their avoidance of me. Neither man pointed any ire my way, instead it was all leveled at their king.

"We guard all this for you and this is how you repay us."

"I pay you in penge," the king grumbled.

"I think I might go to the Southern Kingdom. Perhaps to the Night Folk. No worrying you'll be ambushed by your damn king there."

Kase waved them off and turned back to his queen, a smirk in the corner of his mouth. "All right, you win, Mal."

"I win?" She tilted her head to the side. "I don't believe you finished that statement, Husband. I win *again*. How many turns is this now? Ten? Fifteen?"

"Doesn't matter."

"Someday you will know when you scheme, I will be scheming even more. At least when it comes to this. You're never going to find it. Not until the actual day, Kase Eriksson."

The king was in front of her in two long strides, his arms around her body, the queen pinned to his chest. He kissed her for a breath. "One look, that's all I want."

"No." She pinched his side. "You can wait patiently like the rest of us do on our own birth revels."

My lips parted. "It's nearly your birth celebration?"

Malin snorted. "Kase always tries to find out what I've gotten for him, and every damn turn he gets more annoying with his attempted heists." She pinched him again, shrieking a bit when he kissed her.

"A gift." I wasn't certain if the laugh that slipped through was amused or hysterical, but it came through all the same. "That's what this is about? Finding your gift?"

"I don't like surprises, and I'm impatient," Kase said as though it were nothing.

I held a hand to my head, laughing, maybe sobbing a bit, and slid down the wall.

"Look what you did to her," Malin scolded. "She's not used to this, Kase."

"She was perfect," he insisted. "Rolo and Borg will be talking of her for turns."

I looked back at the two guards, a furrow to my brow. "I'm sorry, I . . . shouldn't have kept you in there that long."

"Princess, it was utterly terrifying. Terrifying." One of the guards frowned. "I have never been more impressed by a magic. Yes, even more than the damn king." He shot his annoyance back at Kase.

Impressed? I looked around the treasury. Folk were arguing and laughing, but no one was backing away from me in fear. No one was horrified that I could devour them whole if I wanted. It was as though it was merely . . . part of the plan.

"Daj!" Jonas's voice echoed through the room, stopping everyone's chatter. The prince strode inside, beelining it to me. "What is this I'm hearing of you forcing Skadi on a heist?"

"Sounds like you know exactly what happened, boy."

Jonas took hold of my hand, urging me back to my feet. "All right?"

Was he disappointed? "I-I didn't really know what it was at first, but your father said he needed my affinity, and I shouldn't hide it, so I thought if the king is at the lead, maybe folk won't fear me and—"

He silenced me with a quick kiss. "I'm wholly jealous." He shot a glare at his father. "You haven't let me in on the birth heist for the last three turns."

"You give in to your mother too easily. You're a liability."

Jonas blustered a bit. "Well, maybe because she includes me."

Malin pressed a hand to her heart, like he'd given her the sweetest praise.

"I'm away for a few clock tolls and my wife turns into a Kryv." Jonas muttered as he brushed dust from my shoulders. "Did you enjoy yourself at least?"

I blinked, still in a bit of a stun, then, unbidden, a laugh broke out. "I stole the guards from their post. That was my duty. I stole them and . . . it wasn't kind, it was a little devious, and . . . I didn't go into the dark. Pain, greed, cruelty, when I use my affinity in such a way, I fade. I felt the pull, but . . . I'm still here."

Gods, I was rambling.

"I imagine you've been told your whole damn life the power in your blood is wicked." The king had his arm around his wife, stern expression in place. "You've been told to be ashamed of it. I'd wager you even believe you should be."

How can we build a life when there is such evil in you? You know what your curse has done before. If you want it gone, prove it.

I closed my eyes against the memory of a knife, of blood, of tears, and twisted praise.

"It is dangerous and evil," I said, voice soft. "My affinity has hurt people."

"All magic has harmed, girl. It is the intention behind it that creates the monster. If you think Malin has not slaughtered folk with her mesmer—"

"Me?" The queen's lips parted. "You're one to talk."

"Fear feeds my magic." He looked back at me. "I'm literally called a Malevolent alver. What is lovely about that? Nightmares feed my sons'. Do you think us dangerous and evil?"

If he knew who had been harmed by my hand, the king might think differently about the woman vowed to his son.

Still, I shook my head. "Dangerous, likely."

"I'll accept that." Jonas nodded as though considering the word.

"Evil? No." I stepped closer to the prince, but spoke to the king. "I don't know how else to see my affinity."

"Useful," the king suggested.

"Impressive," added Raum.

The queen grinned. "Powerful."

"Beautiful," Jonas whispered for me alone.

"Use your affinity without fear here." Kase laced his fingers with his wife's.

There wasn't a sliver of jest in the room. The Norns had never been kind to me with the twists of my fate, but in this—a vow I believed was wretched—I managed to slip into a realm where the darkest edges of folk were accepted, where fear was a constant, where folk loved fiercely through every shadow of their own villainous power.

The alver kingdom felt a great deal like a warm hearth after a cold night searching for a place to rest at long last.

"Daj, if you're finished corrupting my wife, we have a great deal to prepare before we leave for the fading isle in the morning."

The king and queen waved us away, chatter on Kase's failed scheme following us into the corridor.

"Overwhelmed, Fire?" Jonas asked when we returned to our chamber. "Games with the Kryv—no matter how small—have a way of feeling like lives are at stake."

"During, I was a whimpering fool, and I would've embarrassed you."

"Doubtful. You should've seen me on my first heist. I think I asked my father at least a hundred questions and Lynx had to calm my mind until I fell asleep. I woke after it was over."

"I'm not certain I've ever felt this way."

He looked at me, confused. "Meaning?"

I hesitated. "Peaceful."

Jonas didn't respond. For a breath, he held my stare, then took my hand in his and kissed my knuckles.

Peaceful. Strange to realize, days since the death of my parents were locked in fear—fear of my own affinity, fear for my life, fear of never feeling loved again.

There was always something to prove to Natthaven. Prove I wasn't a monster, I wasn't dangerous. I could be a good princess. I could fight. I could defend them.

In this moment, there was no worry for using my magic. Thoughts weren't racing, wondering if this would be the day I proved to be too wretched and banished once more to be alone for good.

"Skadi." Jonas took my face in his palms, thumbs running along the ridges of my cheeks. "You belong here. You have made this palace, this kingdom, my *life,* better. Don't ever doubt that. And I hope—gods, I hope—I might do even a little of the same for you."

I cupped the back of his neck, drawing his lips to mine. The kiss was slow, steady, a new constant I loved.

Here, darkness was beautiful.

Here, we schemed.

Here, family didn't mean blood.

Here, was home.

I woke in Jonas's arms, a vicious sort of gleam in the green of his eyes. "We should've been doing this from the start, Fire. You are my favorite sight in the morning."

"And you are a liar." I buried my face in the pillow, hair in tangles. "I know exactly how I look in the morning and the word you seek is frightening."

"I mean exactly what I said."

I peeked up at him. "We're to go today."

"Off to Natthaven." Jonas tucked a lock of hair behind my ear. "Are you looking forward to returning home?"

"I'm looking forward to showing you some parts of the isle. I'm not looking forward to Cara's insistence I've become a feral royal by the looks of me."

Jonas leaned in, kissing my jaw, the corner of my mouth, his palms teasing the heavy curves of my breasts like a true villain who planned to torment me.

"I like you feral." He pecked my lips then leaned away again, tracing one of the coils of feathery ink that curved around one side of one breast. "Do they mean anything?"

"That words and actions of the past do not need to remain in my sights or my life." I took hold of his hand when he traced a scar. "I know you wish to know, but I don't know how to speak on it. I've never spoken of it."

He pressed a kiss to one tattoo. "Then it is a good thing we have endless turns. When and if you wish to, I will always be here to listen, Fire."

"What do your symbols mean? I know the Kryv motto." I touched the ink of *fight to the end*. "But these are images. Flowers and such."

Jonas sat against the pillows and started near the top of his ribs. "Blades for each of my parents. They are the strongest warriors I know." He pointed at the symbol of wisdom right below. "For Sander. He's viewed as the innocent twin, but he's damn clever and devious when he wants to be. A moonvane blossom from the north for House Ferus—Livia's and Aleksi's house. But my other uncle is consort to their aunt, so we share cousins and family. House Ferus was a second home to me and Sander. As was Mira's, the raven. It is their house symbol. A quill for the fate king and queen. They do not leave their palace much, now even less since their little was born a few months ago."

I looked at each image, following the edges, how they were all connected through vines and briars. "Everyone you love. It is quite a tribute."

Jonas merely hummed and looked to me.

"Are you sore at all?" he asked after a pause. "I bent you up last night."

The way Jonas had my legs twisted around as he slammed into me until I could not even shout his name was a moment I wouldn't forget. "I have never felt better, Nightmare."

Jonas pinched my side until I shrieked and rolled into him. "What did you call me?"

"Nightmare."

"You gave me a lover's name. A horrible one, but I've never had one before."

"It's not horrible. You are my nightmarish prince." I pecked his lips. "And it is one of my favorite sides of you."

"Do explain."

I bit down on my bottom lip, ignoring the frenzy of my hair and leveraged over the top of him. Jonas drew in a sharp breath when my thighs settled on either side of his hips. Beneath my center I felt the thickness of his cock hardening.

"I might've pretended to care for nothing the day we left Natthaven, but when your magic took hold of your eyes and you lashed your words at Cian, if you'd have asked, I might've devoured you right there."

The inky center of his eyes flared. "Princess Skadi, such scandalous words. Your grandfather was present."

I leaned forward, smiling against his lips. "That was the moment I knew you could devour every bit of me if I allowed it."

He cupped the back of my head. "And will you allow it?"

My pulse quickened. Was I bold enough? I scooted down his legs, my fingers trailing over the hard surface of his stomach.

Jonas watched me with a look of stunned heat.

My palms settled on his thighs. "I might be able to answer better, but . . . I think I need a taste of you first."

Jonas took hold of my wrist. "Skadi, you don't have to."

"And that is why I want to." One hand stroked him once from hilt to tip, my thumb running over the sensitive crown.

"Dammit." Jonas gritted his teeth, hips bucking on instinct.

He parted his lips—to argue or have the last word no doubt—but whatever words he planned to say choked off when my lips surrounded the head of his cock. A deep, throaty groan broke over his tongue. He propped one leg, knee bent, and draped an arm over his eyes as though the rush had come on too swiftly.

I dragged my tongue along the underside of his length until he looked down at me with hooded eyes. "Fire . . ." He drew in a few sharp breaths. "Don't stop."

I took him in deeper. The taste of his skin and musk pooled heat between my thighs. My tongue curled around the tip of his length. What I could not take in, I covered with my hand, stroking in tandem with my mouth.

Jonas's breaths were rough, heavy. He wove his fingers through my tangled hair, his head fell back. One glance, and my core throbbed watching the heady pleasure written on his face.

There was a powerful delight that came from knowing I brought those breaths from his lungs, it was my name whispered on his lips.

Jonas moaned when I moved faster. He thrust into my mouth, drawing out a cough when he went deeper into my throat.

I licked and kissed until breaths turned to sharp, staggered pants.

"Skadi, I'm going to come."

I held firmly to his hips, holding him in place until he groaned and spent his hot release over my tongue. When it ended, I pulled back, smiling and wiping my lips. Jonas reared over me, pinning my back to the bed.

He kissed me, doubtless tasting himself on my tongue.

Dark desire still coated his eyes when he pulled back. "What is your decision, Fire?"

"Decision?"

"Will you allow me to devour every piece of you?"

I tugged on his bottom lip. "I'll consider it."

A shriek followed his swift movements. In the next breath, Jonas had one of my knees hooked over his shoulder, the other he kept pressed open on the bed with his palm. He fitted his body between my thighs. "I think there might be more tasting to be done before decisions can be made. Don't move, woman. I have you exactly how I want you."

He was wholly villainous. Impossible not to move beneath Jonas Eriksson's cruel mouth. No mistake when I shattered under his tongue, the entire Black Palace heard my cries.

CHAPTER 35
THE NIGHTMARE PRINCE

To reach the isle, we would sail into the Ever Kingdom again.

With our smaller ships, the dive below the tides to pass through the underwater border between the earth and sea realms was disorienting, but shorter than it had been when sea fae were enemies.

When the stempost burst through the surface, the sun was deeper in the sky, and the winds heavy with more heat than back home. Skadi leaned over the rail near the borders of the far seas and Bloodsinger's domain, smiling as merfolk burst from the sapphire tides over and over.

Their eyes were like bulging orbs, but a little captivating. Iridescent fins caught the sunlight and glimmered like hundreds of gemstones in the water. Lovely creatures until they flashed their needle-like teeth that could tear out a throat.

"Damn fins." The old sea fae who ferried us grunted and bit into a blood pear Ylva sent the whole crew. "Always must be the center of everyone's notice."

I propped my elbows on the rail, grinning. "Bitter toward the merfolk, Nightseer?"

Nightseer earned his name for his ability to sail beneath the stars as clearly as if it were daylight. A simple magic, but useful enough Bloodsinger placed him as one of the lead seamen for the earth realms.

The fae huffed and tossed the core of his pear into the tides, chortling when one of the mermaids flicked it back onto deck with a few gurgled curses. "Not bitter, Prince. Frankly, don't be telling me king, but I don't see the point of merfolk. All they do is swim and try to drown fae who can't drown."

Fair enough.

Nightseer huffed and glared at the sea. A scrappy sort of fae with wiry hair and a beard that had not seen a brush in a few turns, he looked less threatening and more petulant, like a child who hadn't gotten a favorite toy.

"Better to be rid of them now that we be seeing more mortal folk in the Ever. I've told my queenie, her mortal maj ought to take great care with them fins."

I laughed. Livia's mother was mortal and one of the fiercest warrior queens I knew. More than once Elise had kept my mother and father alive. Then again, mine had done the same for the Night Folk king and queen.

"I'm sure your concern is noted and revered by Bloodsinger."

Nightseer's golden eyes brightened. "You'll tell the king, won't you, that I'm doing a pleasing job in the earth realms?"

I gripped the man's bony shoulder and gave him a little shake. "Nightseer, I've not a single complaint, and the Ever King shall know it. In fact, it looks like he is nearly here."

Skadi leaned over the rail a little more, mutely fascinated as she watched the thrashing water boil and bulge until the jagged serpent figurehead shot toward the sky, a sea creature aiming for the sun.

For a few breaths the bow remained airborne before the keel slammed back onto the tides, rippling out its torrent enough our longship rocked violently.

I hooked an arm around Skadi's waist to keep her from spilling over the edge. "Bloodsinger! You almost knocked my wife into the tides."

From the quarterdeck, the Ever King materialized. A black scarf held back his hair from his face. He leaned over his elbows onto the rail, a smug twist to his scarred lips. "Had to test if you were keen on the idea or if you'd prefer she stay dry, Prince."

Bastard. "I am *not* keen on the idea."

Erik opened his arms as though he were innocent. "How was I to know? You've not written to my queen and she's rather furious with you about it."

"I am furious." Livia curled her hand over Erik's shoulder, looking half earth fae and half sea fae. She kept her hair tied back with a scarf much like her mate's, but her gown was wholly Night Folk, simple and hemmed in silver. "Hello, Skadi. I'm not as furious with you, but I am a little."

"Well pardon me, you royal asses," I said. "I've been rather occupied with other things and could not spare the time to write you."

Livia frowned. The sort of frown I'd known since I was born. If we were on land she would tangle me up in roots and vines with her tricky fury magic. Livia could summon practically anything from the soil, even heal deadened land.

I had been a prisoner of her earthen chains more than once.

"Don't look at me like that, Livie. You did not write me when you were with Bloodsinger."

"Well, that was an entirely different circumstance, now wasn't it?"

Erik flashed a wicked grin. "If you wanted to try something different, love, you could fight me like that first night. I could chase you."

Livia returned a heated stare to her lover before recalling she was meant to be angry. "I've written to both of you."

Skadi stepped forward. "In my defense, Queen, I do have a reply at the ready. But I merely didn't get around to sending it before we left."

"A little better." Livia pinned me in her narrow glare. "You are another matter, and I like Skadi more now."

I nodded. "Wise choice, Liv."

"Are we doing this?" Erik grumbled. "I'd like to be on my way. I am told our palace is about to be invaded with more earth fae."

Livia chuckled. "Only Mira."

"Feels like ten souls when she arrives, love."

"The only one to blame is yourself, Erik," I called back. "You brought us all to you by taking Liv. Never forget that."

The sea king tried to look aggravated, but the besotted fool could not whenever he looked at his queen. Like the constant traffic of folk from the earth realms to his solitary sea palace was worth it all as long as he had Livia.

"We'll see you to the shore," Livia shouted down. "Then once this week is up I expect you both to write me some damn letters." She paused. "How are you finding your vows? Better? Hate each other?"

Skadi and I shared a glance. I threaded her fingers with mine and kissed her knuckles. "Blissful, Livie."

Bloodsinger faced his crew and barked orders to light the spears. Curious weapons that burst in flames and shot burning stones with a deafening boom. We did not have such weapons back home, but the Ever Ship was lined in them.

I kept Skadi close as the Ever Ship aimed its hull toward the empty mists ahead.

An echo of the command to fire rolled from Bloodsinger down to a crewman near the bow.

Skadi's hands covered her tapered ears when blasts shot from the ship in fiery clouds of ash and gold. The force of it rattled to my bones, a signal of our arrival.

In moments, thick, stormy mists faded and shadows of mountainous peaks took shape. Dark, sandy shores spilled into the tides. Trees, thick enough nothing could be seen between the limbs, shaped alongside spires of a looming palace in the distance.

Natthaven.

Skadi's smile was genuine and soft, but there was the slightest twitch of unease there.

"I expect to see this hideaway you spoke of, the one where you watch the star showers."

Her eyes brightened with my fire. "Stärnskott will be tomorrow evening. I think you'll love it."

I didn't care what we did; I simply wanted to be with her.

Hells, I was as besotted as Bloodsinger.

"Take care, Prince." The Ever King shouted down, the first hint he might care a little about my life. "I don't trust your folk, elven."

Skadi lifted her chin. "Likely as much as I trusted you, Ever King."

Trust would build. Someday. We could not expect after bitter fighting between clans for everything to be forgotten. The sea folk were attacked by the elven first. Their trust would likely come last.

With a vow to recount every bleeding detail of my life to Livia (which I planned to do until she was lost to boredom from descriptions of how I dressed and ate each day) Nightseer bowed no less than five times to his king and queen, and sailed us toward the shores of the fading isle.

CHAPTER 36
THE MIST THIEF

On the docks was a great huddle of blue and silver robes and gowns. Courtiers and palace guards all surrounded my grandfather who stood in the center of it all.

My spine was as stiff as a tree. Jonas tugged me against his side, drawing his lips to my brow. "What is troubling you?"

"I'm ashamed."

"Of what?"

"I should be overjoyed to see my land, but it doesn't feel . . . like home." I let my head fall to his shoulder.

Jonas led us to one side of the deck, out of the way for the small crew of sea fae to secure the sloop. Near the end of the gangplank, palace guards arranged themselves into two stiff lines on either side of the dock, spears tilted in a sort of tunnel for us to walk beneath.

Jonas watched the uniformity with disquiet written over his brow. He was a prince, he knew how to be regal, but it was not a constant thought on his mind.

Not like it had been for me.

All at once, the difference of my life with my nightmare was stark to what it would've been as Arion's wife. As an elven prince's bride, appearances would be everything. I would be a quiet face in the shadows, compliant to the future king's rule.

The alver clans were at ease around their royals, engaging with them, dining with them, like old friends in the palace.

I leaned in close to speak. "You're to disembark first. The king will greet you and they'll expect you both to walk a step ahead of me."

"They can kiss my ass, Fire," he whispered from the corner of his mouth. "You'll walk with me where you belong."

A bloom of heat filled my chest. "As you say, Nightmare."

Jonas stepped onto the dock, eyes heady with suspicion as he took in the curious faces of the Dokkalfar court. One palm reached for mine, and he eased me down the gangplank. As promised, he kept his stride in time with my own, hands clasped.

"Prince Jonas, you grace our shores." My grandfather approached, arms outstretched. "And my Skadinia, how lovely it is to see your beauty back home once more."

Clad in his finest doublet of blue silk, my grandfather looked like a glittering king. A circlet of bronze topped his smooth, silver hair, and gold adorned his fingers. The bands were cold against my cheeks when he took my face in his palms.

"You look well, dear girl." He kissed my cheek. "Dorsan sent a report that you seem to be acclimating to alver lands."

"They have welcomed me with open arms, Grandfather."

Eldirard made a sound like a hum of delight and gently patted one of my cheeks. "I am pleased to hear it, Granddaughter." The king faced Jonas. "And you, Prince Jonas, I assume the alliance has been favorable."

"I have never been more certain the right moves were made, King Eldirard."

Grandfather studied our clasped hands for half a breath, then opened an arm toward the wood. "Come. Let us take this back to the palace. I wish to hear all you've done these first weeks."

Jonas kept his tone to a playful whisper once the king turned away. "I doubt he wants to know everything we've done."

I jabbed his ribs with my elbow, drawing out his low chuckle.

Courtiers parted and bowed their heads as we passed. I drew in a long breath of sweet honey air from the misty trees. The procession wove through the black wood. Planks and wooden pathways honeycombed across the groves and swamps.

When I did not fall back as my grandfather took Jonas's other side, the king shot me a look. I could feel his annoyance when I ignored it and merely tightened my hold on my husband's hand, keeping right at his shoulder.

Flares of the sunset carved through the lush canopies of dark leaves and twisted limbs. Sun Wings and their flickering bodies winked in the shadows. Chirps of rousing night creatures were a lullaby I missed. Air was cool in the wood below the palace, damp and fragrant enough to taste.

Halfway over a stone bridge, I paused, leaning over the rail to peer down at the swampy ponds below.

Instead of tugging me onward, Jonas came to the rail and leaned over with me. Steps shuffled as the procession came to a halt.

I ignored them all.

"There are such unique trees here," Jonas said. "I never took the time to appreciate them after the vows."

Roots grew in serpentine tangles in the center of black ponds. Over the surface was a thin layer of vibrant moss and tiny clovers, so green they seemed to glow in the dim light.

"I would sit by the ponds after lessons as a girl and read my fae tales. I always had a fascination with fae realms and wondered if they truly existed. Sometimes I thought they might live at the bottom of the ponds since I couldn't see below the surface." I smiled up at him. "Strange that now I live among the fae."

"Better than fae," he said, pressing a kiss to the top of my shoulder. "You live among the alvers. We don't have the strange ears like you pointy lot."

I gasped, feigning offense. "Pardon me, Husband, but I have a very respectable size of ear. Perhaps it is alvers and your stubby, rounded ears that are strange."

"Stubby?" Jonas patted at his mortal-like ears. "You think they're stubby?"

I touched the curve of one, arching into him. "I do, but they are my favorite all the same."

He began to lean forward, like he might kiss me, like he'd forgotten we had dozens of eyes watching us.

My grandfather cleared his throat. "We should carry on."

Jonas took my hand again and we followed through the rest of the wood.

Pathways faded into the thick stone steps leading up to the front entrance of the palace. Jonas's refusal to leave my side had the king walking a step ahead of us, while we were followed by the endless stream of servants and courtiers.

Palace doors were already open when we arrived, allowing for gusts of the twilight air. Marble floors and gold trim made up every corridor and room. Grand tapestries of starlight and dark cliffs covered the wood on the walls, and from the rafters were blown glass chandeliers.

In the great hall, a long table was arranged in the center. Every leg on the table bent and coiled like the roots on the trees outside, and pieces of blue satin draped over the edges. Servants arranged silver plates and forks, crystal flutes and polished horns, in front of each black velvet chair.

"Why the hells would we need so many forks?" Jonas said under his breath, and I wasn't certain he meant to admit it out loud.

A bubble of a laugh wanted to break out. How different feasts here would be compared to the boisterous ordeals of nightly meals at the Black Palace.

"Your rooms have been readied." My grandfather spun into us. "Go and dress. You'll forgive me, but I was preparing dull missives and should see to finishing them. We will meet again soon in the hall."

Dorsan followed behind us, stern as always, but his shoulders were not as tense now that we were back in Natthaven. I thought the king might've placed us in my childhood rooms, but the servants guided us to a second level corridor.

There, waiting, was Cara.

"Prince. Princess." Cara dipped her chin in a greeting. "Gods, child, what is this gown you've selected? And where is your circlet? Your hair is terribly windblown."

Jonas raked his fingers through the tangles of my hair, messing it even more. "Perfect. My feral wife."

Heat bloomed under the neckline of my dress. I needed to get the man alone.

I smoothed the woolen skirt of the simple gown. "It is more comfortable to sail in this than a gaudy dress, Cara. And alver folk rarely wear their crowns." I gestured toward Jonas's empty brow to prove my point.

"True," he added. "They're horribly uncomfortable, and don't you think it's a little pretentious to wear proof of rank at all times? Does anyone truly forget who takes up space in a palace? Gods, we're flaunted about enough."

My mouth twitched in a battle to keep a strangled laugh at bay.

Cara looked at Jonas like he'd slipped into madness. She sniffed and shook any confusion away. "Different customs for different folk, of course. My Lady, I will assist you in dressing. Prince Jonas, your chamber is there." She pointed to a door across the corridor. "I'm sure you'll find it to your standards."

"I'm sure I will," Jonas said. "But I certainly will be sleeping with my wife. In fact, I'll help with her gown. Dressing her is my favorite thing to do."

I was nearly trembling against the exertion not to crumble in laughter in front of Cara's horrified expression.

"Well, that is wildly improper."

"For a man to assist his wife with a gown?" Jonas arched a brow. "All respect, lady, but I fear I've exposed Skadi to sights vastly more improper."

I couldn't keep it in any longer. The laugh rattled through my chest. Cara looked upon me like a changeling had robbed me of my face. I clutched Jonas's wrist and tugged him toward the door to my bedchamber. "Cara, don't fret. The prince has proven time and again to be quite skilled with removing my gowns."

"Lady Skadinia." Cara pressed a hand to her chest, aghast.

Her horror was the last thing I saw before I closed the door behind us and clicked the lock into place.

Jonas laughed first, his brow falling to mine. "You are witty when you want to be, Fire."

"I beg your pardon." I flicked one of his stubby ears. "The words you meant to say were I am witty all the time."

Jonas cupped one side of my face, drawing his mouth closer. "My mistake. Now, let's see about getting you into that gown. Might take some time and I can't promise my hands will keep to themselves during the process."

I curled a fist around his tunic. "They better not, Nightmare."

CHAPTER 37
THE NIGHTMARE PRINCE

I WAS CONVINCED SKADI'S MAID DESPISED ME.

Her eyes dug into my skull from where she stood across the hall during the feast, still appalled we abandoned the room together, in different clothes than when we arrived.

Dull. That is what consisted of an elven feast. It was not the same as the vows where fae folk infiltrated the Natthaven palace with boisterous drums and lyres and raucous behavior.

For what felt like endless clock tolls, we ate dish after dish with countless spoons and forks that I undoubtedly mishandled more than once.

By the time some sort of blood plum sweet ice arrived, I felt like I would need to let out seams on all my tunics and trousers, and could not recall a single topic of conversation offered up by the haughty noblemen who ignored both me and Skadi and spoke only to Eldirard.

Until Skadi squeezed my thigh. "Lord Cathal asked you a question."

"Oh." Across the table a narrow-faced man looked my way. His eyes were seafoam green and as bright as Skadi's, but his nose was so thin, I wasn't certain he could truly breathe through it. "Forgive me. What did you say?"

"I asked what your duties were as a prince of your realms. I assume fae royals have specific duties."

"True, and I'm not fae." I returned him a snide grin to match his own. "Fae and alver royals do have specific duties. Mine fall to the armory of the alver clans."

"I didn't know that," Skadi whispered.

I squeezed her hand, nodding. "I tend to our smiths and weapon trade with other kingdoms. Earth fae warriors are called Rave, and once a turn I visit Rave camps and trainings across the realms to see to the needs of armies through elixirs or alver crops."

"Quite a journey," the nobleman said. "Fae realms are expansive, are they not?"

"They are, but we are bonded clans. I was raised alongside every royal house, visiting neighboring kingdoms often. Most of us have family connections throughout the realms, so I am glad to have another excuse to visit. I plan to invite Skadi on the next one this harvest." I cast her a look. "If you want to join, of course."

"I would." Her smile widened and my fiery wife drifted her palm higher on my thigh, merely to torment me.

"Good. You're much lovelier than most of the company."

Eldirard frowned. Perhaps he was not approving of me being so brazen with his granddaughter in the sight of others. Truth be told, I wasn't certain I knew how to stop.

"You would take your wife?" Cathal asked with a bite of disgust.

"Of course." I pushed a bit of the sweet ice around with one of the delicate spoons. "Skadi's voice would be welcome and respected among all the clans."

Eldirard grunted. "Skadinia was provided a regal education on matters suited for her duties. Surely she can find something more useful to do while you are on your journeys than cavorting about warrior camps, listening to chatter on things she does not understand."

Skadi's shoulders slouched. I covered her hand on my leg and squeezed her fingers.

There was a retort on my tongue, sharp as broken glass, but it was the first damn night. For Skadi's sake, I could keep the peace. At least until morning. "I'll leave that decision to her, sire."

Once more the nobles and the king lost interest in my words and turned back to their conversations about elven clans and plans to potentially move the fading isle deeper into the far seas. Seemed Bloodsinger's nearness unsettled them.

All at once, I choked on a bite of sweet ice when Skadi's hand slid dangerously high on my thigh, her fingers running along the seam of my trousers.

"All right, Prince Jonas?" Eldirard asked.

I pounded a fist to my chest, and held up a hand, nodding.

Skadi shifted in her seat, digging into her own sweet, with a pompous smile on her beautiful lips.

Gods, she would pay for that later.

Somewhere deep in the palace a bell tolled the late hour. Sweaty, naked, and tangled up in Skadi's limbs, I stared at the eaves overhead. Each beam was carved in beautiful symbols of stars and moons and frosted peaks.

"Skadi," I whispered.

"Hmm."

"What interests you?"

She lifted her head off my chest. "What do you mean?"

I tucked one of my arms behind my head, my other hand running up and down the length of her spine. "What we spoke about tonight. Duties, tasks, what sort of things interest you? I was tasked with the armory because I love the Rave. Sander handles trade and textiles because he loves balancing numbers and probably enjoys skimming a few things off the top."

She chuckled and nestled against my heart again. "I don't know. I learned to fight because I was expected to defend myself, but all my lessons were on etiquette, stitching, or languages. They were designed to teach me to be a docile, pious queen to my husband, Jonas."

"Would you want to have a duty in Klockglas?"

Skadi twisted to meet my stare. "You want my involvement?"

"I want you to fill your days how you wish, Fire."

Skadi didn't speak for a long pause, fingers tracing each of my tattooed symbols. "You've mentioned the great fae battles when you were young. Both your men and women take to the battlefield, so I assume some littles lost their mothers and fathers. That is my interest."

Skadi spoke as though her voice were nothing more than a whisper in a storm.

I laughed and pressed a kiss to the top of her head. "What are you saying? You're being bashful about something, and although I do love when your face flushes, I'm a little lost in this."

"Orphans, lost littles. I have an interest in seeing they're fed, clothed, warm, and possibly have a few fae tales to read when they wish to escape to another land. I tried to encourage ideas here, but Grandfather and the nobles insisted such littles were fed in Grynstad young houses. I don't think they are cared for, though. I think the littles are sent to work throughout the light elven lands for the pay of a cot and some bread to eat."

She cleared her throat. "Rumors of those houses were why I ran after my mother and father died. The royal guard came for me, but I was terrified of those places. I want to do better for other littles; I know what it is to be alone in the world."

Unable to speak for a moment, I used one knuckle to tilt her face, giving me access to take those lips. I kissed her, soft and gentle, but her eyes were glassy with need when I pulled back.

"You are soft inside, Fire."

"Not a monster?"

"Be monstrous, be gentle, and be kind. I want you every way." I kissed her cheek, grinning. "You'll want to speak with Von."

Her brow arched. "Why?"

"He works with the Night Folk First Knight and his wife to see that littles who were orphaned during wars as infants, or those littles who lose their folk to disease, are clothed and fed with warm beds to sleep. What else would you want to see done?"

Skadi rolled over me and propped her chin onto the tops of her hands. "When I was brought to this palace as a girl, I could only read a few words. I would want to help with all their needs, but find tutors, perhaps. Possibly books for them, apprenticeships as they grew, so they could learn a skill. Think it's too ambitious?"

I brushed the hair off her brow. "No, Fire. I think you can do whatever you set out to do. Your voice matters to us—to me—I look forward to hearing more of it."

"You are continually unexpected, Jonas Eriksson."

"Good. I hope you never grow tired of me being the same each day." I kissed her sweetly, but sobered. "Do you remember your mother and father at all?"

"Yes." Her jaw pulsed. "They died when I was six turns, but I remember their faces. My mother had pale hair, more golden than mine, and sea blue eyes. My father always carried me on his shoulders, insisting I could touch the stars if I reached high enough."

"Do you mind me asking how they died?"

Skadi's face fell. "They were simply dead one morning. We were treetop folk—the elven who live out in the wood, so I knew well enough how to trust the trees of Natthaven. I kept to the wood until King Eldirard found me two turns later using my mists to scavenge some food."

She cracked a few knuckles. Talk of her fallen parents bothered her.

I pressed a kiss to the slope of her neck. "I am sorry you lost them. It sounds like they loved you a great deal."

"I like to think they would've loved you."

"Of course they would've," I said. "What isn't there to love?"

"Who knows? Easiest thing I've ever done." Skadi laughed and kissed me.

I kept an easy expression, but my blood rushed to my head. I didn't think she realized what she said, but it struck me, a bolt through the chest with a truth I still didn't know how to explain: I was in love with my wife, and I had a bit of hope she felt the same.

CHAPTER 38
THE MIST THIEF

"He seems to be an amiable fae, My Lady." One of the maids of the palace grinned and finished adding a silver chain to my braided hair.

"He is." I peered out the bubbled glass window where Jonas was laughing with the stablemaster as he arranged supplies onto two charges. Dorsan was there preparing a handful of palace guards who would accompany us to the Night Market and Stärnskott. I looked back at the woman. "Although, he'll tell you he isn't a fae, he's an alver. Their magic impacts the body and mind."

She dipped her chin, grin still in place. "If you don't mind me saying, you seem . . . peaceful around the prince."

Peaceful. Another way for her to insinuate happiness without being too bold to assume.

I dabbed my lips in a touch of pink stain, a smile in the corner of my mouth. "I am. I'm fortunate to have such a match when so many arrangements prove to be unhappy."

Before my vows, I rarely spoke to any chambermaids. It was not out of my desire they kept quiet, but most dared not cross Cara or they feared me.

One day here and already Jonas's easy interactions with me had stirred the elven palace. When we were caught laughing or snickering in whispers to each other, odd looks came at first, but little by little trepidation cracked.

More servants added a smile when they greeted me, some looked at me with a new curiosity. Others, like this woman, even engaged in conversation.

"He's not terrible to look at if you don't mind me saying either, My Lady." Her eyes gleamed in a laugh.

I bit down on my lower lip. "No, he's not."

"That's enough, Madeline." Cara clapped her hands. "I will finish with the princess."

Madeline's face paled, but Cara's word was fiercer than mine, and she dipped her chin, practically fleeing the room.

Cara took up a thin cloak and hastily added it to my shoulders, face pinched.

"Something to say, Cara?" I tilted my head. "What have I done to be disappointing now?"

"That, for one." She huffed and placed her hands on her hips. "Speaking like you've no manners at all. I don't know what's gotten into you, My Lady."

I shrugged one shoulder, tying the cloak at the base of my throat. "In alver lands, I am encouraged to voice my thoughts."

"Yes, well, I understand they might be a little wilder of folk—"

"My favorite quality in them."

Cara pinched her lips. "I have worries for you, is all. So many turns you were in my care to guide and shape into an honorable lady, and I do not know what to think of this boldness. You were always such a meek girl."

Inside, I knew Cara's condescension wasn't truly a distaste for me. She, too, was raised to believe a royal elven lady ought to behave a certain way. But she did not understand the lands of the fae, nor the alver clans. Somewhere in her remarks was a fear that if I did not watch myself, they might turn me out, harm me, or worse.

I let my hand fall to her arm. "Cara, I wore many masks to comply here. Jonas has simply asked me to remove them. From the first nights in Klockglas, I was asked to speak freely, to be honest with him. He would prefer to know me, not the etiquette of me, so that is what I am doing. It hasn't made him indifferent to me, I assure you it has brought us closer."

Cara blinked, her hands wringing together. "You know from my missive that I don't . . . I don't want you to be returned to the Ljosalfar, Skadinia."

My face softened. The woman rarely spoke fears of her heart. "I won't. I am vowed to Jonas, and plan to remain vowed to him well into the Otherworld."

"I realize it is treasonous of me to speak poorly of Prince Arion, but after what he did here, after how he allowed that numbness to take you, well, I do not wish to see such a thing again."

Arion watched me fall into my affinity, shouted at me to not let the coldness take me, yet kept forcing my hand to do cruel acts on his behalf, all to keep my bespelled grandfather safe.

"It's not treasonous," I said softly. "I think much the same about the Ljosalfar prince." I offered Cara a small smile. "The alver folk do not fear my affinity. They've been teaching me a great deal how to control it so it does not overtake me."

She blew out a breath, the last of her hidden affection for me breaking through. "Good. That is good, My Lady. Oh, I nearly forgot." The woman reached into the pocket of the smock she kept over her dress and removed a parchment tied in a ribbon. "The king wanted you to have this. An heirloom of the royal house of the Dokkalfar clans."

Warmth bloomed in my chest as I unwrapped the silver chain. In the center was a circular charm with golden sparking stones. The stones were rare and difficult to mine. When they knocked together vibrant sparks glimmered like starlight.

Cara helped fasten the chain. "Fit for a future queen. This marks your ascension, My Lady."

I touched the charm, watching the gentle flashes of light shine. It was the first move that I was Eldirard's heir.

Cara cleared her throat and brushed the hem of my skirt. "Now, you'll be certain to keep your manners in the market, yes? Show your prince the same."

And like that, the old Cara returned.

I hid the few eye rolls, assured her we wouldn't become the downfall of Natthaven, and was finally allowed to abandon the bedchamber.

Grandfather insisted he was embroiled in negotiations in a new trade with King Gerard, so he would not join us to the market. It was familiar. Rarely did my grandfather and I spend leisure time together but for reading or a few meals.

The doors to the palace were open, letting in the pale sunlight and heat of the morning.

Before I stepped into the front drive, a broad figure filled the frame of the entrance. My heart dropped into the pit of my belly.

"Cian."

His eyes gleamed with unsettling malice, like he won a battle I didn't realize we'd been fighting. Cian had his hair tied behind his neck, and a new bronze medal pinned to his guard's cloak.

"Princess." He drew closer, a curl to his lip. "I hoped I might see you at some point during your return."

"Strange, I hoped for the opposite."

For a moment he looked taken back, a little stunned, but arrogance bled through soon enough. "You've grown some claws in these few weeks."

"They've always been there, my husband merely encourages me to use them. Stand aside, he is waiting for me."

The forgotten fear throttled my lungs like a vice, freezing breath, when Cian curled his grip around my arm. "Does he know about you? What you've done? Tell me, Princess, does he know about us?"

Apprehension prickled over my scalp. Simple words and the peace I managed to claim with Jonas Eriksson teetered on the edge of destruction.

"Does he not realize what a risk it is to sleep next to you?" Cian chuckled and traced the point of my ear. "I could offer your husband the same thing I offered Prince Arion. Don't you miss our lessons?"

"Get off me." I tried to yank my arm free of his hand.

Cian only tightened his grip. "You miss them because you know, Skadinia, you know what you are."

"You will remove your hands from the princess, Cian."

A cracked breath of relief sliced between my teeth. Dorsan stalked into the hall, and Cian released me at once. Higher in ranks, Dorsan could level Cian in warrior discipline.

"Forgive me." Cian pressed a hand to his heart in respect. "I was merely greeting our lady."

Dorsan stepped between us, ire in his eyes sharp as a broken blade. "Our Lady is vowed and your nearness is inappropriate. Take heed, I have witnessed the alver clans these last weeks, as powerful as you think you are, offending the prince and his house will be the last thing you want to do."

"Of course." Cian bowed again. "No offense meant. I will keep a proper distance in the future."

Dorsan gestured at me to leave the hall all while keeping his focus on Cian. "See that you do."

I did not wait for the end of their words and bolted into the sunlight.

"Wife!" Jonas raised his hands at the sight of me. "I've had the most intriguing conversation with Barclay, here. I had no idea your horses were trained to walk on such narrow forest paths and tread through swamp lan—oof."

Jonas grunted when I nearly leapt into his arms, squeezing his neck tightly.

"Skadi." He held me close. "What's wrong?"

I pulled back and kissed him. A few gasps at the sudden show of affection filtered through the servants around us.

Jonas's eyes were coated in a passionate glaze when I pulled away.

"I'm not complaining, Fire, but what was that for?"

"No reason," I said, voice soft. "Merely glad my vows were to you, Nightmare."

"Good hells, woman." He yanked my hips, fitting them against the hard planes of his body. "If you'd rather spend the days in our chamber, all you had to do was say so."

I snorted and pecked his lips. "I plan to do a great deal of all that, but I do want to show you some of Natthaven. You are now an heir here, after all. In fact, I am only the heir apparent because of you."

"Is it only the bloodline?" Jonas asked. "If you were born of Eldirard's house would you require a vow?"

"Not unless I desired one. Queens can rule among the elven folk if they are born of the royal house."

"I don't like it. I am not even elven, yet because I was born to a king and queen I have more claim than you on your throne."

"It does not matter to me, not since it is you. I have a voice with you, right?"

Jonas kissed me again, ignoring the second wave of gasps. "Always. In fact, perhaps I ought to start calling you My Queen now."

I accepted his hand to use as a boost onto one of the prepared horses. On the other side of the horse, Dorsan handed me the reins.

"Thank you, Dorsan." I spoke with meaning, one I hoped he understood.

He offered a curt nod. "Always, My Lady."

I turned back to Jonas. "Don't call me Queen. I prefer Fire."

The prince clambered on the stallion beside me, but leaned closer, speaking only for me. "I hope you have a scheme or two in your head on how we'll slip away from our entourage here. The idea of an audience while I shout that name in a more compromising position doesn't sit right with me."

My head fell back with a laugh. "Your mother would be ashamed to hear you speak."

"Wife, come now. You've met my mother and know she is partly to blame."

Despite its name, the Night Market was vibrant. Tucked in a wide clearing in the center of the wood, the market was littered in canopies of rich blue and gold and silver shaped tents and carts.

Jesters pranced about night after night, juggling pomes and knives, and bursting into tunes that encouraged spontaneous dancing.

Jonas was captivated by the owlery. Grand birds with wingspans nearly as wide as my arms perched on thick pegs in a domed tower. I laughed when four of the creatures flew to him instead, settling on his head and shoulders.

"Owls are rare in the fae realms, but my mother loves them," he told me. "I always tried to whittle them for her, since they're seen as good omens."

"Frigg told me of your woodworking talent."

Jonas laughed and paused at a cart with gold bangles and polished stone necklaces. "I doubt Frigg used the word talent. I tried. My daj is actually quite good with building things. He told me when he and Maj were still two unseen orphans, he wanted to apprentice with a carpenter near the docks."

"The king and queen are orphans?"

"They are."

"But she had her brothers, yes?" Bard and Queen Malin seemed close, and I knew their eldest brother was the consort to the Night Folk King's sister, their children shared cousins between the Ever Queen and the alver princes.

Jonas lifted one of the gold bangles, inspecting it. "Their family history is torn up through endless wars for the alver throne. My uncles were there, but no one knew they were truly related. Honestly, my uncles are my mother's cousins, but they all claim each other as siblings. My parents were littles who slept in a hayloft, working for their keep until life tossed them into the streets where it was thieve or die."

He selected four more bracelets, handing the shopkeeper some elven coin Grandfather left for us to use.

"But if they discovered she was the heir, then they must know their family line." I hooked my arm through his as we walked on.

"They do now. Whether Daj wants to admit it or not, he truly is from a noble bloodline. Sander and I are both named after our grandfathers who both died in old alver wars." Jonas flashed me a grin. "As I told you, your desires to help the littles in the realms will be well received."

We wove through the shops, pausing to purchase items here and there: a white iron knife for Sander, Von, and Prince Aleksi from the

Night Folk realms, some silks for Tova and Junius, new pig skin leather from elven hogs that could take properties from foliage—healing or poisons—and add it to whatever was placed in the skin. Jonas planned to gift them to Niklas.

The bangles were for his mother and the women he saw as sisters: Frigg, Livia, and Princess Mira.

"Think Bloodsinger would accept a gift?" He looked at a gold sphere used to gauge dangerous sea storms.

"I think Erik Bloodsinger pretends none of you matter to him save for the Ever Queen, but I saw his concern for you when we came here. I think he would grumble about it, then you would see it on his ship for every voyage."

Jonas laughed and pressed a kiss to my head. "You have him figured out, Fire." He looked to the shopkeeper. "I'll take it."

Later, when only a blood red sliver of sunlight still burned on the horizon, we made our way back to the wood. Elven guards kept in line behind Dorsan. Doubtless they were not keen to spend Stärnskott on duty with a princess they feared. In truth, I was not keen to spend Stärnskott with them.

Jonas wanted a scheme. I planned to give him one. "Dorsan. I think the prince would like to see the Underfalls."

Dorsan's features pinched and he looked to the sky. "Showers will begin soon. Do you not wish to go to the watch point, My Lady?"

"The path takes us straight through."

"But it is quite narrow, and we have the horses."

"I thought we could take it on foot, and you lead our charges to the watch point."

Dorsan gave me a look that hinted I was not fooling anyone. "You would be alone for a time."

"And we are often alone in Klockglas," I insisted. "Besides, as everyone seems to agree, we're both a little wild."

Jonas's eyes sparked with a familiar heat. "I stand with my wife's decision. Wherever she plans to take me, I wish to go."

Dorsan sighed. "As you wish, My Lady."

We passed over the reins to our horses and I took hold of Jonas's hand, leading him through a thick tangle of dark oaks until we came to a web of pathways—some were platforms draped with ropes in the trees, others cut across the bubble and steam of cooling swamplands.

"Tree houses." Jonas tilted his head back, gazing into the boulder thick limbs of the treetops.

Twinkling lights from small windows gave up the endless rows of huts and sod rooftops built into the trees.

"Treetop folk," I said. "This was where I was born. They hunt birds and use affinities to summon medicinal properties from forest herbs. These Dokkalfar know how to survive and how to speak to the magic of this isle."

"They are you." Jonas took hold of my hand. "That's what you mean. These people would see you as you."

I swallowed thickly. "I wish you weren't so perceptive at times, Nightmare."

He kissed my palm, and kept pace with me when the pathways tilted to rocky roads along a peak.

The spray of a nearby waterfall dampened my cheeks, sweet night air filled each breath. The road to the Underfalls was steep and jagged, but Jonas was a skilled climber. Perhaps better than me. He never slipped on loose rocks, or grunted if we hit a challenging ledge.

Jonas moved like a shadow, a man who could be seen or unseen as he desired.

A narrow cavity split into the mountainside. We were forced to turn to the side to squeeze through until the fissure widened into a bulbous cavern.

"Gods." Jonas took it in, lips parted.

The cavern had natural cracks and holes in the stone walls. On all sides streams of the falls spilled over the top of the cave. Some dripped inside, creating small pools, but most thrashed in violence over our heads, creating an illusion that we were encased in the waterfall.

With the sunset nearly finished, and the moon rising, the water shimmered like a thousand crystals. Blue and vibrant, there was a sort of magic in each drop.

"The Underfalls." I spun around, letting the spray mist my cheeks.

"Not many folk enjoy the trek here, so I would come here to read, or simply listen to the falls."

"This is amazing, Fire."

"This isn't my favorite part." I took his hand and led him deeper into the cavern until a giant oak split the rock. An arched opening in the trunk revealed its hollowness. I spun around, walking backward into the open tree trunk. "How are you at climbing trees?"

"A wonder."

"Don't know why I expected a different response."

"Me neither. I would think you'd realize by now, I am wondrous at most things."

I rolled my eyes and turned into the opening. The trunk was thick enough four men could stand shoulder to shoulder inside, and over the turns, I had fashioned small pegs into rungs along the sides. It made for an easier climb, but the damn air always left them slick with water.

At the top, Jonas leveraged out of the narrow opening, his broad shoulders proving trickier than my body. He scooted backward over the crooked floorboards. "What is this place?"

A few satin cushions filled one corner, some stacked books in another. There were quilts and furs, a few ropes that would lower makeshift shades or pop open a flap in the top, to let in the night sky.

"It's mine." A wash of nerves settled like stones in my belly. I'd never brought anyone here before. In truth, I wasn't certain anyone at the palace knew of it.

"Yours?"

"When I ran after my parents died, I found this tree. Far enough elven guards would not come, but not so far I wouldn't be able to forage or slip back to the market. There was an old couple—deep forest elves— who helped me lay the floor as a girl, and the rigging." I tugged on one rope. "They said they didn't care for me, but I found furs, knit gloves, and bread when frost seasons came."

Jonas took in the space with a new sort of reverence. "This is where you lived?"

I hugged my middle and looked around the tree house. "Yes. Even after I was crowned, I came here when I missed my mother and father, or when I felt too frightening for the palace."

"Why do folk fear you, Skadi?" He drew closer. "The king made you his, what is so fearsome about your affinity when you do not use it to harm your people? Your familial bonds do not allow it."

The truth was too horrid, too wretched.

I ran my thumb over his knuckles. "I think most of my people believe since my affinity is different and powerful, it cannot be trusted. In turn, *I* cannot be trusted and must be held at a distance."

Jonas shook his head. "They shouldn't fear your strength."

"Can you blame them? I can take anything, Jonas." My palm rubbed against his chest. "In fact, I can feel the magic of the oath you took, as though my affinity is reaching for the power. It was why you entered this alliance, true?"

Jonas swallowed. "I do feel compelled to protect the lands because of the magic of that oath, but I think there was a part of me that did not want you to be used by Arion."

I kissed the hinge of his jaw. "I can take it. You do not need to be compelled, you can fight simply from the loyalty you have in your heart."

"It is a powerful magic."

"And it holds no chance against my affinity." My palm flattened on his chest, the damp of my power coiled around my fingers. A burn was there, deep in his heart, a remnant of fierce magic.

Once, I thought he took the oath to do anything to protect the sea and earth fae because he craved glory, now I knew it was because of the beautiful heart in his chest.

"No." Jonas took hold of my wrist, his brow dropping to mine. "No leave it. I don't need it to fight for people I love, but . . . it brought me to you. For that, I will always want it."

Bleeding hells. I kissed his lips gently, pulling back my affinity when my hand dropped.

"The same as I do not fear the magic of the oath in my blood," he whispered. "I do not fear yours."

My insides coiled, hard and taut. "You have not seen how unstable my affinity can be when it overpowers me. I have trained tirelessly to never cause harm, but there is always a fear that it will not be enough."

"I'm not afraid of you, Skadi. I am in awe of you."

I clenched my eyes shut. "I think if you knew everything, you would not feel the same."

His fingertips brushed the side of my neck. "I might've once been frivolous with heartfelt things, but I know nothing would change what I feel about you, Wife."

The touch of his lips on the slope of my neck raced my pulse, but slowed my fears. Like my own magic, his touch swallowed them up, tossing them into the Nothing the longer he touched me, the more he kissed me.

Jonas slowly lifted my skirt up my legs. "How long until the guards send out a search for us?"

"I never intended to go to the watch point with so many others," I said through a rough rasp when his fingers curled around the inside of my thigh. "You wanted a scheme to be alone, this was my scheme."

Jonas paused, his fingers viciously close to my center. In the next breath, he drove into me with two fingertips, stealing my breath. "Woman, you are made for me."

My body quaked under his touch. Jonas covered my mouth with his palm when I cried out his name. "The last thing I want is this place filled with guards, thinking I'm killing you. Scream all you want in the palace."

We tumbled to the floor, clothes shredded in a frenzy. I pinned him beneath me, thighs on either side of his hips, and kissed the tender lines of his inked symbols.

Jonas let his eyes close, he gave up control, and allowed me to devour him. He let out a rough gasp when I aligned his cock to my core. I sank over him, agonizingly slow. Brow strained, he dug his fingertips into my hips, shifting with me every time I bucked on his length.

It was a stunning sight.

I took my time, adjusting to the fullness of him.

His verdant eyes locked with mine, reflected starlight burst in a green prism. One hand abandoned my waist and slid up the divots of my ribs until he palmed the whole of one breast.

I bowed my spine, pushing into his palm. Jonas pinched and tugged at my nipple, then fell into his own frenzy. He sat upright and took the other side between his lips, sucking and licking until the peak hardened.

I cried out his name when he rolled the tip between his teeth while his fingers worked the other. I rocked against him, gasping when he bucked his body, striking a new depth.

Heat pooled low in my belly.

My head fell back, his name cascading over my tongue again and again; my body shuddered through my release. Jonas locked on my features, watching my face soften. He held my hips in place and rolled his body against my center until he went taut as he spilled into me.

Spent and breathless, Jonas tucked a lock of hair behind my ear. "We didn't feel there was a choice at the beginning, Skadi. But every day since, you've become the best choice I will ever make. I will never stop choosing you."

I kissed him, deep, needy.

Flashes of white spilled over the small room. I looked up at the open flap in the top. "Stärnskott's beginning."

Jonas grunted—still sensitive from release—when I rolled off him, but settled the moment I curled into his side.

Overhead, endless showers of glistening silver cascaded across the sky, like an army of fiery ribbons falling toward the sea.

I tilted my gaze, watching him. There was a reverent sort of awe in his eyes as he took in the falling stars brightening the elven sky one after the other.

He chose me, and gods, I would never choose anyone else but him.

CHAPTER 39
THE NIGHTMARE PRINCE

THE FINAL DAY BEFORE WE WERE TO RETURN TO KLOCKGLAS WAS SPENT QUIETLY. We walked through the palace gardens, ate by a small creek that wove through the forest. Skadi showed me where part of the trees scorched with a fire Livia started during the start to the battles between elven and fae.

Already trees were shedding the blackened bark and deadened limbs in large chunks, like they knew how to heal their own wounds.

The king had sent a missive to his granddaughter, asking if she would care for a farewell feast. Irritation that the king could not find the time to speak to her personally was there, but kept trapped behind my teeth.

Skadi responded with a firm decline I quickly praised with a few lascivious touches.

Natthaven was fascinating and lovely. I took pride watching Skadi go on about her folk and the forest and the swamps, the light in her eyes always poured out when we were free from the confines of the palace.

In these walls, she was more somber, more reserved. Most of our time was spent in libraries or our bedchamber.

The looks she was given, the hushed whispers that followed her, I was keen to steal her away back to Klockglas early.

More and more it was clear to me, the Dokkalfar people were taught to fear their princess without truly speaking to her, and I didn't understand why.

Skadi peered out the nearby window. "Grandfather might insist we take a whole entourage to the sea tomorrow."

I closed the book in my lap and tapped Skadi's ankle with my toe. "Are you disappointed to be leaving?"

Skadi nestled closer to my side on the velvet sofa, twisting my hair around her fingers. "This was where I once lived, it is a palace, a house, but a house does not make a home." She hesitated. "It makes little sense, but I feel more at home in your cold, misty, devious alver lands than I ever did in this palace."

"My father will weep with joy when he learns you think his kingdom is devious." I laughed and kissed her quickly. "I am glad you feel like it is home, Fire. I hope you always do."

Before I could kiss her again, Dorsan entered the chamber. "Forgive the intrusion, but the king has summoned Prince Jonas. As agreed, each visit to the isle will conclude with a report on the alliance."

I let out a sigh. Part of me hoped the elven king might forget that part. I stood and squeezed Skadi's hand. "See you soon, Fire."

"Tell him what a remarkable wife I've been, Nightmare."

"Ah, then do not plan to see me for days. If I begin to announce your qualities, I will not be able to stop."

She snickered. "Such a bawdy mouth in one moment, then so sweet the next. I do not know what to do with you, Jonas Eriksson."

"Oh, you do, Wife." I paused at the door. "You have proven how well you handle me, night after night, after night, after—"

"Gods, go." She waved me away. "Dorsan is right there."

"Well, he will be the first to hear all my praise of you then."

I wasn't certain, but I thought the somber, infallible elven guard almost smiled.

At the bottom of the stairwell were two guards. One was the sod who always looked at Skadi like he should never be alone with her in the dark. The guard who subtly insulted her after the vows.

There was something wrong with him, an instinct, a tell in his eyes. I wasn't certain why, but I did not want him near my wife.

"He is never alone with her," I murmured to Dorsan. "Understand me?"

The guard nodded. "Cian will always have a fellow guard should he ever be assigned to the princess's chamber, but she will always be with Lady Cara if you are absent. I've already seen to it."

"Good man." I clapped Dorsan on the shoulder, not missing the way Cian watched us pass, like he might be thrilled to see my eyes fall from my skull.

Bastard.

At the king's study, Dorsan opened the door, and held his genuflect until I was inside the room.

Flames of a strange emerald and blue snapped in the inglenook. In these seas, this near the Ever Kingdom, fire gleamed in strange colors. Air was different, warmer, richer, but I had few doubts if Natthaven drew closer to Klockglas the flames would burn in gold and red.

The study was draped in fine white furs, black velvet curtains, and a wide mahogany desk with crystal inkwells and silver quills.

"Ah, Prince Jonas." Eldirard rose from behind a long desk carved to look like thick tree trunks. "Welcome. Please, sit."

Eldirard didn't stride, he floated. Shoulders back, spine in a straight line, I could not match the Dokkalfar king in his elegance.

When my parents made official declarations to our kingdom, Sander and I wrestled at their feet when we were small, then most ended with laughter and too much brän in taverns at the expense of the king if his people vowed not to make him do another appearance for at least two turns.

I was taught to feather step, like a thief in the shadows. Otherwise, I stalked, prowled, whatever it was, my steps were not floating.

Eldirard tossed the cloak from his shoulders, draping it over the back of a sofa, and went to a carafe of elven wine on a tray atop a small table. "Care for a drink?"

"No, thank you." I sat in the chair nearest the fire. "I learned during the vow feast, elven wine does not settle well in my head."

The king laughed, low and deep in his chest. "It is quite potent."

Eldirard took the seat across from me. The man showed most of his age in the corners of his eyes and forehead, but his face had a stern wisdom about it. Not old, but neither was he young. His body had the shape of a warrior once, but had gone trim and lean over the turns of peace.

For a long, aggravating pause, the king merely studied me over the trim of his glass as he drank.

"You seem much more at ease around Skadinia, Highness."

"Jonas, sire. Jonas will be fine." I matched where he placed his hand on his elven blade and rested a palm on the hilt of my own. "And yes, her company is easy to enjoy."

"So she is complying to your ways?"

"Gods, I hope not." I chuckled, but Eldirard didn't smile. I cleared my throat. "What I mean is I don't ask for compliance. I ask for sincerity; I ask for her to be her. That is the company I value—just her."

"I wasn't certain what to expect when I saw you again." The king swirled his dark wine. "But to see you and my granddaughter so cordial was a surprise."

The chair groaned when I leaned back. "Would you rather we detest each other?"

"I always prefer Skadinia to have few worries in her life. Although, I do think it will pain her for a time if this vow is recanted."

"Recanted?"

The door to the king's study opened again. Eldirard looked over my shoulder, face as stone. "Ah, Gerard. You've come to join us."

I spun around, ice in my veins, and met the pompous glare of King Gerard. Like Eldirard, the Ljosalfar king had silken hair, but the color of roasted chestnuts. His high, bony cheeks were lifted in a stupidly pious grin.

"Prince." Gerard tilted his head in a greeting.

What the hells was going on?

I didn't move, didn't look away. Never take an eye off your mark. Daj taught his sons long ago how to hold an enemy in sight, how to study them, how to mark them until weaknesses broke through the cracks.

Gerard held a sleek walking stick in his far hand—likely his dominant. He had no limp; the stick was for aesthetic or a weapon. He was confident, looked down his nose at me.

He underestimated me.

Any thought I could form on the king rolled in my head. "What is this, King Eldirard?"

Skadi's grandfather poured Gerard a flute of wine. "It is no secret Skadinia was once meant to unite the Dokkalfar and Ljosalfar clans."

"Yes," I said, casting a cautious look toward Gerard. "Until they attacked your palace and threatened to overrun the fae realms. Did you forget?"

Eldirard took another sip, chuckling.

So did Gerard.

The hair lifted on my arms.

King Gerard leaned onto his forearms on his knees. "You are a young prince. There are many court politics of elven clans that have been traditions since long before you were even a thought in this world."

I met his stare. "I do not need to be aged to know I signed an agreement with my blood that united the Dokkalfar with the alver clans. Eldirard agreed."

"I did." Skadi's grandfather returned his glass to the table and laced his fingers over his chest. "The legacy of being the first elven alliance with fae, it was more than I anticipated when Skadinia was found and brought to the palace." The king sighed with a touch of whimsy. "I wanted fae lands, I received them by this agreement, but there was always the option of an alliance of the two elven clans. I told you of the condition of choice."

"She has made her choice," I snapped.

"And I am glad for it." Eldirard gave me a look like I was a damn child. "Alas, I cannot deny the Ljosalfar not to attempt to reinstate the first alliance. Whichever way the Norns see fit to secure the legacy of House Naganeen, I must accept. Which is why I wanted to discuss whether you would be willing to sell your marital contract to King Gerard for his son? To simply avoid contention, of course. Don't mistake me, we will still be allies, but this way you will not be required to be vowed."

The king looked at me as though I ought to be gasping in awe. "Listen to me, King. I don't give a shit what legacy is left behind for your house if the price is Skadi. She is my wife, and not chattel to be sold. If you allow anything to interfere with our vows, you will not only lose your coveted alliance with fae realms, but we will destroy you. There will be no House Naganeen."

How could a man who had the opportunity to spend his days with Skadi think of her so callously? How could he not see that beautiful fire that burned in her eyes when her temper flared, when she laughed, when she teased?

King Gerard's lip curled. "You forget yourself, young prince."

"I do not. Your son's mistreatment of Skadi forfeited his right to even breathe near her." I looked at Eldirard. "Why are you allowing this?"

The king tilted his head. "I have no preference toward either alliance. Skadinia is welcome to choose, and you or the Crown Prince Arion are welcome to influence that choice. I would say you have a fine start since you are her husband."

I bared my teeth. "And I will never break my oath to her."

Gerard's eyes darkened. "She is elven and belongs with her folk. She will become a queen of worlds, and you will get your peace. You cannot tell me you love the woman after so short a time."

"I have no plans to tell you anything. Skadi is a queen of worlds as the alliance stands now. I am the heir to my kingdom, but she is now the heir apparent for the Dokkalfar." I shot a look to Eldirard, daring him to refute the truth of our vow. "The light elves would force her to use her affinity in ways she despises. With us, that will never be a concern for her, so piss off."

Gerard didn't deny it. "I suppose we will merely wait until the princess returns on her own accord, or you fail to meet the terms of the agreement and the vows are dissolved naturally."

"I will never give her reason to want to leave."

"But you have a cruelty about you, don't you, Prince?" The Ljosalfar king pinned me in a sneer. "It is only a matter of time before it forces your hand. I hoped it might've ended when poor Villi found his way to you. Unfortunate that the man sent himself to the gods."

It felt as though a dozen fists pummeled my ribs. "Villi? The elven poisoner?"

Eldirard frowned at Gerard. "He was mad, and that act was not sanctioned. It might've harmed my granddaughter."

"You sent one of your men to slaughter a royal household?" My blood felt heavy. Feverish.

"Of course not." Gerard waved the notion away like it was foolish. "Villi was always infatuated with my son. He took it upon himself to retrieve the princess he viewed as stolen from the Ljosalfar. It was simply that no one discouraged him. If you'd have killed him, well, this would already be ended."

Thoughts spun in a cobweb of hate and panic. I was clear-thinking, plotting the deaths of two kings, in one breath. In the next, I could not fashion the next moves.

Eldirard sighed. "I did not wish for such tensions."

"Then you should not have allowed him into your palace. You will need to kill me before I will ever let the Ljosalfar near Skadi."

"Take the land, Eldirard," Gerard said, voice low. "Then tell the girl to return. She's always listened to you."

"Skadinia must choose for herself." The Dokkalfar king sniffed. "So much was taken from her, it was my one demand—when it came to her future house, she would have a consideration."

"Then *strongly encourage* her as you always have. The girl lives to please you."

I was going to murder a king. "You underestimate her."

Gerard scoffed derisively and removed a long scroll. He pointed to intricate designs along the edges. "I suppose we'll leave her no choice and wait for you to destroy the alliance. Do you know how to read ancient elvish, Prince Jonas?"

The tips of my fingers went numb.

Gerard chuckled. "Our old language is clever and keeps the elven clans mysterious. Likely the reason most fae never knew of us. King

Eldirard knew the condition of the princess changing her desires within the first turn was a common clause and a possibility. He also knew of the savagery of fae. Naturally, he saw to it there were protections in this alliance, but written in elder elvish, words that can only be summoned by a king's touch."

The more Gerard held to the contract, the more filigreed words took shape along the edges.

Shit. The entire alliance had terms and conditions my mother had not read. Good hells, she didn't even know they were bleeding words.

Written plainly were causes for dissolution of the vows if any terms were disobeyed in the first turn of the union: no elven—Ljosalfar or Dokkalfar—could be harmed by our hand. If Skadi chose to leave to re-enter her original betrothal with Arion; her desire would take precedence. If she left, the Dokkalfar would still claim a portion of the alver kingdom. Doubtless a way for Eldirard to get his damn legacy of united elven clans and fae connections.

Unwittingly, I'd signed away portions of our lands in blood and gave way for the Ljosalfar to continue manipulating Skadi without repercussions.

"You said nothing of this when I signed," I snapped at Eldirard.

"I was required to give any opportunity to *see* the terms. As I recall, your father refused my offer to read, to even touch the scroll, after your mother."

Skadi would need to forgive me, I was going to kill the man who raised her. "Tell me, King Eldirard, did you have these additional conditions written in elvish because you heard things about my father? There is no possibility this is only a coincidence."

The Dokkalfar king shrugged. "I did not wish to cause any alarm or misgivings. A clause of land transfer is common, Prince Jonas. But we did not yet know each other to gauge reactions, and I did not want it to seem like this was underhanded. Perhaps a few whispers from the sea fae palace—I believe your house is close with the Ever Queen—gave me the idea when it was suggested the alver king could not read."

"He can read, you bastard." I'd always been viciously defensive of my father's struggle with the written word.

"It does not matter." Gerard's mouth curled into a cruel sneer. "The opportunity was given. Had a king held the contract and read it long enough, the words would have been summoned. Perhaps, you should've thought to insist the alliance be written completely in common tongue."

I shot to my feet. "She is my wife and she always will be."

Gerard's cold eyes flashed. "It might not be your decision. Skadinia was once fond of my son, and I believe he is making amends as we speak. Odds are they will soon be paired, so it would make for simpler transitions if she did not hold any frivolous resentments."

Dammit.

I reeled on Eldirard. "Arion is here? After everything he did, what sort of man are you?"

"A king, *Prince.*" Eldirard frowned. "A king who has been securing his peoples' futures since a girl with a strange and powerful affinity was discovered."

I was done listening to these bastards. In three strides, I was at the door.

One hand on the latch, the door half opened, and Eldirard stopped me. "Prince Jonas, this was not meant to be malicious, but I fear you have misread it all."

"I have misread nothing. Your selfishness reigns beautifully over your care for your granddaughter."

"I want Skadinia to have a choice should she no longer find solace in your lands, that is all." The king hesitated. "Still, if you see this as a betrayal, I ought to let you know, you may wish to send word to your people, perhaps to the savage sea folk, but you cannot. There are wards around the isle for the week you are here. Then you may scream and hate all you desire, but it will not change what you signed with your blood."

I looked over my shoulder, jaw tight enough I was convinced my teeth would shatter.

Eldirard softened his features. "Do not fret, young prince. If she reconnects with Arion, you will still have an alliance with elven clans. Her affinity would still not harm your people."

I'd walked the lot of us into a wretched lie. "I'll never give her a reason to desire that light elven bastard. One turn, then your hooks have no power over us. One turn and you will come to regret allowing them back into her presence."

Eldirard stood. "Whatever you think of me, I do want what is best for Skadinia."

"You want what is best for you." Throat tight, I spoke through the grit. "You've always seen her as a woman to strengthen your power, haven't you? If you had taken even a moment to see who she is inside, to see her eyes light up when she reads folktales, or when she laughs, then you would know you were in the presence of the most beautiful heart."

For a moment his stony exterior cracked, there was almost a glimmer of remorse, there and gone. "If you will not see reason, then remember yourself here. Harm an elven—especially a prince—and Skadinia does not leave here with you."

My shoulders heaved, the room dimmed as my eyes blackened. I faced the two kings, enjoying how they flinched at the sight of my mesmer. "We have a saying amongst our clans when someone has wronged us: you have been marked, Kings, and we never lose sight of our marks."

Without another word, I darted from the room straight into Dorsan's chest.

"Prince Jonas." He dipped his head.

I nudged him forward. "Hurry, you sod. Skadi has need of us."

CHAPTER 40
THE MIST THIEF

Cara would not stop fussing over my choice of travel attire, insisting it would be quite impressive to my in-laws should I arrive looking more regal, and not like a passenger off a barge.

I mused to myself, my mother and father-in-law would be more impressed if I found a way to win a pouch of coin off Nightseer without him realizing he'd been duped.

"Cara." I sealed one of the laces on my satchel and faced the woman. "I do hope you'll try to come see me in alver lands. Perhaps then, you might understand what life is like in the Black Palace."

She tightened her mouth as she always did, but buried beneath it all was the slightest hint of a grin. The woman knew she was a little ridiculous, but I thought the week with Jonas, his affection toward me, his questions about her life, her folk, her interests, had begun to soften her rigid heart.

A knock came to the door. Cara nearly swatted my shoulder, stopping me in my tracks before I dared answer the door first.

Gods, it would be welcome to return to days where folk did not take note of every damn step I took.

"Hello, Skadinia."

My heart froze.

I could not draw in a deep enough breath. Slow, like my heels were rusted hinges on a weathered door, I faced the doorway.

Arion.

His face was handsome and sharp in his features. Crimson stubble coated his chin more than it had when he'd overtaken the palace months ago, when he forced me to use my affinity for his benefit, when he threatened to kill my grandfather when he knew the battle was lost to the fae.

His presence was made worse when Cian appeared at his back and closed the door behind them.

Cara kept quiet, occasionally casting me stern looks, mute commands for me to keep my manners. All I wanted to do was run.

"Nothing to say?" Arion approached and reached out one hand, like he might tuck a lock of hair behind my ear.

I jerked my head away.

His grin faltered. "It shouldn't be this way between us. We've known each other so long, *chridhe.*"

I winced. Gods, how I hated his endearment, spoken as though I mattered. It added ice to my veins, so different than the way *Fire* sent my heart spinning when spoken from Jonas's lips.

"You should've thought of how I might view you when you kept me as your prisoner here and forced me into the dark."

Cian clucked, circling around the prince until he managed to crowd me from behind before I could move away. His hands went to my shoulders, holding me still between him and Arion.

Beneath his touch my skin prickled like hundreds of creeping legs crawled under my flesh.

"Did you learn nothing from all our lessons, Princess?" Cian tilted his head closer. "If you did not control your darkness, then the blame falls to you. It shows what you are in the core of your soul."

I squeezed my eyes, trembling, and shook him away. "Do not touch me."

Cara took hold of my arm, drawing me nearer, and stared at Cian with her sharp disapproval. "It *is* indecent." She faced Arion. "My Lord, perhaps you would be better suited to speak to My Lady with her husband present."

"Yes, please do. Perhaps he will cut out your tongue so I do not get blood on my dress!"

"*Skadinia*," Cara chided under her breath.

Arion returned a look of annoyance. "Be reasonable. It has been long enough, and it is time for bygones to be bygones."

The door creaked. "I would be careful what demands you give my wife, you son of a bitch."

My heart jumped. Jonas, eyes dark as fear, leaned one shoulder against the frame of the door.

His breaths were coming too swiftly, his skin too flushed. No. *No.* I tried to get him to break his darkened stare and look to me. His mesmer was growing too strong.

Arion sniffed, holding Jonas's gaze. "You made a poor move by interloping on a long-held betrothal, alver."

"Oh, I made a perfect move." Jonas stepped in front of Arion, nearly a full head taller than the Ljosalfar prince. "Best move I've ever taken. The way I see it, little one"—Jonas chuckled at his own name for the prince—"you are the one who destroyed everything when you thought you could threaten the fae folk and my wife."

Arion puffed his chest. "Enjoy calling her yours. I imagine you've just come from the council of kings and have learned it is only a matter of time before she's nothing but a memory."

What the hells did that mean? I looked over Arion's shoulder, holding Jonas's mesmer-filled gaze.

"Leave us." Jonas said, voice a dark threat.

"I wasn't finished speaking to Skadinia."

"You are. You've bothered my wife and I don't take kindly to that."

"You can't touch me." Arion butted his chest against Jonas.

Jonas lowered his voice, grinning. "Would you like to see the damage I can do without touching you?"

For the first time Arion hesitated.

"My Lady's husband has asked for their privacy." Cara waved her hands, as though shooing the prince and Cian away.

Arion tugged on his blue doublet, mouth tight. "We're not finished with this, Skadinia."

"You are." Jonas stepped between us. "You look like you want to run me through. Go ahead and try. I might not touch you, but there is nothing stating Skadi can't. In fact, she deserves to swallow you up."

Something had gone horribly wrong. Jonas was not a man to shy away from following through on a threat. He was not a man who would merely take an attack against him.

There was a reason he had not drawn his blade.

I straightened my shoulders, summoning the icy damp across my palms.

Arion's eyes widened when the mists coiled between my fingers like diaphanous ribbons. The mists followed my hand when I slid my palm over Jonas's shoulder and tucked close into his side.

Disdain flashed in Arion's eyes, a bit of his true character, and in a flurry he turned and strode from the corridor.

When Cian strode past, he leaned in, the heat of his breath against my ear at a sly angle I wasn't even certain Jonas realized drew him so near. "You smell as perfect as I remember."

Jonas turned and yanked me behind his back. "I will offer one final warning—speak to my wife, touch my wife, come near my wife, and you will not wake the next morning. No contract will stop me."

Cian sneered. "Ah. With a husband like you, I expect to see our princess returned soon enough."

The end of a spear clapped on the floorboards. "Cian. Tend to your royal charge and step back from mine." Dorsan's knuckles stretched white when he tightened his grip on his spear.

"I was just leaving." Cian sauntered down the hall, utterly at ease, and I didn't know why.

Without another word, Jonas demanded Cara leave and Dorsan remain in the corridor, then slammed the door behind us. In the next instant, he clutched me against his chest, his arms choking the breath from my lungs in his embrace.

My fingernails dug into his back, like he might be torn from my arms any moment. "What's happened?"

Jonas tucked his face against my neck, breathing me in. "They'll try to take you from me, Skadi. I won't let them."

"Jonas, look at me." I took hold of his face, forcing him to lift his head. The inky black of his eyes hadn't faded. Truth be told, it seemed to swallow any hint of light in the room. His skin was flushed, heated, and I could not tell if he was going to collapse or attack. "Your mesmer is taking you."

I hurried him into the small wash suite connected to the bedchamber and sat him on the edge of a smaller stone basin than we had in the Black Palace. I made quick work of soaking a linen in cool water in a wooden bowl and placing the cloth on the back of his neck.

He hunched over his knees, but his fingers took hold of the skirt of my dress, like he needed to ensure he had a hold on me.

I lowered to my knees, nudging my way between his thighs, and hugged his head to my shoulder. "What happened?"

It took a moment for him to speak. "We've been played. I pride myself on being able to spot a scheme, but I didn't spot this. None of us did. I failed you, put you at risk, and I can't bleeding think straight. Why is it so damn hot in here?"

He wasn't making sense.

I dabbed another cloth over his brow. "Tell me what my grandfather said."

By the time Jonas's slow, raspy words retold the whole of the interaction, I wished I never asked.

Betrayal was a blade between the ribs, a burning ache I could feel to my bones. My grandfather agreed to Jonas's request while still allowing the light elven to play their games against us.

"This is my fear," Jonas said weakly. His forehead still rested on my shoulder. "A vision of you being taken from me, and I cannot reach you, I can't stop it."

"No." I took hold of his face, urging him to look at me. The green of his eyes was more like slate gray as mesmer faded. "I don't care what they say, do you hear me? Damn a contract, damn the alliance, you are mine, Jonas Eriksson, and I will fight to keep you."

His mouth twitched in a smile that looked more like a wince. "When she is the woman you want beside you on a battlefield, you'll know."

I tilted my head. "What does that mean?"

"The last bit of advice I was given before our vows. You are the woman I want fighting beside me. I suppose that means I know."

My knuckles brushed over his stubbled cheek. "Know what?"

"I'm in love with you." Jonas pressed his forehead to mine. "I do not hold you on the surface of my heart, you are in the deepest pieces where I keep my worst fears. To lose you would mean facing pain so wretched it would destroy me. I would not survive it. Even if I was still breathing, I would no longer be me, and instead would become a cruel, violent, hopeless shell of the man I was."

Tears burned behind my eyes. I kissed him tenderly, slowly, patiently. My lips were wet and cheeks salty by the time I pulled away. "You promised to unravel me, but you've woven yourself into every strand of my soul. I will never love anyone the way I love you. I am yours and that is an honor I will always fight to keep."

Jonas blinked, clearing away the last surge of his magic. "What do we do, Skadi?"

I slipped my arms around his waist, holding him tightly. "We carry on. Our vows are not something they can take away, and we will not give them a reason."

"My folk will want to retaliate. They don't take well to being played."

A bit of beautiful violence dug into my heart. "Then let them when a turn is spent. When we are still vowed at this time next turn, no one can touch us, and I will look forward to the grandest scheme the Kryv can dream up."

Finally, Jonas laughed. It was soft, a little empty, but there all the same. "Look out, Wife. I think we've gone and corrupted you."

"I expect more of your kind of corruption."

I kissed him until he kissed me back, until his fears were put to rest, and his familiar, beautiful viciousness returned to the gleam of his eyes.

CHAPTER 41
THE MIST THIEF

WE WERE AT THE DOCKS BEFORE THE MISTS OF DAWN FADED INTO THE TREES. The palace was quiet and sleepy when we made our way through the trees and waited for Nightseer to arrive by the first light.

Dorsan had seen to it a few servants would be awake to help us carry our packs, so Jonas and I took several to keep our departure quiet. Even Cara still slept. I left her a note of farewell.

My heart had been split in two. The man I thought cherished me was willing to stand aside and allow a cruel prince to use me and entrap me. To Eldirard, I remained a political pawn, and it sent my mind into an endless spiral of wondering if he ever loved me.

"There he is." Jonas nodded toward the thrashing tides in the distance.

The sloop's bow ripped through the surface of the sea, bobbing in the surf until it righted again, and small figures of Nightseer's crew shuffled over the deck.

I blew out a breath of relief. We could be free for a few weeks. Already, we had determined no less than a dozen alvers would join us on our forced return trip, perhaps several sea fae; my folk seemed to still hold a touch of fear for Bloodsinger and his people.

Jonas took hold of my hand and walked toward the end of the dock.

"Skadinia." The king strode briskly from the trees, more disheveled than normal. He wore a simple tunic, no doublet or gambeson, and his circlet was not atop his head. Behind him, royal guards formed a line.

Jonas searched my features, as though waiting for a sign regarding what I wanted to do. I rose up on my toes and kissed him, then faced the water as Nightseer sailed alongside the dock.

"Skadinia," Eldirard tried once more. "You will bid a proper farewell."

I didn't turn around and accepted Nightseer's hand onto the deck.

"Thank you," I said with a nod. "I'd like to leave with haste if possible."

The old sea fae watched the elven king with a bit of trepidation. "At your word, elven lady."

Jonas and Dorsan joined me on deck. There was nothing but unbending loyalty written on my husband's features. He didn't tell me to face my home, didn't look over his shoulder. Where my eyes were aimed, so too, were his.

"Nightseer." Jonas handed the sea fae a folded piece of parchment. "After we've returned home, will you bring this to your king and queen? I've included all the praise for your service at the end."

Nightseer took the parchment greedily. "Aye. Many thanks, dark prince. Many thanks."

Jonas glanced at me. "Felt the sea fae ought to be on their guard."

Violence was brewing in the air, and I wasn't certain a whole turn would pass before blood spilled between elven and fae again.

"Skadinia, look at me." The king moved in the corner of my gaze, striding out on the dock. His voice lowered. "Granddaughter."

My chin trembled. Jonas took my hand and offered a gentle squeeze. I didn't turn around. Nightseer shouted for his crew to catch the wind and take us below the tides.

"This was always for your future, your kingdom," Eldirard shouted, but when I did not turn, the last word was a soft, half-broken, "Please."

I closed my eyes, letting my head fall to Jonas's shoulder when he held me against his side, bracing as the sea tumbled over the deck, drawing us out of the far seas, taking us home.

This was the dreariest I'd witnessed the Black Palace great hall.

The center table was lined with men and women who looked less concerned, and more murderous. The king slouched in the far seat, flicking a knife back and forth in his grip, eyes shadowed as much as his son's.

Ash kept sharpening the curved blade of a curious knife with a hole at the end of the hilt. The rest of the Kryv were equally locked in furious rage. Tova rocked a sleeping Kåre with a strange collision of motherly comfort and bloodlust in her cat eyes.

Kase stood at long last. "This falls on me."

"Daj," Jonas started, but stopped when his father held up a hand.

"It's true, but it's done. No sense wasting breath blaming ourselves. We do what we always do, keep sight of our mark, and we watch their backs." The king pointed toward us. "They will try to sabotage you."

"Why do you say that?" I tightened my hold on Jonas's hand.

"If Jonas retold the tale as it was, they said repeatedly it was only a matter of time before he failed. I urge you to be on your guard."

Gods, a sickening burn turned my insides. If the elven clans succeeded, the alvers would lose their lands they'd fought for long before this alliance.

"Stop it." The king's rough rasp broke my spiraling thoughts.

I faced my father-in-law. "Stop what?"

"Stop being afraid that we're only worried for our kingdom. It's not going anywhere, and that is the least of our concerns."

"Is that what she's fretting over?" Raum chuckled in the back of the room. "Ack, as if anyone could actually steal this land from us. Rather arrogant thinking, if you ask me."

Malin stood next to her husband. "I will send word to the other kingdoms and inform them of the intentions of the elven clans."

"I already sent word to Bloodsinger," Jonas said.

"Foolish, Jo." Sander scrubbed his hands down his face. "Erik is just waiting for a reason to lose his damn mind and slaughter Arion. He could piss crooked and the Ever King would use it as a call to war."

Jonas waved the thought away. "He has Livia to keep him grounded now."

Sander's brows raised, gaze pinned on the floor. "I don't know, I think some of the king's wickedness has twisted up our sweet Livie. She might join him."

A few chuckles rippled through the hall.

Malin approached us, placing a hand on each of our shoulders. "Keep a wary eye, we'll play their games for now. But they will lose in the end."

A week after letters were sent across the kingdoms, days grew calmer with each sunrise. Some mornings, when I woke curled tightly in Jonas's arms, I would forget the truth for a moment.

I'd forget my grandfather loved me more for what I could be for Natthaven—a threat to enemies—and not for the heart in my chest.

I'd forget Arion emerged from his exile, set to take back what he lost.

I'd forget the secrets I still kept from a husband I never planned on loving so fiercely.

It was good to forget. To pretend all was well, it left me time to laugh with the Kryv when we sparred on the field. It left me time to work with Von on ideas for young ones across the realms. I even received a missive from the wife of the Night Folk First Knight in the North. She wanted to meet when Jonas next visited Rave camps to hear ideas about apprenticeships for older children, and books or writing lessons for the littles.

Von and I spoke enough it landed me next to his shoulder, pretending all was well, watching the staff in the cooking rooms.

"This is your chance." I nudged his ribs. "She's alone."

He blew out a long breath, raking his fingers through his short hair. "She's busy. I don't want to distract her."

Brunhild was a gentle beauty. Long hair the color of autumn that reached her waist. Features that were soft but radiant, and a voice that was calm as a summer morning. I wasn't certain the woman knew how to speak louder than a heightened whisper.

"You are being an utter coward." I pinched his arm.

He swatted at my hand. "Watch yourself, Princess. I live with the Falkyns, you might find your bath salts replaced with boil powders."

"Coward."

"I am not."

I fiddled with one of the silver rings on my center finger. "Does it smell a little cowardly in here?"

"Gods. I'm damn glad you're Jonas's pest." In a huff of frustration, Von stalked toward the stone oven where Brunhild crouched, inspecting a platter of oat cakes.

I covered my mouth to muffle my laugh when Von ungracefully announced himself, startling poor Brunhild, and nearly toppling her into the soot-soaked hearth.

Unintentionally, she was entangled in his arms when he caught her. I considered it a success.

To pretend, meant I spent days folding silks and satins with Frigg for her mother's shop, snickering about the princes or trading gowns.

Pretending left plenty of time to lose myself in my library, though I was rarely alone. Most days, Sander would read in a chair, trading questions about my elven lore while I would ask about the fae tales.

I pretended there was no need for unease until I found Jonas sitting on the edge of our bed after the sun faded on the ninth evening, a missive clutched in his hands.

"What is it?"

"The first attempt." He handed me the letter, then pressed his fists against his mouth, staring at the wall.

Skadinia,

I hope you will do me the honor of considering my words.

To the alver prince, you will always be a threat before a wife. We, too, were arranged, but we have known each other most of our lives, does that count for nothing? Do you not recall the warm months riding together, swimming in the falls? We were friends, Skadinia.

I am regretful how the attempt to secure my throne impacted you, and I hope you can forgive me.

I hope you'll consider the idea of returning to your own people and choosing me. If you do, I will let you help the young houses like you always wanted. I will elevate your first familial name to nobility.

Don't forget, the alver prince does not really know you. Not like I do, and after knowing it all, I still want you.

Can he say the same?

—Arion

I crumpled the note in my hands, fury, fear, a bit of violence, collided in a tangle of barbs in my chest.

Jonas pulled me onto his lap and buried his face in the crook of my neck, kissing me there. "You are not a threat at all, Fire. I hope you know that."

"I know. Arion is not who I want, Nightmare. Close, but not quite. I did swoon a bit when he told me he would let me help the young houses." Jonas chuckled against my skin. "Oh, and this part, how he would elevate my familial name to nobility. My parents would wail in the Otherworld. They were treetop folk, the land was their palace."

He laughed a little more and kissed my shoulder. "On the day of our vows, my father told me you were my choice, no matter what brought us together, by taking vows I was making you my choice. He was right." Jonas tilted my face toward him. "I will choose you every day, Wife."

Each word pierced my heart. He needed to know the truth. Arion was right about one thing—Jonas did not know everything about me.

I traced the line of his jaw with my fingertips. "There is something I must tell you."

The chance to tell the most wretched of truths was robbed by the door bursting open and Sander shoving into the room. "Jonas. Oh. Sorry to interrupt, but I thought you should know we're being invaded."

CHAPTER 42
THE MIST THIEF

SANDER SPOKE TRUE. WHEN WE REACHED THE FRONT HALL, IT WAS CLEAR THE Black Palace had been invaded by a few more royal faces.

"Mir. Alek." Jonas laughed and hooked an arm around Prince Aleksi's neck. He moved onto Princess Mira next. The two royals were surrounded by Kryv, and travel satchels were strewn about their feet. "What brings you here? I thought you were in the Ever, Mira."

The princess was dressed in a simple woolen gown for traveling, but a dainty black circlet was braided into her hair.

"I certainly was, but we came to see what in the hells is going on with the alver clans." Her eyes cut back and forth to my hand clasped with Jonas's, then to our faces. "Skadi, so good to see you again. I was told things might look a little different here. You and I will need to speak soon. Alone."

"Want every detail of me, Mir?" Jonas said. "I don't blame you."

She snorted. "I'd like to know the husband side from a wife's perspective. You'll be terribly biased about your own attributes."

At her back the Ever King's cousin stepped into the hall. A blue head scarf wrapped around his brow, and silver rings pierced in his ears, somber as always.

"Heartwalker." Jonas clasped forearms with the man. "Didn't expect you."

"King's order."

"I sense bitterness."

"Oh, he's absolutely wretched." Mira's grin faded.

"Gods, don't get her started," Aleksi mumbled and went to speak with Von and some of the Kryv.

"Oh, please, get me started." Mira reeled on us, a frown curving her full lips. "He's a bleeding child, going on and on about how put out he is being required to escort me."

"I can't imagine Heartwalker as a man who laments outwardly, Mir." Sander said, greeting the sea fae.

"He complains in thought. I can see it in his eyes."

When Jonas stepped aside to speak with Aleksi and Tait about the journey, Mira took hold of my hand, pulling me into an alcove.

"Let's speak. You'll need to forgive my murmurings about my reluctant escort," she said, tossing a lock of hair from her eyes. "Erik finds it humorous to put his cousin as my escort since Tait Hearttalker is the only soul in all the realms who does not like me."

"Could it be that you have not learned his name?" I leaned against the wall. "Isn't it Heartwalker?"

"I know his *given* name, I simply like the one I've bestowed him with much more." Mira flourished one hand. "There are always reasons for my actions, but I never give up my secrets."

"Understood."

A demure smirk played with Mira's painted lips. "So, tell me. Are you truly happy? There wasn't really a worry the alvers wouldn't draw you in, it's what they do." Mira paused. "But I'm curious about your thoughts."

I hugged my middle. "Do you ask for me, or for Jonas?"

The princess glanced to a small, round table pressed against the back of the nook. She lifted a crooked wooden horse Jonas told me he'd whittled for his mother when he was seven turns.

She tapped the misaligned hooves. "Both. I never bothered worrying that Jonas would be a cruel husband, he wouldn't be capable of it, but he does guard his heart. And, perhaps I am wrong, you learned to do much the same."

Apprehension burdened the bright shades of her amber eyes, as though Mira anticipated the worst, as though she were bracing for the pain that would strike her own heart.

Before the vows, I found the closeness between the heirs of the fae realms rather odd. It was true, Arion often spent part of the warm months in Natthaven, and I visited Grynstad with my grandfather during the frosts, but his missive painted our youth as more friendly than it was.

Talk rarely drifted away from chatter of the kingdoms. I could not recall a time when Arion willingly asked me my thoughts. The only reason he knew I had a distaste for young houses was because I merely said so when we passed one on Grynstad.

If memory served me, the Ljosalfar prince mocked my naivety on such things.

I held Mira's stare. "The notion of not being vowed with Jonas Eriksson has become my nightmare. I know how to guard my heart, but not around him. I love him, Princess."

A grin split over her lips, wide and bright. With care she returned the horse, then wrapped me in a throttling embrace. "I knew it. By the hells, the *tension* in both your eyes during the vows was stunning. Ask Livia, I said it was a matter of time before Jonas was utterly lost to you."

"I assure you, it was as much of a surprise to me."

Mira took hold of my hand. "When he loves, it is unconditionally. I've always hoped he would find someone who did the same for him; I am glad he has you."

A separate door opened on the other side of the corridor. The king and queen entered to Mira's shrieks of delight.

"Pardon me." The princess shot a glare toward Tait Heartwalker. "I have others who've missed me, and I them."

"I am not keeping you," he muttered in reply.

I rejoined the others, watching her go, as Jonas leaned into Tait. "What brings you here, really?"

The man took out a tin of paper smokes and rolled one in his fingers.

"Nightseer delivered your note. The queen was going to write until the princess received a missive from her folk during her visit, stating the elven have grown hostile. We met Prince Aleksi on the way and he reported the same. If it is nothing, I'm to ferry the damn princess home because my bleeding cousin finds it entertaining."

I swallowed to keep a laugh inside. Irritation laced each word, but I wasn't certain he was irritated by the fae princess, more by his own reactions for when she was near.

Jonas clapped Tait's shoulder. "There are tensions, but we have them in our sights. We are watching our backs."

The sea fae lit the end of his smoke and drew in a long pull. "Is it anything the Ever should be aware of, Prince?"

"Not yet." Jonas watched Mira embrace his mother, the Kryv, Frigg, then squeeze the king until a smile cracked over his face. "But I wanted everyone to be ready in the event it is."

"You know how the Ever King and Queen feel about you."

"Trust me, I will never be one to shy away from calling in a favor from Bloodsinger."

Mira shrieked, drawing our attention across the hall. "But we *must* celebrate."

"No." The king looked pale.

The princess blew out her lips and shooed him away. "We're all here and we must celebrate the day you were born, Uncle Kase."

Malin snickered behind a palm when the king's eyes darkened to inky black.

He pointed at the princess. "Sometimes you're too much like your father."

"You know he'll preen for that, and since you adore me, he will finally know he has nestled deep in your heart."

Kase closed his eyes. "No balls, no masques."

"A revel? A festival? Musicians?"

"No."

Mira huffed. "A feast. Allow me a feast."

The king paused for a moment. "Fine, one feast. Nothing more, girl.

None of your gold ribbons. Nothing"—he waved his hands, trying to find the word—"shimmery."

Mira tilted her head to one side. "I wouldn't dream of it."

CHAPTER 43
THE NIGHTMARE PRINCE

WHILE MIRA RECRUITED THE WHOLE OF THE PALACE—SKADI INCLUDED—IN plotting against my father and his reluctance for revels, I spent much of the morning in town. Alone, but not truly. The prickle of eyes followed me through the market square, down alleys and through arcades.

More proof the guards of the Black Palace were as sly as the thieves who ruled there. Since our return from Natthaven, they were on edge and watching with more ferocity. Always waiting for a new elven attack.

When I made my way back to where I'd kept my horse before the noon toll, I tipped my chin to one man standing in an arched alley, a hood pulled low, a hand on a black steel seax.

"They're waiting for you, Prince."

"They? This afternoon was only supposed to be the princess and me."

From this angle, I could only make out the smirk on the guard's face under his cowl. "What else do you expect? We're all watching your back, Jonas."

With a groan, I settled over my gelding and made quick work returning to the palace.

On the front drive was a line of more horses packed with satchels of jerky and Ylva's brown rolls.

Skadi was surrounded by my fellow heirs and a few other faces. Hair pulled high and tight, blue satin ribbons tied around her tresses. More glimmer powders on her cheeks, no mistake thanks to Mira.

"What are you lot doing?"

Skadi peeked around the neck of Mira's pale horse. It wasn't only Mira with the aggravating idea of interrupting an afternoon alone with me and my wife. Von, Frigg, Sander, Aleksi, and even Tait were preparing their own charges.

"You really think your parents want you wandering the wood alone?" Aleksi kicked a leg over a black mare. He looked too Rave, too warrior—sword on his hip, and a dagger sheathed on the small of his back.

"I thought I would get an afternoon introducing my wife to Felstad before we're bombarded by the hordes Mira will bring."

"Dramatic, Jonas." Mira tossed her long hair over her shoulder. "I invited a reasonable amount of folk. And don't be sour. You can bed Skadi in the trees later. We don't want anything to happen to you. How awful it is that you have folk who care."

I narrowed my eyes, but led the gelding to where Skadi waited. She leaned into me when I slid off the furs on the horse.

"Mira has a point," she said, kissing the hinge of my jaw. "You were gone long enough, I had all manner of dreary thoughts running through my head."

"I was properly surrounded by blades, Fire. No need to worry. What I am more concerned about are all my salacious plans will now need to wait for tonight."

She tugged on my belt, grinning. "I've no doubt you'll make up for it."

"Best prepare yourself, Wife."

"Jonas Eriksson!" Mira shouted. "If you wish to go, we must leave now or we will be late for the revel."

I helped Skadi onto the horse, glancing at Tait who nervously handled his own charge. "Heartwalker, you've been talked into joining, I see."

There were no horses in the Ever Kingdom, rather strange, horse-like creatures that handled the tides as well as the land.

He glared our way. "I must, seeing as I am the damn escort for her. These beasts are horrendous, by the way."

Mira turned over her shoulder. "The offer to share a horse still stands, Hearttalker. You seem to be struggling."

He glowered. "I'll manage."

Sander kept watch on Tait while I positioned behind Skadi. "I hope you'll be more willing to share a horse, Princess."

"So long as you promise to behave those hands."

I leveraged behind her, my arms caging her between them when I took the reins. I kissed her shoulder. "Never."

"You should."

"I refuse."

"What if I say so?"

"I'll refrain." I paused. "Until I change your mind."

"Doubtful."

A grin spread over my lips. "Trying to get the last word, Fire?"

Skadi hesitated. "Perhaps."

I nudged the horse into a slow trot, laughing. "I wish you luck."

Skadi reached her hands overhead, running her fingers through drapes of willow limbs that opened to a corridor of thick aspens and ever-greens. "This place reminds me of the wood back home."

"Jagged Grove is where vagabonds once lived during wars."

"The Kryv?"

I nodded. "Borders have changed since the earth realms united, but this place is where my mother and father first became a king and queen of thieves."

A few paces ahead of us, Frigg and Sander sang an old folk song, laughing when they went off tune. Von took in the quiet of the grove, occasionally glancing to the west side of the trees with Aleksi.

Mira had grown somber since Heartwalker's charge seemed content to walk alongside hers. It was strange to see these trees as a mere wood. Too many ghosts of fae wars lived here, each with a tale that impacted each one of us.

I wanted Skadi to be part of it now too.

Tall, jagged walls of dark stone broke through the branches. Overgrown with tangles of vines and spindly trees, the ruins had few intact floors and towers, but enough the levels would not crumble should we enter.

"We're here." I kicked a leg over the horse and took hold of Skadi's waist, guiding her down.

I drew her close, planting a heavy kiss on her mouth. She grinned against my lips, arms around my neck, fingers in my hair.

I didn't understand how it was possible, but I was convinced I would never tire of her touch.

"Is this how it's going to be with you two the rest of my life?" Sander frowned.

"It is not my fault," I said. "It is a compulsion to touch her at this point."

Aleksi clambered up on a broken pillar, looking back in the direction of the Black Palace. "If borders were still the same, I think I was found somewhere in that direction. Daj told me it was in a briar shrub."

Skadi's eyes widened. "You were found?"

Aleksi winked. "Abandoned during the wars that won Kase and Malin their crown. I have two fathers, Princess, so no natural littles for them. But the Norns knew what they were doing that day. They took me home to the North, gave me a crown, sort of like your story."

Skadi's eyes brightened and she stared in the same direction, perhaps finding another thread of connection to the folk who mattered most to me, to this place.

This was exactly what I wanted, for her to know she belonged with us.

The others took their own way into the familiar ruins; I led Skadi through an arched doorway that was still intact. "This is Felstad. The first palace, we call it."

A small forest had taken root in the main courtyard of the ruins. Dark walls speared through ferns and trees in levels, like broken teeth of open jaws.

"Your folk lived here?"

"It was the Kryv's haven even before my mother and father were reunited." I helped her over a ledge into the main courtyard. "Daj was taken captive for his mesmer as a boy. They were apart for turns before Maj found him again. Now it's damn near impossible to separate them."

Skadi smiled. "I think it's romantic, never tiring of your lover."

I paused for half a breath, overtaken with the truth—Skadi was the first thought of my mornings and the last of my nights. For the first time, I could see the desire for one heart lasting long after the gods took me to the Otherworld.

I guided us up a set of spiral steps. The staircase opened to a floor overlooking the whole of the ruins. I leveraged onto the edge, letting my legs dangle over the side, Skadi did the same.

Through the cracked and empty corridors voices of the others filtered through the ruins. They would all converge here eventually.

"Felstad wasn't always a joyful place," I admitted. "During the war that earned my parents the throne, their enemies trapped littles here. Von was one of the captives. It was the first time sea fae and earth fae collided, actually."

Tait stood close, inspecting one of the old archways. "Wait, what did you say? This was where he . . ."

I nodded, knowing what he was asking. "The reason the sea fae came to our shores was because Bloodsinger was captured as a tiny boy. He was tortured here."

"Dammit." Tait took in the walls with a new horrible reverence. "I didn't know it was still standing. Has Erik ever returned here?"

"No." I lowered my chin, ashamed for the pain that corrupted the walls of this place. "I think it's why the Ever King avoids our kingdom more than others."

"I didn't know that story," Skadi whispered.

I took hold of her hand. "It is more proof that enemies can become something more, Fire. Bloodsinger once despised us for the pains of his past, but sea fae are found in every kingdom now. They do not hold the past against us, the way we do not hold it against them. I hope you know it is the same for elven folk."

Skadi scooted a little closer, seeming to understand my underlying reasons for bringing her here.

"Speak for yourself, Prince." Heartwalker drew another one of his smokes, but never lit the end. "I still hold everything against you lot."

Skadi snickered. "Yes. Especially Mira."

Tait blanched, and I nearly toppled off the damn ledge from laughing at his back when he stormed away.

"This was a place of pain, and love, and strength. I wanted you to see it because I want you to know, you are part of Klockglas and this clan. Your heart was betrayed, and I want to spill blood for it." I gingerly took one of her hands between mine. "This place is where outcasts became family. If you feel like you have no place, you do with me. You will belong with me, Skadi."

She took my face between her palms, eyes glassy. With her lips over mine, Skadi whispered, "You are the one I would have beside me on the battlefield, Nightmare."

My blood heated. I kissed her slowly. "I love you too, Wife."

We would not be broken, not by games of the elven. Bonds fastened the day I vowed to this woman were too fierce, too rooted in something stronger than any alliance, to ever be torn free. I believed it to my soul.

CHAPTER 44
THE NIGHTMARE PRINCE

MIRA BETRAYED THE KING AS WE ALL KNEW SHE WOULD. EVEN DAJ KNEW IT. The great hall was draped in black and red satin, and curious elixirs supplied by Elixists speckled the rafters and walls with glowing powders that left the hall looking like it had been painted in gold dust.

A crowd surrounded the feast on the table, even if most of the seats were empty. I didn't know if it was living his early turns always on guard with the fear of being snatched for his mesmer, but Daj never did sit long. He perched on the edge of the table, a horn in his hand, laughing with Bard and Aleksi.

My mother stood in front of her place, back to the table, chatting with Lady Shelba about the approaching birth of hers and Ash's little.

Frigg's father tipped on the back two legs of his chair, ankles crossed on the table, an herb smoke between his teeth. Folk would feast by plucking food off platters and moving on to chatter with someone nearby.

It was unorganized in some ways, but wholly familiar. Our halls were packed with the vagabonds my mother and father had collected over the turns. Laughter, taunts, a few spinning couples dancing to the beat of drums, they all were the sounds and sights of my childhood.

One was new, but had become my favorite sight of all.

I leaned against the table, flicking a small knife back and forth in my hand and watched Skadi spin across the hall with little Kåre on her toes. The boy was in love. It was written all over his face whenever Skadi held tightly under his shoulders and spun them around so her skirt billowed out and swallowed him up, then left him wobbling with a dizzy head.

Aleksi tipped a horn to his lips, mimicking my stance. "Never thought I'd see you this way."

"I held that same belief more than anyone."

"It looks good on you." Alek hesitated. "Sander might've let some of your recent . . . confrontations slip."

"And once again my brother proves he has the biggest mouth of us all."

Aleksi chuckled. "Intimidating an elven guard right after the vows?"

"Meet that elven guard and you'll understand. He's an ass."

"Torturing a tavern patron in front of everyone."

"Who thought he had some sort of claim on my drunk wife."

"You marked two elven kings with a threat, Jonas."

I shook my head. "No, I didn't, Alek. Honestly, do you know me at all? Retaliation for breaking Skadi's heart was a promise."

"You're being watched." Aleksi took another drink. "Be patient and calm, or they will use it against you."

I knew this. The constant prickle of unseen eyes watching our every move had not left since we returned from Natthaven.

A wicked sort of darkness had burrowed into my blood, drawing out violent thoughts, a lust for pain and agony I only saw in nightmares. For Skadi, I would enter the terror I kept in my dreams, I'd become the creature lurking in the dark if they forced my hand. No remorse, no regrets.

"I'm being cautious."

"Good." He set his drinking horn on the table. Aleksi gripped my shoulder before he walked away to join the revelry. "But, of course, you know that if caution is forced to turn into something a bit bloodier, I will stand at your side."

This was the reason I loved my folk so damn much.

Across the hall, I caught sight of Oldun.

The woman hugged her middle, a look of fright on her face. Since our confrontation, she'd been cold toward Skadi, and the fault rested on me. Too many turns had been spent taking lovers without much care for their hearts and jealousies.

What was she doing now?

Oldun had never been a lover, but she was one of the few I denied. When I looked again, she was gone.

Arms wrapped around my waist from behind, tearing my focus away from the crowd. "You look a little murderous over here. Not a good look at a celebration of your father, Nightmare."

I returned a grin to my face and pressed a kiss to the top of Skadi's head. "I was just thinking as much as I love my father, I'd like to be alone with my wife."

A pretty little flush pinked the tips of her ears. She traced the lines of my palm, drawing a step closer. "I don't think the king and queen would miss us. In fact, I think your father is searching for the exit now that your mother gave him his gift at last. I do think I'm missing some meaning about it though."

I glanced over her head to where my father was currently, unashamedly, devouring my mother. I no longer flinched at the sight— it was a constant in this palace—but on the table was a stuffed horse.

Inge was explaining to Mira how my mother had slipped out to her shop twice a week for the last months, learning how to make the most intricate of stitches. It added a wash of heat to my chest.

Good hells, if I could be half the lover to my wife that my parents were to each other, it would be a life well-loved.

I tugged Skadi against my side. "The horse is a memory from their childhood, one that was destroyed by those who tried to destroy them. I assure you, it symbolizes more to my father than any coin or any title."

As anticipated, my father tried to end the revel by briskly stating it was simply over. Those who wanted to drink and laugh and feast ignored the king and waved him away.

I dipped my lips to Skadi's ear. "Ready to go?"

She drew in a shudder of a breath when my palm drew scandalously high on her ribs. "I was ready long ago."

In our corridor, I pressed her against the door to my side of the bedchamber. "We should take out the wall, Fire. Do we need separate rooms?" I dragged the tip of my tongue along the edge of her ear.

Skadi blew out a rough breath, shaking her head. "Tomorrow. I'll steal it away."

"Will it bring down the whole palace?"

"I'll try not to."

I laughed and kissed the corner of her mouth, unlatching the door and shoving us inside.

Skadi's breaths grew heavier with each kiss. "You vowed to make up for our stolen moments alone in the wood. I hope you plan to make good on that, Husband."

I didn't need to hear another word. My palms clasped her face and crushed her mouth to mine.

I yanked at the laces on the back of her dress, sliding it off her shoulders. Skadi ripped my belt free with enough force the leather whipped my wrist on its way to the ground. She wriggled free of her gown, only a diaphanous shift underneath. In a frenzy, she shoved my trousers down and had her warm, cruel hands stroking my cock in the next breath.

Her back slammed into the wall. Beside her face, my palms flattened. I kissed her, bit her bottom lip, her neck, rocking against her hand until I was damn-near panting into her mouth.

Next to us was my desk. I cast a glance at the made bed, then back to the wood surface. Gods, no time.

I spun Skadi around, her hips striking the edge of the desk. My palms skirted around her front, cupping her breasts. She whimpered when I tugged the shift down and pinched and rolled her nipples between my fingers.

She bucked into me.

"Bend for me, Fire." I pressed her onto the table, breasts flattening over the wood.

Skadi gasped, her fingers digging into the surface when I rolled up the skirt of her shift and used my knee to spread her thighs. I gripped my cock, aligning the tip with her soaked entrance, stroking back and forth, nudging in, then pulling back out.

Skadi turned her head, her cheek along the tabletop, lips parted as harsh, pitchy breaths heated her cheeks. "Please."

"Please what?" I pressed a kiss to her spine. "What do you want, Fire?"

Again, I nudged the tip of my length inside her, only to pull it away.

Skadi hissed in frustration. "Jonas . . ."

"Words, Wife." I gripped her hair, arching her neck slightly, and took one of the rings pierced in her ear between my teeth.

"Damn you," she cried out. "I want you inside me. *Now*."

I kept one hand tangled in her hair, the other on her hip, and thrust inside in one fierce motion.

Skadi sobbed my name, a sound I would never tire of no matter how many centuries I lived. There was nothing slow, nothing calm about this. I bucked and pounded into her hard. The desk legs scooted along the floorboards with each push.

Skadi cried out, sitting back into me, knees weakening. Her fingernails dug into the wood top, seeking something to hold to as I leveraged one of her knees onto the edge, opening a new angle.

"Jonas, too much." She gasped. "It's . . . it's . . . don't stop."

I was frenzied. Sweat dripped onto my lashes. Fire burned in my veins, pooling low in my gut. Another thrust and Skadi fell apart. She writhed and trembled, her cries shattering the quiet of the room.

Before she caught her breath, I quickened my pace, head lost in a fog.

My heart felt as though it might snap free of my ribs and spill out on the table, bloodied and hers for the taking. My release came in a rush. I couldn't see straight. Hot, endless streams spilled into her. Both legs felt like they might buckle; I braced on the table's edge until the haze in my mind lifted enough to keep upright.

With care, I eased out, helping her off the table, and took her in my arms.

"I can't . . . breathe," she said against my chest.

All I could manage was a nod. Words were too difficult to gather in the moment. I pressed a kiss to her hair. She smelled of sweet spice, and me, and us.

It took a few more moments of standing there, half-naked and sated, before we managed to stagger to the bed. Skadi folded her dress from where it was tossed on the ground while I readjusted the table back into order.

I tugged my trousers back on, but hesitated before taking off my tunic. There was a pathetic piece of me that thought she might think it too much.

"You going to sleep standing up?" Skadi had the quilt tucked over her nose, and her eyes sparkled over the hem.

I let out a rough breath and stripped my tunic.

"Are you wounded?" As expected, Skadi sat up at once. She took a match stick and lit the candle on the bedside table. Her fingers covered the cloth bandage over my heart. "Jonas, what happened?"

"Nothing. While I was out this morning, I visited the inkist."

Skadi let out a gasp. "You got another one. May I see it?"

Jaw tight, I peeled off the cloth, wincing when some of the irritated skin pinched and split.

Skadi looked to me, then back to the design. Gingerly, her fingers touched the area around the new tattoo. "A flame?"

I pressed a kiss to her palm. "It's you."

What I knew of Skadi, I expected her to flush, perhaps grin with a bit of shyness, but I did not anticipate her kiss knocking the air from my lungs.

She kissed me, destroyed me was more like it, as though she might never get another taste. With swift movements, Skadi leveraged over my hips. "I would vow with you again and again, Jonas."

I would never get enough. She was branded on me, not only on the surface, Skadi was imprinted on my damn soul, and I never wanted to be rid of her.

I ought to have known the stronger we grew, the fiercer others would want to tear her away.

CHAPTER 45
THE NIGHTMARE PRINCE

THE WOMAN DID NOT KNOW HOW TO SLEEP AFTER DAWN.

I sighed, my cock already stiff, when she trailed slow kisses along the new flame over my chest, her fingers teasing the edges of my hips. "Woman. Do you ever take joy in sleeping?"

"Not when there is a washbasin large enough for two and not when my husband looks like you."

I chuckled and draped one arm over my eyes. "You make a fine argument."

She rolled out of the bed and covered her shoulders with her satin robe, pecking my cheek. "I'll get the water ready."

"Not at a boil this time."

"I'll settle for a simmer."

"You will cook me alive, Wife."

"I'll make it worth it."

I peeked out from beneath my arm. "I'll hold you to that."

Skadi squeaked in surprise, flashing me a heated stare, when I made an attempt to swat her backside before she disappeared behind the washbasin door. The woman had already arranged for heated buckets before I even woke.

With a bit of reluctance, I slipped out of bed, unthreading the laces

336

on the thin trousers I wore during the night.

"Prince Jonas."

I spun toward the bedroom door. My blood went cold. "Oldun? What the hells are you doing in my chamber?"

The woman trembled, holding another steaming bucket of water. She looked small when she placed it on the ground and removed a pigskin pouch from the pocket of her smock. Thin, linen gloves coated her hands and her fingers shook as she unlaced the pouch. "I knew you were in here, but . . . I'm sorry, My Prince."

There was something wrong here. I took a step back. "You need to leave, Oldun."

"I'm doing this to protect you." Her voice cracked. "They need to take her back."

For such a waif of a woman, Oldun moved like a spark catching flame. She ran at me, a handful of the powder in her palm, ready to toss at me, perhaps shove it down my throat. I dodged, but some of the dusky powder struck my face.

I wiped it away, waiting for a burn or bite of pain.

Nothing came but a bit of haze in my head.

Oldun steadied on her feet quickly and scooped some more. Tears dripped onto her cheeks. "You'll understand in the morning. It is for your good."

"Don't." Gods, I could hardly stand straight. There were moments of exhaustion that left me desperate to crawl into bed and sleep for the better part of a month. But my mind was alive enough to know there was no reason I should be feeling so sleep-deprived now.

But for the unknown elixir on my damn face.

I held up a hand. "I will make you pay, Oldun. I swear it."

She sniffled. "I'm sorry. It's for our folk, for you. I hope you'll come to realize it someday."

Oldun cried out, but the sound was swallowed in a cloud of damp, cold mists. Darkness devoured the woman until her look of terror faded into nothing but a swarm of stormy billows overhead.

"Skadi." I steadied myself with one palm on the wall.

In the doorway of the washroom, my fire held out her palms, a look of vibrant rage written on her beautiful face. The only thing missing was the glow of her eyes.

"Skadi." Her name came out in a rough rasp. "Don't fall into it."

"She tried to hurt you." My wife spoke with an eerie calm. "I have never felt such a rage before."

Wretched feelings—pain, greed, hate—it did something to Skadi's affinity, it pulled her fire into darkness. I started to assure her I was fine, but whatever was ebbing through my blood drained strength with each breath.

"Jonas! Skadi! We heard a scream."

Thank the gods.

Mira, clad in a thin night dress, shoved into our corridor. Aleksi was at her back, then Sander.

Dorsan, with a raised spear was tucked amongst them, but his attention landed on his princess and the swirling mists around her palms.

The endless flow of people kept stuffing inside our corridor. My mother and father were more like my wife, and always rose with the dawn. Daj was already dressed in his typical black, and my mother had a dagger in her hand.

If I was not lost in some bespelled exhaustion, if Skadi had not stolen a woman into her mists in anger and was fading from me, I might've embraced them all.

No questions, and every damn soul in this palace was ready to attack for our sakes.

"She needs to let her go." I fumbled the words, but pointed at Skadi. "Oldun . . . came here . . . I don't know."

"Another woman came to you?" Mira's mouth dropped. She looked from me, shirtless, to Skadi in a silky shift, then to the mists of her affinity still coiling near the washroom. My friend's smile was nothing short of wicked when she looked back at Skadi. "I'm *obsessed* with her."

"Mira." Sander nudged her.

"It isn't only men who wish to kill when the one they love is touched." Mira shrugged one shoulder. "Keep your hands off her husband."

"What is wrong with you?" I was almost certain the voice belonged to Heartwalker, I couldn't see him, but the way Mira snarled in the direction of the voice was proof enough.

Sander came to my side. "What happened to you?"

"Oldun threw something on me." I looked at my wife. "Skadi, let her go. We need to know why."

"She hurt you." Her flat expression found me, she blinked, like she might be recognizing me for the first time.

My mother worked her way into my room and placed a hand on my fire's arm. "Let me speak with her. I'll see it all."

In other words, Maj would take the entire memory of whatever motivated Oldun to come into my chamber.

Another breath, another heartbeat, then Skadi's eyes flickered and she closed a fist.

With a scream Oldun fell in a heap in the corridor. Frenzied, she swiped at her arms, as though the mists were still creeping along her flesh. She wailed and screamed again when she caught sight of Skadi so near.

"Don't touch me! You're . . . wretched and a creature of the hells."

I was going to kill her.

Oldun backed into the shins of Aleksi. My fellow prince sneered down and took hold of her arms, hoisting Oldun to her feet as my mother approached. "Queen Malin. You must listen to—"

"Did you try to kill my son?"

"What?" Oldun's eyes jumped to me, then back to the queen. "No. I-I-I tried to save him. From her." She pointed at Skadi. "She kills and doesn't even know she does it. He told me all about her."

"Who told you?"

Skadi hugged her middle, brow strained.

"I-I didn't learn his name. But he knew things about her. She's vicious, and dark, and a monster. She killed her own parents. Stole their life away as they slept."

No. That wasn't possible. If my mother did not throttle Oldun soon, I would.

At my first step, Sander pushed back on my shoulder. He jerked his head toward Skadi.

Dammit. Her eyes looked more like a somber storm, gray and dull. She backed out of the bedchamber, toward the staircase leading to her library. She was fading from me, she was slipping into the mask of frigid apathy the longer Oldun shouted fears and disdain.

"He told me if she no longer wanted the prince, she would leave." Oldun slumped so Aleksi had to brace her weight to keep her upright. "He told me if I could give the prince the tonic, put him into a sleep, I could make it seem as though he'd chosen me, and she would leave us."

"You went too far, Oldun." The corridor darkened with a flood of my own mesmer shading my eyes. "I've slept beside her for weeks."

Oldun looked stunned. "I-I-I didn't know."

"Because you have *no right* to know what goes on with me and *my wife*." My voice boomed against the walls.

My mother cleared her throat and stepped in front of me, likely trying to prevent bloodshed. "Oldun Aela, you will submit the memory to me, then we will decide your punishment from there. Until then, you will spend your time in the cells under the palace."

"My Queen, please." Oldun was handed to some of the inner guards. "I only wanted to protect the prince."

Her pleas were found wanting. There were few moments when my mother and father showed their regal side, but I was grateful for it now. Daj, in all his untamed rage, shouted for the woman to be taken at once to the cells below and for the rest of the guard staff to start hunting whoever gave Oldun the powder.

"Jonas." Mira dropped a hand to my arm. "Are you steadier?"

I raked my fingers through my hair, nodding. The fog was leaving my skull little by little. Whatever the elixir was, it wasn't enough to hold long.

"Good." Mira pointed me toward the staircase. "Because your wife has fled."

Dammit. I took the stairs two at a time.

"Prince Jonas."

"Dorsan." I wheeled on the man. "I am ready to kill the next person who tries to stop me."

"Understood, My Lord." He propped his boot on the step up. "You should know, what the woman said, well, it is a belief on Natthaven. It is why the princess has been so sheltered."

"You mean shackled." My lip curled. "None of you will ever know how *breathtaking* she is since her people never try to see her. You think one thing for all time about her magic, and it brands her as this . . . this frightening woman. But you don't really know anything about her power."

"Prince—"

"No. None of you ever take the time to see her." My shoulders rose in harsh breaths. "She's a woman who loves too much spice in her icing. A woman whose skin should be boiled off her bones by now for how hot she takes her bath water. Did you know she wakes with the sun all to read in the dawn's light? I pretend to be asleep because I don't want to disturb my favorite part, when she hums along with morning bird tunes."

I laughed, a little delirious. "I don't think she even realizes she does it. You lot don't bleeding see that she would risk her own life to protect all of you, even though what she receives in return is fear and apprehension."

I shook my head in a bit of disgust and turned to finish the journey to the library.

Dorsan gripped my arm. The mask of marble over his straight features cracked. "I agree with you on all counts. I protected the princess out of duty and a belief she had the ability to kill many if she desired. But I have seen *her*, as you say, since we arrived here. I was coming to tell you, I think the coldness might not last if you are there. I have never seen her more alive than with you, Prince. Pull her back."

With a curt nod, I rushed to the library, determined to do just that.

CHAPTER 46
THE MIST THIEF

THERE WAS COMFORT IN THE COLD. RELIEF FROM A FEVERISH PAIN. I REACHED for it, wanted it, but kept spinning back in a strange panic. My fingertips touched the smooth spines of books, the stained shelves he built, the crystal chandelier that reminded me of Stärnskott.

Jonas had done so much—too much.

Another wave of cold draped over my shoulders.

My chin trembled. He deserved more than all this. From the moment he took on his elven wife, the prince's existence had been a torrent of mortification, troubles for his beloved family, now attacks in his own chambers.

In front of the window, the night was a velvet drape of black. Of nothing.

Old thoughts—cruel and dark—slipped into the forefront of my mind. What if I fell into the cold entirely? What if I wrapped myself in the mists and simply faded?

The theory was there, falling so far into the coldness I could not escape the Nothing.

Would it be such a horrid choice? From my youngest turns, wherever I stepped it seemed destruction and pain and heartache followed.

Elven clans were divided because Arion's war—at the heart—was about claiming the mists that could swallow his enemies.

My affinity was why the elven wanted to stand against the fae again. I was the reason Jonas never had a chance at a love of his choosing.

"Skadi."

His voice was silk against my skin. I closed my eyes for a breath and faced him. Did he know how beautiful he was? The ink symbols of his large heart on his bare chest, his wild, tousled hair, those brilliant eyes.

I let the cold pull me back a little more.

"No." Jonas crossed the library, hands cupping my jaw. "You stay with me, Fire. Don't hide, not from me."

"You should fear me."

"I don't." Jonas still held my face, he pressed a kiss to my cheek, my brow. "I don't, Skadi."

"Foolish of you."

"Stop it. Look at me." With a gentle shake, Jonas urged my gaze to meet his. "Stay here, with me."

His hands were so warm, his eyes so inviting. But what replaced the cold ached like a molten blade cutting through my heart.

I pulled away, pulse racing. "Let me go, Jonas. It is safer for everyone. Please, let me fade until it is like I was never here."

"Like you were never part of my life?" His voice croaked. "It's too damn late. You are my life."

I felt every heated word, but spoke like the coldness held me prisoner. "You have the means to forget me."

Jonas looked at me like he battled on whether he needed to kiss me or shout at me. "I don't want to forget you."

Damn him, what the hells was wrong with the man? He could be free of me, he wouldn't have to sleep with one eye open now that he knew the truth.

The mask of ice shattered. "All the things she said are true. You are not safe with me. Already there is someone seeing to it you are harmed in your own walls. Alver lands are at risk, and you are vowed to the monster who destroyed the only people who loved her."

Jonas lunged for me, caging me against the wall. He consumed me with his weight, holding me steady. "You have not destroyed the only people who love you, Fire. I love you. I love you to the point of pain." He placed my open palm over his rapid heart. "Let me in, Skadi."

Emotion pinched my face. Jonas never let me go, only occasionally swiping tears off my cheeks.

"I tried, Nightmare. I tried so hard not to be something dangerous and frightening. I loved . . . I loved my mother and father, and I took them without even realizing. It was more powerful than kinship bonds!"

"But didn't you tell me they were dead beside you? Wouldn't your mists have taken their bodies?"

At that, I paused, but soon shook my head. "I stole the breath from their lungs, likely lost to a dream. It wasn't intentional, but my affinity is unstable, Jonas. That is what I've been trying to tell you all this time."

Jonas's jaw went taut, but he didn't interrupt.

"For what I had done, I thought the king would take my head after he found me. But he told me it was an accident, he told me he would help me tame the darkness. He gave me a new home. I thought maybe it was a gift from the gods, a chance to be something new. When the betrothal to Arion was arranged, I wanted to please both clans so desperately."

I stepped out of Jonas's embrace.

"He said everything right until he had my foolish heart in his hands." My fingernails dug into the meat of my palms. "I thought I'd found my hero, like I read in my ridiculous books."

"Arion?" Jonas tried to take my hand again, but I began pacing without an answer.

"I spent every night with him," I said. "He was so gentle, so kind, and I didn't see the ruse until it was too late."

"Skadi, I don't understand what you're talking about."

My words wouldn't stop, rambling over my tongue in a frenzy I'd never admitted to anyone before. "When I confessed I wanted to please him, he told me the dark power was still too much a piece of me and I needed to learn how to be rid of it before I could be a wife. So, he gave me to another who was willing to show me how I could bleed out the darkness."

Jonas stopped his approach. "You cannot remove magic from the blood, Skadi."

"I know that now." My voice trembled. "But when each lesson was over, he told me everything I wanted to hear. My heart was so bleeding weak, I started to think I loved him more than the prince. When I confessed, he said if I kept to his lessons, he would love me back."

With trembling fingers, I tugged at my dress, showing one of the swirling coils of ink over a scar. "So, I did. I tried, night after night, bleeding out."

"*Fire.*" Jonas's eyes were dark with hate when he looked at the tattoo. "That bastard."

I turned away when my husband reached for me, the prickle of wretched hands reborn on my skin, the cruel words clashing in my ears.

I clenched my eyes shut. "They both started to watch, always telling me to go deeper, to try harder. Only when they thought it was enough would one of them touch me. One said it was to teach me how to please a husband, for the prince it was his way of insisting I know what brought him pleasure. I actually thought I was fortunate two different men wanted my heart. In reality, they both just enjoyed causing pain."

Jonas drew in a sharp breath through his nose, once, twice, then pulled me close again. His thumb brushed over one of the coils of ink. "These are from your own hand."

My knees went weak, but I nodded. "No one did it to me."

"Gods, Skadi, yes they did. You were manipulated into thinking there was something so horrible about you that you needed to bleed it out. Don't you see how wrong that was?"

"Yes. When I started to recognize it would never be enough, I dared ask my grandfather if such a practice would ever prove successful. He was horrified, demanded I never attempt such a thing, but didn't know I already had. It is why I covered them in something that was beautiful to me."

Jonas's eyes darkened, but I didn't think it was his mesmer. "So this was Arion?"

I held his stare. "Some of it. He was the one who sent me to learn how to be a good wife for him."

Muscles worked on both sides of his jaw. "I'll kill him."

"You can't." I reached for his arm. "Promise me. You cannot touch him or any elven, remember? I will not have him be the reason something else was destroyed."

It took him a moment to speak. "If he ever shows his face near you again, I do not give a damn about any condition on a piece of parchment. His head will be mounted on that wall." The prince pointed to where fae battle tomes were stacked. "The perfect place."

"I simply want to forget him."

"Good. He will be forgotten when he is dead. Did you ever tell Eldirard the truth of how he was hurting you?"

I shook my head. "I was ashamed, and Arion was a prince of blood. I was a princess of selection."

To reveal Arion's true heart felt as though a heavy stone had been lifted off my bent spine. He took everything from me, and left me bloodied and broken in the end.

"Who else knew of this?" Jonas stepped closer. "You said they."

"Cian." I lifted my chin. "It was Cian's idea to bleed the darkness out. He is Arion's guard when the prince visits Natthaven, but also his wretched friend. He said he could teach me how to please the prince, but it was all part of their twisted ways of humiliating me."

"You shall have matching heads on your wall."

"Jonas, no matter what happened, it does not change the truth that my affinity killed beyond my control in the past. Perhaps it is better to keep a distance; I would never forgive myself if I hurt you."

"You won't."

"You don't know that!" A sob broke free.

"I do." He took me in his arms; together we slid to the floor. I settled between his legs, my head cradled under his chin. Jonas rubbed a hand across my back. "You are not my kin, you've become a part of my soul, and no magic is more powerful than that."

"Your sweet words are appreciated, but they are your hopes. You don't know."

Jonas kissed me with a new kind of tenderness. "Fine. How about this—if you try to steal my life away, I vow to fight back with my tongue here." My wretched prince dipped his head, kissing my throat, the tip of his tongue running along my pulse point. "Or here." His thumb grazed over the front of one nipple beneath the thin silk shift.

"Jonas." I pressed my forehead to his, breaths rough.

"Or here, Fire." Over my skirt, his fingertips teased my slit, then pulled away. "Until I have pulled you from the mists and you are back with me."

I swallowed, fighting the urge to pin him to the ground and go back to my games of pretend. "Jonas, I mean what I say."

"As do I." He tilted my chin with his knuckle. "The only reason I fear you, is because of how swiftly you had me on my knees. If you've stolen anything from me, it is my heart."

I arched a brow. "Have you been reading some of these books? That sounded rather like a line I've read."

"Perhaps. Do you not like my declarations of devotion, Fire? Too scripted? Too fantastical?"

A soft laugh escaped. "I always want your truth and your honesty. I have trusted too easily before, and I never want to be made a fool again."

"My truth? All right. I am not letting you push me away; where I belong is at your side. The pain you felt tonight, I want you to let me hold some of it—preferably all—if it should take you again. The way you have stood by me when fear overwhelms me, I want to do the same. The truth is I want all of you. Your fire, your tears, your laughter, your hopes. I want them all. You are more than enough for me, Skadi."

Jonas kissed me again. He didn't pull away.

I was lost to him. Somehow we ended sprawled over the rug, clothes cast aside, his slow, deep thrusts filling me, proving with each motion his every word.

There was nothing hurried. We took our time, explored every surface of each other, like this moment created something new—there were no secrets between us, no walls. Jonas held me close, my name like soft prayers whispered against my skin.

My legs locked around his waist, desperate to draw him closer until he became part of the marrow in my bones.

We didn't leave my sanctuary the whole of the day and into the night. I fell asleep against his body, limbs tangled, and to the slow, steady beat of his heart.

CHAPTER 47
THE NIGHTMARE PRINCE

"JONAS." A HAND PATTED MY CHEEK.

I blinked against the dim light. "Gods, Sander." Half-awake, I still managed to see to it my naked wife was covered with one of the knitted blankets from one of the chairs. We'd fallen to the floor of Skadi's library and loved each other until sleep took us. I waved my brother away. "Be gone."

"We found him."

My breath caught. "Him?"

"We know who gave Oldun the tonic and we know where he is."

Careful not to rouse Skadi, I slipped my arms from beneath her body, tucking the blanket around her shoulders, and slid into the trousers Sander tossed at me.

"Someone needs to guard her," I hissed at my brother while I accepted a tunic he'd brought for my use.

"Good thing I'm here." Mira shoved into the library, a stack of quilts and a goose down pillow in her arms.

I pressed a quick kiss to the top of my friend's head. "Thank you."

"Jo." Mira was bright and filled with a vibrant enjoyment for life most days, but there were moments as this when her unseen viciousness bled to the surface. "If he is out to hurt her, make him suffer."

I rushed to my room, gathering blades, boots, and a hooded coat. "Who is it?"

"Maj shared Oldun's memory. I recognize him from the vows, one of the king's guards, but don't know his name. We put the word out, and one of the dock house keepers sent word he thought he saw a strange fae take a room for the night with plans to sail on the post ship to the Ever in the morning."

Only one elven guard had reason to resent this alliance. "Cian. I guarantee it is a man called Cian."

Skadi would need to forgive me. A turn where his head was pinned to the wall would come earlier than planned.

"Jonas." Sander stepped in front of me. "I am at your side, you know this, but there is the alliance to consider."

My lip curled. "An alliance broken first by the elven when they sent Oldun to my room."

With a nod, my brother accepted a dagger, adding it to his own belt. "Still, we do this in the shadows."

"Agreed." As few folk as possible would know the wretched, brutal things I planned to do tonight.

Von and Aleksi were crouched beside one heavy cask, me and Sander at the other. Even without mesmer, Von had lived with the fiercest Elixist in the kingdom since boyhood. He was the best at handling tricky paralytics and the masking powders we'd wiped over our features.

For the better part of two clock tolls, anyone who did not know the powders were there, would see our faces as someone else.

Aleksi joined. He was a Rave, and reasoned this was a threat to all the realms. In truth, I thought our warrior prince had a villainous side he hid beneath duty and honor.

"That's the room." Sander used the hilt of his dagger, pointing at a window above a crooked, weathered dock house workers rented out through trade seasons.

I made certain my hood was in place, nodded to the others, then slipped into the night.

Air was thick with cool brine from night winds off the sea, and torches still lit along the roads layered the corners in dancing shadows. I kept low and slipped into a narrow alley. Sander did the same, but took a wider route. Von scaled the wall of the dock house, crouched on the rooftop. Aleksi danced between posts and crates lying in wait to be loaded on the barges and ships.

A coo, like the call of a dove, signaled us overhead. Von dropped a rope over the ledge of the roof.

I coiled the rope around my wrist. "No feet on the sides."

I made the climb first, careful not to touch my boots to the thin walls of the dock house. The risk of rousing anyone from sleep by the plod of feet on the outer walls was too great, but damn torture for the arms.

When I reached the window, I leveraged onto the sill, balancing my toes enough I could cling to the rope, but reach the lock on the edge. From a notch inside the leather of my belt, I freed a whalebone shard and hook pick.

My mother taught me how to properly use a lockpick by the time I was four turns, the motion was practically rote by now, but I would never tire of the satisfying click when levers and notches shifted.

With a quick tug on the rope, I carefully glided the window pane up. Movements were soundless, feather soft, as I maneuvered into the small room. Furnished in a simple bed, wooden chair, and a shade for dressing, there was little place to hide.

I didn't.

I took my place at the foot of the bed, watching the rise and fall of Cian's chest.

Bastard made a piss poor move stepping foot in this kingdom.

With similar silence, Aleksi and Sander slipped into the room. Von made his way down soon after cutting the rope. Even with his careful moves, scaling the side of the dock house he knocked the walls more than once.

Cian groaned, rousing a bit from the noise. Let him. I took out a dagger from the sheath on the small of my back by the time Von slipped inside the room and closed the window at our backs.

When the elven's lashes fluttered open, I was on him.

Before he could jolt or scream, my palm clapped over his mouth, the dagger pressed against his throat. His eyes were a dark blue, like most Dokkalfar, but they did not have the same shine as Skadi's, like the darkness of his bleeding soul dimmed the shade.

Cian tried to buck me off, tried to thrash, but he went stiff after a few breaths.

Aleksi had his palms out. He lived with the Night Folk, but Alek was a glamour fae with a gift of summoning anything with a beating heart. If Aleksi Bror-Ferus wanted someone—creature or man—to remain in place, they would not be able to move until he released his hold on their blood.

I tossed back my hood. Cian looked befuddled for a moment. The masking powders, no doubt, would make this all rather confusing.

"Hello, Cian. I look different I'm sure." I added a little more pressure to the edge of my blade. "But since you know my wife, I thought it was long overdue for us to get better acquainted."

He tried to kick, but when his body would not move, he cried out, muffled under my palm.

"I'm feeling like you might not want the same." I sighed, closing my eyes for a drawn breath until the force of mesmer chilled the whites. Cian let out a longer shout under my hand when I opened my eyes, blackened like the darkest corners of the room. "Pity. We could've been such great friends."

I lifted my hand only long enough to strike his face, then covered his shouts again and lowered my voice. "Except for trying to separate me from her." Another strike to the other cheek. I covered his nose and mouth and pressed my knee to his chest. "Except for the torture she endured under your watch, your lies, and your hands."

I pulled back the dagger, but in a way that would slash into his skin. Not fatal, only enough to draw blood. I didn't want him dead.

Not yet.

"Sander, I need your help. There are memories in this bastard's head where he thinks he had a bit of control over her, where he made her do things because she trusted him. I want those memories as his nightmares while we work."

Black coated Sander's eyes. He pressed his palms to Cian's head. Von took my place in muffling the guard's cries by shoving a scrap of pigskin into his mouth, while I handled the blade.

Inky veins split like cobwebs around Cian's eyes. He screamed against the gag, staring at Sander's black eyes in a bit of horror. Gods, I prayed he was tormented with the most horrific thoughts. Every memory of Skadi ought to make him piss his trousers in fear.

"Bastard." Sander gritted out more than once. The trouble with my brother's mesmer was while he crafted pleasurable moments of the past, he saw the truth before he coated them in horror.

"She told me," I said, voice rough. "Tell me, is it as bad as I imagine?"

The gentler twin, the kinder soul, Sander was a ghost of that man when he lifted his glossy eyes to mine. Jaw set, hate written even in the nothing of his darkened eyes. "Kill him. Slowly."

I did.

Every mark he watched Skadi carve into her own skin, I carved into Cian's. Each tear she shed under the hands of him and Arion was paid for with his blood. She did not need to tell me every word he spoke to her, I knew this bastard played on the heart of my wife, a girl who'd been desperate to be loved, he'd used her for his own cruel delights.

He was a wolf who'd torn her to pieces, but she had beautifully put them back together despite his bite.

Blood was thick on the floor and linens by the time it wasn't necessary for Alek or Sander or Von to hold Cian in place. Like they knew this moment was between me and the elven alone, they backed away.

Strands of my hair had fallen free over my brow, matted and soaked in his blood and flesh. I had to tighten my hold on the hilt of my dagger to keep it from slipping from my soaked palm.

The Otherworld hovered close. Cian's gasps were wet and strained. Each cough fountained blood-tinged spittle over his lips. I straddled him again, leveling the point of my dagger over his throat.

353

"I want you to know, she will forget you. I will spend each day of the rest of my life seeing to it she never wonders if the man she trusts loves every piece of her heart. You and Arion betrayed her, and there is no room in this land for traitors. Go to the hells, you bastard."

The blade pierced through Cian's throat with a sick rip of flesh and bone. He died with his eyes locked in horror.

I slumped to the side of the bed, dark relief flooding my veins. For a long moment no one spoke a word, not until Von stepped forward. "Dawn's approaching."

With a nod, I stood. "Then we ought to make it so he was never here."

Skadi was waiting for me at the top of the staircase to our wing. Arms folded, unfortunately covered in her satin robe, a hard frown on her full lips.

"Where have you been?"

"Just out, Fire." I looked like the hells spat me back out. Blood still caked my hands, my tunic and hair. Exhaustion begged for sleep, for my bed, for my wife wrapped in my arms.

Trouble was my wife looked ready to send me to the Otherworld.

"You found the tonic trader, didn't you?"

I merely nodded and shouldered my way into our room.

"You killed him?"

Again, a nod. I peeled off the sweaty, blood-soaked tunic.

Skadi hesitated, like she didn't truly want to know the answer. "Was he elven?"

"He was nothing."

"Jonas, I am not teasing."

"Nor am I." I reeled on her. "He deserved every damn strike, and you will not find a drop of remorse in me, Fire. You think you are the wicked partner in this vow, but I assure you that you are wrong. He learned as much tonight."

Skadi kept one arm wrapped around her middle, the other pressed to her throat, like she might be trying to slow her pulse.

"Who was it, Jonas?" she whispered.

"Cian." I brushed a fingertip against one of the inked vines below her sleeve. "He will never torment you again."

"Gods." Skadi covered her mouth, then shoved against my chest. "Why! Why did you do that, you bleeding fool?"

"Why!" My voice climbed. "Because he came for you again, Skadi. He tried to tear us apart, because he put his damn hands on you. That is why. You are angry he's dead? You feel pity for him?"

"Stop it." She practically hissed at me. "I am not angry he's dead, I'm furious *you* killed him. You . . . you broke the alliance and they will . . . they will try to take you from me." Skadi's words came in broken gasps. She was panicking.

Filthy, still overheated from slaughtering a man, I wrapped her up in my arms. "It would take the army of the gods to take me from you. Even then, I would find a way back to you."

Skadi's brow pressed to my chest, her shoulders shuddered. "Why must you be such a nightmare?"

"Would you have me otherwise?"

She shook her head. "Be gentle and kind and nightmarish. I want every piece." Skadi lifted her chin. "But they will come for me now."

"They will never know." I stroked a thumb over her lips. "Cian disappeared. Unfortunate, but seas are unpredictable. Perhaps he should have kept his ass out of our kingdom."

Skadi almost smiled. "They will suspect—"

"Then let all of Natthaven suspect." I kissed her, it was hard and sloppy, but unmanaged anger from the night and delirium from no sleep was taking hold. "You deserve a better man than me, but I will not apologize for defending my wife. What he did in the past was enough to kill him at least twice over. But by sabotaging this vow last night, he played his final hand. I wish I could say, for your sake, bloodlust was tamed, but Arion will earn the same fate when the moment is right."

Skadi studied me, eyes dancing between mine. She was frightened. I could taste it when she kissed me sweetly, when she helped rid me of my bloody clothes, when she gathered them to be destroyed while I scrubbed away the blood.

I sensed her fear when she stroked her fingers through my hair until I drifted toward sleep.

Fear was there, but also the beautiful viciousness of my bride when she whispered as I fell asleep. "You are mine, Nightmare. I will devour worlds to the Nothing if they take me from you."

"Niklas has been studying the powder," Daj said, face hard as steel. He slumped in his official throne, drumming his fingers against the arm, looking entirely murderous. "It was not fatal, but strong enough you could've slept for two bleeding days, and it was not made here."

Skadi sat beside me, fiddling with some of the silver rings around her fingers.

"Elven made?" I pressed.

Maj offered a small shrug. "It's what they suspect. Some of the herbs seemed derived from foliage on Natthaven."

Well, shit.

Skadi gave me a shadowed look. Two nights since I'd slaughtered Cian, but the fear remained.

"Do I want to know where you boys went the other night?" my father asked.

"Better if you don't."

The king arched a brow, but nodded. He knew. There was no way he didn't. Few things escaped the notice of the king and queen in their kingdom.

"Alek, Mira. I do not think it is best for you to be in Klockglas right now." My father turned to me. "In fact, perhaps you ought to take your wife to the Southern realms or Night Folk lands for a time."

It wasn't a terrible idea. I took hold of Skadi's hand. She startled, no mistake still trapped in the fear of the unknown. "Would you want to go to Mira's kingdom until more time passes? Get away from the worries?"

"We need to return to Natthaven soon enough," she whispered. "What is the point in hiding if we must return to keep the alliance?"

I lowered my voice. "We are not held to any alliance, Fire. They broke it as far as I'm concerned."

"You'll enjoy my kingdom, Skadi." Mira said brightly. "We have the most curious fae, if you ask me. The sort from the folk tales with their tricks and glamour magic."

"After what happened last time, we should demand Eldirard bring the fading isle to our shores," Sander snapped. "If he refuses, then we refuse to send Jonas and Skadi. That, or they go with half the Rave Army."

"Both formidable options," I said, trying to keep the tone light.

Skadi almost smiled. "I would like to see more fae lands."

Mira beamed and took hold of her arm. "You will adore the forests and various courts. There are hot springs, and our palace is built half inside a knoll. There are these tiny blossoms that grow and glow like moonlight all along the ceilings. Ash and Shelba could show you her court, they're forest folk. Then there are seers where Alek's and the twins' cousin lives with his wife and littles."

Mira trailed off with chatter over the various fae courts.

My father gave me a half grin. "There is such fear in this palace, I can hardly stand upright against it. They do not get the right to terrify us in our own lands. We'll send word to the elven king and discuss the terms of the next arrival on their isle after all that has happened."

"Maj." Sander stepped closer to the dais. "What will you do with Oldun?"

"Try her for assaulting a prince and conspiring with an enemy against us. For now, after what was done, the elven clans are no allies. I hope that does not cause you pain, Skadi."

Skadi sighed. "It does only because I know it could've been avoided had they not been deceptive."

"In the end," my mother went on, "I expect Oldun will leave this palace without much of a memory of Jonas or his wife."

CHAPTER 48
THE MIST THIEF

By the dawn we would take to the sea and sail toward Mira's kin. Through the shroud of unease, a glimmer of excitement took hold in my belly. The princess had a talent in describing her world with such delight in her voice, it seemed too mystical to be a true land.

Prince Aleksi wasn't due to his Rave post for another fortnight and planned to spend time with his cousin in what Mira called the Court of Stars.

Sander, Von, and several of the Kryv would be joining. The only one who did not seem thrilled with the idea was Tait.

After gathering a few gifts from Frigg and her folk to take to Mira's folk, Jonas and I paused on the staircase leading to our chamber as a new battle of fae broke out in the front entry of the palace.

Mira chatted with Frigg about some sort of pixie legend in wood.

"I still swear I saw one right before my fourteenth turn, remember? We all came for your birth revel."

Mira snorted. "Friggy, I live there. They don't exist, or I would've seen one by now."

"Or you do not have a keen eye." Tait grumbled from the corner.

Mira spun on the sea fae. "I see a great deal more than you, Hearttalker."

"I see plenty."

"And?" Mira came to a halt beside him. "What do you see that is so repugnant to you that you keep an endless scowl in place at all times?"

My arm was around Jonas's waist, but I could not help but look over my shoulder, curious how the sea fae would respond.

Tait freed a soft hiss of annoyance, flashing the points of two elongated canine teeth, and reached for one of the paper smokes in his pocket.

Mira let out a groan of frustration, plucked the smoke from his fingers, and tossed it on the ground.

"Well." Jonas pressed a hand on the small of my back, nudging me up the staircase. "I think that's enough for tonight. Perhaps we ought to get to sleep before fae wars start anew."

With a nip at the lobe of my ear, Jonas opened the door to my side of the chamber. While we were gone, palace staff assured us the wall would be torn down, so we would, at last, claim one wing.

A throat cleared. Dorsan emerged from his chamber. "Sire. I was informed by your . . . brisk cook, there are several travel packs she would like you to approve before journeys begin tomorrow."

"Ah, Ylva. Always thinking we'll find something better beyond these borders." He pressed a kiss to the side of my head. "Be back in a moment."

"You know what I'll want, Nightmare."

He spun around, walking backward. "What sort of fool do you take me for? You adore pickled herring."

I winced. "Do not trifle with my spiced honey cakes!"

His laughter echoed along the stones of the stairwell as he strode away. I glanced at Dorsan, gesturing to my open doorway. "Shall we?"

My guard dipped his chin. Jonas, in not-so-subtle words, had insisted until tensions eased I was not to be alone. Trouble was, we didn't know if tensions would ever ease.

Dorsan took his place between the door and the window, while I settled beside an open trunk packed with my dresses and Jonas's tunics.

I'd only started folding a few more tops when a flash of gold sparked on the vanity. Stones in the heirloom necklace clinked together, shining some of their fiery light into the room. I took off the gift after we returned to Klockglas.

I'd thought the necklace was precious when Cara delivered it for the king, but the sight of it had turned wretched the moment I left the shores of Natthaven. I hadn't put it on since.

But where flashes of brilliant light were common when the mystical chips of stone collided, a growing spiral of light was not.

The bursts of gold spun, faster and faster, until a shield of fiery heat filled my chamber. From the fire, a figure stepped through.

My heart stalled.

Arion materialized in my bedchamber. His red hair was covered in a deep blue hood, two white iron blades were strapped to his belt. White iron did not draw blood like an average blade—it rotted affinities from the heart.

Too deep, too many cuts, and it became fatal when magic was bled out.

Somehow in my stun I managed to scream, and scramble back. Dorsan had his blade drawn in the next breath, but Arion was swifter.

One of his white iron blades flew across the room, the point disappearing deep into Dorsan's belly.

"Dorsan!" I tried to catch his stumble, but my guard's height and weight drew me to the ground with him.

He coughed and gasped. No blood seeped from his wound, only charred skin as the iron rotted his affinity from his heart. I gripped the hilt of the blade, desperate to yank it free, but Arion tore me away.

"Time to go, Skadinia."

I screamed again and kicked and clawed at Arion's arm. Cold bled over my palms, but a lance of pain chased away my affinity before it could take hold. Arion had drawn his second blade and sliced across my hand.

The white iron weakened my affinity as much as others. One strike and my head grew hazy.

"You . . . bastard." I made a weak attempt to snatch Arion's blade, but the prince merely sliced another gash over my arm.

I cried out, falling to the haze of the iron.

"That's enough, Skadinia. You've played your games, but your place is with me."

Through my murky vision, I watched as Dorsan struggled for breath against the cruel blade.

I watched as the light faded from my loyal guard's eyes.

A tear slid down my cheek. The burn of the blade had overtaken my arms, leeched into my throat, and pumped through my blood with every thud of my heart.

I knew a great deal about white iron, knew how fiercely it could incapacitate magical blood. Marks of it were written across my flesh.

Arion waved a palm over the sparking charm on my necklace. "Clever, don't you think? You've kept a way for me to reach you all this time."

All gods.

It was gifted to me . . . on purpose. A second blow of betrayal was sharper than the first. Arion was a powerful Ljosalfar, one of the rare few who could summon enough light and heat with his affinity, it broke through walls, air, barriers, and allowed him to walk through it no matter how small the flare. He could always pull more until it grew into a blaze.

I'd carried the key to his door.

Arion placed a folded missive on the edge of the bed and hooked his arms under Dorsan's unmoving body, and dragged him toward the back of the chamber.

"Alliances were broken, Skadinia. Time to be off. Your husband will soon read your reasons for leaving." He cast a quick look at the missive he'd left on the bed.

The power of the iron boiled the back of my throat in a harsh bile. It was nauseating and suffocating to be touched by the blade. The force of it spun the room, deadened the mind, even with shallow cuts as these.

Arion widened his new fire ring. I tried to scream—perhaps I did— but my head lolled to the side when the prince aimed the white iron blade at my cheek. "Fight me any longer, and the next strike takes a finger. I don't want to rot more of your affinity, Skadinia. It is too valuable to me."

Arion took me into his arms.

Panic choked my breath from my lungs. Heat and light flashed overhead, and he stepped into his fiery wall.

A tear fell onto my cheek.

I love you, Nightmare.

CHAPTER 49
THE NIGHTMARE PRINCE

Ylva must've thought we were leaving for the whole of a turn. I approved half her supplies, and was not allowed to leave the cooking room before I vowed to bring her a bushel of white plums that grew in Mira's kingdom.

I was halfway back to the stairs leading to my wing when Sander's frantic voice called down to me.

"Jonas! Someone bleeding go get him. Why is this damn door locked? Jonas!"

Skadi. I sprinted up the staircase.

My heart was on the outside of my chest, my head empty save for instinct. Voice, screams, pleas, they clashed in my ears.

"I hear nothing," someone shouted.

"She cried out! Hurry. Break the damn lock!" Mira sobbed. I rounded the corner to find her pounding on my bedchamber door, tears on her face, screaming Skadi's name.

Sander was frantically working his set of picks, hands trembling. Von, Aleksi, and Tait were kicking, using their shoulders, trying to break down the damn door.

"Jonas, thank the gods." Frigg, pale and terrified, reached for me, but retreated when I shoved past.

"What the hells happened?"

"I don't know." Mira shook her hands. "We were walking past the stairs and heard . . . I heard her scream. We ran up here, but the bleeding door is locked."

No, no, no. Darkness shrouded my gaze. I couldn't think, couldn't breathe, not until I had eyes on her. I slammed my shoulder against the locked door. "Skadi! Answer me. Work faster!"

Sander didn't waste time shouting back at me, merely added a thinner pick to the hole.

"Stop." He held up a hand. "Don't shake the door."

Von had to hook an arm around my shoulders to peel me back for a breath, two, five. My skin burned and prickled, like it was peeling off my damn bones.

The lock clicked.

I shoved into the room, coughing against the harsh stench of smoke. The room was hardly disturbed, but no Skadi.

I drew my blade. "Skadi!"

"Jonas." Frigg lifted a folded parchment, eyes wide. "For you."

I snatched the parchment out of her hand. It was a short note, but each word sliced across my chest.

Husband,
I cannot go on pretending, not after what you did against my own
people. I wish you respected me enough to stay your hand.
It is better this way, to remain with our own folk.
Skadinia.

This was wrong. I blinked for a breath, then another. Tricksters, schemers, thieves knew how to note the slightest detail. To miss something could mean failure, capture, or death.

I took in the room. *Notice the details, find what is out of place.*

I shook my head, crumpling the parchment. "This is not from Skadi."

"How do you know?" Frigg asked softly.

"She hates being called Skadinia. It is not from her. Where is my wife!" My shout rattled dust off the rafters.

"Prince." Tait tucked his small clock back into his pocket, and tilted his head toward the foot of the bed.

I crouched down. "Dammit. Dorsan."

The guard was pale, cheeks sunken, and a sleek dagger pierced his body. No blood, only scorched flesh surrounded the wound.

"This is an elven blade. We saw them in the battle." My eyes darkened until the room was filled with shadows. "They've taken her."

Numbness flowed through me, until I moved like a haunt in the darkness. No thought, only action. Fear, heady and cruel, clouded all rationale. Nothing mattered, no life, no plan, nothing, until Skadi was back in my arms.

"Jonas." Sander took hold of my arm. I hadn't realized I'd already made moves into the corridor. "Stop."

"Do not tell me to stop. I will not leave her to them, Sander."

"You're not doing it alone or you'll never get her back."

"Natthaven fades. They will hide her away. We don't have time to waste."

"I will go to the Ever," Tait said, a new darkness to his voice. "Merfolk can track the isle. You know the king and queen will stand with you."

All I could offer was a nod of thanks before Tait shoved past me toward the stairs.

"Hearttalker," Mira blurted out.

Tait paused on the first step.

Mira cleared her throat. "Take care as you go. The elven could be patrolling the seas, and I still must be taken home. It was your task, after all. So . . . don't be foolish and die."

The sea fae studied her for a breath, then quit the room with a mute nod.

I reeled back on the others. "I need to get after that damn isle. Now."

It was taking too bleeding long to get free of this kingdom.

I tried to see the progress, but everything moved in a blur.

From the tides, fae of the sea stepped onto our shores—sea singers who could tempt unsuspecting souls into their clutches with their voices, sirens who would do the same, but bury their bones in the deepest abyss. Dark longships were arranged along the docks.

Curious folk watched from tenement windows, cottages, or from inns and taverns as guards and their two princes tossed any blade we could find into the ships.

"Falkyns!" Von shoved my shoulder.

Between a wide alley, cutting through the mists, a swarm of people emerged. At the head, Niklas and Junie were there. Both wore black with kohl around their eyes and down their lips. Over his fingers, Niklas fitted gold rings, some with barbs on the tops.

Junius wrapped us all in a quick embrace.

Niklas looked to me. "I hear there's a fight to be had."

I clapped him on the shoulder and helped heave a crate of what I hoped was poison designed only for elven folk. Niklas was skilled enough with his mesmer, he could likely make a toxin that singled out male elven, leaving Skadi out of harm's way.

Hooves pounded against the cobblestones. Shouts for the Black Palace, the king and queen, echoed through the streets.

A damn army wrapped in shadows filled the streets. A foreboding beat of drums sounded in the night, a tradition in our lands, a way to declare a battle was brewing.

I had not signaled my mother and father, all I could think was getting to the sea and Skadi.

Before his horse stopped, my father kicked his leg over the side. Five long strides had him in front of me. His eyes were pitch as the night when he tossed back a hood.

I straightened my shoulders. "They took Skadi, and I don't know how. I'm going, Daj. You cannot stop me."

He clapped a hand on the side of my neck. "Think I'm here to stop you, boy? Look around, we're here to get her back."

It was the kind of stun that robbed breath from the lungs, realizing the truth of what was in front of me.

Kryv, palace guards, even Frigg's father was there, with swords, daggers, bows, and arrows arranged like war was at the gates.

Many faces were shrouded, and most wore dark tunics and trousers. They had blood painted down their cheeks as though fingers had clawed at their flesh. Others had thick kohl like the Falkyns, or blue and white stain. The drums faded when the final flood of horses joined.

All of them were here for Skadi.

My father was made of darkness, but it was darkness that had shaped me, loved me, and taught me how to stand on my own. When he pulled me into a brisk embrace, I felt like a damn sod for clinging to him until the fear below the surface lost its potency.

"We're not returning without her, Jonas," came his dark rasp, low and meant for me alone.

A promise. My father, in all my memories, had never lied to me. Tonight would not be the first.

My mother came to us, hair braided back, a frightening sort of violence in her gaze. She said nothing, merely pressed a hand to my cheek, then Sander's. A silent assurance she was not missing another fight.

"Mira." Daj gently took hold of Mira's arm. She was dressed in a canvas coat and a little frantic as she helped load the boats.

"I tried to get to her, Uncle Kase." Mira's chin trembled. "I can't lose another one."

An ache cracked down my chest. No mistake, Mira alluded to the weeks Livia had gone missing when Bloodsinger took her for his own revenge.

My father cupped her cheek. "I need you to stay back."

She shook her head. "I can fight."

"I know, but I need you to send the warning to the other kingdoms. We may need the Rave to stand for our shores. You know royal blood ignites the call, so will you do it for us?"

Warning signals fueled by elixirs and natural magic in the soil were erected across the kingdoms. A blazing flame would spark atop towers in every realm in a shade of the distressed kingdom. The towers would burn blood red for Klockglas.

Our tower was tucked into a forest we called Limericks. Too far for us to reach while still having time to hunt the fading isle.

Mira's bright eyes looked about, like she could not think how to walk away from us, but the truth of what my father said was there. Only the royal houses could declare war or troubles that would summon the full force of the Rave.

Aleksi could stay, but he was a warrior. Not even my father could keep him back.

"I'll send the warning," Mira said after a long pause. "I'll do it."

My mother turned over her horse to the princess. Two Black Palace guards and Frigg volunteered to guard Mira as she went, to ready our shores for elven armies if we did not succeed.

Bile turned in my stomach. I couldn't consider failing.

Mira bid us all tearful farewells, but kept her word, and with her small entourage, raced toward the outer edges of our kingdom.

Sea fae took the stemposts of every longship. The fading isle would be in the far seas near the Ever. All I could hope for now was we were not far behind and they had not faded to unknown waters.

I stepped into a ship, looking forward, the heated fear prickling up the back of my neck.

Tonight, I faced my nightmares.

For Skadi, I could not lose myself. The fever was there, burning in my blood, trying to drag me into the pain of my own mesmer.

"I'm at your side, brother." Sander sheathed a blade and leaned over the rail.

I swallowed through the burn in my throat. "This is why, Sander."

"Why what?"

"Why I never settled, why I refused to fall for every sharp, beautiful piece of another's heart." I hesitated, fighting to steady my voice. "I have seen love and what the loss of it can do. I never wanted to risk such a thing, not when my mesmer would destroy me for it."

"Is it not your fear any longer?"

"It is." I drew my sword when the oarsmen shouted a call to heave us into the current. "But I do not fear losing just any heart. What I fear now is losing hers."

Sander straightened and reached for a rope overhead when the stempost tilted to the surface, ready to dive below. "Those fears will never become reality."

True enough. I was getting my wife back tonight.

CHAPTER 50
THE MIST THIEF

ARION'S AFFINITY DID NOT LET HIM CROSS THROUGH FIRE AND LIGHT FOR LONG distances, and he could only travel to places he had seen. The truth of it, revealed he had been watching my chamber for some time. The prince likely came to Klockglas with Cian and knew well who had slaughtered the guard.

The prince summoned light, but he could steal us away through it. Almost like the darkness of my mists, but he was not feared. No. Arion was revered by his clan.

With his arms around me, the prince forced me through a back chamber of an alehouse, to torches near an alley, then lanterns by the sea.

A ship met us at the shore. The white iron began to fade from my blood enough I could stand if I braced against Arion's form.

I didn't.

I let myself drop, tried to claw against the dark sandy shore, tried to scream. Only raspy sobs for Jonas escaped.

From the rowboat, three Ljosalfar warriors forced me into the vessel. Dressed in their golden armor with sleek braids keeping their smooth hair back, my mind accepted them as conspirators in this plot, and tried to be free of them as fiercely as I tried to do with Arion.

When I tried to fling myself over the rail, the warriors bound my wrists with a leather belt and Arion kept hold of it in his grip.

I glanced over my shoulder at one of the warriors. "The prince killed him. Dorsan."

A tug on the leather on my wrists lurched me forward. Arion gripped my face. "They will not care like you think. Dorsan was Dokkalfar, not of my clan."

"You are connected to us." My voice was heavy from the iron. "He did not need to die. I hope it stains your soul."

"Like I said, Skadinia, if it earns me the throne of all elven, a few stains will be worth it."

Cruelty lived in Arion's features. Already his heart seemed twisted with greed. There was no future with him where he did not make me his weapon.

Cold mists enveloped us when we entered the shores of Natthaven. The dark peaks and forests sparkled in lanterns from treetop folk, and the glimmer of the palace in the distance seemed so innocent, so welcoming.

It was a beautiful prison.

When the rowboat slid onto the sand, one of the warriors lit a matchstick. Arion reached for the flame until it danced in his palms. He tossed the fire with a flourish and a violent cyclone of heat and wind fashioned in the darkness.

Arion pulled me through with a firm tug. My hair whipped through the blaze of his hot, biting affinity until I landed on cold stone of the familiar hall of the elven palace, my wrists tucked beneath me.

With a rush of wind, the fire ring closed. Arion stepped past me without a thought.

"I've retrieved her, as promised. She's delirious, lost to some of the alver elixirs. I've no doubt that will explain her odd behavior during the visit. It is as we suspected."

"Liar." I propped onto my elbow, but my breath stuttered. Eldirard was seated on his throne, more haggard than before. He seemed old. By his side, Gerard took a king's seat. Stern and harsh, the Ljosalfar king kept his grip on the pommel of his bronze short blade, and a sneer twisted on his lips.

I managed to rise onto my knees. "Arion slaughtered Dorsan."

My grandfather's eyes went sharp, but the prince held up a hand. "I did not lift a blade, King Eldirard. The alvers caught our escape and poor Dorsan was caught in the middle. We will honor him in both clans."

I was going to end Arion. He'd be tossed into the Nothing, and I would never let him escape it.

"Grandfather, he lies." I tried to stand, but my limbs were made of heavy stone. "Why have you done this? I have always loved you, obeyed you, and you have robbed me of my happiness."

"Like I said, delusions." Arion shook his head as though heartbroken. "There is no telling how long she has been unknowingly taking their spell casts, but they have manipulated her mind to give them undying loyalty."

King Gerard stood. "We will work on restoring the princess, then at last join our clans. Once we are ready, we'll take those boons to which we are entitled from the fae."

"Grandfather, you cannot trust this! You are allowing Arion to bring war to our people. Again! They will come for me. Jonas of House Eriksson will never stop searching for me. You underestimate them."

"Perhaps you underestimate your own people, Princess," Gerard said. "You do not know the half of what has been done to bring us to this moment."

"Grandfather." Strength built; I rose to my feet. "Do not agree to this. I will never be free, not with Arion. They will use me, you know it."

Before Eldirard could speak, Gerard interjected. "Your affinity was gifted to the elven clans through fate, girl. It is unique and powerful, and was never meant to serve fae folk. It was made to serve the elven. Accept your fate, and fulfill your duty."

"I will never serve you," I shouted. A few gasps came from the servants around the throne room. My fists curled at my sides. "*Never.* You will never be my kin in my heart. You can force me to stand before your son as a bride, but I am vowed to another, and I will wait in nothing but ice if I must until the day he finds me and calls me out of it."

At long last, my grandfather stood. "Cara, if you please, take the princess to rest. It seems she is quite weary." He looked to his guards. "Prepare the isle to fade. We go to the deep seas."

"My king." One of the palace guards stepped forward. "The isle . . . well, it seems hesitant to fade."

I barked a laugh. "Because you've betrayed it! It will not bow to you."

My grandfather hesitated. "We will see how far we can go. Cara." He gestured for my lady's maid from the corner. "Tend to the princess."

"See to it she cannot use her affinity," Gerard added. "At least until she can be reasonable."

Two manacles made of white iron were fastened to my wrists. They weakened me, but not the same as a strike from a white iron blade. Mists would not form, and it was another brick in a familiar prison.

I didn't plead. What was the point? They would not listen. I did not have the strength to pull my mists. Not yet.

I said nothing when Cara guided me from the throne room, her features contorted in a sincere worry. I let my heart slow, my indifference take hold. As promised, I would feel nothing of this place until my nightmare found me.

Moments, decades, it would not matter. I would wait in ruthless anticipation, until those hands thawed my heart again.

My old chamber held no joy for me. It was not the long chamber I shared with Jonas with my garden window he gave to me without a thought. It had no abandoned corridor where a dusty, forgotten room had been transformed into a library with tales of romance without complaint that the tales were of no worth.

It did not smell of parchment and deep forest oak.

"My Lady." Cara stood near the doorway. "Why don't we get you rested. You'll feel better by the morning."

"I will not. Do not pretend I will when you do not believe it yourself." I faced her, cold and distant. "I never belonged here. No one will ever see me the way my husband sees me. There were no conditions in House Eriksson, Cara. No masks needed to be worn."

"Do you truly believe such things about your home?"

Time would be wasted trying to explain, and what good would it do? No one would allow me to leave here. "I hope you will find a place to hide when the alvers come."

I faced the window, uninterested in her look of horror at my words.

Out on the sea, clouds rolled toward the shoreline, an army of darkness here to douse the light. Little by little the candles flickered in the room until they died. Wind beat against the bubbled glass, and the sea disappeared behind the wall of night.

There was a subtle tug in the pit of my stomach whenever the isle shifted.

I closed my eyes and let the tear balanced on my lashes fall to my cheek.

Only when light returned to the glass and candles flickered back to life did the king enter my room. Worn and battered, Eldirard dismissed Cara with a look and closed the door behind us.

"Skadinia."

I clasped my hands behind my back. "Did you know I hate that name because it is not mine? It was added upon when you brought me here. My mother named me Skadi."

Eldirard sat on the corner of my bed, arms lax over his knees, his shoulders curved. "I thought you would be clear of these thoughts by now."

"I will never be clear of these thoughts because Arion lied. As I told you, as you chose not to believe. You gave me an heirloom that led him to me!"

My grandfather flinched. "I wanted a swifter way to reach you, my child. In the event, the alliance grew sour and you were put at risk."

"The only risk I have ever faced is by *my own damn people*." My voice was sharp and shrill. Emotion thickened in my throat, forcing me to turn away before I broke under his watch.

"I should never have agreed to these vows." Eldirard let out a heavy breath. "We could have created the legacy without all these toils if I'd kept to the alliance with the Ljosalfar."

I glanced at the floor. "I am forever grateful you agreed to the prince's proposition, even though you have betrayed us both."

"You truly care for him? You have been infatuated with ease before."

"You think I was infatuated with Cian and Arion? I was desperate and alone and terrified I would be the monster you all feared. Of course, I fell for their words. Until they tortured me, laughed at me, took my body, then mocked and beat me when I did not know what to do."

When I looked at him again, shame was twisted on my grandfather's face.

He tugged the circlet from his brow, and ran his slender fingers through his fine hair. "You never said a word, child. Why? I would've protected you."

"Arion was my betrothed, how dare I come to you, the one who gave me so much, and tell you such things about a bloodline prince." The stone mask cracked with a bitter laugh. "How would it have gone? Arion would've been scolded, told to do better. Cian would be reassigned to the other side of the palace, but I would still be betrothed to a wretch of a man for your legacy."

Eldirard looked stunned. No mistake, this was the first time he truly heard my voice.

"This betrayal is proof enough that no matter what you will always give me as a prize to Arion."

"Stop speaking as if you mean nothing."

"I do not matter to you!" Never had I shouted at the king, but it was untamed, and I felt a spark of life in my heart. Jonas's fire. "At least not for what I can do beyond my affinity. I don't understand why you have betrayed the treaty. You have every realm of the fae as your ally, yet you turn them against us for a single elven clan."

The king hung his head. "I wanted to be a king the skald's praised in their tales for generations. Be it through a union with fae or the joining of elven clans, I did not care. I agreed for Arion to bring you home after hearing the suspicions of Cian's death. I truly thought you might be in danger."

"You could think that after you witnessed us together during our visit? You saw how I rejected Arion, yet you did not question why Cian was in alver lands? You merely saw your other option for fame and thought nothing of me and my heart."

"I wanted your name to live on as much as mine, as a glorious queen of the Dokkalfar."

Gods, I did not care about my legacy if it was not written with my nightmare.

"Such alliance was written in legends, my child. A great rise of the Dokkalfar, and when I saw you, I knew you were the answer to my fading bloodline." Eldirard rose and looked out the window with a touch of longing.

"You tore me away from the man I love for a legend?"

"It is more than a legend. The belief in prophecies was enough to form a long-held agreement with Gerard, one written in blood when you were still a babe. Arion unknowingly broke the peace alliance when he came against our isle."

"What prophecy?"

"An old mortal seer spoke of the alliance of the elven, destined to be led by a consuming power that would lead them from obscurity. Arion has strength with the light few in his clan do, and when we heard of the Dokkalfar child who could swallow whole beings, Gerard and I agreed, this was the way to see our clans rise. Now, I wonder if you were always meant for a different fate."

"So you thought you would pair us and we would take battle to . . ." My words faded when a thought burrowed into my skull. "Wait, what do you mean, you heard of the child? You found me by my own mistake."

The king held my gaze. "I found you, but only after I had been searching for you since you ran away. I knew a great deal about you from many meetings with your mother and father."

Sweat coated my palms. "You knew them?"

"They could not be reasoned with. I did what I could to bring them to understand what a benefit it would be for their child to be adopted by the crown and aligned with the Ljosalfar. They were wild hearts, treetop elven, and would not hear of it."

"You asked them to give me up?" I dug the heel of my hand against my forehead, trying to dull the ache building behind my eyes. My heart stuttered when I looked to the king again. "All gods, no."

Eldirard appeared as a broken man. "As king, they were my subjects, practically kin. But Gerard . . . he had his guard take white iron to them, then planned to deliver you to me. You must've woken up sometime through it all, saw the guards, and ran. No one could find you. Then again, treetop folk are loyal and utterly suspicious."

I was going to retch.

"No." I could still hear my father's laughter when he would toss me into the ponds in the wood. I could still feel my mother's gentle touch braiding my hair. "You told me I killed them."

"We had to convince you of your strength."

"You had to crush *the fire* in my soul!" A sob broke from my chest. "You needed your docile princess to see your schemes of domination into fruition. I loved you. I idolized you."

"And I love you." The king's voice broke. "It is why after such loss, I wanted you to always be free of your affinity when it came to your vows."

"To soothe your guilt." Each word was jagged and lined in hate.

"No. So you could voice your thoughts. It is why when a second choice arose with the alvers, I wanted you to have it."

When he reached for me, I pulled away. "You are *vile*."

"Skadi—"

"No." I stepped back until my spine struck the window. "You killed a mother and father who adored me. You've taken me from a man who loves me, just me. Not for my affinity, not for my title, for *me*. So don't you dare tell me you love me, for I know too well what real love is."

Silence fell, its sharp teeth dug into my flesh until I could hardly stand the emptiness between us. A gaping divide of a life I thought I understood. The thoughts, the pain, the fears, they were all lies.

I was not the fearsome beast two kings made me out to be. They were the monsters.

Eldirard placed his bronze circlet on the edge of my bed. "You are right. For turns, I have felt the shame of my actions, and have done all I can to ignore it. It is why I cannot fade the isle alone any longer. I have lost its trust."

"That will be your legacy."

His eyes were rimmed in red and pain. "Greed. It is not the legacy I desire. I grow weary of it all, my girl. You may not believe me, but I do love you fiercely. Forgive me for loving my own ambitions more. Allow me to begin making amends in the only way I can."

The king left me bewildered and unsteady for a moment, but soon he returned with Cara. She was pale, still contorted in a bit of fear.

"Please sit, Cara. I have need of a witness for what I am about to do."

CHAPTER 51
THE MIST THIEF

THE KING POSITIONED CARA ON A VELVET BENCH NEAR THE VANITY, THEN plucked his circlet off the edge of the bed.

He studied the sharp points of bronze. Intricate stars and peaks of Natthaven were etched in the metals. "This has always symbolized the strength of the Dokkalfar clan. Made from the metals of this isle, it is designed to sit atop a leader who cherishes its people, one who is trusted by the powers in its soil.

"It has always accepted you, Skadi." Eldirard offered a sad smile. "I suspect it kept you safe as a child. I am regretful to know how alone you have been in these walls, how misplaced you feel among your own people. But the richest power of elven lives in this land and it bows to you. As I now do."

Cara drew in a sharp breath when the king lowered to one knee, holding up the circlet.

"Skadi of House Sannhet."

I swallowed. He did not use Naganeen, he used the house of my birth. I kept my body stiff, unmoving, in truth, I wasn't certain what I ought to do.

Eldirard lifted his eyes. "I crown you as my heir of Natthaven. Your alliance with royal lines has secured your inheritance and was accepted by this land." On the sharpest point of the crown, the king pricked one finger, spilling a drop of his blood down the point. "Willingly given, my blood is yours, as is this throne. None may take it from you. Claim your birthright."

My palms trembled, but I took the circlet from his hold. The king did not rise as I placed it atop my head. A hiss slid through my teeth when the bronze touched my brow.

"No, leave it." Eldirard held up his hands before I could take the circlet away. "It aches for only a moment. It is a brand, should anyone take into question if you are to be the queen here, the brand will show through and there will be no doubt."

In this moment, I realized how little I had tried to learn about stepping into the throne.

Vague memories during lessons talked of the royal brand, but I never asked. I never asked much at all, too intent on being obedient and not a bother.

Eldirard rose to his feet, hands outstretched. "May I?"

He towered over me, so it was no trouble to pluck the crown from my head. The king gestured to the mirror. Cara had her hands in front of her mouth when I bent to see my reflection.

There, shimmering across my brow was a constellation of stars, almost shaped like a dainty crown. I could not look away as the silver glimmer faded into my skin, hidden beneath the surface. I touched the place, but there was no irritation, nothing to hint it was even there.

"You are my heir, Skadi." Eldirard said. "No alliance with the Ljos-alfar is needed. The man you have come to choose, the life you have chosen, it is more than enough to secure your position here."

Emotion knotted in my chest. I looked back at the king. "You will allow me to return to Jonas?"

"Yes." There was no hesitation. "I have failed you time and again, but I will not fail you now."

"I don't forgive you, not for my mother and father, not for taking me from my husband, the life we had here will never be what it was. But . . . I am grateful for what you have done in this moment."

Eldirard nodded. He opened an arm to the door. "Come. We'll get the key to those wretched things on your wrists and return you to your folk."

"What of Gerard and Arion?"

"I will handle their tantrums." Eldirard did not walk in front of me now. He strode down the corridors shoulder to shoulder, as equals. "They will be disgruntled but will need to make their own alliances elsewhere. The fae lands are too vast, so they will not try to stand against them without the Dokkalfar."

A glimmer of hope took root. I would be with Jonas soon, and as the crowned heir, I could banish Arion from ever stepping foot on this damn isle again.

Ljosalfar guards remained in the throne room where their king and crowned prince sat at a simple meal arranged on the center table. I did not notice any Dokkalfar, but had little time to be discomfited before Gerard drew our attention.

"Ah." Gerard lifted a drinking horn in a greeting. "Is she feeling better now?"

"I believe amends have been made and Skadi knows her place."

"Good." Arion tipped his own horn back. "We'll do swift vows. I want it done with no more delays."

"That won't be possible," said Eldirard. "The future queen is already vowed with House Eriksson."

Air grew cold when both Gerard and Arion lifted their luminescent gazes to the Dokkalfar king. Slowly, Gerard rose from his seat. "I grow tired of your hesitations."

"There is no hesitation." Eldirard lifted his chin. "I have chosen to stand by the alliance, as I agreed in the beginning. Peace can remain with the Ljosalfar and Dokkalfar. Should it, then you will have powerful allies with fae folk, Gerard."

The Ljosalfar king swiped his hand over the table, clattering his horn to the ground. "I do not want allies, you old fool. I want our people to sit at the head of all the lands as they once did."

"What's done is done."

"Undo it," Arion bit out. "You are the king."

Eldirard sneered down at the prince. "And you are a guest who has worn out his welcome. You will never be permitted to take my heir as a wife."

A burn of pride bloomed in my chest. Like a wave of fear was washed away, I felt freer than I ever had within these walls.

Arion shot to his feet and pointed a finger at the king. "You will regret this choice."

I stepped forward. "Leave, Arion. There is no place for you here any longer."

The prince scoffed, flashing the edge of his teeth for a moment. "I think you will find you are quite mistaken very soon."

I blamed my inattention on my reckless burst of arrogance from Eldirard's declaration. I did not see the moment the guards shifted; I took no notice of the blades they lifted.

Not until it was too late.

A bronze short blade sliced through Eldirard's spine until the point broke through his chest. My scream split across the throne room. Betrayed as I was by his actions, the man had been my adopted grandfather most of my life.

Before I could reach him, two guards pulled me away.

"What have you done!" I tugged against their hold. "He's your kin. He's your blood."

Eldirard and King Gerard were distant relatives. This went against all elven customs. It stained the soul too fiercely.

"I did not strike the king." Gerard opened his arms. "Nor did my heir."

I sobbed Eldirard's name when he fell to his knees, blood spilling over his lips. Shouts rose from beyond the doors. Palace guards had been locked out.

Gerard snapped commands for his men to subdue them while defending the palace from any hint of invading fae folk.

"Take the princess to my chambers," Arion said.

"Queen." A wet voice followed. Eldirard tumbled forward, but looked to me, a fading smile on his lips. "She is . . . queen."

I shook my head, tears heating my cheeks when I watched his eyes dim. I wanted to scream, plead with him not to go, I wasn't ready, I needed his guidance before he could go, I needed . . . more time to make sense of everything.

Eldirard drew in a soft breath. He never released it.

Gerard crossed the room. He pinched my chin between his fingers, peering at my brow. The same sting that came when the circlet was placed atop my head lifted under my skin.

"Damn him." Gerard released my face with a rough shove. "No one is to see her. Take her to the prince's chambers, chain her for all I care, but keep her contained." He reeled on another guard. "Summon our remaining guard from the wood and someone rid this hall of all the blood."

"They are coming for you, Gerard." I battled in the grip of the guards. "Arion, you have been marked by a prince of nightmares and he never loses his mark." I laughed, a little frantic, a little broken. "I am the queen of Natthaven, and you have all been marked."

The door slammed on my shouts and I was dragged up a back stairwell to where Arion slept during his stays. It was cluttered and disorderly and smelled of sweat and smoke.

The white iron around my wrists held my affinity back, but I bit and kicked at the Ljosalfar guards until one pinned me forward on the bed.

One guard locked the window and tucked the small key into his belt, then hurried out of the room while his companion kept me suffocated on Arion's bed. When the first guard returned, he carried a thick rope in his hands.

It took time with my resistance, and they were hesitant to strike a woman they knew was branded as a royal. Still, when one of the men grew weary with my trouble, he leveled his fist against my jaw.

Black speckles dotted my vision in a dizzy haze, allowing a sliver of time for them to bind my arms behind my back, then tether me to one of the sturdy bed posts.

When the guards stepped back, sweat was on their brows, and unease lived in their eyes. I tasted blood on my lip and licked it away when they backpedaled for the door. My mouth twisted into a wretched sort of grin.

"You won't survive when they come for me," I said, voice low and harsh.

They fought their composure, kept their stern façade, and without a word abandoned the room, locking the door behind them.

Alone again, I let my heart break.

CHAPTER 52
THE NIGHTMARE PRINCE

Every mark was set.

Warm air, heavy with brine, beat against the sails. The seas rocked our longships, as though the waters knew there was trouble stirring.

"Fins tell me it arrived not long ago. Deepest the darklands have gone." Nightseer peered through the thick billow of shadows wrapped around our fleet.

Raum, draped in throwing knives and dark kohl, stood beside him looking ahead. All I could see were clouds and darkness. Occasionally, Nightseer would hum, pulling out more of his sea voice to wade through the pitch. Raum would squint more when his mesmer blurred his impossible vision.

Natthaven.

They had it in their sights.

"The merfolk saw it appear?" Sander stepped beside the brusque sea fae.

Nightseer gave a nod. "Says they've been watchin' for it since a call was sent from our Lady of Blades after she received a distress."

Heartwalker and his bleeding coherent reason. I'd kiss the fae when I saw him again. Celine Tidecaller was the Lady of Blades in the Ever and could send swift reports through the tides with her sea voice. Her lands were nearest to the border between earth fae and sea fae realms.

Tait made the right call. If Celine spread the word, doubtless the entire Ever Kingdom would already know what happened tonight.

"Think they're going to pull the land out deeper into those unknown seas?" Raum glanced at Nightseer.

The sea fae popped a shoulder. "Could do. Merfolk'll keep watch, but too far and they get disoriented."

"Then we better see to it they have no chance to fade again." My tone was harsh, and I didn't care to soften it. Mesmer held me in its clutches, and I could not shake the heat of it rolling beneath my skin.

Fear was jagged in my blood, and if I gave in, I would fall into a nightmare I wasn't certain I'd escape.

More than once, Von had slipped a few herbs into my palm from the Elixists to stave off fevers, and my father had not left my side, likely tasting every bit of the dangerous fear wanting to pull me under.

Skadi could not afford me wallowing in nightmares. I was the only one in this crew who knew the isle of Natthaven.

While others kept watch on the shores, I hastily made sketches to mark our scheme.

I scratched labels of peaks or swamplands as I recalled them, after the word I would add a symbol or sketch for my father who memorized areas and images simpler than tracking the words that leapt around pages.

It wasn't a weakness; no one learned maps or plans with such frightening accuracy as Kase Eriksson, and once I reported on the scale of Natthaven and the secrets it gave up during the week I was there, my father was the one to shape the scheme.

Not as intricate as other ploys, perhaps, but this was not meant for finesse or elegance.

Our next steps were designed for destruction until we found Skadi.

I sealed a missive in a powdered elixir meant to keep it dry, then leaned over the edge of the longship.

Round, bulging eyes met mine when the mermaid lifted her face half out of the water. Hair like pure jade glistened with mollusk barrettes and pins. Her skin was not scaled, but against a gleam of light it almost seemed to be.

"To the king." I turned over the parchment. "This is important."

She flashed her thin, pointed teeth. "My own hand will see it to him, earth prince. Unless you wish to swim alongside me."

"I'd never see the sun again."

"I could vow it."

Merfolk. Always trying to entice us beneath the waves. "Hurry."

The maid sank into the dark tides and never resurfaced.

"Jonas." Sander nudged my arm. "We're ready."

I detested the first half of the plan, but it was the only way to get through shore patrols and take the palace straightaway.

My mother hid her vibrant hair under a dark hood and stood beside Raum at the rail of the ship. Daggers were tied to both her legs, and she kept one in hand. Maj didn't care for swords or heavier weapons; she preferred lighter weight to sneak and keep her hands free to use her mesmer.

My father only left my side for his wife. He took her face in his hands, drawing her close. "Meet your marks, Mallie."

"Always." She kissed him, fingers around his tunic, then whispered, "Fight to the end."

"Fight to the end," rumbled down the longship, catching wind through the others until the sea was a dark declaration that battles would be won tonight or we would meet to laugh and dine with the gods in the Otherworld.

Sander embraced my mother briefly. I looked to the deck for a pause, despising farewells.

Wars of childhood deepened my fears of loss to the point of debilitation, but even then I could not stomach the fear of a last goodbye.

There will always be another hello, even if it is in the Otherworld. No one ever truly leaves. Words from Silas, one of the fae kings, had soothed me as a boy.

I clung to them now when my mother waited for me to meet her gaze.

I bested my mother in height long ago, and it did not ease the disquiet when she felt so small in my embrace.

"We will find her," she whispered.

I closed my eyes, throat thick with emotion. "You remember the path through the wood? And what to say if any treetop folk stop you? Then the palace—"

"Jonas." She pulled back and clasped my hands. "I know my marks."

I glanced down. "Be safe, Maj."

She stepped to the rail, Raum and Ash at her side. My mother pressed a hand to her heart, a silent declaration to her men that she loved us.

"At first sight," Daj grumbled, a heaviness to his own voice.

Raum gave a meager salute.

There wasn't another word before my mother, Ash, and Raum dove into the tides. Nightseer only hissed once or twice at lingering merfolk to leave them be and watched through the clouds of darkness.

Ten breaths, twenty, time dragged on.

At long last, with a soft hum, Nightseer faced my father. "They be on land."

The king propped his foot on the rail, looking through the shadows of his own mesmer. "Then we wait for her call."

The first mark was set.

We were too close to the isle to shout commands lest we signal the elven we were here. Signals were passed across the longships through lanterns and hand gestures hidden behind the unnatural mesmer shadows.

As the word spread, the glide of steel against leather sounded over the sea.

I faced the shore. *We're here, Fire.*

Time was the cruelest foe of all. Endless pockets of nothing, only the gentle lap of the sea against the hull of our ships was heard. My fingers ached on one hand from clinging to the hilt of my black steel short blade without rest, and my other from keeping my fist clenched.

Sander knelt by the rail, watching the endless darkness. My father kept to the stempost, unmoving, silent, waiting.

Beautiful thoughts of my wife kept me lucid and grounded when fears of what might be happening to her clawed at my mind.

Mere days after I'd shown her the library, I thought she would toss me into the Nothing for daring to mark a place in a book by bending the corner of the page. It took my face between her thighs and an afternoon undisturbed in the washroom for her to forgive me.

Sometimes Skadi could not turn off her mind for the night. I'd grown accustomed to stroking my fingers through her hair until she fell into slumber.

A smile crept over my mouth recalling the morning I caught Skadi in a battle with Ylva. She wanted to learn how to make my favorite savory buns, and Ylva took the request like she was being banished from the kingdom.

In the end, I found the princess muttering curses under her breath as Ylva barked her commands and drank brän while my fire worked.

To think I once planned for my arranged vow to be nothing but indifferent strangers forced into a position we never wanted was laughable.

Skadi was my daylight and nightfall. She was every moment in between.

"She's calling." My father's low, rough voice broke the melancholy. He spun around, eyes blackened with mesmer, and gave me a jerky nod. "They've spotted her."

Pleasant memories were cut away like a jagged blade sliced through me, and made room for the ice of violence and rage. I rolled my shoulders free of the tension and aches of waiting, and took a second dagger into my free hand.

Hooded, blood burning, I faced the shore.

My father raised his palms. The shadows encircling the fleet of longships shifted and spread into one endless wall of inky night in front of each curved stempost on every bow.

Sander adjusted a strap on his shoulder. Aleksi cracked his neck side to side. Von winked.

There were curious bonds crafted by alver folk, simply called alver vows, that went beyond typical vows. They intertwined the magics in the blood of partners. Through their bond, my father could summon my mother's fears; they beckoned him to her.

The shadow wall could take in anyone who held a fear if my father opened it wide enough.

I'd yet to meet a soul who feared nothing.

Skadi was not an alver, but when this was over, I wanted alver vows with her. The same as Bloodsinger had said about Livia at my vow feast, any way I could be bonded to my fire, I wished it so.

By slipping through the darkness, we would avoid the shore patrols, and meet my mother wherever she'd spotted Skadi.

A little longer.

My father bellowed for our folk to ready their blades, to prepare for anything. He shouted for them to meet the darkness. Roars and drums and cries of twisted glee were returned across the sea.

Silence mattered little now. The isle could not run from us, not anymore. The elven kings were marked, and we were about to meet them.

"Jonas. This is your crown and your kingdom. You lead here." My father waited for me to step to the stempost. "We follow you through."

Damn a kingdom, sink the isle, I cared little if it did not bring me Skadi.

I rolled my short blade in my grip once, then stepped over the rail of the longship as though I would step onto solid ground, and faded into the cold welcome of darkness.

CHAPTER 53
THE MIST THIEF

THE KING WAS DEAD. MY HEART ACHED IN A BEFUDDLING COLLISION OF HATE and affection. Eldirard destroyed my mother and father. He was not alone, but had looked me in the eye, day after day, knowing what he'd allowed.

But without him, I would not have Jonas.

It was a wretched sort of pain. To love and hate the fallen.

Eldirard gave me his throne. I was queen here and needed to stand for all Dokkalfar, but I was tethered like a beast about to strike.

My shoulders ached from the way the guards tied my arms behind my back. Cracked calluses were building on my knees, and blood wrapped around my wrists from my constant squirming and writhing to slip my hands free of the white iron.

"You never did think things through well, Skadinia."

My head snapped up. Arion filled the doorway, his narrow jaw pulsed in frustration.

I bared my teeth. "Get out."

"It is my room."

"My palace."

"Hmm. We'll see. We will be fading soon. A few of the Dokkalfar guards have offered to help pull the isle away. It would be better if you agreed to save time and do it yourself."

"It would be better if you slit your throat. Save you some pain for when he finds you. Or perhaps, I'll get the honor of killing you first."

Arion frowned. "Still think your alver prince is coming for you? Don't be a fool. We will make a new alliance to ease worries, divide lands, give them plenty of coin, maybe even a few elven consorts to replace you in his bed. He'll be appeased."

"Do you actually believe the words that come out of your mouth?"

Arion gripped my hair and wrenched my head back. "You have the tendency to think folk care for you more than they do. I tried to show you, tried to prove you would never be seen as anything but darkness, but you still cling to hope someone might see you as more."

"I know what I am, and that is the difference between you and a man like Jonas—he knows exactly who I am, and it is how I know he will come for me."

"You should have learned by now—everyone has reasons for drawing you in. None of them are because of your few charms, Skadinia. Jonas of House Eriksson might come because he sees you as a prize, but we know how to fill that loss easy enough."

One side of my mouth curled. "You can try. But if you do not give up this fight soon, you will not leave this isle alive, Arion."

Arion stepped back and ran his hands through his hair. "Still so dimwitted and desperate for love. I hope to change that during our turns as king and queen." The prince turned to go. "Food will be sent to you. Stop harming yourself; I will still keep you in chains if you cut to the bone."

The door slammed behind him.

Let Arion and Gerard think they could reason and barter with my nightmare. I would relish their screams as he tore them apart.

"Stop touching them, they'll fall off."

"It's starting to itch."

Sharp whispers pulled me from a fitful rest. Somewhere in the quiet, exhaustion overcame me. My neck throbbed from the angle it was resting against the post of the bed, and from my knees to my ankles had gone numb.

Two Ljosalfar guards entered the room, one held a tray of food in his hands. I straightened, unable to fight, but I could snap and bite and curse them like I had done with every other face in this room.

The man holding the tray was tall and lean, his hair was not as satin and pale as most light elven, and the tips of his ears curled out, like they were too heavy to hold upright. His companion was broader with eyes that did not burn brightly, and he glared down at me with such hate, I thought he might draw a blade.

I jolted when the tray clattered on the edge of a desk. "Well, if I hesitated on whether to kill them before, now I have my answer. Poor lovey, chained like a hound."

He yanked a knife from his boot.

"Stop." A bite of shame filled my cheeks. I sounded so desperate, but I did not wish to die, not without at least seeing him once more.

The guard didn't stop.

Not until his blade cut the ropes around my shackled wrists. I cried out and fell forward when my position adjusted so abruptly. The second guard caught me, and placed his palms on my arms, rubbing the agonizing sting of rushing blood away.

"It'll pass, Princess. It'll pass."

The guard who sliced the rope touched his ears and sighed in relief when he plucked off the tops.

I gaped in a bit of horror. When the ears fell to the ground they dissolved like they'd been made of ash.

"Nik needs to work on that little sculpting trick. Feels like damn fleas are creeping along my ears."

Nik? With caution, I looked at the guard holding me. I didn't recognize him, but he too removed the points of his ears, leaving behind a rounded, mortal-like shape.

My heart stalled. They were alvers.

"Hello, Princess. It's Ash. I have on some masking powders that'll wear off soon enough."

Each breath came faster, sharper, tears—unwanted and unexpected —spilled over my lashes. "Ash."

They came for me. I knew it would happen, but . . . I expected weeks, months, not half a night.

Ash patted the back of my head when it dropped to his shoulder.

The second guard picked at a few things on the tray they'd brought in. "When you feel like you can stand, lovey, we best be going. They'll soon discover the two guards with broken necks in the root cellar."

I blinked and lifted my head. "Raum?"

"Clever girl." He clicked his tongue and pointed a finger at me, then turned back to the tray.

"How . . . how did you get in here?"

"I don't think you realize how well I can see." Raum didn't look at me and kept inspecting the offerings on the tray. "Kept to the deep wood and made around the back of the palace. Strangest thing, though, I could've sworn the trees moved. Almost leading us." Raum popped a roasted nut onto his tongue and faced me. "Have I slipped my mind, or is it not so impossible?"

"Not impossible." My voice was small, breathless. "Natthaven aids those it trusts."

Raum shrugged and went back to the meal. "Foolish of the isle to trust thieves."

Ash grinned. "We took over the guards when Raum noticed Dokkalfar palace guards locked in the stables."

"The stables? Damn Gerard." I rubbed the sore skin around the white iron. "He's overtaking the palace. He killed my . . . he killed Eldirard."

"I thought elven couldn't harm their folk."

"They can do whatever they please, but it stains their affinities, brings madness. We call it a soul stain. Gerard is having his guards act on his behalf, believing he will avoid the corruption. I think he was corrupted long ago."

"Hmm." Raum hummed again, mouth full. "We'll want to free your clan's guards, unless they don't stand with you? I know some of your folk like to whimper about darker mesmers—affinities—no, you have mesmer; I prefer that term."

"The palace guards will defend Natthaven. They will not take kindly to the death of their king."

"Good." Raum brushed crumbs off his palms. "Well, blood's about to spill and I don't much like leaving Mal out there alone any longer."

"The queen is here?"

"Of course. Our mark was only meant to catch the first sighting of you, then send word to the others in the sea, but when we noticed the discrepancy of the guards we worked our way inside. Truth be told, I think Mal might've been afraid we'd find you dead if we waited too long."

I didn't understand how they would send word to the sea, but I didn't question. There wasn't time.

"We can't send the signal unless you tell us if you can walk or if Ash needs to carry you. We can do either."

"I can walk." I winced as Ash helped me rise to my feet.

He chuckled. "Reminds me of Shelba when she tries to stand, our little is getting too big."

"Well." I groaned and rubbed against my swollen knees. "If this is how it feels with a little inside, I hope you soothe her aches each night."

"I try." Ash combed his eyes over me in concern. "All right? No shame if you need help, but it's better to know before we make our next moves."

"I'm fine. Where is Jonas? Arion wrote something to him, and whatever it said is a lie and—"

Raum cut me off with a laugh. "Princess, princess, princess. First, Jonas is only a little bit of a fool. Second, if that elven sod wants to plan a scheme, he better learn about his marks. As I understand it, he called you the wrong name in the missive. Foolish mistake. Damn near insulting he thinks any of us would fall for it."

Raum peered into the corridor, then pulled back inside. "Best to take the window, I'd say. Mal can handle the patrols outside, but there are groups of elven in the next corridor. We'd need to kill our way out."

Ash and Raum set to rummaging through a few hidden pouches they pulled from their boots—a knobby, violet candle and powder that looked like crushed charcoal.

"What happened after they took you, Skadi?" Ash asked as they worked with the curious supplies.

I barreled through it all, from Dorsan's death to Eldirard's.

"So I better call you queen now?" Raum said, almost as though he was disappointed.

"Call me whatever you please, I just want the light elven off my isle."

"That we can do."

"Ready?" Ash kept a hand under my arm.

I lifted my wrists. "I can run and fight, but these block my affinity."

Raum grimaced. "There are elixirs to block mesmer that burn like the hells. Does it hurt you?"

"No. In this form it only weakens."

"Don't have a pick on me in this getup, but we'll get them off soon enough." Raum handed me one of his daggers.

I nearly laughed. Whatever potion or spell had masked their features was wearing off and his face looked oddly contorted as his true silvery eyes burned through the false glow.

"I'll light the signal." Ash sprinkled the charcoal elixir over the wick of the strange candle and a poisonous shade of green flicked to life. The flame grew and flashed against the glass of the chamber until the edges of the sill looked stained in vibrant emerald.

Elixirs and potions. I wanted to laugh at Gerard's haughtiness. The Ljosalfar king was not even as skilled with pulling from light as his son, and he thought he could defeat the alver clans into submission.

Their mesmer was wicked, beautiful, and seemed to have a use for any sort of trouble.

A moment later, a small pebble struck the glass.

"She saw it. Time to go if we want to join the fun." Ash nudged me away and slammed the hilt of his sword through the glass, then carved out the shards without a care for the noise. Ash must've noted my hesitation. "Trust us, Skadi. This is not our first time infiltrating a palace."

I held my breath and took Ash's hand. Below was nothing but

shrubs and a narrow pathway guards used to patrol the outer edges of the palace.

"I'm told you're a climber." Ash stepped aside.

I didn't reply, simply reached for a limb of a nearby tree and swung out over the space. No guards. No calls of escape.

The two alvers followed me, carefully maneuvering down the tree until the last limb ended ten paces over the ground. I let go, biting down the cry of pain when my sore legs struck the soil.

When I lifted my gaze, my stomach backflipped. Four Ljosalfar guards sat in a huddle, curiously touching their bright tunics. One studied the hilt of a sword as though he had never seen one in his life.

"Know where I am, lady?" A guard tilted his head and looked to me imploringly.

"She doesn't know where you are. Stop talking, or you might recall what I said would happen."

The guards shuddered as one and looked about with a new frenzy as though something might erupt from the shadows and devour them.

Bleeding gods.

Queen Malin stood between two towering oaks, hand outstretched. Her head was covered in a dark hood, but when she looked my way, her smile was bright against the darkness. "Told them if there is too much noise, nyks with a love of eating eyes will come for them." The queen faced the empty trees again. "It is good to see you safe, my girl. Be ready to use that blade."

She took their memories. The queen had not needed to lift a blade, yet had bested four trained warriors.

From one of the palace towers, a bell clanged in a warning. There were shouts from the inner walls and commands from watchtowers.

"They've discovered you're missing," Ash said. "Or they found the two dead guards."

"Doesn't matter. They're too late." Malin's voice was calm and steady.

Like black threads weaving through the wood, darkness gathered from shadows. It peeled away from the dark side of the trees, from rocks, from beneath the shrubs, and built into a wall of night.

Malin turned her palm as though reaching into the wall, and when she pulled back another hand was clasped in hers. The king.

Darkly clad figures stepped through the shadows, blades in hand, faces lined in blood, kohl, some kept bows on their backs and clambered up the trees to find a position. They spilled into the palace courtyard like a dark tide flowing over the shore.

Breath caught. A few paces away, near the king and queen, a figure broke through the darkness.

It was a girlish dream, to see the hero storming the castle to rescue his beloved.

In every dream where my life might unravel like the romantic fae tales of my books, I never anticipated my hero would be blood-soaked and murderous without a hint of honorable intentions on his features.

He was my sweetest nightmare.

I knew his walk—swift and determined. Those arms held me fiercely and tenderly. His hood was knocked off his head and his hair was windblown and tousled.

A sob croaked in my chest. I gathered my skirt in one hand and rushed in his direction. "Jonas!"

My nightmare spun around. The beautiful green of his eyes was glossy black. Bright or shadowed, I loved it all. I'd take it all. Jonas could laugh and tease, or he could slaughter and torture. If he was mine, what else mattered?

Jonas hesitated for half a breath, then shoved through the rising alver army.

Five paces, two, then my arms hooked around his neck. I clung to him, legs around his waist, face buried in the warmth of his skin.

"Skadi." He held me against him, his mouth against my throat, kissing me across my jaw, my neck, behind my ear. "Gods, let me see you."

He pulled back, brushing hair from my eyes. I gave him a heartbeat to inspect my face before I kissed him. I kissed him the way I ought to have done before watching him walk down that corridor.

"You came," I whispered against his lips.

"Not even an army of the gods would stop me. Remember?"

"Cover!" The shout came from Raum.

Jonas let me fall off his body and raced us behind a thick tree. He cradled my head against his heart in the same moment the air whistled with the sound of arrows flinging into the wood. One steel tip thudded into the trunk in front of us.

Jonas jolted and tightened his grip around my body.

When the shower of elven arrows ceased, alvers in the shadows returned the fire. Their arrows did not merely strike the wall of the palace, they sparked in flames or rattled the stone, crumbling one watchtower.

"Dipped in explosive elixirs," Jonas was quick to explain.

"I can't use my affinity." I held out my wrists.

For a breath, Jonas seemed frozen, his thumb gently touching the bloodied skin around the white iron. "I'll peel the skin off their bones."

"Agreed, but let me help do it."

With a gleam in his black eyes, Jonas plucked his tricky whalebone from his belt and had the levers keeping the manacles around my wrists opened in a few clever maneuvers. He hovered his mouth close, a devious smirk on his face. "Be monstrous, Wife."

CHAPTER 54
THE NIGHTMARE PRINCE

Blood coated Skadi's wrists, a bruise was forming on her cheek. She'd been touched, and I would take the fingers of the ones who'd done it bit by bit—pluck the fingernails first, peel the skin next, then cut through the bone.

Logic reminded me our time apart was brief, but it did not diminish the damage done. The elven fatally underestimated my affections for my wife. Where they thought they could return to the far seas, prepare over time to face the frustrations of the alver clans, now they would realize their mistake.

Within a single night, they had left their marks on Skadi's skin. Doing so sealed their deaths, and brought a new battle they could not win to their gates.

Bells and warnings rang out from the palace walls. Our people were tucked behind trees and shrubs. If I did not already know the curious nature of Natthaven, I might think myself a bit mad. When another onslaught of elven arrows rained over our heads, the limbs thickened, trunks widened, mounds shifted in the soil.

The isle had chosen its side, and I looked forward to the moment the kings realized they did not stand a chance.

My father stepped out into the front of the line when the final arrow thudded into the soil. He shook out his hands. "I wanted a peaceful night and they had to go start a damn war."

From one of the parapets, a warrior with a gilded helmet aimed his arrow at the king. "Alver clans, our king is willing to re-negotiate our alliance in peace. Continue your attack, and you will not leave our isle without grave losses."

"Did he call it their isle?" Skadi curled her fists, the blaze in her eyes like a bursting star.

I chuckled and stepped beside my father. "I believe you've mistakenly claimed this land. This land does not belong to the Ljosalfar."

The warrior aimed his arrow at me. "Highness, you are requested to meet with the king. You'll receive reparations for your troubles."

"I hope you are not referring to my wife as part of my trouble."

"The future king of the elven clans has claimed the princess as his wife, but we do wish to keep the alliance of peace."

Skadi emerged from the trees, waves of her affinity rolling over her palms. "I am not Arion's wife, and I never will be."

The warrior frantically shouted for aim to be leveled at the princess. Skadi raised one hand. It was too swift, but where her affinity was cradled in her palm, now dark mists coated the guard's bow and the arrow until there was nothing but damp air left behind.

"They're all quite afraid to die." My father looked at Skadi, a cruel sort of sneer on his face.

She did not hesitate. "Such a pity for them, Daj."

Shadows snaked around the throats of elven guards along the wall. Stun and fear was written on every face. They tried to flee, but the shadows spread, adding their ankles and shoulders to the web of mesmer.

For a pause, my father inspected his work, then gave a swift tilt to his head. The movement seemed so simple, like it was nothing, but every coil of darkness twisted the throats of the Ljosalfar guards in sick cracks.

Skadi let out a shuddering cry when nearly twenty men toppled in one blow. The ones fortunate enough to make out with their lives, fled the walls, shouting warnings of an attack.

"I warned you, Fire. You belong to a land of nightmares now."

"And I have never been more at home." She blew out a trembling breath, unsettled by the gore dripping off the walls of her palace, but straightened her spine and raised her palms. The mists of her affinity coated the ground like poison in the grass. "There are innocent elven within these walls. If you can, allow them to live."

Mists painted the palace wall like iridescent ropes, fading away stones one by one. She drew in a sharp breath, jaw tight as her affinity worked to pull away the barrier.

Screams rose in the palace when the walls shuddered.

The sound of stones scraping over stones shook the night. Skadi winced. I went to her side, placed a hand on the small of her back, and held her steady until a gaping, crumbling gap was left in the side of the palace.

Crouched in the now exposed corridors were elven servants, covering their heads against falling stones and sconces. A few inner warriors of the Ljosalfar clans tried to use their own magic to summon the flames of outer torches, desperate to light our clan aflame.

Skadi devoured the fire with the swipe of her palm. There was a tremble to her hand. No mistake the lingering impact of those damn bands on her wrists left her fatigued.

I shoved a second dagger into her palm. "Blades for now, Fire."

We raced into the palace, shoulder to shoulder.

My clan were not graceful fighters. We did not study every elegant step to take, nor which strike would fit terrain or blade. We fought wickedly and brutally.

Elven folk raced for alcoves and chambers, screaming when their halls were invaded. They were accustomed to poise and prestige. Alvers and fae raided with blood on their faces and howls of delight for bloodshed over their lips.

In one corridor, Von stuck close to Aleksi. When Alek would use his glamour to summon the blood in a warrior's veins, holding him in place, Von shoved foaming powders down their throats until they choked on their own blood, or made messier work of spilling innards.

The Kryv were masters at cornering their playthings, then torturing with their mesmer.

Bard and Ash kept close to each other, both Rifters, they snapped thighs and shins, breastbones and cracked ribs in two. Tova perched on one of the stairwells firing arrows into the chaos with Junius and Lynx.

My mother and father rarely raised blades anymore. Two formidable forces careened into the center of battles, slaughtering side by side. Most folk feared death. Daj could grant it to them. My mother seemed unassuming, but the slightest brush of her fingertips across an opponent and they tumbled forward, uncertain how to walk, how to lift a sword. Dead before they reached the ground when another knife from another hand would finish the bloody work.

The elven palace was lost in beautiful madness.

Skadi struck at a Ljosalfar warrior, dodging his blows. She parried, he jabbed.

On the first step to go to her aid, and I was met with my own battle. A burly warrior with a gold ring dangling from each ear and blood on his gleaming tunic.

"Hello, there." I rolled my sword in my grip.

The warrior cried out as he leveled a sturdy strike toward my middle. I spun away and crashed the edge of my sword down on his. I kicked at the man's knee, bending it awkwardly. He cursed me and stepped back to reset his position.

"You should leave with your restitution, alver prince." The guard backed up, but tightened his hold on his own weapon. "Prince, it is in your best interests to give the queen to her own people."

He made a sloppy strike for my neck.

I dodged and shouted loud enough my voice rose over the clang of steel against steel. "Fire! I have a question."

"Now?" Skadi managed to catch her warrior's shoulder.

"As good a time as any."

I could practically hear her exasperation.

"What is the"—she grunted and spun out of a blade lock with the guard—"question?"

"Why"—I struck, my warrior dodged— "does this sod call you queen already?"

Skadi sliced and cut her daggers, ripping open the side of her warrior's face with a deep strike. She kicked out one of his feet, knocking him to the ground.

When she pressed her boot over his chest, she paused to look back at me. "Eldirard crowned me."

I ducked another feckless strike. My opponent seemed to be weary. I could use it. My strikes quickened. They kept to his weaker side, until he was panting and a glimmer of fear took hold of his gaze.

"Where is the deceitful king?"

Skadi cried out when she rammed her dagger into the chest of her warrior. She ripped the blade free and spun around. "Dead."

When the elven standing against me stumbled, I palmed his face, forcing the most horrific ways he would die into his mind—torture, severed tongues, plucked bones—until he screamed and the nightmares started to rot his mind.

I cut my sword over his throat.

With the back of my hand, I wiped sweat off my brow in time for another warrior to take the fight with me.

"And . . ." My sword crashed with the elven. He moved swifter than the first, seemed thirstier for blood. "How are we feeling about the death?"

"Conflicted." Skadi shoved a new man off the point of her dagger she had rammed in his belly.

"Understood."

"I'm glad you do."

"Your happiness is always my desire."

"As it should be."

"Agreed." I threw a small knife, lodging it into the back of a fleeing guard.

"Jonas?"

"Fire?"

Skadi spun around to avoid another blow. The man was screaming and tormented in his head. A clear sign of Sander being nearby, corrupting memories with fear. She ended up chest to chest with me. Breaths were harsh between us, sweat and blood painted our skin. There had never been a more stunning sight.

Skadi leaned close. "Just once, give me the last word."

An elven warrior let out a battle roar and raced for us. We stepped apart.

I kicked out a foot, catching his ankle. The man stumbled forward, sprawled out on his stomach. Before he could take another breath, Skadi dug her dagger into the back of his throat.

I gripped her arm and spun her into me, grinning. "Never."

Our people shoved through the elven warriors. Skadi took my hand and pointed toward the king's throne room. "Gerard and Arion were gathering there before they locked me in Arion's chamber."

A ruthless kind of hate took hold. Something cruel and bloodthirsty. I held her against me, my voice as a broken blade. "Did he touch you beyond the shackles?"

Skadi's eyes flashed. "No."

"All I heard was yes."

A small, villainous grin played on her mouth. "I must've misspoken."

"Flawless as you are, mistakes are bound to happen at times."

Skadi raced for the door to the throne room, I followed. We weren't the first inside. Bursts of elixirs snapped and scorched fleeing guards. Rifters twisted spines. Lynx and his calming mesmer had a pile of bodies of those he'd managed to calm into sleep. All their throats were bloodied.

Mesmer was taxing, much like Skadi's affinity. By now, most elven and alver kept to their blades.

A hand gripped the back of my neck. Sander appeared, soaked in blood from his head to his chin. When he smiled his teeth were stained in red. "Spotted the prince using his flames to pull their guards and the king away. They're aiming for the shore to flee."

"No!" Skadi blanched. "They can't go free, not again."

I took hold of her hand. "No worries, Fire."

"Jonas we—"

"We've hit our marks, Wife." I drew my nose along her damp cheek. "We have them exactly where we want them. Now, it's time for you to finish this."

CHAPTER 55
THE MIST THIEF

OUTSIDE THE PALACE, WARRIORS WERE FLOODING DOWN STONE STAIRCASES. From this side, it was the shortest distance to the sea. Arion had used his flames to transport guards and Gerard to the shore.

Raum approached Jonas's shoulder. "The cowardly prince is by those ships. They're readying to flee."

Panic was tight in my belly. I couldn't fight this battle again. Arion brought the fighting to the fae once, abandoned me to clean up the aftermath, and now he and his wretched father would flee again. Hiding away in Grynstad until they recovered and fell upon us again.

But panic halted for a moment when Jonas muttered in a dark voice, "Send the signal."

Raum shoved two fingers into his mouth and whistled, not a simple tune, it rose in pitch, then deepened, a deliberate melody.

Blasts of fiery light burst into the night sky. The boom rattled the ground, it rippled over the tides.

I did not have the ferocious eyesight of a Profetik alver like Raum, but I could see the pause of the retreating prince.

Jonas took my hand and hurried us down the path, but kept glancing out to the sea every few paces.

When the fiery bursts faded against the stars, Arion and Gerard boarded the ships. No. I quickened my pace. Jonas's hold on my hand tightened and he lengthened his stride. What was the plan? Moments ago, my nightmare was at ease, now his jaw tightened and there was tension building over his shoulders.

Until . . .

The surface of the sea churned violently. White tipped tides boiled like a thousand fish thrashed toward the surface. Not only ahead, but to the northern edges of the isle and the southern. As though surrounded, the dark sea shattered.

A gnashing serpent figurehead erupted from below the water. Crimson sails cracked in the wind, and the jagged spikes of bone from ancient sea serpents carved toward the skies.

The royal ship of the Ever King.

More ships rose across the whole of Natthaven's waters. Blue sails with skulls, narrow hulls and pale laths of Gavyn Seeker's vessel. A vicious ship with black sails cut on the other side. Newer than the others, the lacquer on the hull still glimmered beneath the moonlight.

The ship of the Lady of Blades.

Merfolk bared their needle teeth. Sea singers and their gnarled faces and seductive voices beckoned to the Ljosalfar. Sirens joined the call, luring unsuspecting warriors toward the tides.

"Bloodsinger!" Jonas raised his blade toward the sky.

Along the upper deck of the first ship, the Ever King cranked the helm, tilting the bow toward the escaping prince and king.

I laughed, softly at first, then louder with more unbound rage. They were surrounded. Fae answered the call for my nightmare, no care that I was elven, no care that my folk attacked them not so many months ago.

Fire launched from the sides of the Ever Ship. The booms cracked through the night as the king fired his strange spears and burning stones at Arion and his men. It forced the Ljosalfar back onto the shore.

Arion tried to snatch at any light, no mistake, desperate to save his own neck.

From another pathway near the palace, a rush of guards in the blue and silver of the shadow elven raced for the shores, spears and swords raised. Fiske and Isak and the woman I knew as Ash's sister were among them, likely the ones who'd freed my warriors from their makeshift prison.

Dokkalfar blades launched onto the shore against Gerard's weary warriors.

With a new kind of desperation on his face, Arion attempted another spiral of his affinity. I opened my palm free of a dagger and surrounded the spark in dark, creeping mists, wrenching his pitiful magic into the Nothing.

Arion staggered back, barely having time to lift his sword before I crashed the dagger down against him.

"Skadinia!"

"I hate that name." I slashed again. "You tortured me." Another strike. "Mocked me, brutalized me."

"Stop." Arion slashed his sword against me. "I forced you to do nothing. You marred your own flesh."

"Convinced it was the only way to be free because of you!" I nicked his ear.

He cupped a hand over it, dabbing at the blood, and narrowed his gaze. "You will never be accepted here without me. Don't you see that? Your own clan despises you."

I shook my head. "No. My *true* clan came for me. The Dokkalfar and Ljosalfar are welcome to join the alvers once you are dead."

Arion sneered. "I don't think that will happen."

"Skadi, watch it!" someone shouted for me.

I spun around. Gerard rushed at me, blade raised, readied to land a killing blow.

But two paces from me, the king's legs buckled. Black, pulpy veins bloomed from the corners of his eyes, his brow, from his lips. The king cried out in heartbreaking terror.

Both Sander and Jonas stepped onto the shore, eyes blackened, and prowled around the king.

Together, Jonas crafted a nightmare and Sander twisted it into a manipulated memory so deep a soul would believe the horrors to the point of madness. They could break a mind with their forced fear.

The way the twins launched at the Ljosalfar king, never easing no matter how Gerard cried out in fright, was magnificent to watch.

I stepped away from Arion, holding his gaze. For the first time, the prince seemed to consider there was no escape.

Heavy tendrils of mists billowed off my palms, thick enough the cold left frigid droplets of water behind. I was going to be cruel, unfeeling, I was about to cause pain that spurred from my own anger, but I did not feel empty.

I wasn't falling into the cold.

I felt everything—the race of my pulse, the heat of my blood. I felt the wonderment that an entire kingdom went to battle at the first word of my absence. I embraced the laughter we had shared since I stepped foot on their shores. I felt their affection, their jests, and their acceptance.

I felt love. Radiant, burning love for the man who'd taken me as a wife for peace, but had robbed me of every edge of my heart.

It was written like the love in my tales of lore, but so much grander.

Jonas was real.

He was mine.

I felt it all when my darkness engulfed King Gerard where he whimpered and convulsed on the sand from his tortured mind. With a deep draw of air through my nose, I pulled him into the shadows of my affinity, the weight of his soul heavy in my blood.

Sound faded, there were no shouts from warriors, no booms from the sea fae vessels.

A single cry broke out. Arion slumped to his knees, chin down.

"We were meant to lead the elven. You've destroyed our people." The prince's eyes were red and angry when he looked to me, iridescent strands of my magic curled around his face and arms. Arion didn't try to run, merely held me in his disdain. "You destroy everything and always will. He will come to hate you for it, as I have."

A warm palm splayed over the small of my back.

Jonas stood beside me, silent, stalwart.

I closed my eyes and slowly curled my fingers into my palms. Dark mists faded Arion into the void, only his abandoned sword remained.

Pressure stacked on my chest. There was always a moment when I used my affinity as this, to release whatever it was I snared and toss it elsewhere, or to close the gap between this realm and whatever dark Nothing housed the mists.

I tightened my fists and sealed the darkness from returning.

My knees buckled when the force of it lifted abruptly. Jonas curled his arms around my waist, holding me against him. He clung to me, pressed a kiss to the side of my head, and whispered, "There's my fire."

I wrapped my arms around his waist, pressing my cheek to the steady thrum of his heartbeat.

It was over.

CHAPTER 56
THE NIGHTMARE PRINCE

THERE WAS A COMMON KNOWLEDGE ABOUT ALVER FOLK—THEY COULDN'T BE trusted.

Niklas and Junius were found slinking out of the back courtyard of the elven palace with satchels of fallen white iron blades, silk doublets, and even Eldirard's circlet.

I snatched it away from his hands. "That is for Skadi."

Niklas shook his head, as though *I* were the one in the wrong. "It is like I no longer know you."

Worse than the smugglers of the Falkyn guild were the damn king and queen.

The recovered circlet in hand, I made my way toward the great hall only to collide with my disheveled mother and father emerging from one of the chambers.

"What the hells are you doing?" Heat boiled in my face when my bleeding father spun around, still adjusting his damn belt. "You couldn't wait a night, perhaps a day, before defiling the linens?"

"Jonas, really. Emotions run high during a fight. It isn't all that scandalous." My mother had the decency to flush as she smoothed her hair.

Daj patted my cheek. Hard. "I expected a quiet reprieve when you all were going to the South. You think I would let something as trivial as battles stop me from claiming that with my wife?"

"I'm never looking at you again. You're heathens. No regal blood in your veins."

"Thank you," both said in the same breath.

"Hopeless." I shoved into the great hall. "Bleeding hopeless.

The hall was bursting in sea fae, alvers, thieves, and elven. A strange sight, but one I planned to see again and again. Dokkalfar guards were shaken to learn of their fallen king. Elixists handed over strong mesmer-brewed draughts for the nerves while Mediskis tended to the wounded alongside elven healers.

Treetop folk had ventured from their nests and gawked at the towering rafters and spires of the palace. A skittish bunch, but once Raum convinced a few of their elders to taste brän and Gavyn Seeker encouraged the younger elven to tip back sea fae honey rum, the hall had grown as boisterous as a Black Palace feast.

Skadi was not the same woman I observed at our vows not so long ago.

She'd taken up a seat beside Sander and Von and laughed across a table with Livia and Celine. Bloodsinger kept a possessive arm around Livia, but once or twice, the slightest smirk teased the Ever King's lip.

"I'll never forgive you for killing that light bastard," Erik grumbled. "He was mine to kill."

Skadi propped her chin onto her palm, grinning at the Ever King. "I suppose you should sail here a little faster next time."

Laughter followed, and Erik Bloodsinger lifted the horn in a mute acceptance of my wife.

Aleksi spoke with Tait through deep gulps from their drinking horns.

Alver blood smelled like piss, and the hall was rank with it, but no one minded. For a moment, it seemed the collision of worlds was content to sink into peace together.

Even for a night.

Skadi was wild and radiant. Her hair was bloody and tangled, but she held her shoulders straighter than before. Pain was there behind her eyes—pain we could face side by side—but relief and joy burned brighter.

I took my place beside her. The moment I came into her sights she curled her hands around my arm, drawing me as close as possible without sitting atop my lap.

How many turns had I lived fearing this? Someone who cared, and loved, and wanted me. To imagine missing this bond with Skadi because I feared losing it was nauseating to imagine. I held her gaze for a long moment, ignoring the taunts from my friends that I was a lovesick sod.

I was. Skadi promised to watch me burn if I tried to ignite the blaze in her soul, and she kept her word.

From those first moments, she swallowed me whole, and I never wanted to be set free.

The shadow elven did not protest Skadi's ascension as their queen. I wasn't certain if it was the glowering clan of alver folk standing at her back, or the silver glisten of the royal brand that flowed over her brow for her people to see, but the Dokkalfar were quick to bend the knee.

We found her lady's maid hidden in her chamber beneath the bed. Panicked and convinced the alver clans would never allow the woman to live, it took a hefty touch from Lynx and his mind calming before the woman slumped over, relaxed enough she could not keep her eyes open.

"Cara will insist on remaining with me." Skadi shook her head at the door once the woman was taken to sleep off her fears in another room. "Tending to royals is all she's done since she was a girl. To tend to a queen has always been her ambition."

I pressed a kiss to the top of Skadi's shoulder. "She's welcome if she accepts propriety and etiquette mean crass words and overstepping personal boundaries amongst the alvers."

Skadi laughed and wrapped her arms around my waist. "She will be in a constant state of gasping in horror. I think we should introduce her to cook Ylva."

We crawled into the bed, bodies aching, Skadi unbothered by my fetid blood from the nicks and scrapes I'd earned in the fighting.

We spent clock tolls curled beside each other in her old chambers she'd used as a child, talking of the truths she'd learned before Eldirard was killed.

"You deserved more, Fire." I kissed the tip of her nose. "But I am pleased he saw his mistakes in the end."

"I do not know how to feel." She laid her cheek to my chest. "I hate him for the role he played in the death of my parents, in keeping me fearful of my own affinity, but he was good to me in many ways. He gave me a home."

"It will be his regret that he did not love you as you deserved, but you can hold to the love he did offer and hate the rest."

Skadi was silent for a moment, long enough I thought she might have fallen asleep until she whispered, "I am heartbroken over Dorsan."

"He will be honored by our folk."

Skadi kissed the flame on my skin and tucked her head under my chin.

"What do you plan to do now?" I asked. "You are queen here. Do you wish to put a wall down the center of your bedchamber and move me into the other side?"

"I plan for all of us to settle in our home, Nightmare."

In truth, I wasn't entirely certain what she meant, but when her eyes fluttered closed, heavy with sleep, I held her close until I followed.

Before dawn filtered through the trees of Natthaven, Skadi was placed in front of a snobbish looking council of advisors for the Dokkalfar clan.

Beneath the table, she tangled her fingers with mine, eyes heavy with a need for sleep. I was damn close to demanding she receive it, or stabbing another one of these sods if they droned on any more about the succession of her bloodline.

Sander and Von tried to remain steady and watchful, but both had long ago drifted off from sheer boredom. Von's head drooped, but

Sander had toppled to one side on a fur lined bench, softly snoring in the corner.

"What will you have us do with Grynstad?" A wizened man with long, white hair to his waist leaned forward. "Their king and heir have been lost to the battle."

"But Gerard had a queen," Skadi said. "The way I see it, Grynstad and the light elven fall to Valdis's word now."

The man arched a brow. "Yes, the queen, but King Gerard did not often give her a voice—"

"Much like the shadow elven." Skadi's mouth pinched.

Gods, there was something to be said when she locked a man in her stare. It was terrifying and intoxicating in the same breath, and I planned to make my sentiments known the moment these bastards released us from this cramped, stuffy room.

The advisor cleared his throat. "Would you care to arrange a neutral meet with the light elves?"

"I would. We are all elven, and I have grown wretchedly tired of behaving as though we are not."

I squeezed her fingers.

"We have one more matter to discuss." Skadi took the time to meet the gaze of each advisor. "I do not want Natthaven to float aimlessly in the far seas. I do not wish it to fade ever again. I want our land to be known, to be truly aligned with the fae realms." She smiled at me. "That was the purpose of the alliance, was it not?"

"You want Natthaven to become part of Klockglas?" I asked.

"There is a responsibility to the Dokkalfar." Skadi glanced to her council. "But the alver clans are my home. I wish our folk to be united there."

I want us all to settle in our home. She wanted to bring her people . . . home.

This meet needed to end. Too long had my mouth been away from my wife's skin.

When the council tentatively agreed, clearly uncertain how it would be to live permanently beside a fae realm, we opened the doors, and I made quick work of dragging Skadi into the corridor.

"My Lord, a moment." A mousy palace steward dipped his chin when I looked his way. "I wish to inform you, the second throne will be fashioned by the next full moon, I assure you."

"For what?"

The elven blinked his bright cerulean eyes until I considered he might be trying to signal me wordlessly. "Well, for you, sire. You are now. . . the king. By the decree of the alliance, since our queen was not the blood of the royal house, these lands belong to you."

Well, shit. "Fine, as my first act as king, I declare my wife as the blood heir, and the voice of this isle. I will sit beside her, but for gawking purposes and to pique curiosity only."

Skadi pinched my side when he scurried away, more unsettled than before. "You are my king, Nightmare. I want to do this *with* you."

I chuckled and pressed a kiss on the curve of her neck. "I will be honored to be your king, and should you need my voice, or my thoughts, or a shoulder to lean upon, I will be that for you. But you have never had a voice here, and I think it is long overdue for it to be heard."

Skadi pressed a palm to my cheek. "I would vow with you again and again, Jonas Eriksson. I'm afraid I've fallen in love with you."

"I told you hearts were not part of the alliance, but mine will always be yours."

"Seems we failed at our indifferent vows."

"We're terrible at them."

"What a shame."

"A tragedy."

Skadi pinched her lips and arched her body into mine. "Just once?"

I laughed, cupping her face in my hands, and claiming her mouth. Skadi's skin was flushed and her heavy breaths tangled with mine by the time I pulled away with a soft, "Never."

CHAPTER 57
THE MIST THIEF

Natthaven faded for what I hoped would be the final time.

A dozen shadow elven stood with me in the wood, each of us beseeching the trust of the isle to move us to different seas. Called the fading isle, but in truth, if the isle did not wish to abide by the request, it would not go.

I did not know how Eldirard moved the land when I was forced onto its shores. I guessed it was taxing, and I wondered if it was the reason Natthaven did not drift deeper into the far seas where it would have been nearly impossible to find again.

I was the only one capable of forcing the isle by stealing it away with my mists. When fae and elven battled, Arion demanded I shift my land often. The cold was unbearable, there were times I believed I felt the heart of the isle breaking as its will was stripped away.

"I am honored to have gained your trust after such turmoil," I whispered against a tree.

Jonas was perched atop a stone, dragging a knife across a piece of wood. I didn't know what he intended to carve, but after his sleep was tumultuous and heated with a threat of another mesmer fever, I thought he found a bit of calm in whittling.

He lifted his head and gave me a small grin.

Our folk left with sea fae not long before, and the isle felt too quiet.

"Ready?" I asked, not even convinced the isle understood words, more actions.

Trees swayed. Once more dark seas rolled inland, swallowing the shores and lands into a cloak of darkness.

After a time in the damp nothing, it was a relief when the familiar air of the eerie Klockglas docks brushed across my cheeks.

I opened my eyes, once more feeling like I wasn't leaving home, but returning to it. From behind, Jonas wrapped his arms around my waist, holding my back to his chest.

"Do you see them, Fire?" One arm remained around my middle, but he pointed into the distance. "They came for you."

Docks and harbors around the shore were tangled in endless long-ships. Sea fae vessels remained out in the deeper tides, but skiffs and rowboats were tucked alongside the rest at the docks.

All along the shoreline were huddles of people. More than those who fought with us for the isle. Klockglas docks were packed with Rave warriors and fae folk from across the kingdoms. They'd answered the distress of the alver clans and never hesitated to guard our kingdom and stand at our backs with their blades.

Night Folk fae, Glamour fae, mortals, kings and queens, they all greeted the returning fleet of alvers and sea fae. Others gawked at the isle when it settled just along the edge near the warm sea pools.

Within moments of stepping onto the docks, we were surrounded.

Mira raced for us and hooked an arm around our necks.

"I have done nothing but worry. Nothing. Then, I brought them all here, dressed for battle, and waited in the tides even more. When I saw the ships return . . ." Mira squeezed our throats even more. "I have made a decision that I will never remain behind again."

The Ever Queen approached and when I reached for her hand, she did much the same as Mira and wrapped me in her arms. "You have won your crown, Queen."

"Thank you for standing with us," I whispered.

Livia took hold of my hands. "You were never our enemy, Skadi. Know that."

The queen went on to Jonas with harsher words leveled at him for worrying them and still not responding to her missive.

I was left to accept the cold greeting of the sea king. His red eyes were like dark blood, but he did not seem as indifferent on whether I lived or died. The calmer demeanor might've been because Livia's young brother instantly ran to Bloodsinger's side upon their arrival.

No doubt the Ever King did not want to scar the boy with his darker instincts.

"What will you do with it, elven?" Erik tipped his head at the looming isle.

"I don't know. I wanted it to be part of our home here."

"Then make it part of the land." Mira waved her hands in a flourish, as though I ought to understand exactly what she meant.

"Make it part of the land?"

Mira gestured at Livia. "You've met the Night Folk king. The Night Folk fae have magic of the earth and it just so happens their king can bend the soil. Or, you know, fashion some sort of strip of land to the isle."

Livia did not give us a moment to protest before she summoned her father. Behind the Night Folk king were Jonas's mother and father, and the other fae kings and queens in attendance at our vows.

Jonas draped an arm around my shoulders while we all watched with a bit of awe as Livia's father pressed a hand on the soil and the bedrock shifted in a great heave.

Sea floor raised, shorelines shifted, and when it was over, a smooth curve of land had fastened to the edges of Natthaven, securing the isle to the lands of the alvers.

Kase grinned when one of the kings with wheat-golden hair grunted in annoyance. "This should've been discussed. Tell me how it is fair that House Eriksson simply gets an entire isle for their lands and Night Folk have claim to the sea. It will be no time at all before you overrun our humble little kingdom."

Kase chuckled with a bit of smugness. "Arrange vows and you get land."

"You may be right." The second king turned on his heel. "Mira my girl, there is something I wish to discuss with you. I urge you to keep an open mind."

His voice was lost through the chatter and new thrill from the alver folk interested in exploring the isle and the shadow elven tentatively peeking around shops and dock houses in a new land.

"Some Dokkalfar have never stepped foot off Natthaven," I whispered.

Jonas smirked. "They will be corrupted soon enough."

Debauchery of the Black Palace great hall lived on well into the night, long after Jonas urged me back to our bedchamber. The door hardly closed before Jonas had his fingers unlacing the back of my gown in a frenzy.

His mouth demanded mine. I parted my lips, needy for his taste, and I didn't break away when he pinned me down over the bed.

Jonas braced his palms on either side of my head, watching as I unbuckled his belt. Before I could remove his trousers, he pressed gentle kisses to my still-healing wrists and pinned them over my head.

"Hold there, Fire." He kissed across my chest, peeling my gown away as he went until I was bared to him. Jonas tossed the garment aside and kissed and licked his way down my middle.

I shuddered in desire when his teeth nipped at the sensitive skin of my thigh. With a soft moan, my hips rocked against his cruel, beautiful mouth. "More."

Jonas followed his tongue with two fingers, filling me to the point I couldn't draw in a breath.

I writhed and sighed until my thighs clamped around Jonas's head and fell apart with a cry of his name.

My body still burned in pleasure when Jonas reeled back to finish ridding himself of his clothes, then he fitted his hips between my legs.

He shifted into a man undone.

Movements were fast and messy and deep. His breaths heated my throat. I thought he might split me in two, and gods, how I wanted him to.

I moaned and scraped my fingernails down his back, desperate to cling to him as he drove me to the edge again. I shuddered and clawed and reached for him, my head spinning in a delirious fog.

"Skadi," he whispered my name like it was a secret vow. In these moments, when he spoke my name in such a way, I felt as though my heart melded with his, never separate. "Together." Jonas deepened each thrust. "Come with me."

I didn't know if it was his words or his deep movements, but my body bowed into his, shattering against the pieces that had already come apart before. Jonas went rigid, his soft gasps nestled against my neck as his release spilled into me.

For a long pause we stayed that way, tangled up like we'd grown together.

"I always thought if I loved someone this way," he whispered into my hair, "the fear of losing it would be constant. I was wrong."

"How so?"

"I never knew the happiness would outweigh the fear." Jonas rolled onto his shoulder, facing me. "Making you my wife was the best scheme I will ever think up, Fire. I am desperately in love with you, I hope you know."

"As am I." I kissed him gently. "You are my sweetest nightmare."

EPILOGUE
THE MIST THIEF

Mira was given liberties and all the glittering fanfare to transform the gardens of the Black Palace. Bespelled powders from clever elixirs coated branches and leaves, causing the trees and shrubs to shine like starlight.

Even some lazy sparks of Sun Wings had ventured from Natthaven into the groves of Klockglas. The suspicious creatures added a few glows of gold, as if they'd entered the gardens out of curiosity more than anything.

Once more, I stood in a satin tent, waiting.

Unknowns, apprehension, resentment, all of it had twisted my stomach months ago. Tonight, the only knots were beautiful anticipation.

A throat cleared. Jonas's father stepped inside the tent. Someone must've urged the king to look more the part. He wore black as always, but his dark sword was properly positioned in a polished sheath on his waist. His hair was freshly braided off the sides and smoothed down, and he was desperately trying to hide the irritation in his features for his palace being invaded by endless droves of people.

I let out a muffled snort behind my hand. "Surviving, Daj?"

The smallest flick of a grin teased his mouth. "For a moment or two longer."

Doubtless Mira was behind the king's agreeability. The woman could be rather frightening when she set out to organize a revel.

In truth, Cara became Mira's right hand, aiding the princess like a tyrant's minion to create a truly regal event. When Mira insisted I would be clad in a full, elven-style gown, Cara was there to refute my initial protests that it wasn't necessary, and saw to it a gown was commissioned.

I readied to roll my eyes when the garment was delivered to the Natthaven palace two nights ago, but when I saw the silver satin layered in gold and blue stitching and lace, I could do nothing but admire like the rest.

Inge Hob even added new heart glass a few Dokkalfar had polished and prepared for her use.

I smoothed my palms over the bodice, already golden with the race of my heart.

"If you're having second thoughts, I know more than one morally ambiguous sod in there who'd be willing to smuggle you out."

I laughed and hooked my arm around the king's elbow. "Never a second thought, I merely want to skip the production and get the man alone. I know he's your son, but frankly, you lot have yourselves to blame for me speaking my true thoughts. None of you know how to be vague."

The smile spread a little more on my father-in-law's mouth. "Never saw the purpose in speaking untruths."

Thieves, killers, crooks, but they drew the line at lies.

"You have given him happiness," the king said in his dark, low rasp. "I do not say it enough, but that is a debt I cannot repay. You are as much an alver as you are elven, girl."

I tilted my head back, blinking. "Mira is going to be furious at you for making me cry like an infant."

"Then stop."

"Then stop speaking."

"Gladly."

Outside, folk from across the fae realms and Natthaven once more took up chairs and benches wrapped in shocks of gold. There was little divide between them now. Elven folk sat between fae, alvers, and mortals.

Dokkalfar had slipped into alver society with more ease than anticipated. Their affinities to summon healing into talismans and charms intrigued fae folk and healers amongst the alvers.

Some of the bolder Dokkalfar asked for the chance to travel to other fae kingdoms as healers. We hardly cared to grant permission on where they desired to live. It was enough of a step for elven folk to leave the shores of Natthaven.

If they wished to find contentment among all the kingdoms, we would never deny them.

Peace was the intent when I vowed with my nightmare. Our goals had not changed, though so much more had.

Suspicions remained about elvish intentions, but I had hope that soon elven folk would simply be another part of the fae and alver kingdoms.

Kase led me through the crowd. Faces who'd come to matter more than I imagined watched each step.

Aleksi, Sander, and Von offered gentle smiles for me, but tried to get the king to misstep with a few low taunts under their breath. Kase flicked his fingers by his side, and in the next breath Von let out a cry of fright and Aleksi stumbled over the leg of the bench when a burst of shadowy weavers and their hairy legs crawled across their laps.

Mira and Livia snickered in the benches just ahead of them. Livia sat with her king and the sea folk. Tait on one end of the bench, Mira on the other, intentionally lifting her nose away from the king's cousin.

After we'd returned from the battle from Ljosalfar, Bloodsinger reminded his cousin he was still the official escort whenever the fae princess needed to sail.

They'd slipped into tense indifference since.

A little girl with flower-lined braids waved from her family's bench. Teodor and Annetta were healed from the elven poison, and had reunited with their three littles only a week before.

I flashed the littles a smile, reveling in the elven silver they still wore from the night near their longhouse.

Queen Malin sat amongst the Kryv and her fellow royals from the other kingdoms. The expansive households of every royal house took up nearly half one side of the gardens.

Malin wore a gown and even topped her head with her dark circlet for the occasion. She beamed at me, then offered her husband an encouraging smile, as though she could sense he would rather do this without all the crowds.

Seated in a small cluster in the edges was a pale woman with golden hair—the Ljosalfar queen, Gerard's widow.

Valdis was not Arion's mother, who'd gone to the gods at his birth, but when we first met, I didn't know how much affection the woman had carried for the prince.

My senior in age, but not by much. Valdis was a young queen, overwhelmed by being handed a crown.

Only after we sent a missive declaring in blood that we did not seek her crown did Valdis emerge from her lands. Ljosalfar were elven. We wanted peace. We wanted her people to see her as their queen as much as they saw Gerard as their king.

It wasn't long before we learned she hardly knew her husband and stepson, and was often left to solitude in a manor in the upper knolls on Grynstad, living a solitary life as a wealthy woman without a voice and a husband who only visited her once each month.

She did not even know battles had been fought on Natthaven.

Trusted Dokkalfar warriors were assigned to travel to Grynstad with the queen in the coming nights, a way to ensure any noble houses did not attempt to overrule her voice. To the stun of many, Raum offered to keep watch on Ljosalfar lands until the queen found her footing.

Already, the Kryv and queen had been caught in conversation in the courtyards. She was intrigued by his mesmer and seemed more comfortable around Raum than even me. In truth, I couldn't figure if the man volunteered because he wanted to scope the wealth of Grynstad, or he found the queen interesting.

Either way, it was another move toward trust and alliances now that shadow elven and alvers would be friendly with the light elven.

For so long, I'd lived lonely, now I was surrounded by countless brutal, loving people who'd already proved they'd go to war should anyone dare try to bring me harm.

But through them all, I could not peel my eyes from the man standing beneath a vine covered arch. Totems made of bone and runes hung over Jonas's head when he lifted his gaze, the devious smile on his face.

Like his father, he'd been tucked into a fine tunic with crossed blades stitched on the front, and he'd lined his eyes in a touch of kohl as a mark of warriors and strength in the kingdom. Jonas kept shifting in place. He had one palm clasped around his other wrist, but his fingers twitched like he could hardly stand not reaching out and snatching me away.

When I was two paces away, he did it anyway.

He didn't look away from me when his father handed over my palm to his son, and sat beside the queen.

"Fire." My nightmare's eyes combed down my body. "Is all that for me?"

The heart glass blazed over my gown. "Always."

He pressed a gentle kiss to my knuckles. There were no speakers here to lead the ceremony. This was meant to be intimate between a pair.

I leaned closer. "I don't know how to do this."

"No one does. Most of us make it up as we go. There is only one part at the end that is the same."

I dug my teeth into my bottom lip, hiding the grin. Alver vows. A request Jonas asked of me shortly after Natthaven was joined to Klockglas.

Our original contract felt marred and tainted. Jonas took it as the Norns telling us we needed to re-do vows, but add a bit more to them. An alver touch.

"Want me to go first, Fire?"

"As long as you give me the last word."

Jonas chuckled and drew me closer, pressing my body to his, not the standard distance most couples kept. "Skadi, I want nothing more than to walk my days with you at my side. I have been caught in the blaze of your fire, and I swear to you, I will never douse it. You are the thief of my heart, and I will give it to you every day so long as we live, and through the eternities of the Otherworld."

My thumb tugged at his bottom lip. I forced myself to hold steady and not devour his mouth. Not yet.

"You are my sweetest nightmare. A fiend, a thief, a gentle heart, and I will love every side of you forever. I will always be there to take your fears, share your hopes, and give you everything in my heart, day after day."

New power rushed through my blood like the roar of the tides. Something heated that tangled with the ice of my affinity in my veins.

"Now the alver vow."

I didn't know if it would do anything different since I was not an alver, but I suspected it might bond us closer, offer insight and senses of each other that were deeper than unbonded folk.

Last night, when the great hall was packed with visitors here for the new vows, I spoke with Gunnar, one of the shared cousins of Jonas, Sander, Aleksi, and Livia.

He was a Profetik alver who could command another's mind to follow his every demand, even if he desired them to slit their own throat. He'd recited alver vows with his wife, a glamour fae from Mira's kingdom with a gift of sight from celestial occurrences.

Gunnar insisted even though his mate was fae, the pair could sense emotions within each other. When she was troubled, he knew it. Even when she was pained during the births of their two littles, he knew how to help ease her discomfort without a word.

He knew when one of her premonitions was going to take hold, and she had unintentionally compelled a mind to do her bidding more than once.

"Alver vows are sealed in blood, Fire." Jonas took out a narrow knife.

I watched as he carved the rune onto his palm, then didn't hesitate to do the same on my own. Jonas cleared his throat and placed his bloody palm over mine.

"Just repeat what I say," he whispered, then let out a slow breath. "What power I have is yours for all your days."

The tug of power drew me closer, as though my body could not stand to put even the smallest space between us.

My voice was soft when I spoke. "What power I have is yours for all your days."

Jonas laced our fingers together. A bite of heat rushed to my head. Damp mists and inky shadows swirled around our hands, like a burst of the darkness within the both of us could not be contained. The shock of power ended abruptly, and lingering ribbons of mists absorbed into our flesh.

There was silence for a breath, then roars of applause rippled through our audience. Mira had her arms around Livia, shrieking in delight as she bounced on her toes, shaking the Ever Queen enough it drew out an irritated glare from the sea king.

Malin held onto Kase's arm, a bit of glassy tears in her eyes. For the first time I saw the full grin of the alver king.

We were swallowed by Sander and Aleksi before Jonas shoved them away with a grunt of frustration. "Let me kiss my damn wife."

I laughed, curling my fingers around his tunic, and pulled his mouth to mine. Warm, inviting, I kissed my husband a second time after vowing my life to his. In the beginning I thought love that would start wars, that would draw a heart to kill, was only a thing of romantic fae tales.

I never believed my own would unfold when a prince of nightmares dared love the monster in the mists.

Celebrations lasted (to my father-in-law's horror) for a full week. When the Black Palace returned to its quiet mystery, Jonas and I settled in the palace of Natthaven. Close enough we were still drawn into the schemes of Klockglas, but with a new palace to claim as our own.

Raum kept his word and left to Grynstad with Valdis. The alver king and queen did not let on how much they would truly miss the man until Kase damn near threatened Raum with a fearful death if he did not write and return for the Jul revels during the frosts.

Aleksi returned to his Rave unit in the Northern peaks, but with Jonas's harvest duties to inventory the camps, we would see him in coming weeks.

When Livia and Bloodsinger returned to their kingdom, Sander joined after he learned a noblewoman reported a few scrolls and trinkets from the far seas washed ashore on her lands.

There was no telling how long Sander and his curious mind would be gone.

Mira returned to her kingdom with plans to join Sander in the Ever after visiting with her own people for a time. Tait Heartwalker left our shores with a deeper scowl after the Ever King insisted his cousin would need to wait until the princess was keen to return, then he was to be the one to sail her to the sea kingdom.

To others, the man might appear repulsed, but I knew a great deal about hiding truths beneath masks, and I wasn't convinced his lone aversion to Princess Mira stemmed from disdain.

Our palace was constantly flowing with folk. Frigg found the wood of the isle diverting and enjoyed conversing with the treetop elven. Von already insisted he was claiming a wing of the palace for himself (Brunhild joined him often), and most days I barely recognized my own isle.

It was lively and growing rowdier by the day. Soon it would be a mere extension of the spirit of Klockglas. The affinity in the soil seemed pleased. Trees would spread for alver folk, sun wings guided them if they were lost in the forest, and every Stärnskott grew more vibrant the more spectators walked to the isle for the weekly show.

There was still an ache inside for the betrayal of Eldirard, but as Jonas told me, I remembered the love he did give.

With the truth of the past revealed, my husband saw to it three names were added to the alver totem of remembrance and three monuments were erected at the gates of the Natthaven palace.

For my parents and Dorsan.

How different life looked each sunrise. I thought I would find a new prison as the bride of a nightmare prince, but I found my home.

"You should come back to bed." Jonas propped his chin onto the heel of his palm.

I turned over my shoulder once I finished lacing my gown. "You, Husband, promised to teach me how to whittle. I am holding you to your word."

Jonas fell back onto the bed. "I've also told you, my father would be a better teacher."

I knelt over the edge of our mattress and kissed him softly. "I want your hands to show me how it is done."

Jonas started to thread his arms around me, doubtless preparing to pull me back beneath the quilts, when the door opened in a rush.

"Cara!" I startled back. "What are you doing?"

She gasped and tilted her eyes toward the rafters.

Jonas grinned, his cock hardly covered beneath the quilts, and tucked his arms behind his head, displaying most of his bare body.

The delight of his days was horrifying Cara after I confessed she called him a salacious sort of man.

"Forgive me." She closed her eyes and held out a folded parchment. "It arrived just now. Marked as urgent from the alver king and queen."

Jonas sat up and took it, shredding through the black wax seal as Cara bustled out, closing the door behind her.

"Shit." Jonas's mouth tightened as he read.

I propped my chin on his shoulder. "What's wrong?"

"My mother and father received news from the Southern realms. Mira and Heartwalker set sail for the Ever days ago. There was a sea storm near one of the isles, but Liv insists they never arrived. Skadi." Jonas's eyes were black when he lifted his gaze to mine. "Tait and Mira are missing."

WANT MORE?

Want more of our Mist Thief and Nightmare Prince? Scan the code below to keep reading with a bonus scene.

The passion and adventure continues in the Ever Seas with THE STOLEN CROWN, the story of Princess Mira and Tait Heartwalker. Scan the QR code to preorder below.

ALSO BY LJ ANDREWS

Scan the QR code below to begin the bestselling Broken Kingdoms series which follows the parents of the Ever Seas characters, including Kase and Malin Eriksson.

ACKNOWLEDGMENTS

There are so many people to thank. First, I would not have survived writing this book if not for the support of my husband Derek. The man held down the fort night after night so I could write sexy scenes and battles. I love you.

Thank you to the readers of the Ever Seas and Broken Kingdoms. I cannot begin to describe how you have changed my life.

I would not have been able to do this without my beta readers, Kaylee, Katie, and Aubrey. You help me so much in the early phases.

Thank you to my developmental editors Jasmine Mckie of Faye_reads and Sara Sorensen. Remember how many scenes I cut and shifted in this one? Yeah, so do I. Thanks for hanging in there.

Thank you to my other editor Megan Mitchel for taking the book and finding all the typos and weird sentences and telling me to do better in the nicest ways.

Again, I have to do another thank you to the readers. I get teary just thinking of you darlings and your love for fae smut and brutal, villainous men. Who knew it would turn into such a universe as this.

Thank you, thank you.

May we all be the good,

LJ

Made in the USA
Monee, IL
26 July 2024

9a3c1acd-0211-430b-a3d2-76fdbec72ab0R01